CW00498063

FLESH BARGAIN

CURSED MANUSCRIPTS
BOOK 7

IAIN ROB WRIGHT

To my wonderful readers, for sticking by me when I needed them most.

With my greatest thanks to the following:
Suzy Tadlock
Marie Warnquist
Anthony Wilkins
Paula Bruce
Murder Shrimp
Ruth Witcomb
Andrea Oakes
Francis Keenan
Michael Greer
Angela Rees
Philip Clements
Elaine Anderson
KT Morrison
Trudy Meiser
Tracy Burrows
Steph Brown
Julie Adams
Richard Keeble
Sue Jones
Bridgett Duffus
RynoTheAlbinoRhyno
Susan Hall
Marci J Green

Julie McWhorter
Julian White
Wendy Daniel
Fear kitty
Renee Master
Mike Waldinger
Lola Wayne
Sarah Crossland
Lanie Evans
Lorraine Wilson
Sue Newhouse
Dominic Harris
Lindsay Carter
Rach Kinsella Chippendale
Leonard Ducharme
Jonathan & Tonia Cornell
Rigby Jackson
Carmen Hammond
Katrice Tuck
Minnis Hendricks
Kelli Herrera
Terrie-Ann Thulborn
Darrion Mika
Suzy Tadlock
Gillian Moon
Armando Llerena
Stephanie Everett
Ali Black
Angela Richards
Adrianne Yang
Angelica Maria
Kristina Goeke
Andrew Moss

Emma Bailey

Xya Marie

Leona Overton

Susan Hayden

Jennifer Holston

Roy Oswald

Chris Ailchison

Catherine Healy

Carol Wicklund

Lawrence Clamons

Mark Pearson

Dabney Arch

Tracy Putland

Tracey Newman

David Greer

Sandra Lewis

Windi LaBounta

Stephanie Hardy

Janet Carter

Lauren Brigham

Clare Lanes

Cindy Ahlgren

John Best

CHAPTER
ONE

JAKE SLAMMED the car door and stood at the end of the path to his family's new home. The brick wall surrounding the front garden had crumbled in several places, and the grass looked like it hadn't been cut in years. Nothing that couldn't be fixed.

"This is horrible," said Lily, Jake's fifteen-year-old daughter and constant fount of positivity. Her face scrunched up and her arms flapped about like she was about to throw up. "I can't live here. Seriously. My veins are literally filling up with misery just looking at it."

Jake wiped his brow with his beanie hat and stuffed it into his jeans pocket. True, the three-bed terrace in the economically stagnant town of Heathskil was several steps down from their former semi in Bournville, but they needed to accept reality. This was home. At least for a while.

Jake's wife, Maggie, wrapped her arm around his waist and squeezed lovingly. "It's fine," she said, leaning her head against his shoulder. "As long as we're together, what does it matter where we live?"

"It matters," said Lily, swooping her pink-streaked

blonde hair behind her. "Everyone at school's gonna think we're a bunch of tramps. I mean it. I can't live here. It's horrible. Do you want me to kill myself? Because I will. You'll find me with my face in the toaster. In a bathtub. Underneath a bridge."

Maggie put her hands on her hipbones and scowled. "Lily! That's a terrible thing to say. Don't be so dramatic. And nonsensical! How would you get your face in a toaster?"

"I'll find a way."

Jake tilted his head at his daughter and let out a long sigh. "So what's your plan, Lil? You going to live on the streets, or rent some place by yourself? Best get a paper round if that's the case."

Her reply was to fold her arms and look away sullenly. It had been her default response to most things since turning twelve. Perhaps, one day, she would smile again, but Jake was fast losing hope.

Maggie went and gave Lily a hug. "Come on, honey, you know your dad, he'll make this the nicest house on the block."

"Great. We can be fancy tramps then. Maybe build a barbecue out of umbrellas and wasted potential." She folded her arms even tighter, closing in on herself like an imploding star of cynicism.

"Enough, young lady," Maggie warned, evidently realising that getting their daughter to cheer up this afternoon was a losing battle. "You've been a right misery all afternoon."

"All year," Jake added.

"Here we go." Lily grumbled. "Let's all hate on me, as usual. You should have left me at the orphanage."

"Monkey orphanage," Jake muttered. "We got you from the monkey orphanage."

Maggie ignored their banter and rubbed her palms together. "Right, let's get inside and settled, shall we? No more moaning or complaining. We've survived worse than this."

"But at what cost?" Lily said. "At what unbearable cost, Mum?"

Jake was eager to get inside the house too. He'd parked their black Nissan X-Trail on the kerb directly in front of the house, but it was full of boxes that wouldn't unpack themselves. Not only that, he felt oddly exposed out on the street. Watched. Studied.

Unwelcome.

Across the road, sitting on a low brick wall that surrounded the opposite row of terraces, a group of teenagers glowered and snickered like hyenas. Each wore a hoody, while one also had a scarf pulled up over his mouth. It wasn't exactly a welcoming dress code.

Further down the street, a sinewy old man leaned on a cane, chatting to a stooped-over old woman with a giant orange tote bag and wearing an oversized red puffer jacket. Every few seconds, their eyes would dart in Jake's direction.

Maggie leaned towards Jake and whispered, "Looks like we're quite the novelty, huh? Good old nosy neighbours."

"They're looking at me."

They turned to face Emily. The leukaemia had now left her so weak that she needed a wheelchair to get around, and recent weeks had stolen several more pounds from her skeletal frame. Her green eyes had lost their sparkle. Her silky brown hair was gone from months of chemotherapy. But she was alive and still fighting. Their beautiful daughter.

That a seventeen-year-old girl could be so ill made Jake

4 IAIN ROB WRIGHT

want to scream. That it was his own sweet daughter made him want to sob. Neither would do anything to help Emily. "Let them look," he said, glaring back at the boys across the street. "They've got nothing better to do."

"Yeah," said Lily, steadfastly protective of her sister. "Fuck 'em."

"Lily!" Maggie swatted her gently around the back of the head. "Language!"

"English, how about you?"

Jake sighed. "Let's do what your mother asked and go inside. Then I can bring the boxes in to unpack."

"Fine." Lily rolled her eyes again. "I can hardly wait to see my new room. Does it have a private dressing area."

"Maybe," Jake said, and he started up the path.

Without further delay, they all marched, single file, towards their new home. Weeds and long grass brushed against their legs like the unwanted touch of a stranger, causing them to huddle closer together, and while Emily attempted to wheel herself forward, the uneven paving slabs made it too difficult. Lily had to push her all the way to the front door. Jake unlocked it and held it open so that Lily could pull Emily backwards over the step into the hallway.

Their new home's interior was thankfully less neglected than its exterior, but it was still in need of TLC. While the landlord had given the walls a fresh coat of white paint, the cheap laminate flooring creaked when you walked on it and the skirting boards were scuffed and dirty. As a carpenter, Jake could have fixed it all up, but why provide free house maintenance for a faceless landlord?

"It's nice," said Emily, a little out of breath. A bead of sweat ran down from underneath her rose-patterned head-scarf and settled behind her ear. The scent of Vaseline and antiseptic cream wafted from a persistent sore on her neck.

Jake smiled, thankful for his daughter's enduring positivity that never seemed to waver. "I'll build a ramp out front tomorrow," he said, "and we need to put some pictures on the wall – maybe get a hallway rug – but it'll do for now. Everything will be back to normal soon."

Silence fell upon them as they stood there in the cramped hallway. Things would only go back to normal once Emily got better – something all of them prayed for, but none of them could guarantee.

Unwilling to let his mind wander into some dark pasture where everything was cold and hopeless, Jake busied himself by knocking on the walls and gliding a hand over their painted surfaces, checking for imperfections. For the most part, everything seemed solid. Everything seemed—

"Ah, shit!" He pulled his hand back from the hallway wall and put his index finger in his mouth.

Maggie grabbed his arm. "What is it? What did you do?"

He pulled his finger out of his mouth to examine it. A bead of blood slowly emerged, a perfect red circle. "There's a nail sticking out of the wall. Look!"

Someone had obviously tried to pull a nail out of the wall at some point, but it had snapped, leaving behind a sharp, barely visible spike.

He sucked at his finger again, tasting copper.

Lily pulled a face. "Ew, stop being such a vampire, Dad."

"It's my own blood!"

"So what? It's still gross. It's like masturbation or something."

Jake pulled his finger away from his mouth and sighed. "I'll go get the boxes, shall I? Greg's bringing the van round in the morning with the rest of our stuff, but we can at least make up the beds tonight and put the kettle on."

Maggie gave Jake a kiss on the cheek. Her flowery

perfume wafted into his nostrils and made him feel calm. It was the same scent she'd worn ever since their first anniversary, when he'd purchased a bottle at random to give to her as a gift. "I'll put the heating on so Emily doesn't get cold," she said.

"I'm okay, Mum."

"It's a bit chilly in here, honey. The boiler probably hasn't been switched on for a while."

"Or it doesn't work," said Lily, grimacing and holding herself as if she dared not touch anything. "I feel unclean. Who lived here before us? Dirty people? Dirty people with nits? And the nits had mini nits?"

Jake and Maggie looked at each other, shaking their heads and chuckling. Teenage girls, such a delight.

As his family went into the kitchen, Jake headed back outside. For a moment, he just stood at the doorstep with his eyes closed, taking several deep breaths of waning summer air.

They deserve better than this. I wanted more for them than this. It's not fair.

It's temporary. Only temporary.

It'd been an exhausting day, but there was no time for moping – once he allowed himself to wallow, he often struggled to snap out of it – so he opened his eyes and moved to get the boxes.

The hooded youths from before had crossed the road and were gathered around the back of Jake's car. The X-Trail had tinted rear windows, but the boot was still clearly full of boxes.

"Can I help you, lads?" Jake asked calmly as he approached. At thirty-eight, he was a fit, athletic man, confident he could handle himself if necessary. These kids planned on intimidating him? Well, they were going to be disappointed.

One youth, the lad with the scarf over his mouth, stepped away from the car and approached Jake. He appeared to be around sixteen or seventeen, but it was hard to know when so much of his face was cloaked in shadow. "Just having a look, mate, innit? You want some help moving in?"

"I'm good. Cheers though."

"You from round these ends, bruv?"

"Bournville."

"Why you not stay there, bruv?"

"A few reasons. I won't bore you with them. You lads all live here on Tovey Avenue?"

"We live about, innit? Man can't be tied down."

Jake almost chuckled, not knowing if this lad was being serious or not. "I suppose not," he said. "Gotta keep them options open."

"So how old is your daughter, bruv?"

Jake cleared his throat and considered telling the youth to sling his hook, but it was probably better to just play along with his little game. These lads were testing him, seeing how he would react. "Lily's fourteen. Emily's seventeen."

"Which one's the vegetable on wheels?"

Jake tensed. His stomach flooded with bile. His calm blew away on a hot wind. With a protracted sigh, he had to force himself to keep his cool. "Emily has leukaemia. Pray it doesn't happen to someone you care about. Anyway, she's getting better, so she'll be out of the chair and back to normal before long. Okay?"

The youth nodded. "Maybe I'll hit her up when she loses the seat then, innit?"

Don't take the bait; they want to rattle you.

Treat them like adults and maybe they'll act like it.

"Look, my name's Jake Penshaw. I've had a really rough fucking week, so can we move past the pointless posturing and just shake hands like gentlemen? I got no problem with you lads, so let's not get off on the wrong foot, right?"

The youth's eyes narrowed. His friends were slouched against Jake's car, but they perked up now. This was their entertainment. The lad in front of him was their leader.

"Yeah, bruv, of course. No problem here. Just saying hello, innit?"

"Good, then I'm pleased to meet you." Jake offered a hand, confident he'd played things the correct way.

Refuse to be a victim and they can't make you into one.

The two of them shook hands firmly.

The masked youth stared defiantly into Jake's eyes. "Welcome to the neighbourhood, bruv."

"Cheers. What's your name, buddy?"

"Ask around, innit?" The youth yanked hard and pulled Jake off-balance, scoring what he probably thought was a psychological victory. Letting go, he moved back towards his friends, rapping a knuckle against the X-Trail's rear window as he passed. "See ya later, Jakey boy. Make sure you lock your doors at night, innit? Can get proper sketchy round here."

Jake shook his head, trying to unclench his jaw. He waited until the lads were gone and then opened up the boot. He carried the boxes inside quickly. It was going to take a lot for Tovey Avenue to ever feel like home.

———

Dinner ended up being late-night pizza from a takeaway they'd never used before. It tasted fine, but everyone commented how it wasn't as good as their old place in Bournville.

"I'm full," said Emily, sliding her plate across the kitchen's small four-seater table. She'd needed to exit her wheelchair in order to sit around it with everybody else, but the wooden spokes at the back of her chair seemed to cause her pain as she shifted uncomfortably back and forth.

"You've only had one slice, sweetie," Maggie said. Jake's wife had put her mousy blonde hair up in a bun and rolled the sleeves of her red and black lumberjack shirt past her elbows. It was her typical 'I'm done for the day' look. "You sure you won't be hungry later?"

"I feel a bit sick. Leave a slice in the fridge and I might have it tomorrow."

"Okay, my love." Maggie leapt up and put a single pizza slice inside the kitchen's scuffed white fridge. Lily called dibs on the other slice her sister had left untouched and put it on her own plate. The pizza wasn't as good as their old place, but it was still pizza.

Before Maggie sat down again, she asked Jake if he wanted a beer, to which he happily replied in the affirmative. "I could murder one. I'm done in after today."

"Me too. I'm going to pour some wine."

"Can I have some?" Lily asked, a smirk on her face.

Maggie smirked back, her eyes crinkling at the corners. Now and then they allowed Lily to have a small glass of wine, but they weren't about to make a habit of it. "No, young lady, you may not."

"I would have some," Emily said, tightening her headscarf at the back, "but I'm watching my weight."

"One sip and you might double it," Lily quipped, prompting a shared giggle that momentarily lightened the sombre atmosphere inside the kitchen.

Maggie handed Jake a beer from the battered fridge and unscrewed a fresh bottle of white wine, pouring some into a plastic tumbler – their glasses were still buried in a cardboard box somewhere. She plonked herself back down on a creaking wooden chair and took her first sip with a contented sigh.

The laughter slowly faded, and now that the food had gone, the atmosphere seemed to sour. Sitting in silence, they each stared at the wooden table's scratched surface in a shared, quiet daze. Jake wondered if they were thinking about how small and drab the kitchen was compared to their old one. The stylish, granite-topped galley of their previous home had been less than two years old. Jake had fitted it himself. In a house they had all loved.

This was only a setback. He would get it all back for them.

Maggie sipped her wine. Then, leaning across the table, she took Jake's hand and looked him in the eyes. "Lily's back at school Tuesday—"

Lily groaned. "Don't remind me, Mum."

"—so I thought maybe you could go down to the building sites and see if any work's going."

Jake pulled his hand away. "It's not the right time. Emily has appointments. I need to get this place sorted… Maybe in a couple of weeks?"

"We need to bring some money in, babe."

"So you want me to go prostitute myself to the house builders for peanuts? How's that going to help us?"

"It's better than doing odd jobs and decorating. It's coming up on a year since you closed down the business."

"We're doing fine, Mag. What was the point of selling the house if it didn't give us breathing room to take care of Emily?"

"It's just, the longer we wait…" Her words trailed off into a shrug.

"We have time," he said, smiling. "There's no rush."

"Dad…" Emily released a drawn-out sigh, her skin pale, cheeks jagged. "You need to go back to work. Mum can take me to my appointments. I'll be fine."

He shook his head, a fire growing in his belly. "No, I need to be with you, sweetheart. If they miss something and I'm not there…"

Lily tutted. "You reckon you know better than the doctors, do you, Dad?"

"I reckon your sister needs as much support as we can give her." He had raised his voice slightly, and in the cold, cramped kitchen, it seemed to echo.

"Even if it means we lose our home, have no money, and have to live in a house made of broken dreams and crotch sweat?" Lily put her elbows on the table and a pulled a face at him. "Oh, wait, that already happened. And Emily's still dying."

Maggie gasped. "Your sister is *not* dying, Lily. She's getting better, and that's worth all the money in the world. Stop being so self-centred."

"Self-centred?" Lily rocked back in her seat, as if someone had pushed her. "How am I self-centred? My entire life has been turned upside down and nobody gives a shit."

"We do give a… *spit*," Maggie said. "And watch your language, young lady."

"I'm sorry." Emily turned to Lily and reached a frail hand out across the table. "Me getting ill screwed everything up."

Lily's attitude dissolved a little. Her cheeks reddened, and she offered an apologetic smile to her sister. "I'm just mouthing off, Em. You know me, happy and healthy black sheep of the family. Hopefully I'll get a disease next year and then it'll be my turn to get all the attention." She smirked. "Hey, maybe I'll go out and catch AIDS."

Emily stifled a laugh with her hand. "Lil, that's terrible! Anyway, you would be a complete drama queen, so let's hope you never get sick. I still haven't got over you having tonsillitis last Christmas."

Lily stared hauntingly into the distance. "I almost died."

Maggie reached across the table and stroked Emily's arm. "Don't you ever blame yourself for getting ill, sweetheart, d'you hear me? You never asked to get sick, and money doesn't matter." She side-eyed her other daughter. "Whatever Lily might say."

"It'll matter if we end up getting stabbed to death by one of our weirdo neighbours," Lily said. "Half of them are probably shooting up heroin as we speak. Listen, you can almost hear their eyeballs rolling back in their heads."

Jake swigged his beer from the can and put it down slowly on the table. "They're just normal people, Lily. Don't be so judgemental. Besides, I already met the local rabble, and their bark is worse than their bite."

Maggie raised an eyebrow. "Really? Who did you meet? And when?"

"Those lads across the street came over while I was unloading the car. They were fine."

"Oh, well, that's good to know," Maggie said, picking up her wine. "They looked like a right pack of thugs to me."

"Just kids. What else do they have to do, except hang around the streets?"

"Were any of them fit?" Lily asked, her mood lifting as quickly as it had fallen.

Emily was scratching at her arm, but she looked up now and chuckled. "Yeah, I'd like to know too. I won't be in this chair forever."

"You girls…" Maggie shook her head and pretended to be disapproving, but she couldn't help but let a tiny smile escape her lips.

"They were just normal lads." Jake gripped his beer can, forcing a small dent with his thumb. "Anyway, I suggest you both—"

Emily started to hack and splutter.

Maggie leapt out of her seat and started fussing.

Jake froze, exchanging a worried glance with Lily.

Emily's coughing continued as Maggie rubbed desperately at her back. Flecks of blood spattered the table.

"What the fuck?" Lily scooted back in her chair, her eyes growing wide. "Blood!"

"Emily?" Jake reached out a shaking hand. "Emily, are you okay?"

She continued spluttering and coughing but put a palm up to show she was all right. Seconds passed, and she started to get a hold of herself, taking several deep, wheezing breaths. Her rosy headscarf had come loose, and she quickly retightened it.

"Honey, are you okay?" Maggie asked. "Sweetheart?"

Emily nodded, but only managed a grunt into her clenched fist. They all waited until she had recovered enough to speak. "I-I'm fine," she eventually murmured. "Sorry."

"What's with the ketchup cough?" Lily asked, nodding at the bloody spatter on the table. Jake was fixated on the tiny red speckles too. Emily had never coughed up blood before.

"It's just from a cut inside my mouth," she explained. "It keeps opening back up. Look!" She turned her cheek inside-out and showed them all. Sure enough, there was an open sore inside her mouth, oozing blood. "Really, I'm fine. I think I might call it a night though. My chest's feeling tight."

Maggie, still standing and rubbing Emily's back, almost compulsively, nodded earnestly. "That's no problem at all, sweetheart. I'll get you some water and make your bed. Maybe I can find the hot water bottle in one of the boxes. Did you want me to—"

"Thanks, Mum. That'll be great."

Equally shaken by his daughter's unexpected coughing fit, Jake pushed his chair back, its legs dragging on the cheap lino. They were getting worse, more regular. "I'm just going to the toilet," he said. "Then I'll come back and tidy up."

"Upstairs," said Lily, pulling a face. "We have one toilet, and it's upstairs."

He put his hands against his cheeks. "Oh, the horror."

Maggie gave him an understanding nod and waved him off with a wary but supportive smile, then went back to fussing over Emily. When he made it to the toilet upstairs, he locked the door behind him.

Everything was wrong, and he didn't know how to fix it.

Moving over to the sink, Jake faced his reflection in the mirror and struggled to contain the anger and sadness inside him. His cheeks sagged, as if they bore some invisible weight, and his green eyes were bloodshot. In the last eighteen months, he'd aged five years. They all had.

"I just want this to be over," he whispered as he ran both hands over his short, fuzzy hair. "I'll do anything. Just let my daughter be okay." He didn't know who he was begging; he just hoped someone was listening.

———

It took Maggie almost half an hour to find bedclothes, fill a hot water bottle, and help Emily into bed. By then, Emily felt ready to pass out. Merely sitting still was exhausting lately, and her mum's constant attention took its toll as well.

Every day, I feel like another piece of me is gone. Another pound of flesh.

I'm dying and taking my family with me.

At first, getting cancer had terrified Emily, but now she simply wanted it to hurry up and finish its job. She wasn't getting better, no matter what her parents liked to tell themselves, and the endless treatments did nothing besides torture her. She barely had the strength to be afraid of death any more. In fact, every day it grew more appealing.

Acute myeloid leukaemia. That's what the doctor had said to Emily eighteen months ago, with a grim expression on his face. It was only the flickering of his watery eyes that betrayed he felt anything at all about her diagnosis, and ten minutes later he was ushering her out of his office and welcoming the next patient. Strangely, she had an exact memory of the name the doctor had called out as she left. Mr Wilson. She often wondered what had been wrong with Mr Wilson. Had he got bad news too that day, or had he walked away with a prescription for antibiotics to treat a bad throat?

It had been a shock, of course, to learn that she was dying, especially since she had assumed the constant fatigue and sickness had been down to a simple virus or perhaps some kind of deficiency, but no… turned out she had cancer. Whoopee!

But leukaemia isn't that bad, right? Kids get leukaemia and overcome it all the time.

Not AML, I'm afraid, miss. AML is the Real Madrid of cancers. Very hard to defeat.

Apparently, Emily's body was producing a bunch of messed-up blood cells, so goodbye immune system and hello anaemia. And no more being a carefree teenaged girl;

you're a walking corpse now with a zero-effort diet plan. You get to eat and starve at the same time. Instant weight loss!

She stared up at the ceiling, tracing the contours of her bedsheets and wondering where her body had gone. She could probably locate and count every bone if she wanted to. They were easy to find.

Getting cancer sucked about as hard as anything *could* suck, but getting an extra rare kind that she shouldn't have even been at risk for sucked even worse. It was like the opposite of winning the lottery.

At least the chemo had stopped for a week. The doctors said she deserved a break, but she knew dogshit when she smelt it between her toes. The chemo wasn't working – the treatment was killing her faster than the cancer – so the doctors needed a new plan. It meant Emily got a few days of not puking her guts up every five minutes.

Lucky me.

She lay now in a rickety bed, with an open book in her lap and a small pile of pills cluttering her bedside table. It was pointless taking most of the meds, but they helped with the pain slightly, so she swallowed a couple with the glass of water her mum had left for her. It felt like forcing down broken glass, her throat red raw. The pain was nothing new, though, and barely concerned her.

What did concern her was her parents. Her mum never relaxed for a second any more – always on high alert and ready to leap to attention if Emily so much as sniffled – and her dad was wasting away the same way she was. He barely worked, never saw his friends, and, worst of all, had stopped telling jokes. Emily had always thought his humour cringeworthy, but she realised now how much she missed it.

To see him smile like he used to.

And then there was Lily. Emily suspected her younger sister was slowly coming to hate her. She never said so – and Lily was always on hand to help whenever Emily needed her – but their relationship had changed. Her sister was angry. She'd never been angry before.

She's angry at me. She wants me to hurry up and die.

No, she loves me. They all do. That's what makes this so hard.

It would be better if I were gone. Then they could move on with their lives.

Occasionally, whenever Emily slept deeply enough to dream, her mind conjured images of the past. She and Lily were always youngsters, pushing each other on the garden swing that their dad had built for them. It was always the day Emily had taught Lily how to propel herself, kicking out her legs to go forward and tucking them in to go back. Lily had been so proud of herself when she had finally mastered swinging herself, and so had been Emily. It was the time in her life when she had most felt like a big sister. She often thought about that massive hug Lily had given her afterwards.

You're the bestest sister ever, Em.

Movement outside Emily's bedroom window caught her eye, but it was only the gentle swaying of a bushy tree growing in the small back garden. Its branches split the moon's silvery rays and caused broken slivers to settle on the cream carpet. It was beautiful; in the way most things seemed to be lately. Just simple. Simple and beautiful.

Rapidly approaching sleep, Emily picked up her book and decided to read for a little while before her eyelids betrayed her. She was halfway through *Dracula*, which ironic, she supposed. Prior to her diagnosis, she had read only when required for school, but now it was one of the few activities she could easily manage. Initially it had been autobiographies, but after picking up a copy of *The Cellar*, by Richard Laymon, she had acquired a taste for the macabre. The escapism of a book took away her pain almost as much as the painkillers did.

Footsteps sounded on the landing. They paused at Emily's door.

"Lily? Is that you?"

The door opened with a barely audible creak. Her sister appeared at the threshold and stepped inside. "Hey, I'm going to bed. You need anything?"

Emily glanced at her leather-strapped Mickey Mouse watch, which hung off her bony wrist like it was ten sizes too big. "It's only nine," she said. "Early for you."

Lily shrugged. "I'm gonna faff on my phone for a bit. Mum and Dad are drinking, so it won't be long before they annoy the shit out of me."

"Yeah, they chat rubbish with the best of them when they're tipsy, huh?"

"That they do." She went to turn away, but lingered in the doorway.

"Did you want something?" Emily pushed herself up on her pillows with great effort.

"Yeah, um, I think I'm getting my period. Can you give me something for the cramps?"

Is that what she came in here for? Did she actually want to check in on me at all?

"Oh, I'm not sure I have anything. Mum has my pill bag."

Lily glanced at the side table, and the few pills remaining there. "You have some *co-codamol* or something though, right? Can you spare one, please? I think it's gonna be a baddun."

Emily gave a thin-lipped smile. "Sure. Just… find some *paracetamol* next time, yeah? These are really strong."

Lily strolled over and took a little white pill from the pile, popping it into her mouth and swigging from Emily's glass. "You know me. I like the good stuff."

"Uh-huh. Well, guess I'll see you tom—" Emily put a hand to her stomach, enduring a wave of discomfort. "Urgh!"

"Hey," Lily touched her on the shoulder. "You okay?"

"Yeah. Yeah, it's just a flutter." She took a breath in and let it out. "Like going over a hump in the car."

Lily grinned. "I love that feeling."

"I've been getting them all the time lately. It gets old, believe me."

"I suppose it would after a while. Well, if you need anything, I'll be right next door in my tiny bedroom. Sleep well, sis."

"You too. See you in the morning – if I'm still alive."

Lily giggled and walked over to the door. "Night."

"Goodnight."

Once the door closed, Emily looked over at her remaining pills and scooped them into her hand. After a moment's thought, she tucked them underneath her mattress. The less she had on show, the better.

CHAPTER
TWO

JAKE PLANED HALF a centimetre off the right-hand side of the ramp and then it was perfect. He bolted it to the brickwork beneath the doorstep and gave it a shove to ensure it was stable. It didn't move a hair as he ran his fingertips appreciatively over the sanded woodgrain. The smell of freshly cut cedar filled the crisp morning air, and the soft hum of a distant lawnmower added a comforting soundtrack. A trickle of sweat ran down the side of his face, well earned.

In the bright light of day, Tovey Avenue didn't seem so bad. Instead of bleak and uniform, the Victorian terraces now revealed their personality. While all had twin bay windows, tiled roofs, and stubby chimney stacks, there were a few key differences between them. Some had painted wooden doors, while others had more modern PVC – one or two even had expensive slate-grey composite. One house had been rendered completely white, in contrast to the russet clay bricks of its neighbours. Some gardens were wild and overgrown, while others were mown and flowered. One house, a few doors down, had a dozen gnomes lined up along its garden wall, each one fishing, sleeping, or posing happily. People lived here, and people were okay.

"That's very fine work," said a voice behind him as he sanded one of the ramp's edges. "I'll have to get you round my house to fix a few things."

Jake looked over his shoulder and saw an old man leaning on a cane. He couldn't be sure, but it might've been the same gentleman he'd seen chatting at the end of the street yesterday. "Um, hello there."

The old man smiled, eyes crinkling at the corners as if it were a well-worn expression. Broad-shouldered and tall, he wore a baggy, green knitted vest over a light blue button-down shirt. His black dress shoes were so scuffed they were almost grey. "Sorry to sneak up on you," he said, "but I wanted to welcome you to the neighbourhood. I'm George from number fifty-two."

Jake wiped the sawdust from his palms on his jumper and stood up to shake the man's hand. "I'm Jake. We just moved here from Bournville."

Where we were happy.

"Work for Cadbury's, did you?"

Jake forced a polite smile. "Contrary to popular belief, there are other jobs in Bournville besides making chocolate. I'm a carpenter."

The old man pointed at the cedarwood ramp he'd just made. "Which explains the fine work. Is your family settling in all right?"

"We're missing our old house a little, but I'm sure we'll adjust soon enough. My kids lived there their whole lives, so it's a bit strange for them to be somewhere else. Fresh start though, right?"

"It's not such a bad place," George said, casting a sweeping glance along the road. "I've been here twenty years. Seen it all, I have – people coming and going, kids growing up, parents growing old. The faces change, but the street never does."

"And is it…?" Jake didn't know whether it was rude to ask.

The old man frowned, oversized ears twitching either side of wispy grey sideburns. "Is it what?"

"Safe? There was a group of youths hanging around here yesterday. It felt like they were up to no good."

"Oh, them? Yes, well, you're best off staying clear of that lot. Vincent and his rabble cause most of the mischief around here, but if you keep out of their way, they'll mostly keep out of yours."

Vincent? So, that's his name.

Jake looked past George for a moment. There was no one else around on either side of the street, so all was quiet. In fact, things had been surprisingly quiet all morning, as well as during the night. Jake had held secret fears of rowdy neighbours playing music and arguing at all hours, but there'd been no disturbances at all. Perhaps, like Lily, he was guilty of being judgemental.

Is it really unreasonable to expect the worst when the worst keeps happening?

"Your daughter…" said George, his smile fading to sympathy. "Did I see she has mobility issues?"

Oh great, he's the resident busybody. Just what I need.

"Um… Emily has leukaemia. She's getting treatment for it."

George added more sympathy to his face, which was unwarranted. Jake didn't need strangers prying about his daughter. She was going to be fine.

The old man seemed to sense Jake's offence, because he put a hand up defensively. "I only ask because my own daughter spent some time in a wheelchair as a littlun. Used to get the worst seizures, she did. Her spine would bend like a banana and her eyes would roll right back in her head."

"That's terrible," said Jake, realising the man might actually know how he felt. "It must have been traumatic."

"Oh, it was." He gave Jake another smile. "Fortunately, she grew out of it. Kelly's a nurse now, up in Sheffield. Pops down a few times a year to see me, she does, but mostly has her own life. I wouldn't change it for the world."

Jake nodded. "You're happy she's happy."

"After the suffering she went through as a nipper, yes, very much so. There was a time when all I wanted was for her pain to stop, no matter the cost. Never even considered there might be a happy, normal life for her at the end of it all."

Jake nodded wistfully, knowing exactly what he meant. "I can't wait for the morning when Emily wakes up not dreading the day ahead. She's been through so much and yet…" He shook his head and cleared his throat. Why was he spilling his guts out to a stranger? "It's just a tough time for us all right now, but we'll get through it. Anyway, thanks for welcoming me to the street… George, you said?"

"That's the one. And I welcome you *all*, Jake." He straightened his shirt cuffs and opened his arms wide. "I welcome you all to Tovey Avenue. There're no trees here, but I believe there used to be, hence the name, but what we lack in greenery we make up for in character. Hey, how about you pop round for a glass of whisky later, so I can welcome you properly? I can't afford the good stuff, but it goes down well enough."

Jake grimaced. "Yeah, I'm not really sure if I'll be able to—"

"What? Drag yourself a few doors down for half an

hour? I'm sure you'll make it. Wouldn't be neighbourly to refuse, would it?"

For a moment, Jake didn't know if he had rankled the old man, but when he saw those playful creases at the corners of George's eyes, he knew there was nothing more going on than a friendly invitation.

"Okay, I'll come have a quick one. What time?"

"Any time! I'm retired, so be prepared to see me in a dressing gown and three sheets to the wind at any time of the day or night. We're an informal bunch around here."

Jake chuckled. "Hey, you worked your entire life, right? Why not enjoy it?"

"Exactly."

"What did you used to do, by the way?"

George held his hands up, palms out, rough with calluses. "Used to be a butcher before the supermarkets came along. Worked in an abattoir after that. Dirty, horrible work, but there's a lot of skill to it."

"Yeah, I bet."

"You're not a vegan, are you, Jake? Seems to be the fashion these days."

"No, my family and I are all devoted carnivores. Although I have teenage daughters, so it's subject to change at any moment."

George chuckled. "You don't have to remind me what it's like. Anyway, I'll see you later – sooner, if you need anything – and by all means bring the wife and kids. I'm sure I have something non-alcoholic lying around somewhere."

"Sure thing, George. Nice to meet you."

"Likewise."

Jake watched the friendly old man totter away on his cane and felt something he thought might be relief. He had dragged his family away from all that was familiar and friendly, but for a moment George had made him feel at home.

"Nice guy."

Jake went back inside the house and called out to his family, ready to show them the cedarwood ramp. It felt good to build something after watching so many things fall apart.

———

Greg didn't turn up with the van until ten past twelve. He'd arranged to be there at ten. Still, his ex-employee was doing him a favour, so Jake could hardly complain. They unloaded boxes and furniture now, chit-chatting as they went.

"So how you finding it?" Greg asked him while carrying a battered Dyson vacuum in one hand and a hair dryer in the other.

Jake picked up a heavy suitcase full of clothes. "Only moved in yesterday afternoon, mate, but I suppose it's going all right. Lily thinks her life is over because we don't have a downstairs toilet, but she'll survive."

Greg chuckled. He was only in his early twenties, so he had always got on well with Lily and Emily, especially since Lily constantly flirted with him and told him how handsome he was. "You'll get it all back," he said. "Just remember all my help when you restart your business."

"Of course I will. I still feel bad about letting you go."

"Hey, I get it. You gotta be a dad first, right? Wish my old man gave a shit. If I got cancer, he'd probably be glad and turn my bedroom into a wanking den."

Jake grimaced. Greg wasn't the most eloquent of speakers, but he was always sincere. "I'm sure he'd be gutted if you got ill, Greg."

"Eh, maybe."

They headed up the path.

Jake had rented the house furnished, so most of their furniture was in storage for the time being. Even so, a dozen boxes and various knick-knacks filled the back of Greg's van.

Greg set the bulky vacuum down in the hallway as if it were a stapler. The kid was strong as an ox. "You met the neighbours yet?"

"A few. Friendly old guy named George came by to say hello this morning." He pulled a face. "And the local troublemakers sized me up as soon as we arrived."

"Yeah, I hear it's a bit rough round here, mate. Didn't a bloke get stabbed last year at the Aldi on the corner?"

"I don't know about that." Jake set the suitcase down at the bottom of the stairs with a grunt and ran a clammy hand over his head. "I just wanted somewhere cheap, so I don't have to worry about bills for a while. Once Emily's better, I'll look at getting a mortgage for some place nicer. We'll manage until then. I grew up in a place scarier than this."

"Just keep yourself to yourself, yeah? Stay out of trouble and hopefully it won't find you."

"What exactly do you think I'm planning to do, Greg? Join a gang?"

"I dunno. For all I know, you might have moved here to start up a drug empire to make ends meet."

Jake cackled, and they went back to the van to grab more stuff. "Maggie would kill me if I became a delinquent. She still takes the micky out of me for having a pierced eyebrow when we met."

Greg grabbed an armful of picture frames from the back of his van – Emily and Lily's smiling faces peering out from the top of the pile. "You met at college, right?"

"Yep. Childhood sweethearts. I was doing my NVQ and Maggie was doing 'Hair and Beauty'."

"How did you hook up if you were doing different courses?"

"We both used to spend our lunch breaks at the same cafe near campus, so we knew each other a little. One day, she got stung by a huge wasp and started panicking, so I grabbed a sachet of vinegar and came to the rescue; put it on her sting to help ease the pain."

"That actually works?"

"God knows, but I was confident about it. Anyway, it got me a date, and the rest is history. Married at twenty-one, had Emily the same year. Probably all happened a little too fast, really, but it worked out okay in the end."

"And here's me, still living at home with no girlfriend in sight."

Jake grabbed a box full of photo albums. "Not everyone lives the same life, mate. What fun would that be? Besides, the world is different for you. Getting a house, falling in love, having kids… it's tougher now. I don't envy a guy your age."

Greg tittered. "You sound like an old man."

"I *feel* old. Been a rough year, mate."

Greg seemed to want to say something, but he simply nodded. What *could* he say? The things Jake was going through couldn't be understood, especially not by someone so young.

"You're a good kid, Greg. I appreciate you helping me move."

"No problem at all. I learned a lot from you, and I haven't forgotten it."

"Well, thanks." Jake had only employed Greg for eighteen months as an apprentice carpenter, but the kid had learned fast and given it his all. When Jake eventually restarted his business, he genuinely hoped to rehire him, but who knew what the future held? One thing the last couple of years had taught him was not to plan on anything.

They continued unloading the van and stacking everything up in the hallway. Maggie was out with Lily, getting supplies to stock the kitchen, but Emily was resting on the living room sofa watching a cookery show. She seemed to enjoy watching food more than she did eating it lately, and she was stick-thin. Earlier, when Greg had popped his head around the corner to say hello, her emaciated appearance had clearly shocked him, but bless him, he had done his best to hide it. Emily even smiled when she had seen him.

He used to be part of the family.

When did I last even see him? When did we last have a beer together?

Once they finished unloading, Jake offered Greg a cup of tea, but the lad declined. He was due to meet some mates in town to play snooker. "Just give us a shout if you need any more help, mate," he said, as he started heading down the garden path.

"Will do." Jake walked with him, patting him on the back. "You sure I can't pay you for today?"

"What, for two hours of helping out a mate? No way."

"I owe you one, then."

"No worries." He shut the back of the van and moved towards the front. There, he paused a moment, seeming to battle with something. "Hey, Jake, is Emily going to be okay?"

Why is he asking that?

Because he cares. That's not a crime.

Jake forced a smile to his lips. "Of course she is. The treatment's rough on her, but it's working. She'll get better."

Greg sighed with obvious relief. "I'm so happy to hear that, man. I really hope she feels good again soon."

"Me too. Mind how you go, okay?"

"I always do." Greg stepped into the road towards the van's driver's side.

A horn blared.

Greg leapt back onto the kerb just as a black Range Rover sped past far too quickly for the type of road. Its driver leant on the horn for an obnoxiously long amount of time.

"Jesus Christ," Greg shouted. "Bloody moron almost flattened me."

Jake watched the Range Rover speed down the road and come to a screeching halt about a hundred metres away. One of its rear doors opened before the car had even settled on its springs, and someone hopped out onto the road.

Vincent.

The young lad had his scarf away from his mouth and his hood down, but somehow Jake recognised him from their brief encounter yesterday.

"One of the troublemakers I was telling you about," he told Greg.

Greg pulled a face. "Like I said, steer well clear, mate."

Jake watched while Vincent chatted to someone through the Range Rover's open driver's side window. A few seconds later, the large black car sped away, leaving the lad standing in the middle of the road. Vincent looked around, as if checking to see if anyone was watching. When he spotted Jake, he seemed to smirk.

"I am going to steer clear," Jake said quietly. "I've got enough to deal with."

Greg attempted to get safely to the van's driver's side again, and this time he made it. Leaning over the stubby bonnet, he gave Jake a wink. "Give my love to Lily and Maggie, yeah? I'm sorry I missed them."

"We'll have you over for dinner one night soon, buddy. Soon as we get settled in. Should only take a year or so."

"You'll feel right at home before you know it, mate. See you later."

"See you later, Greg."

Jake watched his friend – slash former protégé – turn his van around in the road with a twinge of sadness. Greg had been a part of Jake's old life, the time before Emily had got sick. The lad reminded him of happier times.

Jake turned to go back inside the house, but he noticed that Vincent was still standing in the road, smirking at him.

You better steer clear of me too, kid.

————

When Jake mentioned George's invite, he had expected Maggie to want to come along and say hi – she was the gregarious one in their marriage, after all – yet she had declined. "I'm too tired to socialise," she had said, rubbing her eyes and yawning. "Maybe another time, but you should go."

Likewise, Lily had rolled her eyes at the suggestion of visiting an old man, which was entirely predictable, but surprisingly, right as he had been about to walk out the door, Emily had asked to come. "I'm feeling okay," she said, "and I could use a change of scenery."

So Jake had helped her off the sofa and was now wheeling her up the pavement towards George's house – number fifty-two. Funny how life could surprise you, and he couldn't deny he was happy to spend some time alone with his eldest daughter.

Because I might not get the chance for much longer.
Stop it!

"Are you warm enough?" he asked her. Emily had a cotton blanket across her lap – she couldn't bear anything scratchy – but sometimes she shivered no matter how many layers he put on her.

"I'm fine, Dad. Don't fuss, please. Just let me feel normal for once."

"Okay, okay, just checking. So, how are you finding the house?"

She shrugged. "The sofa's comfy and the television's pretty big, so it'll do." She wrinkled her nose playfully at him, and it filled his heart with joy to see her happy and mostly pain-free.

Since the beginning of her illness, Emily had had good days and bad. At the start, she had sometimes found it hard even to get out of bed, or she would lie in a cold bath for hours trying to break a fever, but other times she could feel fine for an entire week. Perhaps if her illness had been more consistent in the beginning they would've visited a doctor sooner. Later on, as the cancer had progressed, Lily would spend days plagued by migraines and aching bones, while on other days she could be full of energy. Lately, however, the bad days far outnumbered the good, and the high-dose chemo had added debilitating nausea and weakness to the mix.

But today was clearly a good day – which meant it was a good day for Jake too.

"Was Greg shocked to see me?" she asked, not in an embarrassed way, more just curious.

"He just said he hopes you feel better soon. Maybe he's planning on taking you out on a date."

Emily groaned. "He's way too old for me, Dad. Plus, Lily would tip my chair over if I showed any interest in him."

"You're right, he probably is a little too old, but he's a nice lad. Would be good for him to meet someone."

"But not me."

"Fair enough."

They headed a little further along the path, but they slowed down as they passed by an odd-looking house. A strange array of oddities decorated its well-kept front lawn.

"Please, tell me this isn't George's house," Emily said.

Jake checked the door number. Forty-four "No. It's not this one."

"What is all this stuff?"

"I dunno."

The property's front gate had a pair of clay monsters to either side of it, sitting atop the brick wall. Upon closer inspection, they appeared to be dragons, like the kind waved around as kites in Chinese parades. The house itself had a red-painted front door marked with strange black symbols, and there was a plaque with Chinese writing attached to the wall on the left. Planted in the front lawn, a five-foot wooden pole held a brass plate with a burning candle, despite it being only seven o'clock and the sun still being out.

"It's very… Chinesey," Emily said, reaching out to touch one of the clay dragon's noses.

"Shush." Jake put a finger to his lips and stifled a grin. "We shouldn't gawk. Come on, before we disturb whoever lives here."

They carried on, and a moment later, they were outside George's front door. While many of the properties on the street needed a little sprucing up, this house was prize-winning in its dereliction. Thick grass competed with stinging nettles and thistles for sunlight, and the resulting tangle climbed almost to chest height. The front door might once have been blue, but it was now a chipped, faded slab of wood inside a crooked frame. A black rubbish bag sat just outside the front step.

The doorbell didn't work. Jake had to knock.

Emily gawped at him in horror. On their old street, the neighbours had competed in unspoken competitions for 'best driveway' and 'neatest lawn', but not here. This was a different section of society altogether.

And we shouldn't judge. In fact, I should offer to help George get his front lawn cleaned up. He's probably too old to do it himself.

The door moved an inch in its frame and then became wedged. It took a couple more tugs from the other side for it to fully open and a smiling George to appear. The man wore a fluffy grey dressing gown, and Jake was relieved to see he was also wearing trousers and slippers.

"Hi, George."

The old man's face lit up. "Come in, come in. Oh, you brought your beautiful daughter. Emily, right?"

Emily blushed and nodded.

Jake turned Emily's chair around so he could get her up over the doorstep. "I just need to…"

"Oh. Oh, how silly of me. Let me get out of your way."

"It's no problem." Jake lifted Emily inside and just about found room to turn her around in the hallway.

George's home was lovely. Old-fashioned, but also homely and warm. He clearly took far better care of the inside than the outside.

"It's a bit of a jungle out there," Jake said, feeling George could probably take the joke. "I almost had to call for rescue."

"Ah, I can't stand gardening, never could. Also, it keeps people out. Surprising how a few thorns can deter a burglar."

Jake swallowed, unnerved by how casually the old man spoke about crime and the possibility of it happening. Was it just a fact of life here on Tovey Avenue?

Do I need a cricket bat next to the front door?

"Follow me," said George, hobbling off down the hall on his cane. The door ahead was already open, and they passed through into a lounge with an awful green carpet. Again, everything was old and out of fashion, but well looked after and solid. Jake positioned Emily's chair next to the arm of a blue floral two-seater sofa and then sat down on it. The cushions sagged, enclosing his hips, but he quickly made himself comfortable.

George sat down in an armchair opposite Jake.

"You have a lovely home," said Emily, smiling warmly in that rare way she only did when she was briefly pain-free. "I love your furniture. Everything made today is so cheap and flimsy."

"You're not wrong, my dear, but a lot of this stuff is nearly as old as I am. I always meant to redecorate, but… well, I suppose it just doesn't matter that much to me, being on my own as I am."

"Were you ever married?" she asked, leaning forward a little in her chair.

"Of course. I'm not an ogre!"

"Oh, oh, I'm sorry, I didn't mean to—"

He waved a hand to show he was only joking. "No, no, I'm being silly. I married at twenty as it goes, but my Leanne… Well, I lost her before I turned forty."

Emily put a skeletal hand across her heart. "That's such a shame. I'm sorry."

"Me too, my dear, but the decades have long healed those wounds. Leanne died of a sudden brain aneurism when our daughter was twelve. Can happen to any one of us at any time, I remember the doctors saying, but it didn't offer much solace."

Jake knew the feeling. Emily's doctors regularly spoke about how unlucky Emily was – how rare her cancer was – as if it somehow made things better.

As if we should feel special for beating the odds. Or for the odds beating us, more like.

"So you never remarried, then?" Jake asked. "Not sure I would either if something happened to Maggie."

George gave a sharp laugh. "It was a miracle I got one woman to marry me, let alone two. I courted a little, here and there, but nothing ever really went anywhere. Eventually, I reached an age where I was too set in my ways to share a house with anyone else. Nope, I'm better off alone. Saw my Kelly married off, healthy and happy, and that was me done. Seeing her get well and recover to live a normal life was all the blessings I needed."

Emily sat up in her chair, her interest clearly piquing. "Your daughter was ill?"

"Oh, I forgot to say," said Jake, turning to her. "George's daughter was in a wheelchair for a time too. Epilepsy, did you say, George?"

"The doctors were never quite sure. Something was wrong with her brain, but it fixed itself eventually. Thank the stars."

Jake went to pry further, to ask how she had miraculously recovered, but George suddenly stood up and broke the conversation. He wobbled for a moment before grabbing his cane from where he'd propped it against the side of his armchair.

"Where are my manners?" he said, putting a hand to his forehead. "Let me get you that whisky, Jake. Emily, what can I get you?"

"Um, just water, please," she waved a hand, "but don't go to any trouble."

"When fetching a glass of water for a lovely young lady becomes too much trouble, it's time for me to leave this place."

Emily chuckled. The two of them watched George hobble out of the room.

"He's sweet," Emily said. "Friendly."

"I think it must get a bit lonely living by himself. Neighbours are probably important to him."

"I don't think we even knew the names of our old neighbours back in Bournville."

Jake frowned. "That's not true. There was John, opposite, and, um, Sharon, with that lovely purple TVR."

"We never went inside their homes though, did we? No one ever invited us round for a drink."

"Well, they all worked a lot. George is retired."

"Suppose so."

George returned with two tumblers of whisky and a ceramic mug clamped between his fingers and thumb. He set them down on the hardwood coffee table and plonked himself back down in his armchair. When his cane toppled over and fell flat across the carpet beside him, he went to grab it, but instead started to cough and splutter.

"You okay there?" Jake asked.

The old man caught his breath. "Just getting over a cold. Things don't shift as easily at my age. Enjoy being young while you can."

"I don't think I qualify as young, George."

"Wait until you're my age and then you'll think differently. Anyway, bottoms up."

Emily picked up the mug from the coffee table in front of her. It had a picture of Mr Happy printed on one side, and it made her smile. When George saw her chuckling, he blushed. "I don't entertain many people your age. Most liquids in this house come in glass bottles."

"It's fine. Who doesn't love the Mr Men?"

"Exactly." George leant over and handed Jake one of the glass tumblers. There was no ice inside, and the golden-brown liquid gave off sickly fumes.

"Cheers," Jake said.

"Cheers."

They clonked their glasses together.

The first sip burned Jake's throat and made him gasp. The second went down a little easier, but it still caused George to chuckle at him. "What's wrong? You never had Aldi's finest Scotch before?"

"I'm just more of a beer and wine drinker."

"Have a little class, Jake. A man your age should be enjoying the finer things in life. Whisky or claret, that's what you want. Distinguished tipples."

"Claret? Right. I'd best get myself down to Aldi then."

The three of them chortled. George had an impressive talent for pushing away awkwardness and making people feel at ease. There was no forced politeness with the man. He seemed genuinely happy to have company in his home.

"So Emily…" he asked, "what are you interested in? Music and boys, I suppose?"

"Ha! Music – yes. Boys… maybe when my boobs grow back."

Jake blushed. "Emily!"

"No, I'm serious. I used to have boobs, George, but now I look like an ironing board. Losing my hair was bad enough, but I really have no chance of pulling a lad now, do I?"

George looked at Jake questioningly. Then he burst out laughing. "Well, lucky for you, my dear, there's a costume shop in town that sells wigs and stuffed bras. Get yourself down there, pronto."

"How do you know it sells bras and wigs?"

George burst out laughing again. "Never you mind!"

Jake started laughing too. Both his daughters had a way with words, but if George didn't mind a little cross humour, then neither did he.

The time passed easily.

Rather than beating a hasty retreat, Jake found himself agreeing to a second whisky. The first had given him a taste.

"Can I have one too?" asked Emily, sitting up in her wheelchair and raising her eyebrows cheekily.

Jake jolted. "No way. You're not old enough, and you're—"

"Ill? Yeah, don't I know it? As for my age, I'll be eighteen in six months – hopefully – and most kids my age have been drinking alcohol for years. Let me live a little, Dad. I've never tasted whisky before."

George chuckled. "Don't let us silly men fool you, my dear. It tastes like cat's piss."

"How do you know what a cat's piss tastes like?" She said it with a smirk, but then she drilled Jake with a pleading stare. "Please, Dad. Today is a good day. Who knows when I'll get another? Who knows *if*?"

"No, Emily. Absolutely not."

"Then just kill me now." She slumped back in her chair and folded her arms. "If I'm never going to experience anything new, then there's no point to anything, is there?"

He shook his head in disbelief. "Jesus, Em, that's a bit dramatic. Have you been spending too much time with Lily?"

"It's not drama, it's the truth. If I wasn't in this chair, I'd be out with boys, drinking and doing God knows what. Let me live a little, instead of always treating me like I'm dying."

George let out an audible sigh, either from awkwardness, or agreement with Emily. Did he feel her frustration, or did he want them to stop arguing in his house?

"Come on, Dad. Please?"

"But… what if it makes you bad, Em? You're fragile."

"You think I can't manage a shot of whisky after months of chemo? Dad, I can probably drink you under the table."

George snorted.

Jake shook his head and sighed. Everything about saying yes felt wrong, yet his daughter deserved to be a normal teenager for once, didn't she? She definitely shouldn't drink, but that was the point, right?

What's the worst it can do?

I don't want to think about it.

"Don't tell your mother," he warned. "And only one."

Her face lit up. It made Jake feel three stones lighter.

George looked at Jake. "You sure?"

Jake nodded.

"Then here's to bad decisions." George poured three more whiskies and handed them out.

"No," said Emily, taking her refilled Mr Happy mug and grinning. "To new friends."

"Cheers to that!" George beamed as if the gesture genuinely touched him. "To new friends."

"To new friends," Jake said, wondering how much trouble he was going to get in for this.

———

It was dark outside when George saw them to the front door. The soft glow of a nearby lamppost cast an amber hue across his overgrown garden, lending the grass a warm sheen.

Or perhaps that's just my head.

Jake could feel the third whisky in his legs. Emily had clearly hated the alcohol, her face contorting with every sip, but she wore a contented smile now, and seemed brighter than she had done in ages. She even stepped out of the front door by herself rather than be wheeled out backwards in her chair.

George leaned on his cane in the doorway. "We should make this a weekly thing," he said. "Drinking's always better with company."

"We'll see," Jake said. "Thank you for tonight. I can't believe we've been here for…" He checked his watch. "Damn, an hour and a half. I only intended on being thirty minutes."

"I'm a wonderful host," George said.

"You are," Emily agreed, giving him a delicate hug before plonking herself down in her wheelchair. "I had fun."

"Any time, young lady. Any time." He stifled a belch and then wobbled back and forth on his cane.

Jake waggled a finger. "But only water next time."

George crossed his heart with his free hand. "I had to welcome you to the street properly. You're one of us now. I'll introduce you to Mary and some others once you've settled in."

There was a rumble of an engine, causing them all to look towards the road.

It was the black Range Rover again, its bright red brake lights melting the night like a pair of searing hot irons. Vincent and his mates appeared and huddled around the driver's side, talking to whoever was inside. They all had their hoods up.

"Who's that?" Emily nodded in the car's direction.

"Best you don't ask," George said. "Not everyone on this street is as charming as me."

"That car was here earlier," Jake said. "I'm assuming it's drugs? Is that the local kingpin or something?"

George grunted. "I don't care who it is, and neither should you."

Jake turned back towards the house and shrugged. "I don't care. Not my business." But he couldn't help glancing back, watching as Vincent seemed to take a small package from whomever was driving the expensive car.

"Most souls on this street are good people," George said, side-eyeing what was going on in the road. "Hard workers, retirees, and a few people down on their luck, but we take care of one another mostly. Don't worry, okay?"

"I'm not worried." Jake folded his arms. "I'm looking forward to meeting everyone."

"Who lives in the Chinese house?" Emily asked. She craned her neck to look down the street.

George frowned. "The what now?"

"The house with the dragon statues."

"Oh, you mean Mr Cho? Lovely man. Jing's seventy-nine now, so doesn't get about like he used to, but he's been here longer than anyone. We all love Mr Cho. He's done us all favours at one time or another."

Jake frowned. "What do you mean, favours?"

"Well, Jing's a bit different from the rest of us. Came here from Hong Kong in the eighties, he did, and brought his strange ways with him. You got a wart needs removing? He'll give you a cream to have it gone in a day. Headache? He'll make you some wonderful mint tea to see it right off."

"Holistic medicine?" Jake frowned. "I've never really believed in that stuff."

The truth was that he'd given Emily all kinds of herbal

remedies and magical supplements that random people on the internet had sworn by blindly, but none had done anything to help her. She had only got sicker, with the added misery of having to drink foul-tasting concoctions three times a day.

"It's not new age hippy stuff." George shook his head. "It's traditional Chinese remedies. Honestly, Jing Cho is a miracle worker. Ask anyone."

"Wonder if he can fix me?" Emily asked, chuckling to herself.

George smiled at her, but he wore the expression strangely, as if he were having to force it into place. "If you have a bad head in the morning from my finest whisky, then yes, Mr Cho has a remedy for that. Think he puts dried penis in it."

Jake grimaced. "The penis of what?"

"I find it best not to ask." George eyed the black Range Rover again, which was now driving away. Once it had gone, he put his hand against the door frame. "Well, I'll bid you folks a good night. I'm an old man and I don't last long these days. Don't be a stranger though, you hear me? Either of you."

"We won't," said Emily, pulling her blanket up over her lap.

"Then goodnight to you both. May you dream happy dreams and hold your bladder till morning." George gave them one last bleary-eyed smile and shut the door.

Jake wheeled his daughter down the overgrown garden path and headed for home. "You feeling okay, sweetie?"

"Better than I have in a while. Whisky is disgusting though. It really does taste like cat's piss."

"God yes. That's why I drink beer and wine. If your mum finds out I let you drink, she'll kill me."

And I'll have no excuse. What was I thinking?

She's happy. Happier than she has been for ages.

"Well, if you don't want me to tell Mum, you better do exactly what I say from now on."

"Don't you blackmail me, you cheeky bugger." He picked up speed, racing his daughter along the pavement. She cackled loudly, probably disturbing the neighbours, but Jake didn't care. Tonight was a good night.

He didn't slow down until they reached number forty-four again. Neither of them could help but gawp at the strange red door, especially after what George had told them about Mr Cho.

A flickering orange glow came from the house's front window, but net curtains stopped them from seeing inside. Beneath the moon's silvery glow, the twin dragons looked particularly menacing, their clay teeth shining. The candle still burned on its hanging brass dish.

"You really think he knows ancient medicine and stuff?" Emily asked. "Like, stuff we don't have in modern medicine?"

Jake pulled a face and spoke quietly. "Mr Cho might have an acne cream or a balm to treat athlete's foot, but herbs and roots can only do so much. It's probably just a placebo effect – people get better on their own and think it's him. More power to the guy, if it helps people get by."

"I want to meet him. He sounds interesting."

"Probably best not to bother him, sweetie. He might put a spell on you."

Emily laughed – even harder when he started racing her chair again. By the time they reached home, it was past nine o'clock, and Maggie eyed the two of them suspiciously, asking what on earth they'd been up to, and why Jake was sweating.

CHAPTER
THREE

SCHOOL WAS as bad as Lily had feared. First thing that morning, and after a summer of long lie-ins, she had wanted to kill herself. It had taken every ounce of mental strength to peel herself away from her pillow and hop into the shower. Then she remembered that they no longer had a shower, only a mildewy old bath. So, after contenting herself with a flannel wash, she had slapped on as much make-up as her parents would allow and put on her school uniform, which felt tighter than it had when she had tried in on two weeks ago in Tesco.

By ten thirty, the tiredness had gone away, and she was actually glad to be back at school with her friends. Some of them she had hung out with a little during the holidays, while others she hadn't seen for weeks. Of course, she had declined to mention her move to Heathskil, but some of her closer friends, who had already known, had spilled the tea and told everyone that Lily now lived in the ghetto. The ridicule had begun from there, growing and taking shape like a piss-covered snowball. While none of the kids at her school were posh, they couldn't resist the chance to kick someone when they were down.

Everyone thinks my sad life is hilarious.

Are they even my real friends?

The day had finally ended, and she was now sitting on a bus back to Heathskil, hoping her mum had made something nice for dinner so she could eat her misery away. She was starving. In fact, lately, it felt like she had a constant hole that needed to be filled. Sometimes she joked that she was stealing all of Emily's weight.

I best stop if that's the case, because she's got no more left to give.

How much longer can she hold on?

Lily rubbed at her temples, a fuzzy feeling behind her eyes. She needed another one of Emily's pills to take the edge off. Problem was, her sister was getting weird about sharing them.

Treats me like I'm a bloody junkie or something.

Maybe she would just go into Emily's room later and grab a couple for when she needed them. The doctors handed them out like Smarties anyway, so where was the harm?

Mum and Dad drink every night. What do I have to relax?

The bus stopped at the end of her street. The doors opened with a hiss and the suspension lowered. She shimmied past a few old people sitting at the front and hopped out onto the pavement. The sky overhead was turning grey as if it were preparing for a downpour. The threat of rain matched her mood.

"Summer truly is over," she said as she started towards her house.

It was a wonder she even knew the way after only a few days, but Tovey Avenue was a simple straight line with a small Aldi supermarket nearby to use as a landmark. As for her house, it was impossible to spot from further down the road, as the terraces were identical, but she could easily follow the door numbers until she reached it.

"Hey there, baby girl." Someone hollered from several metres back, causing her to turn around. A group of lads were walking behind her. They had hoods up, but the one in front lowered his as he caught up to her. His shaved hair had a slice running through it, and there was a similar gap in his eyebrow. A wispy brown beard made it obvious that he was only a little older than she was.

She stopped and put her hands on her hips. "Who are you?"

"You haven't heard about me? Girl, you need to ask around."

"Or you could just tell me."

"Fair enough. I'm V. This is Mikey, Doser, Kaydon, and this fat fuck here is Ryan."

A short lad at the back, who wasn't particularly fat at all, pulled a face. "Fuck off, V!"

"Nice to meet you," Lily said. "You live around here?"

"Next street over, but I do my business all around, innit?"

"You the next Alan Sugar, are you?"

He sucked at his teeth. "More like the next Scarface."

"Uh, huh? We just moved here. I think you already met my dad."

V turned to his buddies and laughed, then turned back to Lily and smoothed down his fledgling goatee. "Yeah, I reckon I met your old man. Offered to help him with some boxes, but he didn't want no help apparently. Bit rude actually. Man was a little vexed."

"What man?"

"Girl, this man. You're a cheeky one, innit?" He smirked

at her, and it brought out a matching response despite her attempts to resist. The lad was a bit of a numpty, but he was cute. Maybe he was just trying to impress her by acting cool? He certainly seemed eager to talk with her.

"I gotta get home," she said, and turned to start walking away. "But maybe I'll see you around?"

"For sure. But yo, you never told me your name, blondie."

"Ask around."

"You bet I will. And, hey, mention me to your sister too. Your old man says she's gonna be out of that chair soon."

She stopped and turned back. "What?"

"Your sister, Lightning McQueen? I wanna meet her too, innit? Man wants to be welcoming."

"You stay away from my sister, you dickhead. She's ill."

"Not forever though, right?" He winked. "I never got with sisters before."

"Gross! Show some respect, you fucking moron."

"Ooh," said the one V had called Ryan. "You made her mad, fam."

"Such language for a little girl," said another, a young guy with dreads.

"She's into you, V. She's proper into you."

"More like disgusted," Lily said, her stomach churning with a desire for violence. "What's your fucking problem, you saddo?"

Vincent wiped the smirk off his face and seemed a little shocked by her anger. "Yo, I apologise. For real. I was only fucking about, but you're right, that was bang out of order. She's gonna be all right, yeah? Your sister?"

Lily shrugged. "I don't know."

"Shit. No joke?"

"Well, she's not getting any better." It felt strange to

admit the truth out loud to a stranger, but good. Lying to herself was exhausting sometimes. "But what do I know?"

V took another step, getting close to her. "Probably more than most people. I feel bad for you."

"You know nothing about me."

He folded his arms and leant in, speaking as if he were letting her in on a secret. "My mum got MS when I was little, so I get it. I had to watch her wither away and die, not being able to do nothing about it, you get me? And my old man weren't no fucking help either. Twat disappeared with some tart and left me to deal with shit all on my own. Luckily, I got an uncle who took me in, so the situation got right in the end. I can't complain, innit?"

Lily looked into his eyes and saw something. Pain. Like looking into a mirror. "Well, I don't have anyone to take me in," she said, "so I'm stuck here on this shitty street."

"Tovey Avenue ain't so bad. 'Specially now a tidy piece like you lives here." He made a clicking sound inside his cheek, as if he were trying to call over a horse.

She rolled her eyes. "I'm going now. Don't speak about my sister again, okay? I mean it. I'll kick your balls in."

He held both hands up in defence while his friends sniggered behind him. "Warning received. Hey, if things get rough and you need a friend, me and the boys are always around. Come hang sometime, yeah?"

"I'll think about it. Catch you later, V."

"Soon, I hope."

Lily walked the rest of the way home, trying not to smile.

Play it cool, Lil.

Maybe this place isn't so bad after all.

———

Dinner was spaghetti bolognaise, which Jake was just in the mood for. There was nothing quite like a simple, carb-filled meal, although being off work had caused him to plump up, so he really needed to think about going on a diet. His forearms, usually rock hard from sawing wood and turning screwdrivers, seemed half the size they had been a year ago.

I feel tired, sluggish.

And starving.

They all sat down at the small kitchen table and pulled in their chairs. Last night, after George's soiree, Emily had grown tired and gone straight to bed, awakening that morning to another bad day. In pain for several hours, she had snoozed the afternoon away on the living room sofa. At least she was awake for dinner.

"You have an appointment with Dr Kwami tomorrow," Maggie said, sliding her hand out across the table and getting Emily's attention. "Try your best to eat, so you have your strength up, okay?"

Emily nodded gloomily, a little green around the gills. "I'll do my best."

"It's at three," said Jake, turning to Lily, "so there'll probably be no one home when you get back from school. We won't be long though."

Emily tutted. "You don't have to come, Dad. Mum and I will be fine on our own."

"I want to come. What if they decide to change your treatment?"

Lily curled some spaghetti around her fork. "It's fine, Em. I'm a big girl. I'll just sit in my room and contemplate the shittiness of my life. Or masturbate. I'm getting really good at it lately."

"Don't be disgusting," Maggie chided her. "Did you not have a good day at school today?"

"It was okay, I suppose."

"Just okay?" Jake raised an eyebrow at her. "Was it not good seeing all your friends again after the holidays?"

"Everyone found out about me living on Benefit Street, so I'm pretty much a leper now. I might last a week if I'm lucky. Bury me in Bournville, okay? Right in the middle of the Cadbury's car park where they have all those big milk tankers."

Jake and Maggie glanced at each other and sighed.

Emily sighed too. "I used to think I hated school, but I miss it now."

"You'll be doing your A levels next year, sweetie." Maggie smiled and scooped up a forkful of pasta. "Just as soon as you're feeling better."

Emily moved her food around her plate and muttered. "Can't wait."

"You still want to be a teacher someday, don't you?"

She shrugged and didn't reply.

Jake reached out to his daughter and put the back of his hand against her forehead. "You're warm, sweetheart. Are you getting a fever?"

"Don't think so. Just tired. I… I'm sorry, Mum. I really don't think I can eat this."

Maggie looked at Jake with concern, but then smiled again at their daughter. "Okay, sweetheart, maybe later. You could have a protein shake instead?"

"That would be better." Emily blinked slowly. "I don't think my stomach can take anything solid."

Maggie got up and pulled out a tub of bodybuilding supplement from beneath the sink. Jake hated the smell of the stuff, but it was the best way for Emily to get the protein she needed. Maggie mixed it with tap water inside a shaker and set it down in front of their daughter. "There you go, honey."

Emily sipped the liquid gingerly, accustomed to the taste enough now that she no longer grimaced when she drank it. "Thanks."

"I met those boys," Lily said through a mouthful of spaghetti. "V and co."

"What?" Jake turned to her. "You're talking about Vincent? When did you see him?"

"After I got off the bus. He was just hanging about."

"Did he bother you?"

Lily flicked her hair back over her shoulder and shrugged. "Not really. He just wanted to get to know me."

"Well, forget about that. He's bad news."

I know because I was a young lad living on an estate once too.

"Oh chill out, Dad. V's all right. He even apologised after he upset me."

Maggie frowned. "Why did he upset you?"

"Oh…" Lily licked her lips and glanced at her sister.

"What?" Emily frowned, clearly puzzled. "Why are you looking at me?"

"Vincent was being a bit of a perv about you, sis, so I told him to shut his mouth or I'd kick his nuts in."

She pulled a face. "Why would he be saying things about me?"

"I suppose he's thinking about the day you'll be out of that chair. You used to be really fit."

"Oh thanks, that's so nice of you to say." Emily rolled her eyes.

"You know what I mean. Once you're better, the boys will be all over you."

Emily smirked and straightened up a little. "You'll have to give this V my number, then. I've obviously still got it."

"Sex on wheels." Lily winked at her. "But V's mine. I'll get you the number of one of his ugly friends."

"Bitch."

Jake slapped the table and made everybody flinch. "Neither of you is going to spend any time with those lowlifes, do you hear me?"

Lily pulled a face. "Seriously, Dad? Are you going to send us to a nunnery if we don't obey? What's got into you?"

Maggie shook her head as if Jake were a fool. "You know the more you tell them not to do something, the more they'll just go ahead and do it. What are you getting so het up about?"

"I demand better for my family." He banged his fist on the table and made everyone flinch. It was unlike Jake to lash out, but it felt like all three of them were ganging up on him, which wasn't fair when all he ever did was worry about their safety. Even so, he was sorry for the outburst and tried to show it. "Look, our fortunes may have taken a downturn recently, but that doesn't mean we have to lower our standards."

Lily stacked her hands neatly on the table. "Oh, I didn't realise we were snobs." She looked at Emily. "Did you know we were snobs? What happened to our butler?"

Emily chuckled. "I think Dad buried him under the patio. That's why we had to move."

Jake raised an eyebrow at Emily. She was only having a giggle – trying to feel like a normal, insolent teenager – but she knew as well as he did that Vincent was bad news. "Have you forgotten about the black Range Rover last night, Emily?"

Lily looked at her sister. "What black Range Rover?"

"There was this dodgy car last night," Emily explained

with a shrug. "Vincent and his mates were talking to the driver. Dad thinks it was a drug deal."

"What else do you think it was?" he demanded.

"I dunno. Just a bunch of lads chatting, maybe?" She rubbed at her eyes, making them red. "It was probably nothing."

"It was drugs!"

Lily shook her head and snorted. "Jesus, Dad. You wanted us to give this place a chance, but you're the one who's being judgemental."

Jake placed a hand against his forehead and groaned. "I'm just watching out for you, Lily. I don't want you associating with people who are going to get you into trouble."

"Then who am I supposed to associate with? You moved us here."

"I had no choice."

"Yes, you did."

"No, I didn't."

"Yes, you did."

"Lily, no!"

"You *did* have a choice, and you chose Emily."

The silence seemed to explode, throwing everyone back in their chairs.

Jake opened his mouth to speak, but he couldn't get any words out.

Is she seriously complaining that Emily gets more attention? How can I have raised someone so self-centred?

Eventually, Maggie broke the silence. It clearly took effort to keep from raising her voice, but she managed to stay calm. "What are you talking about, Lily? Explain."

Lily opened her mouth, about to explain, when there the front door's letterbox clattered – and then clattered again.

Jake growled. "Who the hell is that?"

"Just go see," Maggie told him, reaching out and stroking his arm. "Take a breath."

He slid back in his chair and got up. He didn't so much as walk into the hallway as stomp, the fury inside him like an unborn child, growing and growing.

The front door was locked, so he grabbed his keys from the hook on the wall and slid the right one into the lock. After a few seconds, the key stopped fighting him and the lock turned. He opened the door.

Nobody there.

Only a slight breeze whistling through the gaps in the brick wall around the front garden. Amber light flickered from a nearby lamppost.

Jake stepped out onto the front path and looked around. Tovey Avenue was deserted.

"What the fuck?"

Had somebody lifted the letterbox and run off?

Seriously, do kids still play that game?

Jake felt a breeze against his cheeks. It cooled him, calmed him, and allowed him to unclench his fists. He took a few seconds of fresh air, then went back inside.

When he re-entered the kitchen, he sat down without a word.

"Who was it?" Maggie asked.

"Nobody. The letter box is a bit flimsy. I think the wind lifted it."

Maggie nodded, then glared at Lily. "Good, then that means Lily can explain herself. What exactly is your problem, young lady?"

Lily shrugged.

Jake snorted air out of his nose. "You're not getting off that easily. You clearly have a problem, Lily, so spit it out."

She glared at them each in turn, her expression

suggesting they were all idiots. "Fine. Emily got sick and everything went to shit. Mum, you turned into a nervous wreck – like mental ward patient level – and Dad, you totally fucking lost it. You didn't need to close the business, and you didn't need to force us to move house. It's not that we needed the money, it's that you can't keep your shit together long enough to do any work. Emily got sick, sure, but that didn't mean life had to stop for us all."

"It's only until Emily gets better," Maggie said, shaking her head in confusion. "Lily, how can you—"

"She's not getting better!" Lily turned to Emily. "Sorry, sis, but I can't keep acting like you're on the mend. You're not. Shit, I've seen zombies healthier than you."

Jake shot up out of his chair, unable to sit still any longer. "Lily? What the hell is wrong with you?"

"Nothing's wrong with me. It's *you* lot who are crazy."

"I… I can't deal with this right now." Jake leant forward and put his hands on the table for support. "Do you think I asked for this? Life took a dump on us, Lil, and it stinks to high heaven, but what can we do except stick together and get through it?"

Maggie nodded in agreement. "You might think your life is over, Lily, but you're fourteen years old. You have your entire life ahead of you, for Christ's sake."

"Unlike me," Emily said. "In cancer years, I'm like ninety-seven."

Everyone gawped at her.

"Come on," she said weakly. "That was funny."

Lily started laughing and shaking her head. "Fuck, sis."

"Lily!" Maggie chided. "Seriously, your potty mouth is getting worse."

"Don't fight." Emily rubbed at her temples as if she had a headache. "Please. It makes me feel horrible."

Jake was still standing at the table, so he moved over to Emily and studied her closely. "Sweetheart, are you—"

Emily lurched forward and threw up across the table. It was mostly liquid – the protein shake she'd just ingested – and it covered the entire table, racing toward the edges.

Lily slid her chair back and yelped. "Gross!"

Maggie leapt up and grabbed a tea towel from the oven door handle.

Jake put a hand on Emily's shoulder. She was trembling. "Easy, sweetheart. Easy."

Emily threw up again, this time a little solid mixed with bile. Then she retched emptily, sounding like a wild animal caught in a snare. Nothing else came up, but the slick puddle on the table gave off rancid fumes.

"I… I'm okay," she said between heaves.

"Yeah," said Lily, covering her mouth and nose. "You really seem like it."

Maggie started wiping the table with the tea towel, but it was insufficient for the task, and she ending up pushing most of the frothy liquid around. It drip-drip-dripped onto the floor.

Emily started crying. "I-I want to go to bed."

"Okay, sweetheart." Jake scooped her hair back tenderly and placed it against her back. "Let me help you."

He tried to lift her under her arms, to hop her over to her wheelchair, but she was a dead weight, even as thin as she was. "I can't move, Dad. I… I… I can't. Just… just want to go to bed."

He shushed her. "Okay, honey, I've got you. Daddy's got you."

Jake bent at the knees and scooped his daughter up into his arms. Carrying her to bed was the easiest and the hardest thing he'd ever had to do.

———

"Is she okay?" Maggie asked, pouring two large glasses of wine. The kitchen oven's clock read 10:10. Settling Emily to sleep had taken almost an hour. Just like when she was a little girl, she had insisted Jake sit on her bed and gently tickle her tummy until she fell asleep. It felt good to care for her in such a way – a way he'd thought long behind him – but at the same time it seemed to signify some kind of surrender in his daughter. Rather than a growing woman, Emily had become a child again, unable to drift off to sleep unassisted. The feel of her ribs jutting out beneath his fingertips had put tears in his eyes.

Jake spoke, but became dismayed when a sob interrupted his words. He had to take a moment to steel himself and try again. "She's asleep. The nausea went away, but…"

Maggie nodded. Neither of them wanted to say it.

She looks awful.

Maggie passed him a glass of wine, which he downed half of in one go. It tasted sour, but his emotions dimmed. The panic, the sadness, the anger – they all retreated a step. The problem was, they always came back before long, shouting and hollering like a roomful of unruly children, requiring him to chase away their voices with a second large glass of wine. And then a third.

I'm drinking too much.

It's the only way I can cope.

"We'll speak to the doctors tomorrow," Maggie said. "Demand them to help her."

Jake took another swig of wine, almost finishing the glass. "They need to change her treatment. All they've done is make her sicker. I swear, I don't even think they know what they're doing half the time. We should start looking into private treatments – experimental treatments."

Maggie blinked slowly, one of her tired gestures he knew well after two decades of marriage. "You're right, I agree. We'll discuss it tomorrow, but…" She shook her head and sighed.

"But what?"

"Lily? What she said tonight…"

"She's just being a teenager. She'll adjust. Everything'll be fine."

"I know that, but what if she has a point? We're ruining her life, babe, and if we start throwing money at experimental treatments for Emily – which might not even work – are we not sacrificing her future even more?"

"What are you saying? If there's a chance we can help Emily, then we have to—"

"But what if we can't help her? What if it's hopeless?" Maggie's voice turned shrill, almost shouting at him now. "We've already lost so much. I think… I think we might need to start preparing for the worst."

"Mag…" Jake shook his head, blood pulsing in both his temples. Why was she saying such dreadful things?

Why was she giving up?

She reached out and took his hands in hers. "She's not getting better, honey, and while I intend to give the doctors absolute hell tomorrow, I don't want to forget about our other daughter. Lily has suffered too."

"Not like Emily has."

"Of course not, but Lily deserves a normal life. We can't let cancer take both our girls."

Jake finished his glass of wine and pushed the empty glass towards his wife. She refilled it from the bottle beside her and pushed it back. She'd barely even sipped from her own glass, but once she got started, she would steadily hasten until she was drunk. They ran a different race, but they crossed the finishing line at the same time.

We're both drinking too much. I don't even know when it started.

"I can't think right now," he said, rubbing at his throbbing temples. "I just want to shut off."

"I know, babe. Me too."

"What did we do to deserve this, Mag? We had all these hopes, all these dreams. Everything was going exactly how we wanted it to."

"Maybe that's the point." She ran a chewed fingertip back and forth in the groove beneath her bottom lip. It'd been a while since she'd last painted her nails, and she never used to bite them. "Life isn't supposed to go exactly how we want it to, is it? Life does its own thing, and we just have to roll with the punches. We'll survive, whatever comes, but I worry what'll be left of us afterwards."

Jake wanted to give her some sort of reply, but he didn't know what to say. In fact, he didn't fully understand what she was saying.

What will be left of us?

"Mum? Dad?" Lily entered the kitchen, her pink-streaked hair tied up in a ponytail. After dinner, she'd sprawled out on the living room sofa with her phone glued to her hand. Had she been listening to them talk?

Maggie smiled. "Yes, love?"

"I'm going to bed, but I have a bit of a headache. Do we have any painkillers?"

"Oh." Maggie stood up. "I think there might be some paracetamol in the cupboard. Hold on."

Lily eyed the glasses on the table. "How about a sip of your wine?"

Maggie glared at her, but then she chuckled. "You have school tomorrow, young lady. One sip!"

With a great big smile, Lily trotted up to the table and took a swig from her mother's glass. A big swig.

"Hey, young lady," Jake said, prodding her in the ribs. "Put that down before it's all gone."

Lily put the glass back down on the table, half of it now gone. The look on her face was the picture of mischief, and he loved it. Although, he thought to himself, both his daughters had now drunk alcohol in the last twenty-four hours. He felt a pang of irresponsibility about that.

Maybe Maggie's right. Are we failing Lily?

Maggie went into the cupboard and brought out a foil packet. "Just one pill. You're not supposed to drink with them."

"I had one sip of wine. It'll be fine."

"Do as your mother says, *you*." Jake prodded her ribs again and made her giggle.

Maggie handed Lily one paracetamol, which she took to the sink and swigged from the tap like an urchin. Wiping her mouth with the back of her hand, she bid them both goodnight. "See you in the morning, DNA-givers."

"Sweet dreams, honey." Jake tilted his head, marvelling at how beautiful she was. He reached out and pulled her into a hug, which she broke away from after just two seconds. It was longer than he usually got.

"Night night," said Maggie, also stealing a quick cuddle.

Lily left the kitchen and creaked up the stairs.

After a moment, Maggie bit her bottom lip. "You think she was listening to us?"

"Probably," Jake said. "But I'm sure she won't hold it against us."

They looked at each other and laughed.

While sipping her wine, Maggie let out an enormous yawn, mouth stretching wide.

"Jesus," Jake said. "I can see what you had for dinner."

She covered her mouth and playfully jabbed him on the arm. "I looked online," she said. "They collect the bins tomorrow. Can you take out the recycling?"

He groaned. "Seriously? Wish you'd told me earlier."

"You're still dressed. It won't kill you. There's only a bit of cardboard from the move, along with a few empties." She refilled her glass and slid the empty wine bottle across the table.

"All right. I'll do it now before I forget." He stood up.

"You fancy a cuppa before bed?"

He snatched the empty bottle and wiggled it in his hand. "No, I fancy another glass of wine. There's more in the fridge."

"I'll join you."

Jake went into the hallway and unlocked the front door again. A full moon shone down on the roof tiles of the houses opposite, and the street seemed even quieter now. In fact, he winced when he tipped the green recycling bin onto its wheels and caused glass bottles to clink together inside.

"Hang about, it's daddy dearest. How's it going, bruv?"

Jake wheeled the bin to the end of the path and looked around. It took a moment for his eyes to adjust, but he soon spotted Vincent – scarf around his mouth – and two other youths sitting on a wall two houses down.

"What are you doing out here?" Jake demanded. "Haven't you got anything better to do?"

Vincent yanked the scarf from his mouth. "Yo, what's your fucking problem, bruv? Man is just out here chilling, and you're being rude. Again."

"You're outside my house, and you've been pestering my daughter."

Vincent moved closer, an absurd swagger to his walk. "I've been what now, bruv?"

"You harassed Lily after she got off the bus."

"Harassed her? It was just chat, so back off, yeah, because man is getting seriously vexed." He raised a hand and made a gun shape with his fingers and thumbs.

Jake marched the remaining steps to confront the lad. He saw an anxious flicker in Vincent's eyes and took joy in it. "You think I'm scared of a little prick like you? Think again. If I catch you talking to my daughter again, I'll wipe the floor with you, innit bruv?"

"Daughters."

"What?"

Vincent looked back at his mates and sniggered, before turning back to face Jake with a smirk on his face. "You got two daughters, bruv, so don't limit man's options. Wheels she can stay sitting and still impress me, you know what I mean?"

Behind him, his friends cackled and whooped like gibbons.

Jake's hand was moving before he even realised it. He was going to knock this kid's block off – screw the consequences.

Vincent ducked out of the way with plenty of time to spare. In fact, the young lad dodged Jake's half-drunken swing so easily that he was able to throw a punch of his own in reply.

A fist struck Jake underneath his ribs so hard he feared he'd been stabbed. He crumpled to the pavement, gasping and clutching his chest. He couldn't get air. Couldn't breathe.

Vincent seemed slightly shocked by what he'd done, glancing around as if he expected to be pounced on or apprehended, but once he realised no one had seen – or cared – about his attack, he became emboldened. Puffing out his chest, he glared down at Jake on the floor. "Dickhead! Swing at me again and I'll end you, bruv."

His two mates behind him continued cackling, flicking their fingers and making snapping sounds. "You proper dropped him, fam," one of them said. "I reckon he's gonna cry, for real."

Vincent stood over Jake and glared. "You wanna live here, bruv, you better show mad respect from now on, you get me? Only reason I ain't stompin' your ass into the pavement is because it would upset Lily, and if she's upset with me, she ain't gonna want to put that little mouth of hers to work, is she?"

Despite being sprawled on the ground, groaning and gasping, Jake launched himself at Vincent's legs. "Bastard!"

Vincent hopped back and delivered a swift kick to Jake's ribs, reigniting his agony and taking away the last morsel of breath he had left inside him. He collapsed face down on the cold, dirty pavement, moaning in misery.

"Fucking wasteman," Vincent said, spitting at Jake. He then walked away with his mates without looking back, their laughter echoing down the street.

Jake lay still and groaned, waiting – and hoping – for his lungs to start working again.

Maggie came out and found him fifteen minutes later, still lying on the pavement.

CHAPTER
FOUR

"ARE you sure you don't want to call the police about last night?" Maggie asked him as they grabbed their jackets from the cupboard beneath the stairs. Summer was waning, and it seemed like Autumn wanted to start early.

"What would be the point?" Jake grabbed his wallet from the shelf above the hallway radiator and shrugged at her. He tried to ignore the searing pain in his ribs and the difficulty in breathing. "Even if I report it, the police won't do anything. That's why you have troublemakers like Vincent in the first place."

"I can't believe he just attacked you. What if he tries again?"

Jake tugged on his jacket and turned away, unable to look his wife in the eye. "I'll worry about that later. My mind's on Emily right now." He checked his watch. "She really needs to get up or we're going to be late. It's past two."

Maggie nodded. "I know. I left her sleeping because of how she was feeling last night. Hopefully the doctors can change her medication to something stronger."

"Any stronger and she'll be sleeping round the clock."

"You want to go wake her up, babe? Oh, and take her some water. She's always thirsty when she wakes up."

Jake went into the kitchen and filled a pint glass with water from the tap. Then, passing by Maggie in the hallway, he started up the stairs. "Honey," he called. "Are you awake?"

No answer. Emily could sleep through a hurricane.

"Sweetheart. We need to get going to make your appointment. Time to wake up." He looked back at Maggie, standing at the bottom of the stairs. She gave him a reassuring smile.

It wasn't unusual to have to jostle Emily awake, but she hadn't woken at all today, which was strange. She usually had at least a few hours late morning where her strength was up.

It's fine. She just had a rough night with her tummy.

Jake approached his daughter's bedroom and nudged open the door. Immediately, his eyes fell upon the bundle of soft blankets on the bed, and then to the fallen copy of *Dracula* lying on the floor. He went to call out again, but didn't want to startle her, so instead he crept around to the side of her bed and reached out.

"Sweetheart?" He rocked her gently by the shoulder. "Emily?"

Silence. His daughter didn't move.

He shook her again, calling out a little louder.

Emily still didn't move.

"Come on now, sweetheart, wakey-wakey. Emily? Open your eyes. Emily?"

He shook her roughly, something he would never usually do. His fingers dug into her bony arm. She was breathing – he was certain of it – but…

Wake up, Emily. Please.

Jake's legs turned hollow. His hands were shaking.

There was watery vomit on Emily's cheek.

She wouldn't wake up.

"M-Maggie?" Jake tried to shout, but his voice emerged as a pathetic croak. He had to clear his throat, close his eyes, and try again. "Mag," he bellowed. "Mag, come here quick. MAGGIE!"

Maggie raced up the stairs. "What is it? What is it?"

"It's Emily. She won't wake up."

His wife flew into the room and almost collided with the bed. Jake had to leap out of her way as she raced to Emily's side. "Come on, sweetheart," she said. "Wake up now, it's Mummy. Wake up!" She shook her by the shoulder. "Emily! Wake up, wake up, wake up!"

Jake fell back against the wall, unable to support his own weight. As Maggie's hysteria increased, and Emily remained unconscious, he reached into his pocket and grabbed his phone to call an ambulance. He could barely speak when they answered.

––––––––

Jake stood on the pavement, watching the paramedics lift Emily into the back of the ambulance. Maggie buzzed around the road like a drunken fly, weeping and calling out for their daughter. "She doesn't have her headscarf," she cried. "Let me get her headscarf. Emily? Emily, it's going to be okay. Be careful with her."

Jake leant against the garden's crumbling brick wall, his legs vague and uncertain beneath him. He pulled his grey woollen jacket around himself, trying to keep from shivering but quickly discovering that it had nothing to do with the cold. In his hands, he held an oversized jumper for Maggie, but she wouldn't take it from him, too hysterical even to dress. He'd barely managed it himself, pulling one arm into his jacket and then the other over several surreal, slow-moving minutes where he seemed to move through ice-cold sludge.

Emily's still alive. They said she was breathing.

But for how long? There's barely anything of her left.

Emily, please hold on.

The ambulance had turned up with its sirens blaring, which had attracted attention. Curtains twitched on both sides of the street. Vincent and his followers were watching too, loitering at the end of the road with colourful energy drinks in each of their hands. At least they had their hoods down for a change.

It took all Jake had not to yell at everyone to mind their own fucking business.

Do they find this entertaining? My daughter's suffering?

"Jake? Jake, is everything all right?"

Jake turned to see George hobbling down the pavement towards him, his cane tap-tapping on the pavement like a scuttling insect leg.

"George?"

"What's happened, Jake? Is it one of the girls?"

"Emily. She… She won't wake up."

George said nothing. He just stood beside Jake and watched while a paramedic slammed the ambulance's rear doors, enclosing Emily inside. The lights continued to flash silently on the boxy vehicle's roof. Jake stared into them, unable to blink, even as the glare hurt his eyes.

Maggie turned away from the ambulance, sobbing, and staggered over to Jake. When she saw George, she glared suspiciously.

"This is George," Jake explained before she shooed him away for being nosey. "He came to check on us."

"Oh." Maggie nodded at George but didn't bother to say hello. Instead, she gazed vacantly at Jake through glassy eyes. "We need to follow them. They're taking her to the Queen Elizabeth. You need to drive. I… I'm in no state."

"I'm not sure I can drive either," he said. He held out his hands. Both were trembling.

"Just take it slow," George said, putting a warm hand on Jake's back. "I would offer to drive you both myself, but I haven't been behind the wheel in a decade. Arthritis in my knees and the vision of a mole."

"It's okay, George." Jake gave his wife a nod. "I'll drive. I can manage."

But he just stood there, inert, unable to get going.

Maggie grabbed his hand and looked at him. "Jake? Let's get in the car, okay? We have to go."

"Yep. Yep, I'll just grab my keys."

As soon as I can move my feet.

Move.

Come on!

Using all of his willpower, Jake staggered into the house and grabbed his keys from the hook beside the door. Then, hurrying back outside, he fumbled with the key fob until he succeeded in unlocking the X-Trail. Its sidelights blinked with a friendly bleep.

The ambulance took off, sirens wailing, blue lights strobing almost invisibly in the mid-afternoon sunshine. Within seconds, it reached the end of the street and swung around the corner, out of sight.

Emily was gone.

"Jake, come on," Maggie urged. She hurried around to

the X-Trail's passenger side and yanked open the door. "Get in."

Jake failed to move again until George put a hand on his arm and made him flinch. "She'll be okay," his neighbour told him with a positive nod. "That's all you need to tell yourself, okay?"

Jake took a step towards his car, but then paused. "Lily! She'll be home in an hour. I-I'll text her to let her know what's going on, but can you—"

George put a hand on his back and gently pushed him. "I'll hang about and check on her. You just get going."

"Thank you. Thank you, George." He nodded to himself. "Right, I'm going. To the hospital."

He opened the driver-side door and slid in behind the steering wheel. For a second, he just stared vacantly through the windshield, but eventually he forced himself to press the button and start the engine. Once he put the car in drive and pulled away from the kerb, his nerves began to settle. He could get them to the hospital in one piece, he was sure. The problem was, the ambulance had sped away so quickly that Emily would arrive there first.

She's going to be on her own.

What if the worst happens and we're not there?

No, she's going to be okay. That's all I need to tell myself.

She's going to be okay.

She's going to be okay.

As Jake pulled onto the main road, he glanced across at Maggie. "She's going to be okay, honey. She's going to be okay."

Maggie nodded and smiled, but there were tears streaming down her cheeks. After a moment, she repeated his words. "She's going to be… to be… to be okay."

Jake nodded and stamped his foot down on the accelerator.

————

Lily got off the bus after staring at her phone for the previous ten minutes. Her dad had texted her just as the last bell had rung at school, the afternoon's maths equations still half-finished in her book.

Emily rushed to hospital. Will call you. Neighbour George will check on you. Dad x.

The short message had left her numb.

It felt like she'd spent the entire last year waiting for her sister to suddenly die. Was today the day it finally happened?

Is Emily gone?

Do I not have a sister anymore?

Lily walked along the pavement towards home, not quite knowing what to do. Should she try to get to the hospital somehow? Call her mum and dad? Or should she just go home and wait? If Emily was in a bad way – or worse – then should she be there or not? Did she even *want* to be?

She told herself not to jump to conclusions. Her dad's text message had said nothing specifically, so there was no reason to freak out and assume the worst.

Emily could have chopped her finger off for all I know, or fallen down the stairs. She's always been clumsy.

As she took off her school tie and stuffed it in her blazer pocket, she picked up the pace, wanting to be inside with the door closed where she could think about what to do privately.

Best thing to do is wait for Mum and Dad to call.

With good news or bad?

She sent a text reply to her dad.

Am almost home. Is Emily okay? Please let me know what's going on.

She put a kiss at the end, then deleted it. Somehow, it felt inappropriate.

Outside her house, Lily spotted V standing alone. She didn't know if she was glad to see him right now or not, and she was confused about why he was staring at her glumly.

"Hey," he said. "You okay?"

She frowned. "Yeah. I'm just going inside. What are you doing here?"

"I wanted to check that you knew about your sister."

"Um, she's gone to the hospital, right? Do you know what happened?"

"There was an ambulance." He rubbed his hands together near his stomach. "I don't know what happened, but your mum and dad were in a bad way. I didn't know if they'd got hold of you yet, so I wanted to make sure you knew."

She allowed herself a second to study him, to try to figure out why he was acting as though he cared. She didn't find an answer. "My dad texted me," she said. "Thanks."

"All right, cool." He suddenly seemed uncomfortable and started fidgeting even more, grabbing at his fingers and popping his knuckles. "I, um, guess I'll leave you to it then. I'm really sorry about your sister, L."

"I appreciate it," she said.

"No worries." He half turned away, but hesitated to leave. Turning back, he spoke again. "Despite what people might think about me, I'm not—"

"Get away from her!" An old man with a walking stick came hobbling towards them. "You buzz off, Vincent. Do you hear me?"

V put his hands up. "Whatever you say, Limp. Was just being neighbourly, innit?"

Lily gave V the briefest of smiles as he stepped backwards into the road. "I'll see you later," she said. "Maybe."

"Sure thing, blondie." He winked at her and gave her the cheekiest of grins.

V crossed the road as the old man came closer. "I'm George," he said, out of breath and leaning on his cane. "I told your dad I'd check on you. It's Lily, right? Are you doing okay?" He turned and glared at V on the other side of the street. "Was he bothering you?"

"I'm fine. Do you know what happened to my sister?"

"All your dad said was that Emily wouldn't wake up. An ambulance came to collect her."

"Wouldn't wake up?" Lily felt woozy. To keep from falling, she sat down on the wall outside her front garden. "Not waking up is a pretty bad thing, right? As in, this might be it?"

George leant against the wall beside her, grunting slightly as he bent. He held his cane with both hands, propping it between his legs. There was a dull glass globe on the handle that was actually pretty cool. "Don't assume the worst, my dear. Life is much better when you choose hope."

"Hope doesn't fix anything though, does it?"

"Nor does assuming the worst, but at least hope feels better."

She nodded. There was wisdom in that, she supposed, but why was this old guy even talking to her? Emily's illness was a private family matter, and she had never even met him before. "I should go inside," she said. "Thanks for checking on me."

"No problem at all. I'm very sorry things are so tough for you right now, Lily. For all of you."

"You have no idea."

"No, I probably don't." He gave her a warm smile, the corners of his eyes crinkling. "I'm happy to listen though, if you'd like to talk for a minute?"

The old guy was badly dressed, in a grungy blue jumper that was a few sizes too big and tatty black trousers that looked like they had been around before mirrors were invented. He also had the craziest grey sideburns, but at the same time, he had a kind face and a reassuring smile.

"I'm not much of a talker," she muttered. "In fact, talking about Emily is the last thing I want to do right now. My whole life revolves around cancer, and I don't even have it." She expected him to say something to that, but he didn't, so to fill the silence, she spoke again. "Mum and Dad have forgotten I exist."

"Parents have a weakness," he told her, staring into the dull glass globe on the end of his cane, "and that weakness is worry. It fills us up, you see, makes it hard for us to focus. Right now, your mum and dad are so filled with worry that they can only deal with one crisis at a time."

Lily rolled her eyes. "My sister. Always my sister."

"Your sister is their biggest worry, so yes, their focus is most probably on her. Take it as a compliment."

"A compliment? How is it a compliment?"

He looked up at her and smiled, his eyes so faded they were almost grey. "They don't worry about you as much, Lily, because they can trust you to take care of yourself. Don't you think that could be the truth of it?"

"You really don't know me, do you?" She chuckled ruefully and pulled her blazer around herself. "Emily's always been the sweet daughter, the smart daughter, the well-behaved daughter. Her cancer has only made her more of a saint. She doesn't lash out or get angry about it, she doesn't blame or hate. No, she just plods along like the plucky little trooper she is. My sister has been ill for so long now that it just feels normal." Shaking her head, she let out a breath. "But it's over now, and… and part of me is glad. Does that make me evil?"

George kept the soft, reassuring smile on his face. "I don't think you're evil, my dear. I think you're probably exhausted and scared and confused and an all manner of other things that are hard to deal with."

"But I'm relieved my sister might be dead." For some reason, she wanted this stranger's blame. She wanted him to confirm what she knew about herself.

That I'm horrible and selfish, just like Mum and Dad think I am.

"It's perfectly reasonable to feel relieved," George said. "Tomorrow you'll feel something else, and the day after that, something else again. Emotions don't define us, Lily. They come and go. Like sneezes."

She frowned. "Sneezes?"

"They're intense for a moment, sure, but once you let them out, they're gone."

"And sometimes they leave snot everywhere."

He raised a bushy eyebrow at her. "We should probably leave the metaphor there before you spoil it any further. Are you okay, Lily? Do you need anything?"

He's too nice. I don't like it. It's weird.

"I think I'm good." Lily stood up from the wall and brushed her hands over her backside. "I'm going to go inside and wait for Dad to call. Thanks for the chat."

"Anytime, my dear. I'm at number fifty-two if you need anything. Old men like me don't have much to do except be of use to others."

"Fifty-two, got it. Nice to meet you, George." She

wandered up the path and put her key in the lock, but the door was already unlocked, so she simply let herself in. Let herself into a cold, dark, empty house.

It's like the inside of my soul.

She had felt a little invaded by George, although part of that was probably due to having spilled her feelings to a stranger, which was so embarrassing she could die. She didn't know what had got into her. The old man had a harmless, disarming quality about him, but now he was gone, she felt tricked into talking. Or manipulated. Or… she didn't really know.

He's probably a child groomer, and he just used his powers on me.

Why the hell did Dad ask him to check on me, someone I've never even met?

She went into the kitchen to make herself a cup of tea. While the kettle was boiling, there was a knock at the door. Clearly George wasn't done with her yet.

I'm going to kick his cane.

Hissing to herself, she went back out into the hall and opened the front door. "Yes?"

V stood there with a sombre expression on his face that did not suit him at all. "I, um, never got to properly say goodbye because of Limp interrupting us," he said. "Just wanted to see if you needed anything."

Lily stood in the doorway and thought about it for a moment. Eventually, she had an answer. "Some company?"

Vincent smiled.

CHAPTER
FIVE

EVERY MINUTE FELT LIKE TEN, so the two-hour wait was pure torture.

Jake and Maggie sat on opposite sides of a small private room at the back of A&E. Maggie had a plastic cup of water in her hand, taken from the dispenser in the corner, but Jake had gone and got himself a hot chocolate from the hallway vending machine. He always found it a calming drink, even more so than tea. He remembered drinking cups and cups of it seventeen years ago when Maggie had been in never-ending labour with Emily.

She's always been a stubborn one, refusing to come out for twelve hours.

I need you to be stubborn now, dear daughter. Don't give up.

Lily had texted twice to say she was okay, but Jake hated the fact he hadn't been able to reply with any good news. The doctors had been with Emily since the moment she'd arrived, but they hadn't come out even once to provide an update. Now and then, a nurse would rush by the window at the top of the door, but no one came in. No one spoke to them.

His daughter was still alive. If she wasn't, they would have heard something.

She's fighting.

I just wish I could fight with her.

"I need to know what's going on," Maggie said, chewing at her thumbnail. Her left knee bobbed up and down frantically. "They can't just keep us in here without a clue of what's happening."

"They're focused on Emily. That's good."

She tutted, and then spat out a piece of nail. "They can't spare one nurse to come and let us know she's okay? I'm going out of my mind here, Jake. What do we do? We can't sit here another two hours."

His wife was really suffering. As much as Jake went inside his own head during times of stress, Maggie did the opposite, letting out a bunch of nervous energy like a rapidly expanding star. If he didn't calm her down, she would eventually explode.

He put his drink down on the coffee table, grabbed his jacket, and stood up. "I'll go find someone, honey. Just relax. Everything's going to be—"

The door opened, allowing glaring white light to spill into the small room from the corridor beyond. A nurse smiled at them both and stepped inside. "Sorry to keep you both waiting."

Jake sat back down, his heart thudding in his chest. "It's okay. I-I was just coming to find somebody."

"Is she okay?" Maggie asked. "We've been waiting here for hours. Tell us, is she okay?"

The nurse nodded. "Emily is stable."

Maggie and Jake looked at each other and deflated in unison. Jake had never felt relief like it. His bladder almost released itself.

"Oh, thank God," Maggie said, running her hands through her dishevelled, mousy blonde hair. "Thank you so much, Nurse. Thank you for helping her."

"Of course." The nurse offered another smile. "Now, if you don't mind waiting a few more minutes, the doctor wants to come talk with you."

Jake didn't like the sound of that. "Is that normal?" he asked. "Or is something wrong?"

The nurse continued smiling, but the expression never reached her eyes. "It's perfectly normal. The doctor just wants to update you on your daughter's current condition."

"Do you know what happened to her?" Maggie asked, her voice fraught with anxiety. Her thumb was bleeding from where she'd been gnawing at it, and a tiny red smudge stained her bottom lip. "Why wouldn't she wake up earlier?"

"The doctor will explain everything. Can I get either of you anything in the meantime?"

Jake shook his head. "We'll wait for the doctor."

"He won't be long." The nurse left them alone again.

The air in the room changed. Jake felt sick, like he was breathing in poison. He tried to separate the smells. Chlorine and old carpet. Tepid hot chocolate. His wife's sweat.

What is the doctor going to tell us? How bad is it?

The next ten minutes passed even slower than the two hours before, and when a doctor finally arrived, Jake's entire body had gone numb. His mind, however, was alight with fizzing fireworks, each one exploding into embers of worry and concern.

"Hello, folks," the doctor said. He was a very tall man with short auburn hair. "I'm Doctor Erikson. How are you both doing?"

"We're nervous wrecks," Maggie said, rubbing her palms

against her knees as if to dry them. "Please tell us Emily is okay."

Dr Erikson closed the door and moved into the centre of the room. "You've been dealing with your daughter's illness for quite some time, I understand?"

"Eighteen months," Jake said. "At first, it looked like the treatments were working, but the last few months have seen her get worse and worse. She needs help."

"I understand. Oncology isn't my expertise, but I believe Emily's form of leukaemia is particularly nasty. The chemotherapy hasn't been successful."

Jake didn't like the man's tone. It sounded more like he was making a statement than asking a question. Maggie however, gave him an answer. "No," she said. "Her doctors stopped the chemo a week ago. They're going to try something else. In fact, we were heading to an appointment today when Emily wouldn't wake up."

Dr Erikson laced his large, bony hands together in front of him and nodded. "I'll contact her care team as soon as I leave here and inform them about her present condition."

Jake folded his arms and looked the doctor in the eye. "What's wrong with her, Doctor? Why wouldn't she wake up?"

"May I sit down, Mr Penshaw?"

"Of course." He tried to swallow, but there was a lump in his throat. "P-please."

Dr Erikson took a seat next to Maggie, which prompted her to hop across and sit next to Jake on the other sofa. Almost automatically, their hands found each other.

"I'm afraid," Dr Erikson began, "that Emily's organs are shutting down. The lack of healthy blood supply is starving them of oxygen, while at the same time her immune system is virtually non-existent. I believe this has led to an infection in her kidneys."

Maggie leaned forward and nodded. "Okay, so what can we do about it? How do we help Emily?"

Dr Erikson smiled softly and shook his head ever so subtly. "I'm sorry, Mrs Penshaw, but Emily's body is just too weak to continue fighting. Even if there were some alternative treatment available, she doesn't have any time left."

"What?" Jake let go of Maggie's hand to keep from crushing it. He put his fists against his knees, driving his knuckles painfully into his patellae. "What are you saying? She's not giving up. Just give her what she needs."

"She's been fighting for eighteen months," Maggie said. "She's beating it."

Dr Erikson sighed. "Mr and Mrs Penshaw, I'm going to move Emily to a high-dependency unit where we can keep her comfortable for the time being, but I fear there's little else we can do. I'll update the lead oncologist on her case and have him contact you to discuss options going forward. I think I saw Dr Kwami was in charge of her care plan. Is that correct?"

"Yes," Maggie said in a shaky voice. "Dr Eugene Kwami."

"Good. I'll speak to Dr Kwami as soon as I leave here. Perhaps he can come across and speak with you now."

The cancer centre was a separate building across the road, so it would only take Dr Kwami ten minutes or so to reach the Queen Elizabeth. Whatever was going on with Emily, Jake wanted to hear it from the cancer expert who had been treating her for the last year, not this stranger sitting on the sofa opposite.

"Okay, please call him now," Jake said. "I want to talk with him."

Dr Erikson stood up, his gangly body unfolding. "Of course. I'll contact him right away. In the meantime, is there anything I can get for you?"

"Can we see Emily?" Maggie put a trembling hand to her mouth. "Can we see our daughter, please?"

"She's still sleeping, but I'm happy for you to see her before we move her upstairs. I'll have a nurse come fetch you in a few moments."

"Thank you, Doctor."

Jake grunted, his jaw clenched so tightly he couldn't speak.

Dr Erikson exited the room and left them both sitting on the sofa.

Maggie erupted into tears.

Jake held her in his arms, wishing there was something more he could do. He'd never felt so powerless.

———

Jake felt it perverse that the room's acrid odour evoked being at the swimming pool, a place of fun and laughter – a place he had used to take his girls every Saturday afternoon when they were little. But this was not a place of fun and laughter, and the chemical stench existed only to mask the odour of death and misery.

Emily lay beneath a thin blanket on a wheeled operating table in the centre of the room. A massive aluminium lamp hung from the ceiling above, held in place by a folding metal arm, and a stainless steel trolley parked nearby held various instruments and gadgets. A large paper towel covered half the tray.

Hiding the bloody tools they used on Emily?

"She's still asleep," Maggie said, moving up beside their

daughter and placing a hand against her cheek. "Cold. Jake, she's so cold."

He moved up and placed a hand on Emily's forearm. She wasn't so much cold as room temperature, like some inanimate object. A frail, lifeless thing. Jake paid close attention to Emily's breathing. Every pause between her chest rising and her chest falling was a promise of death, a single second where she might simply slip away. But she was a fighter, and sure enough, every time her chest fell, it rose again in reply.

"She needs to wake up," Maggie said. "I need to talk to her, Jake. I need to tell her how much I love her."

Jake held his wife and kissed the top of her head. Despite the medical stench in the room, he could detect the comforting scent of her perfume. "She'll wake up, Mag. She's been fighting this thing too long to give up now."

A tear spilled from her cheek and stained the blanket near their daughter's chest. "We're going to lose her. Our baby."

No. No.

No!

Part of Jake wanted to shove his wife to the floor for saying such a terrible thing, but another part of him wanted to break down and sob in her arms. Looking at their daughter now, shrivelled up and in pain, it almost seemed kinder to let her go – to give in and finally say goodbye.

But the other night she was laughing. Laughing and joking at George's house. She was fine. Happy.

Only for an hour. She was happy for one single hour.

"We just have to stay strong," he said. "As long as she's still breathing, she's our daughter. She's alive."

Maggie nodded silently and slumped against him. "We need to get Lily. She should be here."

"I know. Should I try to get a taxi to pick her up?"

"No. We're probably going to be here late, so take her to go get some food. You look like you could use some air."

He shook his head. "I can't leave Emily."

"She's asleep, Jake. They're just going to move her somewhere more comfortable, so go get Lily and take a breather. I'll be with her the whole time."

"What if something happens?"

"Honey, you need to listen to me. Go be a dad to our other daughter. Explain what's going on and make sure Lily's okay. This will be hard on her too, so we need to be strong – like you said. Be there for her, okay?"

Jake looked at his wife and wanted to beg her not to expel him, but her words made too much sense. Lily couldn't deal with this by herself. She needed to see that her father was strong and in control.

The thought of leaving Emily alone, however…

Not alone. Maggie will be here.

I need to think about Lily.

"Okay, I'll go fetch her," he said, "but if anything changes here, you need to call me straight away." He drilled her with a stare. "Straight away."

Maggie nodded. "Of course. Do you think I wouldn't? Go on. Sooner you leave, the sooner you can get back here."

Hesitantly, Jake exited the bleach-stinking room and went back out into the busy corridor. He avoided the sympathetic smiles of doctors and nurses as he hurried for the exit, wanting to cry out and tell them to stop looking at him.

My daughter is going to be okay.

Emily is going to be okay.

————

George sat in his armchair, feeling the ache in his knees. Every year, another part of him seemed to go on strike. Last year, his left elbow had started locking up. Today, he felt a terrible discomfort in his stomach. He was only sixty, but the way he had lived his life had put another decade on him, at least. Most people assumed he was collecting his pension, but he had a long way to go, and in fact, he wasn't ever going to get there.

Is this the price tag of growing old? If so, I can't afford it.

I've lived long enough, seen enough…

But poor Emily.

He had only met the girl once, but she had made an impression on him. Perhaps it was the injustice of him being an old man, and her a dying child, or perhaps it was because she reminded him so much of his Kelly. He and his daughter spoke little these days, but when she'd been young, George's little girl had been a defiant, headstrong battler. So full of fire.

Emily has that same spark inside her. I saw it in her eyes every time she smiled.

But unlike Kelly, it didn't seem Emily was going to get a proper chance at life. As charming as she had been the other night, drinking whisky and making jokes, the girl had been frail and delicate, withering away before his very eyes. Seeing Emily wheeled into that ambulance today, her bald head exposed like a shameful secret, had given him little hope that she would be coming back home.

His heart ached for Jake. There was a buried anger inside that man – sharp edges sticking out like a broken bottle tossed on a beach – and George recognised it well. Recognised it because he had once felt that very same anger. Anger at the universe. Anger at whatever counted for God. If there were any rules to existence, then keeping children from getting sick should be number one on the list.

What price would Jake pay to take away his daughter's pain? To save her life?

The same price I paid?

"No, George. Don't even think about it. Some things are not supposed to be interfered with. Some favours should not be asked."

But she's just a child. A child who should have a lifetime ahead of her. Why does a wretched old man like me get to live a full life while a sweet young girl has to die?

"You can't do anything about it, George. It's not your problem. It's not your place."

He turned to his wife, standing in the corner and glaring at him. Her anger was a beautiful thing – passion and vibrancy written in the lines of her face – but he missed her smile terribly.

Twenty years since I saw it last.

Her nose had been bleeding again, her mouth and chin stained berry red.

"It's not right, my love," he said. "Not right at all."

"Nor is what you're thinking about." Blood droplets dripped from her chin, but disappeared as soon as they hit the carpet. She never left any mark of her presence.

George clutched the arm of his chair and sighed. "That poor man, though? What horrors is he going to endure?"

"Horrors that you, fortunately, have never known. Leave him be, George. Let him suffer as he needs to. Don't interfere."

"I *do* know those horrors, Leanne. We lost two babies before our Kelly came along, don't you remember? We'd almost given up hope of ever being parents. Kelly was our little miracle."

His wife still didn't smile, but her glare was a little less harsh. "She was."

"And it was a miracle that saved her too, my love. How can one miracle be a blessing and another one not?"

"Because the miracle of her birth was natural. The miracle of her surviving was a perversion of how things were meant to be."

"You wish our daughter had died as a child?" He enquired without anger, for he knew what a pointless emotion it was. "You wish she had died in pain?"

Silence. It was a question she never answered, no matter how many times he asked her.

So he asked another question. "Will you be there when it's my time? It's not long now."

"I don't know, George."

"Are you really *you*, Leanne? Or has this all just been my guilt haunting me all these years? Why do you visit me so often?"

"Because you are my husband, even in death."

"That's true, my love." He smiled at her, but it quickly became a frown. "I'm afraid, my darling. Afraid of dying without ever doing anything to make up for what I did."

"Don't interfere, George."

He lowered his head and sighed. "I won't."

"Good. Accept what fate has in store, as we all must. Your misery is well earned."

"I know." He turned to look at her again, but she was gone.

His wife had left him alone with his tears and whisky, as she had done for many nights over the last twenty years.

CHAPTER
SIX

JAKE GOT BACK to the house in record time, having driven faster than he really ought to have. He was ashamed, thinking about all the other daughters who could have ended up in hospital if he had caused an accident.

I need to stay calm. I'm getting…

Angry. I feel angry.

Jake didn't know why he was feeling such an unhelpful emotion, but perhaps it was the only mental state that allowed him to keep going. If he gave in to sadness or panic, he risked ending up on the floor, a quivering mess.

He had to stay strong for Lily.

The front door was unlocked. He pushed it open and went inside. Immediately, he started calling out for his daughter.

But Lily didn't answer.

"Are you here? Honey, it's Dad." He peered up the stairs. She wouldn't have gone to sleep at this hour, nor could she have really gone anywhere – she didn't know anyone in the area.

He checked his phone. The last message from Lily had

explained she was at home and fine. Afterwards, George had sent a poorly typed text to say he had checked on her and all was okay.

Huffing irritably, he dialled his daughter's number and put the phone against his ear. The call went straight to voice-mail. He hung up and tried again.

Voicemail.

Dialled a third time.

Voicemail.

"For God's sake." He waited for the beep and left a message. "Lily, it's Dad. I need to take you to the hospital. They're keeping Emily in, so we have to be there for her. Call me back immediately. I don't understand why you're not at home. Where are you?"

He ended the call and stood in the hallway, perturbed and unsure about what to do next. Then he felt a spark of panic.

What if she's hurt herself? What if the shock of her sister being rushed to the hospital has made her do something stupid? Based on her outburst last night, she was clearly unhappy.

How long has she felt like that?

Jake checked the living room and kitchen, shouting out his daughter's name again, but she wasn't there. The house was eerie – too quiet and still – not like a home at all. Next, he checked the bedrooms, growing ever more worried as he found them all empty. Finally, when he found no sign of Lily anywhere, he decided to check the bathroom. His mind tortured him with images of his baby girl lying pale in the bathtub, her wrists opened up and her beautiful blonde hair soaked with blood.

The bathroom was empty.

Jake stood in the doorway, hand on his chest, and let out a long, whistling exhalation of hot air. After his heartbeat returned to normal, he was once again perturbed. "Where the hell are you, Lily?"

George! I told him to keep an eye on her. He must have invited her to his house.

Certain he had solved the mystery, Jake rushed out of the house and raced along the pavement. The street was quiet, unlike earlier when curtains had been twitching and faces had peered from doorways. The memory of his gawking neighbours caused his fists to clench.

People need to get lives of their own.

He slowed for a moment, almost as if some invisible force was pushing against him. He was passing by Mr Cho's house, and he couldn't help but stare. The candle was still burning in its brass dish. The twin dragons still sat atop the wall.

A chill slithered down the back of his neck.

I need to find Lily.

He shook himself free and broke into a full-on sprint, desperate to find his daughter. It took a few seconds to make it to George's house, and he immediately starting banging on the rickety blue door.

It was almost a full minute before George opened up, and by that time, Jake had battered his fist against the wood several more times.

"J-Jake?" George appeared nonplussed, and a little worse for wear. From the bleary look in his eyes, he'd clearly started on Aldi's finest whisky a little early today. "Is everything okay? How's Em—"

"Is Lily here? Have you seen her?"

"What? No. No, I haven't. I-I checked on her like you asked, but that was about an hour and a half ago. Is everything okay? It sounded like the drugs squad was about to burst through my front door."

Jake put his hands to his face and groaned. "Where the hell is she?"

"Who?"

"Lily. She's missing."

"Jake, I'm sure she's fine."

He threw his arms down by his sides, whacking himself on the thighs. "There's nowhere she could've gone, George. She doesn't know anyone around here."

"Maybe she caught the bus and went somewhere else."

Jake rubbed at his forehead and groaned. "She could've gone to see a school friend, I suppose, but why would she do that when her sister is in hospital?"

George put a hand against the door frame, as if he were getting weary of standing. He held his cane in the other hand. "Go easy on her, Jake. It's a lot to deal with for a girl her age. If she went to see a friend, it's probably because she needed to."

Jake nodded, but his mind was already racing ahead. "I'll check her social media. If she's with a friend, they'll probably be posting selfies by now." He reached into his pocket and slid out his phone. It buzzed in his hand before he even managed to unlock it.

Jake looked up at George, eyes wide. "It's Lily."

George smiled. "Her ears must have been burning."

Jake opened the new text to read it.

Went for a walk to clear my head. Coming home now. Twenty minutes. Lily x

Jake gritted his teeth, but realised he had no reason to be angry. It was just stress and frustration putting him on edge; he needed to let it go and calm down. He smiled weakly at George and cleared his throat. "She's okay. She's on her way home."

"You see? I told you she would be fine."

"Least that makes one of my girls, huh? Shit!" A sudden sob escaped him, and he tried to stifle it. "I'm really sorry for coming here like a maniac, George. What must you think of me? I might be having a breakdown."

"Oh, Jake, come on now, it's going to be okay." George looked like he wanted to reach out to him, but he kept a hold of the doorframe and his cane.

"I don't think it is going to be okay, George. Emily still hasn't woken up. They… they're moving her to the HDU. Her organs are failing."

George slumped further against the door frame. He appeared slightly winded, either by the news or something else. "You think…" He shook his head and sighed. "You think this might be it then?"

"You mean the worst day of my life?" Jake closed his eyes and shook his head. "I used to think Emily getting diagnosed with cancer was the worst day of my life, but it's not, is it? The worst day of my life is still coming. I'm standing on the train tracks, facing it down, and it's about to hit me."

What am I saying? Emily needs me to be strong.

I've tried to be strong this whole time. It's done nothing to help her, and I'm tired. So tired. I can't be strong any more.

"Come in," George said. Some of the bleariness had cleared from his eyes, replaced by an intense stare.

Jake waved a hand. "No, no, I have to get Lily and head back to the hospital."

"Tell her to meet you here. I need to talk to you about something."

"I don't have time."

"For this, you do."

Jake put his hands on his hips, irritated by the old man's vagueness and insistence – something he had zero time for right now. "What are you talking about, George?"

The old man took a deep breath, then let it out through flared nostrils. "I'm talking about how I can help turn the worst day of your life into the best one. Please, Jake. Just come inside and hear me out."

Something about the way George was staring at him kept Jake from refusing. Whatever his neighbour wanted to tell him seemed important. So, confused and irritated, Jake stepped inside and closed the door behind him.

———

"I need to go," Lily said, hopping down off the middle of the seesaw and landing on the soft bark chippings. Hanging around a playground was such a chavvy thing to do, but here she was anyway, slumming it with a local lad.

But V was surprisingly sweet, and the smile he gave her as she turned to leave was sincere. "That's a shame," he said. "I like spending time with you, L."

"Me too, but my sister…"

"Yeah, of course. Go take care of her."

"You mean go say goodbye?"

He hopped off the seesaw and walked after her. Taking her hand in his, he looked her in the eyes as he spoke. "You don't know that, but whatever happens, you're gonna be okay. Just keep your head up."

"Wow. You should be a therapist. I feel so much better now."

He backed away, embarrassed. "I'm just tryna say the right thing, innit?"

"Why?"

"Because it seems like you need someone on your side."

"You think there's no one on my side?"

"I'm not saying that, exactly. I just mean someone who

has your back no matter what, right or wrong, you know what I mean?"

"And you're offering to be that person, are you?" She raised an eyebrow, suddenly finding him ridiculous. "You're just a player, aren't you? I bet you smooth talk every girl you meet." She flipped her pink blonde hair over her shoulder and sneered. "But I'm not that easy, bruv."

He tutted and turned away. "Think what you want, innit."

She paused and asked herself why she was being so mean to him. He'd done nothing to deserve it, at least not in the last half hour. She just felt so vulnerable, easy to take advantage of.

It would be stupid to trust a lad she had only just met, and one who was most definitely trouble. Better she keep her guard up. Safer.

"Look, I need to go," she said. "Dad's gonna go schitz as it is." She turned and strode across the playground, determined not to look back and betray that she gave the slightest shit about whether or not V was watching her.

She already missed the intense stare of his brown eyes.

Damn, do I actually fancy him? This is not good.

It was hard to decide about V. Was he really bad news, or was he just a rascal with a bad reputation? There was something about him that was so…

Kind? I feel like he might actually care about me.

That's stupid. We only just met. I'm being played.

"Hey, L, wait a sec."

She stopped and turned around, huffing irritably. "What is it?"

V marched up to her, his face alarmingly earnest. For a second, she thought he was going to try to kiss her, but instead he planted his feet and stood just in front of her.

"People around here…" He looked away and grunted. "They think they know everything about me – all the bad things I've done, plus a bunch of things I didn't – but with you…"

She frowned. "What? What about me?"

"It's just nice having a new friend," he said, seeming to blush. "Someone who ain't judging me for shit all the time, you know? You can trust me, L. I've got your back."

"How do I know you're not just a fuck boy?"

"I guess I'll have to prove it to you."

She studied him for a moment, trying to read his expression – trying to see a smirk or an insincere twinkle in his eye – but she saw nothing but honesty, and behind that…

Sadness?

"We'll see, Vincent." She used his full name as V suddenly didn't seem to suit him. "I really have to go now."

"Yeah, yeah, of course. I hope your sister's okay, for real."

"Me too." She turned to walk away again, but spoke over her shoulder as she left. "But hope doesn't change anything, does it?"

"Well," he called back, "if hope don't make shit better. Try weed. Hey, I'm gonna put that on a T-shirt."

She stopped dead and then turned around. "What?"

Vincent took a step back. "Huh? It was just a joke. Sorry. Stupid of me."

"No, I could use something to take the edge off. Do you have anything on you?"

"What, you mean weed, like?"

She stepped towards him. "Or something stronger?"

"Well, um…" He shifted uncomfortably. "I'm always holding, innit, but what do you want exactly?"

"Pills? Just something to zonk me out."

"Shit, I dunno, L. Maybe it's not what you need right now. I don't wanna—"

She stepped closer to him, staring him in the eye. "Don't tell me what I need, Vincent. You want to help me, then help me."

"I do want to help you. I do."

She thrust out a hand. "Then prove it. Help me deal with all the shit that's going on in my life. Be my friend. Have my back."

"Shit…"

"Please, V. I need something to keep me from spiralling."

Vincent sighed and shook his head. "I hope I don't regret this."

With obvious reluctance, he reached into the pocket of his hoodie and showed her what he'd got.

———

"George, I really don't have time to sit down for a chat."

George grabbed a bottle of whisky from the middle of the hardwood coffee table and attempted to pour two glasses. Jake stopped him and told him he needed to drive. He kept his jacket on in a bid to get away quickly.

"One won't hurt. You're going to need it, I promise."

Jake sighed. "Fine, but just a very small one to help my nerves. What do you even want to talk to me about?" He checked his phone again, anticipating a text message from Lily. He'd sent her another text, telling her to come to George's, but she hadn't yet replied.

"I told you my daughter, Kelly, was very ill as a child?"

Jake nodded. "Right."

"So you know I understand how you're feeling? That burning knot in your stomach that never goes away, the constant taste of acid at the back of your throat while you try – hopelessly – to fall asleep every night. The anger and frustration at being a father, unable to help his child. I understand all of it."

"I know you understand, George, but how does that help me? How does it help Emily?" He pinched the bridge of his nose. "God, please let her be okay."

"Don't leave it up to Him, Jake. He's the one who made her ill in the first place."

Jake had no real faith in Heaven; it had just been a figure of speech. "I'll pray to the doctors then."

"The doctors can only do so much, and sometimes medicines and a scalpel aren't enough. Sometimes, certain bargains have to be struck." George took a swig of whisky and topped it back up from the bottle on the table.

"What is this about, George? Please, get to the point so I can go to my daughter."

The old man swigged his whisky again, gulping loudly. He put the empty glass down and slumped back in his armchair. "Getting to the point quickly will send you running for the door, Jake. Allow me a few minutes to get this out."

"Get *what* out? What do you want to tell me?"

"I want to tell you what I did to cure my Kelly after everything else failed."

Jake opened his mouth, closed it, then opened it again. He decided to just be quiet and let George speak.

George licked his lips and continued. "Like Emily, Kelly wasn't getting any better. Every week was worse than the last. Every day she grew weaker and frailer. The seizures were slowly killing her, Jake, eating away at her bit by bit. She lived in constant fear of the next awful fit, knowing every moment of happiness could instantly be shattered by an agonising convulsion. Towards the end, she just stopped taking part in being alive. She didn't wash, wouldn't eat… just waiting to die, she was. The doctors and God had done all they could, and it wasn't enough by far. Kelly was sitting cross-legged outside death's door, waiting to be let in. It broke me, I can tell you, Jake, knowing I was going to lose her."

"I'm sorry." Jake knew exactly how George must have felt. An unbridled fury at somebody or something you could never hold accountable.

"Don't be sorry, Jake. That broken father is long gone, but I see a reflection of him in you. It's like looking in a mirror at the past. Emily, too, reminds me of those days. She has the same spark Kelly had before she eventually gave up."

Jake took a small sip of whisky, resisting the urge to down the whole thing in one go and ask for another. "I know you get it, George – you're the only person who does – but how did Kelly recover? You said you did something to cure her?"

"I made a bargain."

"With who?"

"I wish I knew, but whoever it was, it was a deal I was happy to make. It gave me back my daughter and gifted Kelly with the long life she deserved."

Jake blinked slowly. "You've lost me, George."

"Mr Cho!" George suddenly turned manic. He spoke quickly, making it difficult to interrupt him. "I told you the man works miracles, didn't I? Well, it's true. Jing Cho saw Kelly's suffering and offered to help – and help he did, Jake. Within days, my little girl was back to her old self, laughing and playing, and putting on weight like there wasn't enough junk food in the world. After Jing helped her, Kelly never had another seizure again – not ever. That was twenty-two years ago."

Jake finished the rest of his whisky and put a hand on the sofa to get up.

"Don't leave." George put both hands out, his mania dissolving as suddenly as it had appeared. "Listen to what I'm telling you, please. There's a way to save Emily. You can cure her, Jake. It's everything you want and more – the miracle you've been desperate for. You just have to trust me."

"How? How can I trust you? I don't even know you, George, but you're clearly a drunk."

"Aye, that I may be, but it doesn't make me a liar. I'm offering you a chance to save your girl. Don't you at least want to humour me? What if there's the slightest chance what I'm telling you is true? Do you truly want to get up and walk away?"

Jake eased back down on the sofa. He wished Lily would knock on the door and rescue him from this ridiculous conversation. Until that happened, he felt trapped. "Fine," he said. "Tell me how I can cure Emily. What do I have to do, George?"

"First, you come with me to Mr Cho's house. Then you do everything he tells you to do. Agree to that, and by this time tomorrow, you and your family can restart your lives, cancer-free."

"You're insane."

"I promise you, I'm not. This is real."

Jake shook his head and tutted. "You really expect me to believe some spooky old medicine man, on Tovey Avenue of all places, can cure my daughter of cancer? George, come on."

"You put your faith in doctors, didn't you? How is this

any different? I'm just asking you to try something new – something older. Science doesn't know everything, Jake. Don't be a fool and think it does. Emily doesn't have to die. You don't have to lose her."

Jake shot to his feet, almost kicking the wooden coffee table over in anger. The conversation was offensive, a waste of his time, and a cruel attack on his emotions. "Enough, George. Enough."

George remained seated in his worn armchair, but he looked up pleadingly at Jake, visibly teary-eyed. "Please, Jake. Let me help you. I need to fix this for you."

Jake paused, his fists clenched and his stomach churning. Suddenly the room seemed tiny, shoving him and this obscene old man together, separated only by ancient furniture and muggy air.

What if he really is trying to help me?

What if he can? Emily…

"Okay," Jake said, almost inaudibly. "Take me to Mr Cho's miracle parlour. I'll humour you."

George leant on his cane and eased himself up out of his armchair with a grunt. Once he was balanced, his eyes narrowed at Jake. He was old, but not frail. In fact, looking into his eyes now led Jake to believe that George was younger than he seemed. "Don't mock me, Jake. I thought long and hard about what I'm telling you right now. If we do this, you need to take it seriously."

"Jesus, George, I don't know what you expect me to say?"

"Then say nothing. Just listen and do what you're told."

"I…" He shrugged. "I don't know."

George hissed. "You're still not convinced? Right, stay there. I'll be back in a minute."

As soon as he was alone, Jake checked his phone again.

Still nothing from Lily. He was eager to get back to the hospital. What if Emily needed him? What if she was…

George returned quickly, clutching a small yellow and blue envelope in his hand – photographs. With a shaking, bony hand, he pulled out the first picture and handed it to Jake.

Jake took the photo and immediately winced. It showed an emaciated girl with uneven shoulders and a strange twist to her neck. She was lying across a pretty young woman's lap, probably her mother. If not for the weak, pitiful smile on the girl's face, Jake might have thought he was staring at a corpse. He also recognised a lively spark in her eyes.

Emily has it too. It's life. This girl is hanging on to life.

"I'm sorry your daughter was so sick, George."

"That was Kelly's eleventh birthday. Check the back."

Jake turned the photograph over. Sure enough, it had a date on it, along with the words: **Kelly, 11th birthday.**

George handed over a second photograph. "This one was taken exactly one year later on Kelly's twelfth birthday."

Jake looked at the more recent photograph and was astonished. It was clearly the same young girl, but this time she was two stone heavier, and her shoulders were properly aligned. The twist to her neck was completely gone, but so too was the smile. In its place was a distant, faraway gaze that suggested the girl was deep inside her own head about something.

She's troubled. Healthy again, but less happy.

"The woman isn't in this picture," Jake noted. "Was it Kelly's mother?"

George's head lowered, and he stared at the ancient green carpet beneath their feet. "Leanne died between the two photographs being taken. I got my daughter back, but I lost my wife. I wouldn't trade it, but it was tough on us both for a long while."

Jake could almost see the pain etched on the young girl's face – but he could also still see that spark of life in her eyes. It was brighter now, more vibrant.

She has her whole life ahead of her.

"And this is Kelly last year," said George, handing Jake a third photograph. "At thirty-three."

This picture caused Jake to smile. Even with decades having passed, it was obvious this elegant young woman was the same person as the poorly young girl. This time, however, her smile was wide and beaming. In each arm, she hugged a young boy, and from behind, a handsome gentleman held her around her waist. A happy family.

Like the one I used to have.

"Two sons and a loving husband," George said, "instead of a tragic, premature death. Do you want that for your daughter, Jake? Do you want Emily to grow up and have a family?"

Jake studied the photo for a few more seconds before looking up at George and nodding. "Yes. Yes, I want that."

George sighed with apparent relief. "Then come with me, Jake. While there's still time."

CHAPTER
SEVEN

LILY KNOCKED on the door and then turned around to face the overgrown front lawn. It was probably the worst kept frontage on the street. Typical that her dad had chosen a weird old man to be their friend.

We know nothing about this George. He could be a murderer or a U2 fan for all we know. You can't trust anyone these days.

The front door opened almost immediately, and it made her jump. Her nerves settled when she realised it was her dad who had answered. "Lily," he said, his eyes wide like he was seeing a ghost. "You're here."

"Well, yeah, you told me to meet you here. Has George infected you with Alzheimer's or something?"

"There's nowt wrong with my mind, young lady," George said, appearing from behind her dad. "Sharp as a tack, always have been."

"Right…" Lily felt a little embarrassed for getting caught making the comment, but she was unwilling to show remorse. "What happened, Dad? What happened to Emily?"

"She just wouldn't wake up, honey. She's at the hospital."

Lily blew air into her cheeks and let it out slowly. "So, are we going, then?"

Her dad turned to George, and something seemed to pass between them. Then George whispered something. It sounded like: *This might be the only chance you get.*

Jake turned pale, and when he looked at Lily, he seemed to force a smile onto his face. "I just need to run an errand, honey. Get changed out of your school uniform and wait for me at the house. We'll leave soon, okay?"

"What errand? What do you need to do?"

"Just something I need to take care of. Anyway, where exactly have *you* been?"

She shrugged, hoping her face didn't betray her guilt. If her dad knew she'd been hanging out with Vincent, he'd go mad. "I just walked a few streets to get some fresh air. I was freaking out in the house all by myself."

The look he gave her was one she knew well. Mistrust – his default way of dealing with her lately. Slowly, however, that mistrust fell away. "Okay," he said, "that's fair enough. Wait for me at the house, okay?"

She nodded. "Fine. Just don't be long."

"I promise. Can you grab a few things for Emily while you're there? Her phone and a book, some pyjamas?"

Her dad was acting strange, trying to be calm, but Lily detected the stress in his voice.

And where the hell is he going with George of all people?

"I'll see you in a bit, then?" she said. "Don't be long."

"I said… I promise."

She turned to leave. Walking down the garden path felt like trekking through a jungle, and she was glad to make it back out onto the main pavement. As she headed home, she was careful not to look back; not wanting to get caught for being nosey. For whatever reason, she was sure her dad was up to something.

And I want to know what.

She made it several houses down before finally stopping and looking back. Her dad and George were creeping down the garden path, clearly having waited for her to be far enough away before leaving. If she wasn't careful, they would spot her standing and watching.

She bolted into the garden of the nearest house and knelt down behind the brick wall surrounding the lawn. From her hiding place, she watched Jake and George stroll down the pavement, passing by the various houses.

They eventually stopped, turned, and went up the garden path of a specific house about six or seven numbers down from George's.

"What the hell? Has Dad joined a neighbourhood cult or something?"

Now she knew where he was going, Lily could confront her dad. Emily was dying in hospital, so why the hell was he wasting time visiting neighbours?

She exited the stranger's garden and headed back up the pavement. Jake and George were standing in front of a strange house with two weird dog-monsters either side of its gate. A candle burned on a hanging metal dish, which was weird seeing as it had only just started getting dark. Also, candles burning outside were just weird in general.

It's definitely a cult. They probably pray to the gods of Jobseeker's Allowance.

Jake and George moved up to the front door, which was painted red and marked with strange black symbols. "What are you doing, Dad?" she demanded, sneaking up behind him.

He spun around and gasped, then grabbed at his chest. "Lily? I told you to go home."

"Yeah, you did, but I decided to see what sketchy shit you were up to instead. What's going on? Whose house is this?"

"Mr Cho's."

"Mr Cho? Who the fuck is Mr Cho?"

"Lily, watch your mouth."

George sighed and tugged at her dad's sleeve. "We don't have time for this, Jake."

"Time for what?" she demanded. "What's going on?"

"Go home, Lily. I'll be there soon."

"No. I want to know what you're doing. Why aren't we going to the hospital right now?"

"We are! Just… in a little while."

George tugged at him again. "Jake…"

"Yes, George, give me a minute." He glared at Lily. "Go to the house and wait for me there. I'm trying to help your sister."

"How? How are you helping Emily?"

"You just have to trust me."

She folded her arms and planted her feet. She was pushing it, she knew, but she was so angry. Angry that her dad wasn't taking her straight to the hospital, or even giving her a straight answer. "I don't trust you, Dad. So, whatever you're doing, you're going to have to do it with me here."

"Lily, do what you're told for once, please."

"I'm not leaving. You're not going to just…" She lost a little of her resolve, her emotions swaying back and forth. "I don't want to go sit inside that house by myself, okay? It's not home, so please don't make me."

"Lily."

"No. No, I mean it. I'm sick of being told what to do and

expected to just go along with everything all the time. Include me in what you're doing, or forget about it. I'll go in there and piss all over the floor and embarrass you and do all kinds of insane shit until you regret me ever being born."

"For crying out loud, Lily!"

George cleared his throat. "We need to do this now, Jake, in case the worst happens. You'll have to bring her inside."

Jake shook his head. "No. She can't be a part of this, George. I… I don't even know what *this* is myself."

"Mr Cho's a lovely man. There's nothing to fear. Lily will be fine."

Lily watched, bemused, as her dad put his head in his hands. "I need to go," he muttered. "This is madness."

What's madness? What is he doing here?

George put a hand on his shoulder. "Remember Kelly," he said. "Remember the pictures I showed you. Emily can live a long, wonderful life, but we need to knock on this front door first, okay?"

"Dad?" Lily shivered, a breeze against the back of her neck. "What is this?"

He looked at her, but instead of answering, he banged on the strange red door and stood back from it. "We're about to find out what this is," he said, "and hope for the best."

Almost a full minute later, the red front door opened.

———

Mr Cho was tiny. Jake didn't know if it was old age or if the man had always been short, but it wasn't close to what his imagination had conjured in anticipation. Jing Cho wasn't a wizened, wizard-like stranger, with long grey moustaches and a pointy beard. He was just an old man, wrinkled around the eyes and mouth, and slightly stooped over.

Clean-shaven and bald, he was well dressed in black trousers and a grey button-up shirt tucked in at the waist.

"H-hello?" The old man squinted. "George, is that you?"

"Yes, it's me. Sorry for knocking on your door so late in the evening, Jing, but we really need your help."

Mr Cho bowed slightly. "It is no bother, my friend. Are these the new neighbours I saw move in at the weekend?"

Jake nodded and offered a hand. "My name's Jake Penshaw. My family and I just moved into number twenty-six." He half turned back. "This is my youngest daughter, Lily."

"Welcome to the neighbourhood," Mr Cho said, shaking his hand and bowing once again. His voice was soft and a little hard to hear.

"Jake has another daughter," George said. "She's sick. Very, very sick."

Mr Cho's eyes focused on George intensely. "I am sorry to hear that, but I do not see what it has to do with me."

"Yes, you do, Jing." George met the other man's concerned stare.

"George…" He let out a long sigh, seeming to shrink down even smaller on the doorstep. "I hope you're not suggesting what I fear you might be."

"You're the only one who can help Emily. If there were anyone else…"

Mr Cho closed his eyes. "George, we agreed Kelly was to be the last. What happened that day was—"

"Twenty years ago," George interrupted. "It was twenty-two years ago. Please don't make Jake's family suffer for my mistakes. They've been through hell."

"I am sorry, George." The old man started to close the door.

Jake put a hand out and blocked it. "Wait!"

Mr Cho paused and blinked wearily. He allowed the door to remain half-closed but kept a hand on it.

Seeing this might be his one and only opportunity – to grasp at something he didn't even understand, but which could help Emily – Jake begged the man to help him. "If it's within your power to do something for my daughter, I'm pleading with you to help her."

"Dad?" Lily stepped back, retreating down the garden path. "I don't understand what's going on."

Jake turned to her and smiled thinly. "George thinks Mr Cho can help Emily. If he *can't…*" He shrugged. "Then it's over, honey. Emily's organs are shutting down. She can't fight any more."

Lily's eyes widened in disbelief. Her upper lip quivered for a moment, but then it curled in derision. She shoved past Jake and positioned herself directly in front of Mr Cho. "My dad's lost the plot," she said. "In fact, he's been losing his marbles for a while now, ever since my big sister got sick. He loves Emily so much that his tiny brain is melting at the thought of her actually dying." She folded her arms and growled. "Sometimes, I wish Emily would just hurry up and kick the bucket."

Jake gasped. "Lily."

She ignored his exclamation and continued standing in front of Mr Cho, locking eyes with the small bald man. "Emily's in pain all the time – like, every second – so it's better if her suffering just ends. If she's gone, then Mum and Dad might go back to how they were before. They might help me with my homework again and take me to the cinema." She let out a bitter chuckle. "God, even a game of Monopoly would be amazing after how little attention they've paid me this last year. I miss them, Mr Cho. I miss my parents, and maybe with Emily gone, I can have them back."

Mr Cho nodded, blinking slowly.

"But," Lily said before anyone else could interject, "if you're telling me there's a way my sister can be healthy again, that she can be free of cancer, then I choose that, okay? If it's really, truly an option, then I want Emily to be okay. She's better than me, Mr Cho, and she should never have got sick in the first place. It's not fair – and if you can help her, then you absolutely have to."

Mr Cho seemed a little stunned by the sudden, forceful speech levelled at him by an unknown teenager on his doorstep, and when his hand went to the door, it seemed like he was going to close it. Instead, he pushed it open and stood aside. "You'd all better come in," he said.

Jake's stomach fluttered with uncertainty – uncertainty, confusion, and fear – and when Lily turned to face him, he didn't quite know what to say to her, other than, "You really feel all of that?"

She shrugged and turned to look at George. "I feel a lot of things, but emotions come and go, right?"

George nodded. "That they do."

Lily took a breath. "Dad, whatever this is, Mum is gonna kill you. You get that, right?"

"Only if it fails," Jake replied, and then went inside Mr Cho's house. "Only if it fails."

———

Mr Cho led them through a hallway into a candle-lit lounge. The layout of his home was identical to George and Jake's, but the decor was different. Watercolour prints of forests, meadows, and waterfalls adorned the light blue walls, while peculiar ornaments cluttered every surface. Tall candles hissed and crackled in brass dishes around the room, creating a warm yet eerie atmosphere. "Did you paint these yourself?" Jake asked, admiring a framed sunset made from orange and yellow swirls.

"Yes," Mr Cho replied. "I like to surround myself with nature. Reality is what one makes it, after all."

"They're beautiful."

"Thank you. Please, take a seat. Jake, was it?"

"Jake Penshaw, yes." He turned around to ease himself down into a small armchair, but as he lowered his backside, a disgruntled snort caused him to leap back up again. He turned around and gasped. "Jesus!"

A chubby black pug gave Jake a lopsided frown. The animal was curled up on the armchair cushion like a tired old man.

"Not there," Mr Cho chided. "That's John's seat."

"John?" Jake raised an eyebrow. "The dog's name is John?"

"So he tells me. Anyway, John sits there, so choose some-place else."

Jake eyed the pug, but the fat, wrinkled creature put its head down on its paws and went back to sleep, immediately snoring.

Lily couldn't keep herself from going over and stroking the dog a few times as it dozed away. "So cuddly," she said with a coo. "He's like a stinky teddy bear."

Three armchairs filled the room, but there was no sofa. Nor was there any television. A low coffee table sat in the centre of the room, upon which sat an ornate teapot and a small pot of burning incense that gave off a stench of damp cigarette ash. Plump cushions lay on the floor on either side of the table.

Mr Cho sat down on one of the floor cushions, remarkably spry for a man about to hit eighty . Then, from on the floor, he bowed at Jake. "Your daughter? Tell me about her condition."

"Of course." Jake's voice was shaky, his stomach increasingly unsettled. "Emily has a rare form of leukaemia, one that's very hard to treat. It's been eighteen months, but… but the treatment has stopped working. Her organs are shutting down."

He felt sick admitting it. The disgusting incense only made his nausea worse.

"She's in the hospital," George added, obviously seeing that Jake was struggling. "She won't wake up."

Jake pulled out his phone and showed Mr Cho a picture of Emily taken at Alton Towers. It was her first week in a wheelchair, but they had focused on the positives and skipped all of the ride queues. It had been one of her last truly good days. She was smiling in the picture.

"A pretty girl." Mr Cho handed Jake back his phone. "Is that Oblivion in the background?"

Lily, sitting in an armchair at the side of the room, snorted with laughter. "Wait, have you ridden it?"

"Many times. Although not recently. I don't get around as well as I used to, so I tend to remain at home nowadays, but when I was younger, one of my favourite things to do was head up Stoke-way to ride the Nemesis. One must push the senses as often as possible. To feel alive is to be alive."

Lily was clearly dumfounded, but an amused grin slowly found its way onto her lips. "That's wild. Did you ever get to ride the Smiler?"

"Alas no. In fact, the last time I was there, they still had the Ripsaw. A travesty that they got rid of it."

"Right? I only rode it once, but it rocked."

Jake grumbled, his impatience growing. "George said you can help me – help Emily."

Mr Cho looked at him. "George should not have made such promises on my behalf, Mr Penshaw. The things my old friend speaks of are from a past long forgotten."

"I'm sorry, Jing," George said, sheepishly. "I know the promise we made, but I've met Emily. She's a sweet girl, and she deserves a chance at life."

"But at what cost, George? To meddle with the tapestry of life is a dangerous thing, you know this. Bargains must be made. Flesh bargains."

Lily groaned. "I'm not gonna have to blow anyone, am I?"

Jake glared at her. "Are you serious?"

"Not very often if I can help it."

Jake turned back to face Mr Cho, trying to ignore his fourteen-year-old daughter's obsession with saying things she shouldn't. He slipped himself off the armchair and placed himself down on the remaining floor cushion opposite Mr Cho. His knees clicked painfully as he crossed his legs in front of him, but he ignored it. "Mr Cho, whatever the cost is, I'll pay it."

The old man leant across the table and looked Jake in the eye. "Fifty thousand."

Jake flinched. "Wh-what?"

"Fifty thousand pounds, cash, and I'll help your daughter."

"I don't… I can't… Oh… Oh, now I get it." Jake turned to glare at George. "This has all been one big scam, huh? Take advantage of the new family on the block. Wow, you must have seen me coming."

George turned pale, candlelight flickering on his face. "What? Jake, no…"

Mr Cho gave a chuckle and rapped a knuckle against the coffee table to recapture Jake's attention. "I am toying with you, Mr Penshaw, although it appears you would be unwilling to exchange money for your daughter's health, which is concerning."

"I thought I was being scammed!"

"Why should I believe you would be willing to make a true sacrifice, if simple money is too great a cost?"

"If you can genuinely help Emily," Jake said firmly. "I'll pay you every penny I have. But you need to give me more than your word."

"Where is your faith, Mr Penshaw?"

Lily shuffled in her armchair at the side of the room and tutted. "Come on, mate, be fair. No one in their right mind would believe you can cure my sister, but…"

Mr Cho raised a wispy grey eyebrow at her. "But what, child?"

"But we're here, aren't we? Isn't that enough faith? We've come here to ask you to, I dunno, perform a spell or something, yeah? What exactly are we talking about here?"

"A bargain," said Mr Cho, his soft voice suddenly forceful. "A bargain made with entities beyond our understanding. Entities that care very little for mortal desires. Entities that—"

"Well, these en-titties say bring it on," Lily said, jiggling her modest boobs beneath her school shirt. "You're talking about the Devil, right?" She rolled her eyes. "So cliché."

"You speak of Christian ideals, young lady, but I am not a Christian. In fact, my home is a place of no religion."

"You're an atheist?" Jake asked, finding it odd. He looked around the room at all the candles.

"I have faith in the universe," Mr Cho answered, "and the powers that keep it spinning, not the fairytales created by men to make their nights seem less dark. The deeper truths of existence remain unknown to us all, as they should, but we can reach out beyond the veil of our perceptions and plead for intervention from beings greater than ourselves."

"So you don't know who you're talking to?" Lily started playing with her hair. It was a nervous habit of hers. "Have you ever tried, like, asking? Hey, hello dark spirit, what's your Instagram? Where were you born?"

Mr Cho's mouth rose at the corners. "Think of it like sending a signal into space, young one. A distant, advanced civilisation might pick up our message, but it doesn't mean they'll send a reply. If only it were as simple as asking a name."

Jake rubbed at his temples, trying to avoid drifting off into a confused daze. "How do you know these *other beings* will help Emily?"

"Because he's done it before," George said, giving Mr Cho an apologetic look. "Like I said, Jake, a lot of people around here owe Jing favours."

"From a long time ago," Mr Cho quickly added. "I live a quiet life now, George. The secrets of my family will die with me. The world no longer has need of them."

"Wait," Lily said, perching forward on the edge of her seat. "You have the power to heal my sister, but you just, like, choose not to? That's pretty shitty, man."

Jake was about to chide his daughter, but decided he actually agreed with her. It was pretty shitty not to help someone when you could.

Mr Cho sighed. "It's not that simple, child. It is unnatural for me to interfere in the way things are meant to be. Not only that, it is… draining. It takes an amount of strength I fear I no longer have."

Lily glared at the old man, the flickering candlelight

lending an infernal sheen to her face. "Then why invite us inside?"

"I invited you to talk."

Jake reached out across the coffee table, almost knocking the pot of incense onto the plush grey carpet. "I'm not interested in talking," he said. "Whatever you want from me, you can have it. Anything."

"It's not about what I want, Mr Penshaw."

Mr Cho let his words hang in the air and the room fell to near silence. Only the soft crackle of burning candles and the rhythmic snores of John the pug disturbed the solitude.

Jake glanced at George.

His neighbour just shrugged.

"Do you truly want this?" Mr Cho asked. "Are you willing to make a flesh bargain?"

"I don't know what a flesh bargain is, but I'll do anything to save my daughter. Help me. I'm begging you."

Mr Cho maintained eye contact with Jake for what seemed like minutes. Eventually, the old man exhaled and looked away. "Very well. Then we shall begin." He slapped his palms together and all the candles in the room flared. John, the pug, grunted and sat up on the sofa, but quickly flopped back down and went back to snoring.

CHAPTER
EIGHT

MAGGIE WATCHED HELPLESSLY as they wheeled Emily down the corridor. She still hadn't woken up. No one would say if she ever would.

Will I ever get to talk to her again? This can't be it.

Come back to me, sweetheart. My baby.

The nurses had led Maggie into a waiting area and left her there. No one else was present, and it left her feeling like the unluckiest person in the world. Only she had a child who wouldn't wake up. Only she was there, unattended with her tears.

Feeling utterly abandoned, she pulled out her phone to call Jake. Sending him away had been necessary, but she regretted it now. Going through this alone was too much. It was only a matter of time before she collapsed from the emotional exhaustion of it all.

She called her husband and got his voicemail. *"Hi, it's Jake. Leave a message. Or don't."*

He should've been back by now. Knowing Jake, he would only have taken Lily to a Burger King or a McDonalds, not a sit-down meal, so there was no reason for him to be taking this long.

Unless something has happened. Is Lily okay?

Maggie wrapped her arms around her knees and leaned forward, rubbing her ankles as she sat alone on the plastic chairs. There was enough to worry about as it was; she couldn't take on any more.

Lily's fine. If any young girl can take care of herself, it's her.

Emily's cancer had changed all of them in several ways, but it had possibly affected Lily most of all. She had once been so carefree and positive, but now she was sarcastic and cynical, forced to grow up too fast. And as for Jake…

He never smiles any more, and we have nothing to talk about except cancer appointments and pill dosages. I don't even know if we still love each other. There's no room in our lives for joy or happiness.

A distant beeping noise snapped Maggie out of her thoughts. It was accompanied by a garbled message from overhead speakers. Moments later, a pair of blue-uniformed nurses rushed past in squeaking shoes. One of them placed an ID card against a sensor and prompted a pair of double doors to open. It allowed them access into an adjoining area of the hospital.

Urgent chatter erupted. Panic.

It's Emily. Something's wrong with Emily.

Maggie leapt out of her seat and rushed over to the double doors the nurses had gone through, but they closed just as she got there. She banged on the wood with both fists. "Hello? Hello, I need to speak to somebody. Is my daughter okay? Emily? Is Emily okay? Hello?"

Nobody came. The urgent chatter in the room beyond continued. Another call went out over the speakers. More beeping.

Code blue. Code blue in trauma room one.

"Emily! Emily, hold on." Maggie screamed at the top of her lungs. "Let me in. Let me in. Emily!"

————

"There are certain rules," Mr Cho explained as he lit a pair of candles on the coffee table. He had asked Lily to extinguish all the others around the room and also to close the curtains. The thick red drapes were like something from a Chinese palace.

Jake nodded. "Okay. Tell me the rules."

"First, you may not bargain for your own personal benefit. To do so requires a sacrifice far too great to consider. To ask a favour on behalf of another, however, requires a lesser bargain."

"That… makes sense."

"Second, the favour you ask will only be made permanent once you fulfil your side of the bargain."

"Fine. What do I need to do?"

Mr Cho reached underneath the coffee table and pulled out a hidden drawer full of tiny glass bottles and small cloth bags. From inside, he produced a needle about the size of Jake's index finger. "One end of this pin must taste your blood. The other, the blood of another. Make no mistake though, Mr Penshaw, this *other* will suffer. Death and sickness leave a scar that cannot be healed, only passed on."

"Wait," Lily said, sitting in near total darkness since she had snuffed out the candles. "Are you saying we can give Emily's cancer to somebody else? Who? Who would we even give it to?"

Mr Cho glanced at her briefly before returning his gaze back to the coffee table. "That is not for me to answer."

Jake swallowed a lump in his throat. Giving a person cancer on purpose…

It's murder.

This can't be real.

What am I doing here?

"Do you accept this bargain, Mr Penshaw?"

Lily moaned. "Dad…"

"I accept. Let's just get on with it." He swallowed a scratchy lump at the back of his throat and took a deep breath. "I accept."

What choice do I have? Emily is all that matters.

Mr Cho glanced at George, but George failed to make eye contact. These two men had history, but it was of no interest to Jake right now. He just wanted this to be over with. He just wanted his daughter to be better, and if there was a way…

"Your phone." Mr Cho reached out a hand. "I need a picture of Emily, so there's no confusion about whom we seek to benefit."

"Of course." Jake unlocked his phone and opened up a recent picture of Emily. She was lying in bed, clutching a copy of *The Exorcist* and pretending to pull a scared face. He placed the phone in the centre of the table, screen up. "Is that okay?"

"Yes, that is perfect. Okay, close your eyes and we shall begin." Jake did as he was told and Mr Cho began. "Ob-la-de, ob-la-da." He took a deep breath. "Ob-la-de, ob-la-da, life goes on, brah!"

Jake opened his eyes and frowned. "The… The Beatles?"

Mr Cho sniggered. "Sorry, I wanted to lighten the mood. We should not proceed upon this path with grief weighing us down. Keep your eyes and heart wide open and know exactly what it is you are doing."

"No more games," Jake snapped. "My daughter is dying."

"Not for long," Mr Cho replied. "Now, we shall truly begin."

With a sigh, Jake asked himself again why he was there. Mr Cho could be a loon for all he knew. In fact, it seemed likely.

George must have sensed his reticence, because he spoke from the shadows at the edge of the room. "This is real, Jake. Stick with it."

Jake nodded resignedly.

Mr Cho clapped his hands together, and like before, the candles flared. A gentle breeze drifted through the room, followed by the most appalling smell.

"Whoa," said Lily, pinching her nose. "What the hell is that?"

Jake pressed his face into the crook of his elbow. "That's bad. That's really bad."

Mr Cho tutted and shook his head. "John! Now is not the time."

The sleepy pug lifted his head and frowned at Mr Cho. Then, slowly, his eyes closed and his head fell back down onto his paws. Within a few seconds, the pug was once again snoring soundly, unconcerned with the stench of his own fart.

"I apologise," Mr Cho told them. "John is nineteen years old and flatulent. Did you know pugs were originally bred and raised by Chinese royalty? They are one of the oldest breeds in the world." He wafted a hand in the air. "But boy do they stink."

"I…" Jake felt his eyes watering. He had to blink. "I didn't know that. Is it important?"

"Is anything? Okay, I shall begin again."

"Please do."

Mr Cho took a deep breath and placed his hands down flat on the table. "Kings of old and ancient, those who came before, those who live here now, please hear us. Kings of old and ancient, wise and true, please acknowledge us." He reached into the drawer again and threw a pinch of something at the nearest candle on the coffee table. The flame hissed and turned green. "Kings of old and ancient, with powers untold, we beg you to help us in our need."

The other candle, the one closest to Jake, began to hiss and flare. Mr Cho had done nothing to it, but it began to change colour. Eventually, it settled on an identical green to the other candle.

Mr Cho nodded at Jake. "The ancient ones hear us."

"Um… good." He looked up at the ceiling. "Thank you."

Both flames flared, green and unnatural.

Mr Cho took something else out of his drawer, some kind of dun metal token, like two holy crosses fixed end to end, with each tip coated in a lighter material, like silver. He placed it on top of the phone, on top of Emily's picture. "Ancient kings of mercy, we ask that you give mercy now to the one whose image we have placed before you. She is a child without a thread. We beg you to restore it."

Both flames flickered and changed colour again. Green became blue.

"We ask a boon, not for ourselves, but for another. Selfless deeds cannot be ignored, yet we offer flesh in return, as has always been the way."

The candles flared again, as if in response – so wildly that the entire room lit up for a moment. Jake noticed Lily's pale face as she seemed to slip something into her mouth, chewing gum or a sweet.

The darkness returned.

Mr Cho raised the sharp needle in the air. His hand was shaking, as if the pin weighed as much as a bag of sugar. "Blood is given: a contract offered by he who wishes to bargain. By tomorrow's end, the blood of another shall be shed and the contract shall be complete. In this, we promise, lest all bargains be broken."

Jake's stomach danced a samba of acid and undigested food, causing him to grab his guts. He nodded to Mr Cho, showing that he agreed to proceed despite his obvious discomfort.

This can't be real, right? I'm taking part in a seance. It's nonsense, superstition.

But what if it's not? George's daughter got better. Kelly's alive and well.

In the centre of the table, Jake's phone buzzed and vibrated. Maggie's picture came up on the screen, partially obscured by the peculiar metal token. "Damn it!" He reached out to grab his phone, but Mr Cho slapped at his hand.

"It is no matter," the old man said. "We offered Emily's picture first. There will be no mistake. Let it ring."

Jake rubbed at his throat, which suddenly ached. "W-what next then?" His mouth was dry. Anxiety perhaps? Stoked by his wife's unanswered and persistent call?

What if she's calling with news of Emily?

What if this is all too late?

"We offer you blood," Mr Cho said, and he thrust the needle at Jake. "We offer you blood."

Jake got the hint and pressed his thumb hard against the end of the needle. The sharp flash of pain was so intense that his body automatically forced him to recoil.

But the job was done.

His thumb bled from a deep hole. A crimson bead glistened on the tip of the needle.

Mr Cho reached into the tiny drawer again, and this time pulled out a small plastic wallet. He dropped the pin inside the wallet and sealed it with a brass popper sewn into the fold. The material appeared thick enough to keep the needle from accidentally pricking anybody.

"The bargain must be fulfilled before tomorrow's end," he told Jake, and then looked up at the ceiling. "We thank you kings, merciful and wise. We leave you now in thanks. You may take your payment."

The candles flared and blinked out, casting the room into total darkness.

Mr Cho grunted in pain.

"L-Lily, my young friend. Would you… Would you be so kind as to relight the candles in the room? You'll find matches on the table beside you."

"Sure." Lily picked up a rattling box of matches and struck one alight. In the aura of its flame, she went around the room, lighting the candles.

"Actually," Mr Cho said, "just switch on the big light. It'll be easier."

"Oh, okay."

A moment passed, then Lily switched on the room's main light. In the harsh glow of the bulb inside a red fabric shade, everything appeared crimson. It took a moment for Jake's eyes to settle on the room's finer details.

The air turned cold. Everyone seemed to shiver in unison.

"Th-that's better," Mr Cho said.

Jake frowned. "Are you okay? You sound like you're in pain. Is something the mat—"

Mr Cho had a deep gash across his forehead. Somehow it

wasn't bleeding, so it looked like a hungry baby's pink gaping mouth.

Lily gasped. "Mr Cho, what happened to your face?"

Mr Cho lowered his head, weak and weary. "Phone calls are not free, child, but they took less than they usually do." He pulled up one of his shirt sleeves and revealed an arm ravaged with potholes and pits, the deepest of scars. "I will not show you my back."

George sighed, as if it were something he'd seen himself.

Mr Cho handed Jake the needle inside the plastic wallet. "It is done, Mr Penshaw. By midnight tomorrow, you must prick someone with the other end of this pin. Then, and only then, will your daughter's future be assured."

Jake took the wallet with a shaking hand. "And what'll happen to the person I prick?"

Mr Cho raised an eyebrow at him. "You know what will happen to them. This is your last chance to consider what it is you're asking for. Do nothing, and all will be as it was always meant to be. But take another's blood with this pin, and you'll alter fate in your daughter's favour at the expense of theirs. The decision is yours alone."

Jake stared at the needle inside the wallet, struggling to put his thoughts in order. This was all nonsense, surely? It had to be.

But if not, whose blood did he take?

Who do I kill?

———

Maggie couldn't believe her eyes. Her daughter was a vibrant, strong, wonderful woman.

But now they said she was dead.

The lifeless body in front of Maggie didn't look like

Emily at all. She was different somehow. Wrong in so many ways.

"There's no more pain now, sweetheart." Maggie stroked her dead daughter's forehead. A cold sheen of sweat coated her flesh. "You can rest now."

She'd tried calling Jake as soon as she'd found out Emily was arresting on the table, but he hadn't answered his phone. She'd called him every two minutes since. He hadn't answered.

His daughter is gone, and he doesn't even know it.

He should be back by now. How can I ever forgive him for not being here? Not being here when I need him the most? What excuse do you have, Jake?

Maybe it's my fault for sending him away. Perhaps he'll be the one blaming me.

Will we survive this?

What did it matter? Emily was gone, and the misery of the last eighteen months had all been for nothing, and the only thing that lay ahead was even more misery.

The nurses kept peeking in through the window at the top of the door. Maggie had needed to fight to even see Emily, and even though the staff had eventually allowed it, they kept a close watch on her. She didn't know what the normal procedure was for this kind of thing, but she felt as though they wanted to take Emily away some place.

The morgue.

She's grey. Why is she so grey?

"Mummy's right here, sweetheart. I won't let them take you. Not yet." She wiped tears from both cheeks. Emily belonged to both Maggie and Jake, but in this moment, she didn't want anyone else to be there. The bond between a mother and a daughter was primal, and it was something Maggie felt in her guts right now. It was a bond that should never be broken so tragically. It was wrong. So wrong.

"You were strong, honey. You never stopped fighting. Even at your worst, you managed a smile for the rest of us. You never wanted to be a burden." She took a deep breath and let it out slowly, trying to keep the howling winds of hysteria at bay. "My first baby," she moaned. "I'll never stop loving you, Emily. You'll always be with me."

Emily sat bolt upright, gasping for breath. "Mum?"

Maggie screamed and leapt back from the bed, smashing into a bank of equipment nearby and collapsing to the ground. Her hip struck the cold, hard tiles like a hammer and knocked the breath out of her in a wailing gasp.

What is happening?

Emily was sitting up on the bed. She craned her neck to see her mother on the ground. "Mum?" she said again. "Mum, where am I?"

Maggie couldn't breathe. She blinked over and over, trying to trust her eyes. It was only the chaotic pounding of her heartbeat that let her know she was truly awake.

With a shaking hand, she reached out. "E-Emily?"

"Mum? Something's wrong."

"What? What is it, honey? What's wrong?"

"I don't know. I just feel…" She frowned and glanced around. "Where am I?"

Maggie tried to get up off the floor, but she yelped and fell back down when the door burst open. A portly nurse came rushing in, and when she saw Emily sitting up in bed, the shock hit the woman like a punch in the mouth. "My… My…" She turned to look at Maggie, still laying on the ground. "I'll fetch the doctor. I'll… I'll go get him."

But the nurse didn't move for a moment, turning to gawp at Emily.

Then she took off like a racehorse.

Maggie clambered off the floor and went to her daughter's side. "I'm dreaming," she said, grabbing both of Emily's hands. "I thought… I thought…"

I thought you were gone.

Emily yanked on Maggie's hands and pulled her into a hug. Maggie was shocked by her daughter's strength as they held each other tightly. Even the smell of her was different. She smelled…

Healthy. Alive.

"Mum?"

"Yes, sweetheart?"

"Where's Dad and Lily?"

CHAPTER
NINE

JAKE WAS GETTING ready to leave. As friendly – and as strange – as Mr Cho was, the old man suddenly seemed irritable and clearly wanted them to leave. George had gone into the kitchen to make his old friend a cup of tea, but he was back now and helping to patch up the open wound on his forehead.

It was nearly nine o'clock.

Maggie must be going insane, wondering where I am.

I need to get back to the hospital. I need to see Emily.

Standing by the table in the centre of the room, Jake turned to Lily, who was still sitting in an armchair at the side of the room. "We need to go," he said. "Your mum is going to have a fit if—"

His phone rang in his pocket. With all that he'd been through in the last half hour, his nerves were completely frayed, so much so that he flinched at the sudden noise as if a gun had gone off.

It was Maggie, calling again. Twenty minutes since the last time.

A numbness spread throughout his legs, and he flopped

down in one of the armchairs, almost dropping both his phone and the wallet with the needle in it. He placed the wallet down on the armrest carefully. It felt like evidence of a crime, and he didn't want to be holding it while he spoke to his wife.

He answered his phone. "Maggie, look, I can ex—"

"She's okay. Jake, she's okay." From the sound of her voice, Maggie was obviously in tears, but she went on. "It was bad – really, really bad – but then she was okay. Jake, where are you?"

"I'm with Lily. It's hard to explain, but I'm heading to the hospital right now. What happened with Emily?"

"She died."

He almost dropped the phone, and kept hold of it only by squeezing it in his fist so tightly that the plastic threatened to snap. "No. No, Maggie, she can't be. She can't be dead, because—"

"No, Jake, listen to me. She died, but then she came back. It's a miracle. The doctors said she was completely gone – and she was, Jake. I was there, I saw her. But then she suddenly woke up and hugged me like nothing had happened. She says she's feeling better than she has in a long time. The doctor said her organs are functioning again, and her infection is easing. I… I don't think they can even understand it themselves. Somehow, our baby kept on fighting. Our little girl won't give up."

Jake swallowed, wanting to shout down the line that he had done this, that he had saved their daughter. But, at the same time, he knew she would think him crazy. He barely believed it himself. "Have the doctors said whether she's going to be okay?"

"Not exactly. I don't think they know. Jake? Why aren't you at the hospital? Did something happen to Lily?"

"No, nothing like that. She'd gone for a walk, so I had to wait for her. Then we…" He glanced at his daughter. "Then we went to, um, grab a burger. Sorry it's taken so long."

"Just get here now, babe. I'm going out of my mind without you."

"I'm leaving right now. I… I love you, Maggie."

She was silent for a moment. Then: "I love you too. Just hurry."

Jake put the phone back in his pocket and took a moment to take stock of things.

George, a man he had only just met, had convinced Jake to perform some kind of weird ritual to cure Emily's cancer. Then, in that very same hour, Emily had died and miraculously come back to life. It couldn't be a coincidence. Had Mr Cho's magic truly worked? Had the ancient ones cured Emily?

And who the hell are the ancient ones? To whom do I owe my thanks?

Jake's stomach was so awash with anxiety that he thought he might be sick, but he slowly realised it was a good feeling. Excitement. Hope. Happiness.

"Emily's going to be okay," he told the room, unable to keep from gushing with joy. "She's doing good."

George was still fussing over Mr Cho in the corner, but he turned around now. "Was that Maggie on the phone? Emily's okay?"

Jake nodded. "Things were bad at the hospital, but she pulled through. Sounds like it was a miracle."

George gave him a knowing smile, a hint of pride about him. "That's the best news, Jake. I'm so glad."

"Thanks." He nodded at Mr Cho. "Thank you, to you both."

"Better poke someone with the pinny-pin-pin," Lily said

in a lilting, dream-like voice. "Gotta give Emily's cancer away, like a lovely little gift."

Jake groaned as that part of the ordeal came back to him. If he didn't prick someone in the next twenty-four hours, Emily's miraculous recovery would be reversed. That was the deal, right? If not for the ritual, would she be dead right now? Did he now hold her death on the end of a pin, waiting to give it to somebody else?

I can't lose her. Not now I've found a way to save her.

"Lily, we need to go. We'll figure everything out later. Your sister's still in the hospital, but she's—"

"Cured?" said Lily, giggling like a half-asleep idiot. "Because we summoned the Devil to fix her."

Mr Cho grunted weakly. "I already told you there are no devils here."

"Just magic." Lily laughed again. "Pick a card, any card."

Jake frowned. "What are you talking about, Lily? Are you…?" He put a hand to his head and groaned. "Lily, have you taken something?"

George came over from the other side of the room. "What's wrong?"

Jake ignored him and studied his daughter's face. In the flickering candlelight, her eyes were like jet-black sequins. Her bottom jaw jutted out as if she were trying to do an impression of an alligator. "Lily, what the hell have you taken?"

She shrugged. "Summin' to help me cope, innit? Been a rough few days, Dad."

"A rough few days? Lily, have you any idea what you've done?"

George put a hand on his arm. "Go easy, Jake. There's a lot going on."

Jake whipped the man's hand away, not wanting to be

touched. "Stay calm? I have one daughter dying in the hospital, and the other one – fourteen years old, by the way – decides it's a good idea to try drugs for the first time."

Lily snorted. "Not my first time, Dad."

What happened next, Jake seemed to witness from outside his own body. He watched himself snatch at his daughter's arm and drag her to her feet. Lily could barely keep on her feet, but rather than show pain or fear, she just kept giggling like an imbecile.

"Stop laughing," he demanded. "What have you taken, Lily? Tell me!"

"Jake." George reached out to him again, but didn't touch him this time. "Come on now."

"Stay out of this." He grabbed Lily by both arms and shook her. "What have you taken? What have you taken? What have you taken?"

"I dunno," she said, smiling like an idiot. "But it's goooood. You should try some, Dad. You need to relax. When was the last time you gave Mum a good seeing to?"

He shook his head, barely able to comprehend what he was hearing. "Do you have any concern for someone other than yourself? Do you even… Do you even… Wait a second…" It dawned on him, what he had seen when the candles had flared. "I saw you put something in your mouth when I was sitting on the floor. Lily, you've taken a goddamn pill. Are you trying to throw your life away?"

She shrugged petulantly. "You got to live a little, right? Who knows when you might get cancer and die?"

He raised a hand to slap her, something he'd never done before. Thankfully, George grabbed his wrist, stronger than the old man looked. "Don't do something you'll hate yourself for later, Jake."

Jake pulled his wrist free and made no second attempt to

hit his daughter. Instead, he stepped up to Lily and glared at her. "Tell me where you got it? Who gave you the pill?"

Lily still showed no fear. In fact, she seemed bored and sleepy. "He didn't want to give me it," she muttered. "I made him hand it over. Reckons he fancies me, Dad. Maybe I should go thank him properly." She gave Jake a revolting wink.

Jake felt his fists clench into balls of fire. "Who gave you the pill, Lily?"

She pressed her lips together.

Mr Cho cleared his throat from the armchair at the back of the room. "I would like you to take your problems outside. This is ungracious behaviour, and I am tired."

Jake turned to glare at the old man, but realised Mr Cho had every right to be upset. He unclenched his fists and apologised. "Come on, Lily, we're leaving. I'll deal with you at home."

She yawned, completely unable to care. As if to keep Jake from grabbing her again, George stepped between them both and took Lily gently by the arm. "Come now, my dear. Let's go get some fresh air, eh?"

Jake followed the two of them out into the hallway, knowing he could kill someone right now if he wasn't careful. He'd never felt fury like what was bubbling away in his guts right now. It almost distracted him from the fact his other daughter might actually have received a miracle tonight. A desire for justice had pushed away any excitement, and all he could think about was retribution.

Whoever gave Lily that pill is going to pay.

———

"Are you sure you wouldn't like me to keep you company?" George asked as they stood at the bottom of Mr Cho's garden path.

Jake knew his neighbour was worried about what he was going to do to Lily, but it was none of his business. "I can deal with this," he snapped. "Thank you, George."

"I know you can, Jake. I just want you both to be okay. There's a lot going on. Do you want me to look after her while you go back to the hospital?"

"No. George, I appreciate it, but we barely know you. I need to take care of this myself." He put his arm around his half-asleep daughter to keep her from falling down.

George seemed a little hurt, but that didn't make Jake's statement any less true. "Very well, but you come get me if I can do anything at all, okay?"

Jake nodded and led Lily away.

"Jake?" George called after him.

"What is it?"

"Emily. You'll let me know she's okay?"

With a sigh, he nodded. "Of course, George."

"Oh, and you forgot this." He pulled something from his pocket and offered it out. It was the plastic wallet with the needle inside.

"Shit! How did I…?" Jake reached out to take the wallet, but hesitated. Now that he was outside in the fresh air, the entire ordeal inside Mr Cho's house seemed surreal and farcical. Reality wasn't magic and miracles, it was drugs and alcohol, and rebellious teenage daughters. It was misery and pain.

But Emily made an unexplainable recovery. The doctors don't understand it.

Because it had nothing to do with medicine.

Jake took the wallet and quickly slid it into his jacket pocket. "Goodnight, George."

George simply nodded and turned away.

Jake went in the opposite direction with Lily, his teeth grinding and a knot forming in his stomach. He didn't even know what to focus on first. He desperately wanted to reach the hospital, to be with Emily, but Lily was in no state to be left alone.

"I can't believe you did this, Lily," he said, seething. "How could you be so utterly stupid?"

She groaned, staggering back and forth, and only kept moving with help from his guiding arm. "What d'you care? You expect me to look after myself. Let me."

"I do not expect you to look after yourself, Lily. You're fourteen."

"Whatever."

They staggered further down the pavement, but Lily couldn't go on. "I… I need siddown. Gon' puke."

"Jesus Christ." Jake eased Lily down onto the brick wall outside one of the terraces. She swayed back and forth, her eyes rolling about in her head and an ominous bulge in her throat. As angry as he was, Jake couldn't stand there and be mad while she was feeling ill. He rubbed her back gently. "Just take some deep breaths," he said. "It'll pass."

She nodded and did as she was told. In the moonlight, the pink streak in her hair looked like blood. Her pale skin appeared silver. It would've been easy to mistake her for a ghoul.

"Wish I was dead," she mumbled.

Jake put a finger to her chin and forced her to look at him. "No, you don't, Lily. Don't you ever say that."

"S'true. My life's shit."

Jake bit down on his instinctual reaction, which was

to shout at her for being so selfish – and to remind her that her sister was seriously ill. Instead, he took a few moments to consider. Perhaps it was time to listen to his younger daughter, even if he didn't like what he heard. "Why do you think your life is shit, Lily? Tell me."

She let her head drop. "You'll just have a go, like you always do."

"If you're unhappy, I want to know about it."

With effort, she lifted her head back up and sneered at him. "You *already* know. Don't act like you don't."

Again, he wanted to lash out, but he was starting to realise he'd been doing too much of that lately. Lily clearly didn't trust him enough to be honest about her feelings, and that hurt. He could only blame himself. "I won't have a go," he said softly. "I promise."

She looked him in the eye – as much as she was able to – and seemed to scrutinise his expression. "What about me taking drugs? You gonna make my life hell about it?"

Yes, absolutely! I can't believe you could be so stupid. I can't believe you—

He shook his head and exhaled. "We'll keep it between us. As long as you never ever do it again, I won't bring it up."

"Seriously?" She eyed him suspiciously. "You're not even going to mention it?"

"I'll do my best to just forget about it. I know things have been tough for you, Lily, so let's talk about it. Let's sort out whatever it is making you unhappy."

"Everything." She almost shouted the word at him. "Everything makes me unhappy."

Jake glanced at the window of the house they were loitering outside of, worried about disturbing the occupants.

"Can you break everything down a little so I can understand it?"

She shrugged. "Sometimes, I wish I was the one who was ill. Emily doesn't have to do anything. She doesn't have to worry about school or friends or making you and Mum happy."

"She does have to worry about her body shutting down and killing her. I think it's a little unfair—"

"You see? You'll take her side no matter what I say." She glared at him, a little more focused and a little less sleepy. "I know she's ill, Dad – and I wish she weren't – but you're my parents too. Why can't I just be right for once? When do I get to be the centre of attention? When do I get to be important?"

He took a deep breath and stroked his daughter's face with the back of his hand. "You are important, Lily. You have no idea how much."

The fact she looked shocked by his statement was heart-breaking. Hearing that she mattered should not have been a revelation. "I've let you down," he admitted, feeling the last of his anger ebb away. "You're acting like a little shit, but I guess we've left you no choice. If you can forgive me, I'll try to do better."

She opened her mouth to speak, paused, and then said, "We can go. My stomach's okay now."

"Let's just sit another minute or two. No rush."

She continued taking deep breaths, and gradually her cheeks found some colour. Whatever she had taken had hit hard and fast, but now she just seemed dozy and relaxed.

"Do you think you can make the hospital?" he asked her.

She shrugged. "Not sure. I really wanna go to bed."

He nodded. How on earth he might explain it to Maggie,

he didn't know, but he needed to do whatever was best for Lily.

"Dad?"

"Yeah?"

"Do you really think Emily's cured? Did all that weird stuff work?"

He turned and looked back towards Mr Cho's house, but he couldn't see it from where they were standing. "It's been a strange night, that's for sure."

"This place isn't so bad," Lily said, rubbing at her eyes. "The street, the house… it's all right. I'm sorry for complaining."

He leant forward and gave her a hug. She was still clearly high, but more or less seemed like herself again. "Whatever happens, Lil, your mum and I will always love you, okay?"

"I really want to go to bed."

He hooked her around the arm and helped her to stand. Then, together, they strolled along the pavement, passing beneath clouds of insects buzzing around lampposts.

When they reached the end of their own garden path, Jake readjusted his grip on Lily and tried to examine her. "I don't know if it's safe for me to leave you sleeping. What if you choke? Or swallow your own tongue?"

"I'm okay, Dad. I just want a big glass of water and then I'll be all right."

"I don't know. Perhaps I should go back and fetch George to watch over you."

"Don't you dare! Just go to the hospital, Dad. You have no other choice."

"Thanks to you, Lily. I can't believe you—"

"Hey!" She wagged a finger at him. "You promised you wouldn't bring it up."

"Fine." He let go of her arm to test her sobriety. She

stayed standing by herself, which gave him a little hope. "What do I tell your mum when I turn up without you?"

"Just say I couldn't bear to come. Tell her I was in tears or something."

"When are you ever in tears?"

She shrugged. "First time for everything."

"Come on." He shook his head. "Get inside, you little druggie."

"Dad!"

"Last time, I promise."

―――――

Jake texted Maggie, informing her that Lily was an emotional mess and didn't want to come to the hospital. She texted straight back, telling him to hurry to the hospital with or without their youngest daughter. The kisses at the end of her message were a good sign that things were okay with Emily.

Rather than leave in a hurry, Jake stayed and sat with Lily for ten minutes. He had helped her sip from a pint of water and then placed her in bed, with pillows tucked either side of her to keep her from rolling onto her front or back and choking. Within a few minutes, she was snoring away like a—

Pug. Snoring away like John the pug.

What a strange night.

Even after Lily had fallen asleep, Jake lingered by her side. He was afraid to leave, afraid to go to the hospital and see for himself that Emily had miraculously recovered. It would mean the world didn't obey the rules he thought it had.

Is there really magic in the world? Powerful beings watching us?

It's insane.

Eventually, Jake had no choice but to leave. It was ten o'clock, and he'd been gone from the hospital for several hours now. It was unfair to leave Maggie alone to deal with everything by herself any longer.

"I'm on my way," he said to no one, and then headed out the front door.

He unlocked the X-Trail – its lights flashing – and was just about to open the driver's side door when he saw someone standing on the other side of the road.

Vincent.

You bastard.

Jake put his car keys back in his pocket and crossed the road.

When Vincent saw him coming, he glanced left and right nervously, and even took a step back. Despite the lad's physical victory the other night, he seemed unnerved by Jake's approach.

He's not so tough without his mates backing him up.

"Hey," Vincent said in an oddly neutral tone. No insults. No stupid street slang. "What's up?"

Jake stepped up onto the kerb and came to a halt in front of the lad. "What are you doing out here, Vincent?"

"Just got some business to take care of." He shrugged, but he couldn't look Jake in the eye. His usual swagger was completely absent. "Um, how's your daughter?" he asked, sounding as if he actually gave a shit. "Is she okay?"

Jake fought to keep his hands by his sides. The hair on his neck prickled. "Do you mean Emily? Or are you asking how Lily is after you gave her fucking drugs?"

Of course it was him. Why wasn't it obvious the second I thought about it?

Vincent stepped back, glancing back and forth again, as if looking for help. "Hey, man, look, I didn't want to give her nothing, but she forced me to, innit?"

Jake stalked after him. "She forced you to? A fourteen-year-old girl?"

"She's pretty pushy, bruv."

"Are you a man or a fucking mouse?"

"Listen, right?" Vincent put his hands up in defence. "I gave her the weakest shit I had on me. Just a little downer to help her relax. She's been having a hard time, so—"

Jake couldn't control himself any longer. He lashed out, grabbing Vincent by the shirt and tossing the lad sideways off the kerb and into the road. He landed hard, rolling onto his side with a groan and clutching his elbow.

"Don't tell me how my fucking daughter is doing," Jake growled. "You know nothing about Lily."

Vincent shuffled backwards on his rear. Despite his obvious fear, he talked back defiantly. "We hung out while you were at the hospital. She's unhappy, bruv. I just wanted to help."

"By giving her drugs?"

"By being her friend. Who else does she have?"

"Get up! Get up now so I can knock you back down."

Vincent stopped scooting and put a hand up to protect himself. "You and me got off on the wrong foot, bruv, but there don't have—"

"The wrong foot? The wrong fucking foot?" Jake bared his teeth. "How about this foot?" He swung his leg and booted Vincent square in the ribs. Air exploded out of the lad like a punctured tyre, and his agonised moaning was music to Jake's ears. So he kicked him again, this time in the meat of the thigh. Then a third time, once again in the ribs.

Vincent's howling puttered out, replaced by a low groan. He rose onto his knees and clutched his stomach, desperately trying to take a breath but failing.

"A little winded, are we?" Jake had no compassion for the pain he was inflicting on the lad. How many innocent people had Vincent and his pack of thugs attacked? He deserved a taste of his own medicine.

A deep grumble erupted at the end of the road.

Jake turned to see growing headlights, a pair of angry, white eyes opening wider and wider.

Brakes bit. Tyres screeched.

Jake shielded his eyes as a large vehicle skidded to a halt less than six feet away from him, headlights blinding, engine puttering like an idling thundercloud.

A car door opened.

The silhouette of a man entered the glaring cocoon of the headlights.

And then a voice said, "The fuck is this bullshit?"

"Who are you?" Jake asked, lowering his arm, stepping backwards and trying to see. He recognised the car. The black Range Rover.

A square-shouldered man with a goatee, slicked-back hair, and thick metal bracelets on each wrist stepped into view. He peered over at Vincent, who was still lying on the ground. "Off your arse, V. You're embarrassing yourself."

"I said, who are you?" Jake repeated.

The stranger kept his attention on Vincent. "Who the hell is this guy?"

Vincent climbed gingerly to his feet, clutching his ribs and wheezing. "It... It's all right, Unc. Just leave it."

"Leave it? I come here to handle some business with my nephew and find some piece of shit giving him a kicking."

"He had it coming," Jake said, almost spitting. He saw another person sitting inside the Range Rover, which meant he was outnumbered three to one. Probably best he lower his tone, but it was a challenge to control his temper. "He gave my fourteen-year-old daughter drugs."

The stranger flinched and then looked at Vincent again. "That true, V?"

Vincent couldn't meet the man's glare.

Jake sighed. At least it seemed the stranger understood his anger. Maybe they could work this out here and now. So long as Vincent stayed the fuck away from Lily. "He gave her pills. He could've killed her."

The man walked over to Jake and stopped two feet away. He leant in, his face getting close, and asked, "Who the fuck cares?"

What?

Jake didn't even know a punch was coming until it hit the side of his jaw. His vision tilted, and his legs couldn't tell which way was up. The road came up to meet him, hard and unkind, biting into his back and scraping away the flesh from his elbows, even through the fabric of his jacket.

Time seemed to pause.

Jake didn't know where he was or how he had got there.

But he heard a voice.

"Leave it, Unc, please! He ain't worth it."

"Too late, V. You represent me. If people see you getting a kicking from some no-mark, it's gonna give 'em ideas. Can't have it. Gotta send a message."

"You have sent a message. He's hurt."

"Not nearly enough."

Jake could hear the words, but his mind wouldn't make

sense of them. It was like a jumble inside his head. All he could focus on was getting back to his feet. He refused to stay down and be a victim.

No more of this. No more letting life shit all over me.

Jake put both hands on the sharp surface of the road and pushed. It took a moment to get his feet underneath him, but eventually he made it back to standing. "W-who are you?" he mumbled, confused and disorientated by a pounding in his head.

The stranger glared at Jake, his eyes like coal glistening in two sunken pits. "I'm the fucking lord of this manor, sunshine, and you've been found guilty of breaching the peace."

Jake frowned, his mind muddled, his legs uncertain beneath him. His throbbing jaw felt too large for his head; he could barely move it.

"Uncle Dev, don't!" Vincent cried out from somewhere nearby, sounding like a frightened child. "Don't!"

The other man grabbed Jake by the back of the neck and punched him twice in the stomach. The vicious blows knocked the air right out of him, but unlike when Vincent had been winded, Jake made no sound other than a weak grunt. Alarmed and confused, he turned and started walking away.

Need to be away from here.

Jake couldn't take a breath, but he felt no pain. He was okay, and didn't feel the need to fight back. His anger was gone, and all he felt was a disorientated, desperate desire to get away.

He kept trying to make sense of what had happened, but he couldn't figure it out. Why was it so hard to remember something that had happened only a moment ago?

Vincent's uncle had arrived to find Jake attacking his

nephew, that much Jake knew. Had the man then punched him in the jaw? Things got murky afterwards.

Jesus, am I okay?

Jake glanced back over his shoulder and saw Vincent standing in the road, watching him leave. In the glarc of the Range Rover's headlights, the lad seemed childlike and afraid. His uncle moved up beside him and lifted a phone to his ear.

Jake carried on walking, not sure where he was going, but certain that any direction was better than standing still. He needed to get home…

With every step, he seemed to grow dizzier. His temples pulsed, a drumbeat in both ears. He felt a chill, but at the same time was sweating profusely.

I'm sodden. What's wrong with me?

He reached down inside his jacket and grasped his stomach in the place where he'd been punched. A dull ache emanated from the centre of his torso.

I should've stayed and fought. Things will be even worse now I'm walking away.

Behind him, the Range Rover turned around in the road and sped off. Vincent was gone, too, which must mean he had got inside the car with his uncle.

Stay away from Lily, you lowlife.

Jake stopped and tried to take a breath. He was breathing shallowly, which was probably why he felt so dizzy. As he held his tummy, he felt a hot, wet sensation between his fingers. For a second, he thought maybe he'd wet himself, but the warmth was coming from too high up.

He brought his hands up in front of his face to examine them. They were slick with a viscous, black liquid. To get a better look, he stepped beneath a lamppost. Its glow added colour to the world and revealed that his hands were stained red. Jake could barely understand what he was seeing. There was blood all over the front of his shirt. How?

"I've… I've been…"

I've been stabbed.

Jake staggered and almost fell, but he knew, somehow, that if he did, it would all be over. He couldn't stop. Had to keep moving.

Home. I need to get home. Need to get help.

Help me!

He reached into his pocket and pulled out his phone. He tried to unlock the screen, but he couldn't. His trembling fingers smeared blood all over the glass, and his wet thumbprint wouldn't work. Nor did the facial recognition, because his jaw was twice its normal size.

"I-I need help." He tried to yell out, but hot coals inside his guts took away his breath.

His legs shook as he zigzagged back and forth across the road.

Where was home? Where was Lily?

Too far away. So close, but impossible to reach.

Jake realised he had wandered, in a traumatised daze, halfway down the street in the wrong direction. Home was now a hundred metres behind him. His legs buckled. He would never make it.

George's house?

Also too far away. Thirty or forty metres, at least.

I'm going to die out here in the middle of the street. Somebody, please…

Then Jake saw a familiar door, illuminated by a flickering candle on a brass dish.

Mr Cho. He can help me.

He can do miracles.

Jake was sinking towards the ground, his vision growing dark, his legs getting shorter.

Time was running out.

He staggered across the road and made it onto the pavement.

I can't die. I can't…

My girls…

As he stumbled between the two clay dragons, Jake's legs finally gave in. Hot blood ran down all the way down to his ankles. He shivered, almost uncontrollably. His mouth filled with copper.

Please…

He collapsed onto his knees.

But he wasn't dead yet.

Like a wounded dog, Jake crawled his way up the garden path towards Mr Cho's front door – towards the tiny slither of salvation from a near stranger. The only hope Jake had left.

I can feel myself slipping away.

Heaving and shuddering, Jake put one knee in front of the other and reached forward with both hands, dragging himself along. The path was short, but it felt like a marathon ahead of him. Never had it been so painful to move so little.

But as long as I keep moving, I'm still alive.

Jake made it to the doorstep, still conscious but quickly fading. Weakly, he banged his fist against the bottom of the red-painted door, over and over and over again. Desperate. Dying. Begging.

"Mr Cho," he whimpered. "Please… open your door. I… I've been stabbed."

CHAPTER
TEN

THE DOOR OPENED and Jake slumped sideways across the step, coming face to face with a pair of slippered feet in the hallway.

"Mr Penshaw?" said a soft, barely audible voice. "What has happened?"

"Stabbed. Need help."

"My word. H-hold on, I'll call an ambulance."

Finding a last reserve of strength, Jake lifted himself enough to grab Mr Cho's ankle and prevent him from leaving. "Need help now."

Mr Cho pulled his leg away and gasped. "You need a hospital."

"F-flesh bargain. Only… chance." Jake grabbed the doorframe and pulled himself up, fighting nonstop until he was standing. This was his only chance, the final few minutes of his life – unless Mr Cho helped him.

Mr Cho stared at Jake's bloody torso and grew pale. "Y-you don't know what it is you're asking for."

"To live," he said weakly. "To live and protect my girls. The man who did this…" He fell forward, his vision suddenly tilting. Somehow, the diminutive Mr Cho managed to catch him and hold him upright. "Please… don't let me die."

"Let's get you inside," Mr Cho struggled to reach out and close the door while also propping up Jake. "We'll figure it out."

"Help me."

Mr Cho looked him in the eye. "If you truly want this, Mr Penshaw, I take no responsibility for the price you have to pay."

Jake exhaled, worried his words were all spent. "H-help me."

"So be it." Mr Cho shoved the door closed and helped Jake stagger down the hallway into the living room. There, he attempted to ease him down onto a floor cushion, but Jake collapsed awkwardly onto his side and sprawled across the carpet. Mr Cho left him lying there.

The old man hurried and sat on the other cushion, then reached into the drawer beneath the coffee table. He lit the two candles and threw dust onto them.

He began the ritual, beseeching the same ancient gods as before.

Jake lay on his side. The words floated in and out of his head. His eyelids were heavy; he had to fight to keep them open. All he wanted was to stop fighting and drift away, a powerful force tugging at his consciousness and promising peace and comfort. A soft cloud made only for him, where worry and pain did not exist. If only he would just give in and allow that force to take him.

No, I can't leave my girls. Not like this.

I brought us here, to this street. They're not safe. This place is not safe.

Mr Cho continued to petition the beings beyond human

perception. He tossed more dust at the candles and dropped that same strange metal symbol onto the coffee table as before. A bell rang inside Jake's skull. He realised his eyes had closed. Oblivion was carrying him away.

"Mr Penshaw? Mr Penshaw, are you still here?"

Jake forced his eyelids open, pulling himself back from the claws of whatever darkness had been about to swallow him whole. He saw Mr Cho staring at him from across the table.

"You ask a favour for yourself, Mr Penshaw, something I caution strongly against, something I have never before facilitated. Do you truly want this? Sometimes, it's better to accept fate's plan."

One of Jake's eyes closed, but he fought with everything he had to keep the other one open. "Save. Me."

Mr Cho sighed. "Very well. May the universe have mercy on us both, my friend."

Jake could fight no longer. Both eyes closed, and he plummeted into an inky black void, searching out that soft, peaceful cloud he was promised.

———

Vincent had given Lily his mobile number yesterday at the park, but after texting him all morning, he'd not replied even once. It made no sense. If he was a player, then surely he would've waited until after he got in her pants to ghost her?

Lily also didn't understand what had happened to her dad. He'd tucked her into bed last night and made sure she was all right—

He was really sweet actually.

—but then she had fallen asleep and not seen him since.

The only person she'd spoken to that morning was her

mum, and she claimed not to have seen or heard from her dad either. In fact, she'd been frantic when Lily had called, having been alone with Emily at the hospital all night. Apparently, she had been leaving message after message for Lily and her dad, but neither had replied. Underneath her mother's tears, Lily detected a bubbling fury slowly heating up. There was going to be hell to pay.

Where the hell are you, Dad?

Are you okay?

It was that second question that tied knots in Lily's empty stomach. Last night had been…

A trip, in more ways than one.

It all felt like a dream now, but she remembered following her dad and George into Mr Cho's house, and how the weird old man had performed some crazy ritual to help Emily. Had it worked? According to what her mum had told her earlier, Emily was doing fine. Better than fine, in fact.

The other issue swirling around Lily's aching head was the fact her dad had caught her taking a pill – not that she'd tried to hide it. The memory brought a chuckle, and she marvelled at her own audacity. It had been a ballsy move, but in that moment, she just hadn't cared about getting in trouble. She had just wanted it all to stop. The noise. The drama.

The feelings.

The high was like nothing she'd ever felt before, but disappointingly brief. She still couldn't believe her dad had promised never to mention it, doubtful he would ever be able to keep his word. At least he was doing his best to stay chill about it.

He listened to me, she thought, flashes of last night still coming back to her. *I let him down badly, but he didn't shout. Just listened.*

Lily texted Vincent again, desperate to hear from someone other than her exhausted, mentally unstable mother. Someone who could tell her that everything was going to be okay, and that she didn't need to freak out.

V, pls text me. Things r weird and I need to talk to u.

She reached over to her side table and drank what was left of her water. No matter how much she sipped, though, her thirst wouldn't go away, and she'd been refilling the glass constantly for the last hour. Time to stop monging on her bed, but she couldn't seem to shake her body awake. If she closed her eyes, she would probably fall right back to sleep.

Whatever Vincent had given Lily last night had certainly relaxed her, but her sluggish mind was now awash with anxiety. Everything felt wrong, and a deep loneliness hung over her like a guillotine about to drop, threatening to sever her fuzzy grip on reality completely.

Mum, Dad, Emily… I need you.

Her mum had told her to get a taxi to the hospital as soon as she was ready, but Lily had so far delayed doing so. Mainly because she didn't know what to tell her mum about what she had been doing for the last twelve hours.

If she finds out I got high, she'll ground me until I'm thirty.

Lily yelped as her phone vibrated in her hand. When she looked at it, her mood instantly lifted. Vincent had finally messaged back. Tentatively, she opened the text.

Soz, bin dealing with stuff. Everything ok? x

She typed back immediately. **My dad is missing. Have u seen him?**

What? No, y would I have sin him? He at hospital? x

Deflating slightly, Lily took a moment before replying:

Not at hospital. Been missing since last night. I'm worried. x

It took a few minutes for him to come back to her again, and she sat on her bed, biting her nails and pulling at her hair until her phone vibrated.

Maybe he went an got drunk? x

Lily considered the theory, and couldn't reject it outright, but it didn't feel like the right answer. Her dad hadn't gone down the pub in months. He was much more likely to overdo the booze at home.

Maybe… she typed. **Gotta go hospital now. Meet later?? xx**

Again his reply took several minutes.

Not sure. Bit busy. maybe.

Lily frowned, disappointed by his answer. Before she sent a reply though, another text came through.

Hope sis is ok. x

She let out a sigh, relieved at his concern. Perhaps he really was busy. She was expecting too much, coming on too strong.

Thanks, V. Speak later.

He didn't reply.

Lily tossed her phone down on her bed and scooped her knotty hair back behind her ears.

End of conversation, I guess.

"Where the hell are you, Dad?" She said it out loud, unnerved by the silence. "If you don't turn up soon, you're a dead man."

———

"You keep your goddamn mouth shut, V!" His Uncle Dev was often angry, but this was worse than usual. He swung his fists in the air, his gold bracelets rattling on his bony wrists as he stomped back and forth on the worn carpet. "If you kept your fucking head down instead of prancing around like the big man all the time, shit like this wouldn't happen."

V knew better than to argue – he'd already got enough of a beating last night from Jake – so he kept his head down and tried to stay calm. Shit was precarious.

Last night, he'd thought for sure that Jake was going to kill him.

But it went a different way.

Last night, Dev had driven V home and ordered him to stay inside until morning, which he had done without complaint. He hadn't slept a wink. Trying to keep his tears at bay, he had rotated through emotion after emotion – fear, guilt, anger, shame – unable to keep his mind from crying out in misery. Then, as the sun had finally risen behind his curtains, and commuters filled the nearby roads, Mikey and Doser had rang his uncle's doorbell. V had met them fully clothed and half-asleep.

The boys had been sent to come and collect V for 'a meeting' down at the snooker club. It was clear they knew nothing about what had gone on, but they seemed excited by any potential drama. Even now, Mikey and Doser were waiting outside the snooker club for him, no doubt eager to get the score. Not that it was any of their business.

The beef between V and Lily's dad had got out of hand. Admittedly, V had played a part in things – he'd fucked with Jake when he had first arrived on the street and said some things he shouldn't have – but it wasn't supposed to have gone this far. In fact, V had been intending to bury the hatchet with the man, for Lily's sake.

But the guy had anger issues. He didn't have to come at me like that.

"I'm sorry, Uncle. I fucked up." He was standing at the back of the snooker hall that his uncle used to do business, very aware of how far away the exit was.

His uncle glared at him. "You'd just better hope none of this winds up on my fucking doorstep, V, or you'll be doing a long stretch at Winson Green."

"What?" V gasped. "Man did nothing wrong, bruv. You shanked the guy, fam, not me."

His uncle fronted up to him, his sickly aftershave polluting the air. Several feet behind him, Bekim folded his thick, tattooed arms and glared. Vincent hated the stupid fucking Albanian, but the guy was a complete psycho, so he avoided making eye contact. Right now, his uncle was the biggest threat in the room.

"Don't you speak that stupid roadman shit with me, you little cunt." He reached out and grabbed V by the chin, squeezing hard enough to make his jaw ache. "Listen very carefully, nephew. I had to sort your fucking mess out last night, so whatever happens, it's on you."

"You never had to stab him, Unc. You never had to—"

V swore as the back of his uncle's hand collided with the side of his head.

"Don't answer back to me, you useless prick. You'd be in the gutter sucking cocks if it wasn't for me, so you do whatever the fuck I tell you to do when I tell you to do it. If I say get down on your knees and blow Bekim, you do it. Understand me?"

Bekim blew V a kiss.

His uncle slapped him again. "Do. You. Understand. Me?"

V shied away, an arm out in front of his face. "Fuck! Yeah, I understand you, fam."

"Good. You want to be a real gangster, V, then shut your

mouth and get to work. You're going to be hustling day and night until I say otherwise. Now get the fuck out of my club."

V took off as quickly as he could without breaking into a full-on run. While he was terrified of his uncle, it would be a mistake to show it so blatantly. Fear got you killed in this game.

Once he'd moved to the other side of the nearest snooker table, and he was sure Bekim wasn't following him, he slowed into a purposeful march, trying to disguise the pain in his thigh and ribs.

If Jake's dead, I'm screwed. I'll go down for murder.

But what if he's still alive? Lily says he's missing, not dead.

So where are you, bruv? How d'you walk off a pair of stab wounds?

V limped down the stairs and shoved his way out of the exit. Mikey and Doser were sitting on the wall outside, waiting for him to return. Kaydon and Ryan had also joined them since V had gone inside. Kaydon was smoking a joint, but he stamped it out now, only a butt left.

Mikey probably called everyone to let them know there was drama going down. Big-mouth bitch.

Doser stood up and turned to face V. His friend was wearing a navy blue D&G tracksuit worth more than most people made in a week, but it made him look like a Smurf. "Geezer? What did bossman want to see you for?"

"Shit man," said Ryan, standing up as well. "You look pale, bruv. Did your uncle ream you out?"

"Shut up, you fat fuck." V glowered. "You don't know shit."

Ryan rolled his eyes and huffed. "I ain't fat, bruv, so stop with that shit."

Kaydon chuckled. "Come on, Ry-Ry. One more Nando's and man will be sharing the stage with Lizzo."

Ryan snatched at Kaydon's dreads and yanked on one hard enough to make him yell. "Yo, let go, you wasteman."

Despite the obvious jolt of pain, Kaydon laughed off the assault. Out of all of them, he was the most chill, and probably the only one V would trust to have his back in a bad situation. Too bad he spent so much of his time completely baked.

"So, why are we all here so early, bruv?" Doser asked, zipping his tracksuit jacket up to his neck. "We got some new gear coming in or summin'?"

V hissed. "Not in front of the club, idiot. Anyway, it weren't about no business, bruv. Just family stuff, innit? Private shit, you get me?"

"Wait," said Mikey, squinting at him through his dodgy eye that never seemed to look where it was meant to. "Bossman has me and Doser come get you at the crack of dawn just to chat family shit? Don't you two live together, bruv?"

"Uncle Dev ain't ever home, is he? Roots down here at the club most nights." He turned back to face the snooker club and looked up at the old steel-framed windows. "Let's get out of here and go grab a Maccies. Man's paying."

"Sound!" Ryan patted him on the back.

V started walking, wanting to be away from his uncle and Bekim. "Only one hash brown for you though, yeah Ry, you fat fuck."

Ryan groaned while the others laughed at him. V did his best to laugh too, but in the back of his mind he couldn't stop imaging the worst, like turning the next corner only to find a bunch of uniforms waiting to arrest him for murder.

A murder man didn't even fucking commit. Shit is messed up.

"Why are you limping, bruv?" Kaydon eyed V as he

walked a step behind. "You mashed up your leg or what?"

V had forgotten his friends didn't know that he'd got a kicking last night, and he wasn't about to explain it to them now. "Oh, yeah, just slipped in the bath after too much of uncle's tequila. Max shit, bruv."

Kaydon winced. "Lucky you didn't bang your head, V. Gotta be careful around water, you know what I mean?"

"Listen to *him*," said Doser, pointing a thumb and sniggering. "Fam wants to become a lifeguard and keep us all safe at the pool."

"Shut up, wasteman." Kaydon scowled at him. "Man is just showing concern for his brethren."

V put a fist out and bumped knuckles with Kaydon. "Safe, bro, but I'm good. Just a dead leg."

They crossed the road and walked past the grotty windowless shops leading up to the town centre. It slowly grew busier, but thankfully no police arrived to arrest V. He told himself to stay calm. If the heat was on him, the police would have kicked in his door first thing that morning. They always liked to catch man sleeping.

I need to see Lily and find out what she knows.

And make sure she's all right.

"You all right, V?" Mikey asked as they crossed the road towards McDonalds. He sounded genuinely concerned, which he might've been since they went back all the way to first school. "Stuff with your uncle got heavy, yeah?"

V nodded, wishing he could tell his friends what had happened. But that wasn't the way things worked on the streets. The more people knew about your shit, the more they could fuck with you. Mikey and the others couldn't know what went down last night. They couldn't know about Jake.

"It's all good," he told them all. "We just need to bring in a good score this week or bossman is gonna come down hard. He thinks we can shift more than we have been."

"Shittin' hell, bruv." Kaydon sucked at his teeth. "Mandem is already pushing his luck as it is. Pigs are gonna be on our case if we ain't careful."

"So we'll be careful. We move more, we make more. It's worth the risk."

Especially if I'm on the hook for murder. What's a few more years added on for dealing? Maybe I can even get sent to a prison far away where my uncle can't get at me…

No chance. Whatever happens, he's never going to… going to—

V lurched forward and heaved. He'd not eaten breakfast, but the water he'd drunk that morning ejected from his mouth, spattering the chewing-gum-covered pavement.

"Whoa!" Ryan hopped out of the way, clutching his pot belly. "The fuck, bruv?"

V wiped his mouth and reached out for support. Kaydon grabbed his arm and helped him over to a brick wall running around the Halfords car park. "Sit down, V. Take some deep breaths, innit?"

"You sick or something?" Doser asked, pulling his zip up the final few centimetres as if to seal himself away from a biohazard.

"Must have a stomach bug or something," V said. "Sod it, I can't do breakfast, lads. I'm gonna go back home and get some sleep."

Doser grinned. "Maybe you can get that new blonde piece to come nurse you back to health, fam? Unless you ain't interested, in which case man might take her for a ride himself."

Vincent leapt up off the wall and fronted up to Doser. "Lily's off limits, d'you get me?"

"What?"

"I said: Do. You. Get. Me."

Doser backed off with a frown. "Yeah, bruv, chill. Why is you so vexed?"

Because I like the girl, and I think I got her dad killed.

V realised he'd overreacted – his mates were looking at him like he was a mental case – so, exhaling, he sat back down on the wall and lowered his head. "Sorry, Ry. Girl's just dealing with a lot because of her sister, innit? Don't be giving her no stress, yeah?"

Doser nodded and backed off. As much as they were mates, V kept them in line when he needed to. He was his uncle's nephew.

Mikey batted his eyelids and started blowing kisses. "We never knew you had a heart, V. When's the wedding?"

"Behave, bruv. I'm just being a gentleman, innit? It'll pay off later, you know what I mean? No weddings though, for real. Not man's style." V tried to give them an honest laugh, but it was a struggle. It wasn't weddings he was worried about, it was funerals.

CHAPTER
ELEVEN

MAGGIE'S SCREAMS were like daggers in his ears. It might have been old-fashioned, but as a man, Jake felt it his duty to love and protect his wife. Right now, however, she was in the worst agony of her life and there was nothing he could do about it.

"Push, my darling." The nurse squatted at the end of the bed like a wicketkeeper. "I can see her head. She's finally coming."

"About bloody time." Jake sighed, exhausted. Their daughter had taken eleven hours to reach this point. Multiple complications had slowed things down, and at one point, the consultant feared the umbilical cord had been wrapped around the baby's neck. That had instilled a type of dread in Jake that he'd never felt before. Suddenly, the kicking lump inside his wife's tummy had become a living, breathing thing. And it was in peril.

But that was all in the past now.

Their daughter was finally coming.

"Push," the nurse urged again, and Maggie let out another of those ear-dagger screams. In the last hour, she'd made an all manner of noises Jake hadn't known she was capable of making. The worst part was how she had drifted away some place in her mind, beyond communicating with. She didn't acknowledge anyone else in the room. His wife was a vacant, screaming beast, covered in sweat and blood.

Jake stayed near his wife's head, understanding that the business end wasn't a place for him. All the same, he couldn't help but lean over and take a look. What he saw was bizarre, gruesome, and amazing. A thatch of slimy blonde hair filled the space between Maggie's legs, and it had a thin metal rod poking out of it, which the consultant had attached for some reason. It was an odd thing to see – a tiny, misshapen mass not resembling a human being at all, but then, inch by inch, a little girl emerged.

A miracle. This is a miracle.

Ten minutes later, a bloody, pink, mucus-covered baby rose into the air and landed with a slap on Maggie's naked chest, put there by the no-nonsense nurse.

Despite what Jake had expected, their newborn daughter didn't cry. She just looked up at Maggie's face with bleary grey eyes, seeming both blind and all-knowing at the same time.

"Hello you," Maggie said with a smile. Her agony was gone, extinguished in an instant, and she was once again back in the room. "Are you the one who's been causing all this trouble?"

Jake felt sick. In fact, he feared he might pass out as his heart clattered in his chest. He should probably take a seat on the chair in the corner, but he couldn't bear to leave his family – not even by a few feet. To keep from falling, he gripped the railing at the side of Maggie's bed and took some deep breaths. It had been an exhausting, torturous, endless day – for Maggie most of all – but it was finally over.

We have a daughter. A safe, healthy daughter.

"She's beautiful," Jake said, looking his sweaty, half-delirious wife in the eyes and loving her more than ever. "You both are."

"Emily," she said with a far-off smile. "I want to call her Emily."

Emily.

Emily.

Jake muttered to himself, eyes closed, his body heavy. "Em… ly."

Delicate hands pressed themselves down against his chest and a soft voice soothed him. "You're okay, Mr Penshaw. You've been asleep."

Jake peeled his eyes open and saw the concerned face of a wrinkly, bald Chinese man. It took him several seconds to make sense of that. "Mr Cho?"

"After what we've done, you should probably call me Jing. May I call you Jake?"

Jake sprang up, hinging at the waist. He found himself lying on an old carpet with his woollen jacket draped over his legs like a blanket. A seat cushion sat behind him on the floor, acting as a pillow.

Mr Cho – Jing's – living room.

None of the candles were lit any more, and the curtains had been pulled back from their windows, allowing in sunlight. Dust motes drifted lazily in the air. It felt like early morning.

Jake tried to force the fuzziness from his eyes by blinking. "How… How long have I been here for?"

Jing was resting on his knees, hands folded in his lap. "About ten hours. I remained with you all night while you recovered."

Jake saw the tiredness in the old man's eyes and felt

guilty. Had he sat on the floor the whole time? Why? What had happened?

Why am I here?

Confused, all Jake could say was, "Thirsty."

Jing bowed slightly, then reached around behind him and picked up a glass of water from the coffee table. Jake accepted the water greedily and downed it in one go. With a gasp, he wiped his mouth on his forearm and nodded gratefully. "Th-thank you."

"You are welcome."

"What happened, Jing? Why am I here?"

"You don't remember?"

Squinting, Jake tried to recall. His thoughts were blurry and out of focus, offering only glimpses of last night. Then, as if cracked by a whip, his mind awoke with a start. "Emily? You… you helped her."

"I helped her, yes, but that is not the part you should remember. Jake, you returned to me last night. Alone and in need."

Jake tried to delve deeper into his murky memories. Despite having just downed a glass of water, he remained parched. His head was pounding. "I should be at the hospital," he muttered, thinking about Maggie there all alone. "Why am I here, Jing? Why didn't I…?"

Slowly, last night came back to him in stark, white-hot flashes, like photographs pinned to a wall in a darkroom, illuminated by a swinging lightbulb. Hands shaking, Jake reached down towards his stomach.

His shirt was damp with blood, the smell of it acrid and undeniable. Prodding himself firmly with each of his fingertips, he searched for the source of the bloodshed, but no pain jolted him. No puckered flesh presented itself.

"I-I was stabbed…"

"Stabbed, yes," Jing said, "but no longer."

"How?"

"You asked something terrible of me. Forgive me, but I said yes."

"Why? Why help me if you didn't want to?"

Jing sighed and seemed to think about the question seriously before answering. "Helping someone in need is never a choice, Jake. If I could have helped you another way, I would have, but you would've died long before an ambulance arrived. You are a father and a husband, and I am just an old man. I couldn't refuse you, but the consequences are yours."

Jake closed his eyes, trying to silence the drum beat inside his skull. "What consequences? How did you help me? It… It's hard to remember."

"I helped you the same way I helped Emily, but with one important difference."

"I asked a favour for myself…" Jake suddenly remembered it all. Like a dam bursting, the events of last night flooded over him. Vincent and his uncle. Getting stabbed. Crawling his way to Jing's doorstep and begging the man for help. "I asked you to save my life."

Jing nodded. "My family is long gone – most of my relatives having never left China – but their teachings remain with me. The number one rule passed down through my bloodline is never to grant a favour to one seeking to directly benefit themselves. It is a rule I have never broken – until last night."

"So what'll happen?" Jake rubbed at his throat and licked his lips. So thirsty.

A pig-like grunt sounded beside him, and something wet started scraping against the back of Jake's right hand. He flinched and looked down to see John the pug voraciously licking him.

"Don't fight it," Jing said flatly. "And he'll want the other hand after he's done."

Jake frowned, but allowed the plump little dog to continue licking his hand. Sure enough, after a few minutes went by, John went around and started licking Jake's other hand. It was awkward, and it stopped the conversation dead.

Jing rose stiffly to his feet, his knees seeming to bother him. He went over to his coffee table and pulled something from the drawer. It was that strange metal symbol again – two stubby crosses, affixed end to end, with silver points. He offered it to Jake. "The blessing of my family, Cho Zhou. May it keep you safe as it has done me."

Jake examined the object, surprised by its heft. "I can't take this, Jing. It's yours."

Jing waved a hand. "I have dozens of them. You think my family made only one?"

"Is it…" Jake blushed. "Magic?"

"Magic? I have no idea. But…" He sat back down on his knees and offered a hand for John the pug to lick. "It is my belief that certain objects connect us to our ancestors. Symbols, heirlooms, even simple diaries. If your ancestors are wise and just, and favoured by the forces of the universe, then that goodwill can be passed down and inherited. I have lived a peaceful life, Jake. I hope you get to do the same."

Jake wrapped his hand around the symbol and thanked Jing for the gesture, but then loosened his grip as he felt a twinge of pain shoot up his wrist. To keep from losing the gift, he placed it inside his jacket pocket. "The conse-quences," he said, licking the back of his teeth as he looked at Jing. "You still haven't told me what they are."

"Because I do not know. Perhaps fortune will shine upon you, Jake, and the cost of saving your life will be minor."

Jake studied the old man's expression, the wisdom of age in his every wrinkle. "You don't believe that, do you?"

"No. I believe the cost will be equal to the favour granted, and saving your life was no small request."

Jake nodded. A part of him still doubted all of this mystical mumbo jumbo. For all he knew – and utterly feared – Emily had recovered only temporarily in the hospital, and merely by coincidence. It was possible that when he finally spoke to Maggie, she would give him the worst news.

She died. She died and you weren't here.

I hate you. You let us all down.

Pushing the terrible image away, his mind turned to something else. He thought about being stabbed last night – stabbed by Vincent's uncle. There was no doubt in his mind that he had been dying – he had felt his life slipping away – and he could still feel, in vivid detail, the sensation of warm blood soaking his hands. He'd been fading away, falling backwards into an abyss. Jing Cho had yanked him out.

And if he saved me, then he saved Emily too.

I owe this man everything.

"Mr Cho—"

"Jing."

"Jing, if there's anything I can ever do for you…"

Jing shook his head, a mixture of gratitude and sadness written on his face. "I seek not a life of reward, Jake, so do not worry yourself with payment. John, however, loves to chew on a small deer antler. So, the next time you happen to pass by a pet shop…"

Jake glanced at the chubby black pug, still licking his owner's hand – or maybe not owner and merely an equal companion – and smiled. "John will get all the antlers he ever needs. You have my word."

"Do you hear that, John?" Jing smiled and petted the dog on his head, but then he wrinkled his nose and turned his head away, gasping. "You'll have to excuse John. He's not very good at saying thank you."

Jake tried to wave the dog-fart away, but it was impossible. You could have cut it with a knife. "If that's a thank you, he can keep it."

"Indeed."

Jake turned onto his side, wanting to get up. He expected to find himself weak, or to be wracked with pain, but he sprang to his feet with ease. He felt well-rested and alert. If only he didn't have such a raging thirst…

Putting on his jacket to hide the worst of the blood on his shirt, he put a hand out to Jing. "I suppose I'll take my pin then."

Jing frowned. "I'm sorry."

"The needle. Isn't it part of the ritual?"

"There is no needle, Jake. For this, you take all the consequences upon yourself. You can't pass it on."

"Oh, that makes sense. As much as any of this does."

"Emily's needle?" Jing narrowed his eyes, turning serious. "Have you shed another's blood? Have you completed your side of the bargain?"

Jake had to think for a moment, then shook his head. "Not yet. I… I never got a chance."

"Jake, you have until midnight. If you don't shed the blood of another by then, the deal made to help Emily will be reversed. Where is the needle now?"

"Shit!" Jake patted himself down in a panic. For all he knew, he could have lost it when he had attacked Vincent. Why had he got so sidetracked from what truly mattered?

His temper.

I beat the shit out of a kid.

What the hell is wrong with me?

Jake's hand slid inside his jacket pocket, moving past the Cho Zhou family symbol he'd put there and groping deeper until his fingers fastened around the small plastic wallet. He exhaled with relief and gave Jing a confirmatory nod. "I have it here."

"Use it," Jing said. "Or don't. But whatever you decide, you must live with the decision."

Jake nodded, unsettled by the warning, but in no doubt about what he was going to do. "I have to get to the hospital. Do you know if Lily is still at home?"

"It is still early. Perhaps she is still sleeping."

"Thank you, Jing. I…" He shook his head, unable to put into words what he was feeling about last night's events. Life. Death. Miracles. Blood. If he thought too hard, it would drive him insane. "I'm truly grateful."

Jing smiled, but his eyes glistened with worry. "I fear your gratitude will be short-lived, Jake, but I wish you well. Don't get into any more trouble."

"I won't."

"And don't forget about John."

Jake glanced down at the pug, who had now jumped up onto his armchair and gone to sleep. "Deer antlers. Got it."

Jing saw Jake to the front door. The morning sunshine was blinding.

———

Lily stepped out the front door to get some fresh air and call a taxi. The house had grown stuffy and claustrophobic, like the walls were closing in on her. She needed to get out.

Am I paranoid because of the pill I took, or just losing my mind?

Is there much of a difference?

When she first saw her dad hurrying down the street towards her, his shirt covered in blood beneath his open grey jacket, she had to blink to convince herself he was real. When he spotted her and picked up speed, she almost ran back inside the house out of fear.

"Lily," he called, placing a hand against his chest and slowing down. "Thank Go… Thank Go…" He couldn't seem to get his words out. "Thank the stars you're okay."

She hopped back a step and put a hand up. "Dad, you're covered in blood!"

He looked down at himself and grunted, as if it were something he was unaware of or had forgotten. "Oh, yeah. I need to get out of this shirt."

"What the hell happened to you? Are you all right?"

"Yeah, I…" He stared at her blankly, and she knew he was trying to make something up to tell her. "I'm not hurt, Lil, but I can't really explain it right now. Have you spoken to your mum? Is Emily okay?"

Lily frowned, wondering whether she was willing to just let him skirt past being covered in blood. "Mum's doing her nut, but she said Emily's okay. Are you going to explain what—"

"You spoke to her this morning?"

"Yeah. I called as soon as I woke up. I had like fifty missed calls from her. She's going to kill us, Dad."

"We'll just have to take what's coming to us. As long as your sister's okay, that's all that matters."

She tutted. "Yep, that's the only thing that matters, as always."

"Hey, come on now. We did it, Lil. Last night, we saved Emily."

"With a magic spell? Dad, do you really believe that? We haven't even seen her. We don't know she's any better."

"She is." He said it forcefully, almost aggressively. "We did it, Lil. We saved her. Mr Cho is the real deal. Trust me, okay?"

She folded her arms and sighed. "Fine, whatever you say. Can we just go to the hospital now? And you need to call school and tell them I'm not coming in today – or maybe all week." She winked at him.

He patted himself down and pulled out his car keys. Heading down the path, he called back to her, "Yeah, of course. I'll call them on the way. Let's go."

Lily remained standing where she was. "Dad?"

He spun back around energetically, as if he'd drank a ton of Red Bull. "What is it?"

"Your shirt. Are you going to change it or what?"

He looked down at himself again. "Oh, yeah. Hold on, I'll be two minutes."

She looked him up and down, seeing that his hands were also stained with dried blood. "Take your time. Seriously."

He smiled at her and hurried past, heading for the front door. "Two minutes, all right? Call your mum and let her know we're on our way."

"I'll wait until we're in the car," she said. "Then she can shout at us both."

"Fair enough." He hurried inside and disappeared.

Lily sat down on the wall surrounding the front garden, feeling dizzy and sick.

Why the hell is Dad covered in blood?

Is it his? Or someone else's?

Neither answer offered any comfort.

———

Jake took the stairs two at a time, partly because he was in a rush, but also because he had so much energy. Somehow, being magically healed had left him feeling energised and alive.

Nothing like a miracle to start your day.

But it wasn't a miracle, was it? It was a bargain, and he still didn't know what he owed.

Any price is worth paying. Any consequence is better than dying and leaving my girls.

Jake hurried into the kitchen and removed his shirt. There were no mirrors on the ground floor, so he couldn't examine himself fully, but there were zero signs that he'd been stabbed. His rounded stomach was smooth, his flesh unaffected by even the slightest bruise. When he pressed his fingertips into the area where he was sure it should hurt, there was only firm, healthy muscle. The sensation of being sharply punched was like a phantom in his mind now, as if the knife had never entered his abdomen at all.

Perhaps it didn't. Perhaps I dreamed the whole thing.

He picked his bloody shirt up from where he had tossed it onto the kitchen table and stretched it out in front of the window. Eyes darting back and forth across the stained, bloody fabric, he found what he was looking for. Two clear rips on one side, letting through daylight. Stab wounds.

Momentarily stunned, Jake took a breath. The lingering smell of pizza calmed him slightly, allowed him to focus on something as mundane as food.

Wait? We had pizza the night we moved in. Days ago.

How can I still smell it?

And why am I still so thirsty?

His raging thirst was only getting worse, so before he did

anything else, Jake went over to the sink and took a glass from the draining board. He filled it up and downed the contents three times in a row until his swelling stomach begged him to stop.

Still thirsty.

He needed to get going – needed to make it to Maggie and Emily. The only thing causing him to hesitate was the complete lack of a reasonable excuse he could provide for why he had been AWOL for the last twelve hours.

Just have to be a man and get it over with. It'll all be worth it in the end.

Jake reached inside the tumble dryer at the back of the kitchen and pulled out a clean T-shirt. Putting it on, he went and grabbed his jacket and rejoined Lily outside.

When Lily saw him, she seemed to snap out of a daze. "You ready?" she asked, rubbing at her eyes. "I was falling asleep out here."

"Rough night?" He knew the answer was yes. Intoxicated sleep wasn't a patch on sober sleep. "We'll get a coffee at the hospital."

"Before or after Mum kills us?"

"I'll take the flak. I'll think of something."

"Can't wait to hear it." She pointed at his thighs. "You've still got red on you."

He glanced down at his jeans and saw a few patches of blood. Fortunately, the denim was dark, which would make it easy enough to explain the stain away as simple paint or oil. If anyone asked, he'd tell them he'd been bleeding a rusty radiator or something.

Wasting no more time, he unlocked the car and both of them got in. When he started the engine, he felt it rumble throughout his skin, and when he gripped the leather steering wheel, he could feel the individual pores beneath his palms.

Why am I so buzzed?

My daughter's in hospital and my wife is probably gonna divorce me, but I feel…

Good. I feel really good.

Jake put his foot down and sped away from the kerb, hoping the wonderful feeling lasted and that nothing came along to ruin it.

CHAPTER
TWELVE

EMILY HADN'T FELT this good in a long time. No pain. No sickness. No tiredness. For the first time in over a year, she felt like leaping around the room. She felt strong, not old and withered.

"I feel great," she told Dr Kwami as he questioned her for the tenth time. The nurses had just brought her back from X-ray, but her oncologist had been waiting right at the door to meet her, clipboard at the ready.

"That's marvellous news," he said, studying her as though she were wearing clown make-up. "Your blood tests came back. Your T-cell count is substantially improved. So is your liver and kidney function."

"I feel great," she said again. "Can I go home?"

Maggie was standing in the corner of the room, and she spoke up now. "Honey, you need to rest."

"I really don't. This is the best I've felt in ages."

Dr Kwami sighed, then studied his notes for a moment. "It's possible this is some kind of spontaneous bounceback. You were in bad shape last night, Emily, so your body may have thrown out everything it could to keep on going."

Maggie stepped further into the room and faced the doctor. "What does that mean? Is she going to get better?"

"I can't make promises like that, Mrs Penshaw. There's a possibility this marked improvement in Emily's condition will be brief."

"Brief?"

"Temporary."

Emily shrugged. "I'm not expecting miracles, guys. We all know this cancer is going to get me one way or another, so I might as well make the most of feeling good for a change, right?"

Dr Kwami turned to her and smiled. He'd been trying to help her for over a year now, but his attitude over the last few months had been flat and defeated. It remained so now. "I think, after so long fighting this horrible thing, you should do whatever it is you want to do, Emily. I'm glad you're feeling well today."

She smiled. *In other words, you're dying, so what does it matter, kid?*

"However," he added, "allow me to run my tests and find out for sure what is going on. One thing I have learned in my many years as a doctor is that even the sickest patient can get better, so let's get some answers and go from there."

Hanging around the hospital while they prodded, scanned, and pumped her full of foul-tasting liquids was the last thing Emily wanted to do, but when she saw her mother holding herself anxiously, she agreed to stay in bed.

"Good," said Dr Kwami, patting Emily's knee beneath the sheets. "I will put a rush on everything, okay? Today, you are my number one patient."

"I should think so," she said. "I've been waiting for you to fix me for a year now."

He frowned, his eyes showing hurt.

"I'm joking," she said. "I couldn't ask for a better doctor."

It's not his fault I got the cancer from hell. The only way I'm surviving long enough to legally watch a Saw *movie at the cinema is if Jesus comes to visit me himself.*

Jesus, or that big guy from The Green Mile.

She chuckled to herself, continuing to enjoy the rare total lack of pain. Even if death was still coming for her, she could at least be grateful for today. Especially since she got the impression she'd almost been a goner last night. Nobody said it plainly, but yesterday didn't exist in Emily's mind, which must have meant she was unconscious for most of it. Or worse.

Dr Kwami looked at her for another moment, appearing as though he wanted to speak. Instead, he shook his head with a confused smile and left the room.

Maggie poured a glass of water from the beaker beside Emily's bed and handed it over. Perching on the edge of the mattress, she said, "I know you feel good, honey, but you still need to take it easy."

"Why? I'm either still dying, or I'm not."

"You're not dying."

"Mum, come on."

"You're not."

Someone walked into the room. "Your mother's right, Emily. You're not dying."

Jake stood in the doorway, with Lily peeking out sheepishly from behind him. Emily didn't need to be an empath to recognise that her mum was angry with her dad for not being at the hospital sooner. She'd been popping in and out of the room all morning, calling his phone. It was a relief to see them both together, but she sensed a clash incoming.

"Where have you been?" Maggie demanded.

"It's hard to explain," Jake said. "Just let me—"

Lily stepped in front of him. "I got high. I'm really sorry, Mum. It was stupid and selfish and really fucking stupid, but it's all my fault. Dad had to look after me all night because I was a mess. I… I, like, pissed myself and stuff."

Emily watched her mum's mouth fall open. The shock on her face was almost comical, like a cartoon character whose soul was about to leave their body.

Jake appeared shocked as well. He turned to Lily and tilted his head slowly, as if he wasn't sure if he had heard her correctly. Emily knew, right then, that he'd intended to cover for Lily with some made-up story.

But Lily owned up. That's not like her at all.

"Don't be mad at Dad," Lily said. "I asked him not to call and tell you."

Maggie shook her head repeatedly. "I can't believe what I'm hearing. Bad enough you do something so utterly reckless at the worst possible time, but to hear nothing from either of you all night long…" She put a hand against her forehead. "Honestly, I'm disgusted with you both."

Jake took a step towards her. "Maggie, please? I know you've probably been going nuts here, but—"

She backed away and put a hand out to block him. "Oh, you have no idea. I thought I was going to lose Emily. I thought…" She couldn't complete the sentence, her voice trembling so much. She had to take a moment to calm herself before she could speak again. "I was here on my own, while you two were off doing God knows what. Did either of you even think about me for a second?"

"Emily's okay," Jake said, oddly confident, as if he knew something they didn't. "She's going to be fine."

"Don't. Don't talk to me like you know anything at all, Jake."

"Honey…"

Emily lay quietly, wondering when they might include her in the conversation, since it was partly about her.

Also, I need to pee.

Maggie ignored Jake and glared at Lily. "What did you take, huh? And where the hell did you get it?"

Lily shrugged, which didn't help her mum's mood at all. Emily worried her sister was about to get a slap across the face.

Jake stepped in front of Lily and held up both hands like he expected Maggie to suddenly charge at them. "She got it from that little yobbo, Vincent, but it doesn't matter. We're all okay. Everything's going to be better from now on."

"Why do you keep saying that? You know nothing, Jake. You haven't been here."

Emily had never seen her mum this angry before. It shocked her. "Mum, calm down. Don't fight."

She looked at Emily, pulling back her rage a little. "Don't fight? Honey, I thought I'd lost you last night."

"I'm fine, Mum."

"I know you are, sweetheart." She smiled, but the anger stayed in her eyes. "There's no one on this whole planet as strong and as kind as you. I'm so proud of you for not giving up." She started sobbing. "So proud."

Jake stepped towards her. "Maggie? I know you hate me right now, but can Lily and I give you a hug?"

"We really love you, Mum." Lily was growing teary-eyed herself. "And I really am sorry."

Maggie didn't reply. She sagged, shoulders slumping, and continued sobbing. Both Lily and Jake approached her like an angry lion, stepping cautiously, hands raised. Emily was relieved when they wrapped their arms around her without being walloped.

"I'm sorry," Jake told her, squeezing tightly. "We let you down, Mag. You shouldn't have had to deal with this all by yourself."

"You asshole," she spluttered, face buried in his chest. "I ought to divorce you."

"I was kinda expecting you would."

"Does that mean two Christmases?" Lily asked. "And you both trying to buy my love with lots and lots of presents?"

Emily sniggered in her bed, glad to see everyone calming down. "And twice as many holidays, Lil."

Lily snapped her fingers. "Hell yes!"

"It would mean an orphanage for you, young lady," Maggie told her, eyeballing Lily with only half a smile on her face. "Don't think this is over. You're grounded until you're thirty."

"I knew it! I should've let Dad cover for me."

Jake cringed.

Maggie glared at him. "Can't believe you didn't tell me right away. I have a right to know what our daughter is up to."

"Everything's fine. I handled it."

"Guys?" Emily put her hands on top of her bedsheets and patted her sides. "Since I'm not dying right this second, can I get in on the hug?"

Everyone broke apart and came over. They enveloped Emily in a mass of loving arms until she was giggling her head off. Considering she might have died a little bit yesterday, today was a good day. She just hoped it lasted a while longer before things went back to normal.

"I need to pee," she said.

———

Jake and Maggie left the girls alone to chat for a minute, the sound of them giggling in the room behind them like music. Despite Lily being worse for wear after last night's intoxication, her mood had lifted as soon as she had hugged Emily. It was a relief to know their sisterly bond remained intact.

Jake smiled, almost gushing with joy, so brimming with relief.

Emily's better. Just looking at her, I can see it clearly. Her cancer's gone.

Mr Cho was everything George had claimed him to be.

I need to do something for George. If not for him…

Maggie shoved Jake in the arm as they rounded a corner and entered a small waiting area with vending machines. "Who the hell do you think you are?" she growled, venom in her glare. "Our daughter takes drugs and you try to hide it from me? How dare you? How fucking dare you?"

He jolted, blindsided by her vitriol. "W-what? Maggie, I thought we were okay?"

"You think a group hug fixes everything? Jake, I can barely even look at you right now."

"Wow…" Not knowing how to respond, he moved past his wife and went over to the vending machines.

That blasted thirst still hadn't gone away, so he keyed in the number for a bottle of water and swiped his debit card against the payment sensor. Standing patiently, he watched while the metal arm twisted and slid a bottle forward. The tiny motors inside made a droning noise that set his teeth on edge.

The bottle hit the glass and wedged in place.

"Are you serious?" Jake growled in frustration, striking the see-through panel with his palm. The glass cracked. The bottle fell free.

"What the hell?" Maggie moved up beside him and

stared at the broken pane in horror. "What the hell is wrong with you?"

Jake studied his palm to see if it was bleeding. It wasn't. The spiderweb crack on the glass pane was small, no longer than his index finger, but it was the kind of rupture that would probably gradually increase until the whole thing shattered. "The panel must be weak," he said, pulling the bottle of water out of the drawer. "I barely pushed on it."

Maggie shook her head and reached out to take the water from him. "Can you get another bottle? I'm thirsty too."

"Sure thing." He paid for another bottle, and this time it fell into the chute without issue. Taking it from the drawer, he immediately twisted off the cap and downed the contents in one go, gasping when he was done. Maggie eyed him suspiciously.

"I was thirsty," he explained.

"Are you hungover? I swear, if you spent last night drinking—"

"I didn't have a drop," he snapped. "I don't know what's wrong with me, Mag. Just can't seem to get rid of this thirst." He scrunched up the plastic water bottle and tossed it across the room right into a bin.

Maggie's eyes narrowed. "Jake, you don't seem right. You're all on edge."

How could he possibly tell her what had happened last night? That he had stared death in the face and survived? That some psychopath in a Range Rover had stabbed him, but he had walked it off and was now fine?

And why am I not worried? Vincent and his uncle are still out there. They're not going to just ignore it when they see me walking around with a spring in my step.

"I'm just trying to be strong," he said. "Emily's going to

be okay, Mag, I promise. It's time to put this family back together again."

Maggie sipped from her water and let out a long, tired sigh. "What if it's too late?"

"What?" Jake tried to look her in the eye, but she turned away from him and moved over to a nearby plastic chair, leaning against its back. He spoke to the side of her head. "Maggie, we'll get through this. We just need to talk to each other."

She turned back to him, the corners of her mouth pointed downwards. "My head's a mess right now, Jake. It feels like we've been drifting through life ever since Emily got sick. Barely talking. Drinking more and more. I just… I just don't know what connection there is between us any more."

"Maggie…" He stepped towards her and reached out, but then pulled back his hand without touching her. "We moved house, uprooted our lives… Why didn't you talk to me sooner?"

"Because I'm human, Jake. Thing don't always make sense the moment you need them to."

"Look," he reached out to her again, and this time took her hand in his. He was trembling, so shocked and terrified at the thought of Maggie not being his best friend any more. "This last year has been about keeping our daughter alive. Of course we've drifted apart, but let's not give up on our entire lives until we're at least in a better headspace. Who knows what we'll be this time next year? Marriage isn't a straight line, but we've been together since we were kids."

Maggie shook her head slowly, staring at the floor. "Just don't ever disappear on me again like you did last night. I mean it, Jake. It's a red line."

He pulled her into a hug and gave her a promise. If only she knew why he hadn't made it to the hospital sooner. Then she would understand that he hadn't wilfully disappeared on her, that he'd been doing what he needed to do for their family.

He winced in pain and eased Maggie away.

"What is it?" she asked, putting a hand on his arm.

Jake rubbed his temples and moaned quietly. "That bloody vending machine. The noise it's making."

"What noise?" She frowned. "I don't hear anything."

He turned to face the damaged vending machine and homed in on the sound it was making. "It's the cooler," he said. "It's making a high-pitched whining noise. Giving me a headache."

"I really don't hear anything, Jake."

"Seriously? It's so loud." He sniffed. "And what's that smell? Is it… blood?"

She backed off and looked around. "Blood? Where?"

He sniffed again. "It's blood. Maggie, are you hurt?"

"No, I'm fine. Stop being a weirdo." She stepped back again, glancing around like she was looking for an exit.

A noise made them both look towards the adjacent corridor.

Someone entered the waiting area, shoes squeaking loudly on the polished floor as they shuffled along. It was an old man with a bandaged arm. Blood leaked out from underneath his dressing, staining the adhesive tape holding it in place. The smell was… sweet. Almost cake-like.

Maggie nodded and said hello to the man, but then raised an eyebrow at Jake suspiciously. "Are you telling me you just smelled that old man's blood, you freak?"

He gawped at her, not knowing what to say.

Maggie rubbed at her forehead and tutted. "We're in a hospital. There's probably blood everywhere. Let's just go see what trouble the girls are getting into. Emily will need to sleep soon, so that horrible nurse in charge of her will probably send us home."

Jake nodded, but he couldn't help glancing over at the old man, who was getting a drink from the cracked vending machine. Somehow, Jake knew his arm wound was bad, a cut almost to the bone. It seemed to throb beneath the bandages, making the air vibrate.

Maggie pulled at Jake's arm. "Stop acting weird."

I feel weird.

I can smell that old man's blood, and…

And I'm still so goddamn thirsty.

"Hold on," he said. "I just need to get another bottle of water."

Maggie sighed, but she waited while he went back over to the vending machine and queued behind the old man. He couldn't help but take several long inhalations of breath, enjoying the sweet odour in the room.

The smell of blood.

Maggie's right. I am a freak.

———

George hacked and coughed. Blood spattered the arm of his chair. He'd never felt so ill, but he faced it the way he faced most things – alone and with a gut full of regret. At least the whisky still tasted good. He was halfway through a bottle of Aldi's finest, which wasn't bad for eight o'clock at night.

The stomach cancer was invisible to everyone except the doctors with their scans and blood tests, which made it easy for George to keep his condition a secret from others. He couldn't abide the thought of sympathy, nor did he want to squander his last days being fussed over. While he had plenty of splendid memories from decades living on the street, he had forfeited his happiness long ago. His end was long overdue.

"Stop moping," his wife chided from the corner of the room. Her neck was broken, and her left arm snapped backwards at the elbow. She often appeared in such a way when she was in a bad mood. "At least you got to grow old."

He put his whisky down on the old oak coffee table and looked over at the image of his wife. "If I could change the past, I would. You know I would."

"I only know what you say, husband, not what you'd do."

"Have I ever not been a man of my word? I might not be worth much, but you can allow me that."

She looked away, bulging eyes flickering with disdain.

"I love you, Leanne," he said. "I never stopped. Soon, when I finally join you, I hope to find that you still love me too."

"Love doesn't exist where you're going."

He picked up his glass and took another swig. "I don't believe that. Love exists everywhere, even in the darkest of places."

She sneered, oily tongue slipping out between her bloody, chewed lips. "Love gets you killed, George. I'm proof of that."

"It wasn't my love that killed you, dear. Just plain stupidity."

"You've always been stupid, George, even now. You should never have got involved with that family's problems. There'll be consequences. There are always consequences when you interfere with the way things are supposed to be."

"If children dying is the way things are supposed to be, then I'll accept the consequences of interfering."

"You're a fool."

George did something he rarely did. He got up out of his chair and faced down his dead wife. Beneath the chewed lips and distended eyeballs, he still saw her beauty. He still saw his Leanne. "What happened back then was a mistake," he said, his voice firm but compassionate, "but the woman I married – the real Leanne – would forgive me for what I did. Our daughter lives. Kelly is happy and healthy."

"Happy only because she has nothing to do with you."

He reeled slightly, her barbs finding flesh. "That's not true. She visits."

"Out of guilt. You're a chore to tick off her list, George. She doesn't love you, not after what you did."

"I did it for her."

"And she hates you for it. She'll celebrate the day you die."

George threw his whisky, shocked by his unexpected rage, a rage he'd not felt since the days of helplessly watching his daughter waste away in agony. The glass went right through Leanne and shattered against the wall, taking a chunk of wallpaper with it.

The spectre of his wife grinned obscenely. He knew she wasn't the real Leanne, just an aspect of his guilt – or a phantom tasked with ensuring the ongoing torture of his soul – but despite that understanding, he had welcomed her presence over the years, comforted by the visage of the woman he loved.

"Thank you for keeping me company," he told the spectre, which seemed to confuse it. It flickered in and out of being, Leanne's face scowling and grinning in equal turn. "You'll have me soon, my dear, and I don't care what it is you do to me. I atoned for the past, whether you like it or not. I helped that poor family, and you can't take it back.

Whatever happens to my soul, I found a little happiness right at the end. You failed."

Leanne smiled at him, her wounds gone and her beauty back in full. "You silly fool."

There was a knock at the front door.

Leanne glared at George through blood-red eyes. "Your consequences are here, honey. Better go and let them in."

CHAPTER
THIRTEEN

JAKE COULDN'T KEEP STILL. He knocked on George's door and waited.

As Maggie had predicted, the hospital staff eventually urged the family to go home in order to give Emily some time to rest. It had taken a lot of persuasion, but eventually Maggie's tiredness had won over and she had reluctantly agreed to leave.

Emily's tests kept coming back normal, prompting the baffled Dr Kwami to commit to working throughout the night in pursuit of answers. The man was apparently unwilling to accept that her cancer could actually be gone. Emily had groaned at the prospect of being kept in, but she was used to hospitals enough by now to grin and bear it.

Only Jake and Lily knew that her cancer was really well and truly gone.

Jake's persistent thirst had finally eased a little, but it was still present, along with a slowly escalating headache that had been plaguing him for the last few hours. Every light and every sound was like a needle in his brain. At least the sun going down in the last hour had seemed to help a little, as had the silence in the car on the way home.

It must be a migraine, he told himself. *Or a blood vessel in my brain about to explode and kill me.*

It was now a little past eight at night, and Jake found himself knocking on George's door, wanting to thank the man for what he'd done. Maggie had been aghast when Jake announced he was leaving the house, obviously still holding a grudge for him not making it to the hospital sooner. She had relented only after Jake told her that George had helped take care of Lily last night. It wasn't the complete truth, but at least it allowed her to understand why Jake needed to show the man his gratitude.

He had picked up a bottle of whisky at the petrol station on his way home – a forty quid bottle of Glenfiddich, which he hoped tasted better than Aldi's finest.

He knocked on George's door again, fidgeting with his clothing and stepping from side to side. He was still strangely hyperactive, overly alert.

The full moon seemed to thrum in the starless black sky above, calling out to him. Whispering.

Distant traffic droned. Lampposts buzzed. Insects chirped.

Jake knocked a third time and then held open the letter box. "George?" he shouted through it. "Are you there?"

He was sure he heard a voice inside.

Reaching out to bang on the door again, he paused instead and tried the handle. It was unlocked. The stiff, misshapen door took a hefty shoulder barge to open fully, but Jake let himself into the hallway.

"George? Are you here? It's Jake."

"Yes, um, come in, Jake. I'm in the lounge."

Jake frowned. George's words sounded slurred, which

probably meant he'd been drinking, but his neighbour also sounded…

Weak. Breathless.

Jake went into the lounge and found George standing with the aid of his glass-topped cane in the corner. It appeared he'd already been on his feet when Jake had knocked on the door.

George smiled at him warmly. "Emily? She's okay?"

"The doctors haven't admitted it yet, but she's cured. Her cancer's gone. I just need to complete my end of the bargain. That's why I'm here, actually. Well, *that* and to give you this…" He offered the bottle of whisky.

"Wow," George raised a tufty eyebrow and adjusted his grip on his cane. "That's the good stuff. Reckon I've had enough for the minute, though."

When he realised George wasn't going to take the bottle from him directly, Jake placed it down on the wooden coffee table with a soft *clunk.* "Can we talk for a minute?"

"Of course." George hobbled over to his armchair and collapsed into it. The impact of hitting the cushions so hard caused him to lurch to the side and cough.

"Are you okay?" Jake asked, reaching out. "Can I get you a glass of water?"

George caught his breath and waved a hand. "I'm fine. Just a little under the weather. W-what do you need to talk to me about?"

"I wanted to thank you for Emily, of course. I owe you everything. If not for you…" He shook his head, unable to say it. "Thank you, George. Truly."

"It was my pleasure. In fact, helping Emily is something I'd been waiting a long time for. It warms my heart knowing she's going to be okay."

Jake smiled, marvelling that George could care so much

about Emily when he had only met her once. "Why did you choose to help her?" he asked. "I mean, I'm not saying you had an agenda, but…" He shrugged. "You don't owe my family anything."

"I owed it to the universe, Jake. When I saw Emily moving onto the street, sitting in a wheelchair just like my Kelly used to, it was like a sign. She came here so that I could help her, and when I learned she had cancer, it all made perfect sense."

"What do you mean? Why did her cancer change anything?"

"Because I have cancer too, Jake." He patted his stomach lightly and wheezed. "My stomach, kidneys, and who knows where else. Doctors gave me twelve weeks."

Jake shook his head. "No. That can't be true. You're still as strong as an ox, George."

"Do you know what I used to enjoy doing before we met, Jake?"

"No, what?"

He patted his stomach again. "Eating. Takeaways, microwave dinners, sweets. This time last year I was eighteen stone. I'm thirteen now. The only reason I'm not rail-thin is because the cancer has its work cut out for it." He pulled a face. "I also never bothered with the chemo or any of that. Truthfully, I haven't felt too bad. The whisky helps with the stomach pains, and I rest a lot to conserve my energy, but I haven't kept any food down in a fortnight, and it's getting harder and harder to rise out of bed each morning. The monster started out slow, Jake, but it's a glutton now, chomping away at me day and night." He let out a sigh. "Anyway, none of that matters. Cancer might be ready to take me, but it won't take your Emily. It's a fair trade."

"Not really," Jake said. "I'd rather see you both fine."

"Nonetheless."

Jake sighed, needing to explain the true reason he was there. Time was running out, and he was beginning to panic. "I haven't used the needle on anyone yet. If I don't do it in the next few hours, Emily's cancer will come back. That's what Mr Cho said, right?"

"You don't need to worry," George said.

"I *do* need to worry, George. I have less than four hours to prick someone with the needle or Emily will die. Where does Vincent live?"

"What?"

"Vincent. Where does he live? He's the one I'm going to stab with the needle."

"He's just a boy, Jake. He doesn't deserve to die."

"He deserves to die a hell of a lot more than Emily does. Please, George, just tell me where he lives. I need to complete my side of the bargain."

George sat there for a moment, wheezing quietly and licking his lips. "Y-you don't have to worry, Jake. It's okay."

"It's not okay." He clenched his fists atop his knees. "I won't lose Emily, so tell me where Vincent—"

"Jake, listen to me." George sat up, leant forward, and looked him in the eye. "It's taken care of. Emily is going to live a long and happy life."

"Not unless I use the needle."

"You don't have the needle, Jake. You never did."

"What? What are you talking about? It's right here." He reached into his jacket pocket and pulled out the plastic wallet. Holding it up to George, he raised both eyebrows. "See?"

"Do *you* see, Jake?"

Jake didn't understand, but George sat there patiently, as if waiting for a penny to drop.

What am I missing?

"Stop playing games, George. You say I don't have the needle, but it's right he…"

The plastic wallet was empty.

How had he not noticed?

Because I shoved it in my pocket without checking when George handed it to me last night.

Jake glared, wondering if this was some kind of trick after all – an extortion with real life magic at its centre. Was George going to demand money now, in exchange for Emily's life?

"Where is it, George? Where's the needle?"

"On the table right in front of you."

Jake turned his eyes downwards. All he saw on the table was a nearly empty bottle of cheap whisky and a brand-new bottle of Glenfiddich. But then…

The needle sat innocuously in the centre of the table. Its slender profile and dull grey metal had kept him from noticing it. A tiny speck of blood stained the gnarled oak surface at one end.

"I don't understand."

George held a trembling hand up in front of himself. A tiny red bead dotted the meat of his palm. "I pricked myself with Emily's needle twenty minutes ago, Jake."

"H-how? How did you take it from me?"

"You never had it. When I handed the wallet to you last night, I had already slid the needle out and put it in my pocket."

"George…" Jake shook his head. "You can't."

"It's already done. Emily will be fine."

Jake tried to speak.

"I'm dying," George said, with a resigned sigh. "This way is just a little faster, and with one hell of an upside."

Jake still couldn't speak. He just stared at the bloody needle on the table.

George waved a hand. "I think now is a good time to open that bottle you brought me. Jake, can you get us a pair of glasses from the kitchen, please? I don't think I can make it back up to my feet again."

"O-of course." Jake sat there a moment, unsure how to communicate with his legs. Eventually, he made it up and went into George's kitchen.

The room was like the lounge, old but well cared for. The cabinets were painted white, with thick shaker doors, while the worktop was a cheap wood-effect laminate. A small cooker sat in the middle of the cabinets, but appeared barely used. In the corner was a microwave, and atop the microwave was an old photograph inside a ceramic frame decorated with flowers.

The picture showed a young George – perhaps only in his late twenties – and a beautiful young woman of a similar age. Both were smiling in what looked to be a zoo, a giraffe peeking out from the background. Jake realised then how sad his old neighbour was. The beaming, carefree young man in this picture was not the George sitting in the other room.

He died when his wife died.

Rooting around the cupboards, Jake located a pair of glass tumblers and took them into the lounge. By the time he returned, George seemed to have aged another five years. A sheen of sweat coated his brow and his hair had turned lank and brittle.

"Would you… Would you do the honours, Jake?"

"Of course." He put the glasses down on the oak coffee table, avoiding disturbing the bloody needle, and then peeled the packaging from the bottle's slender neck.

Twisting off the cap, he poured two generous helpings of whisky and handed one to George, who took it with a badly shaking hand.

Jake took a swig and winced at the fire in his throat. The scent of the liquor was intoxicating, almost nauseating.

George took a swig too, a tiny one, and it caused him to grumble and cough. Bloody spittle stained his lips. He seemed unconcerned and grinned merrily at Jake. "A perfect tipple to go out on."

"Do I need to call for help?" Jake asked. "What's happening exactly?"

"You know what's happening – and no, please don't call anyone. Just have a… have a drink with me. Nothing like a b-bit of company at… at m-my age."

George's eyes turned bloodshot. His hair fell free of his scalp, strand by strand, settling on his shoulders. Jake swallowed, his throat tingling from the whisky. "You're dying, aren't you? I mean, right now. George…"

"We're all dying, my friend. The only thing that matters is the burdens we leave behind when we're done."

"Why did you do this, George? I don't understand."

He sipped his whisky again, then held it in his lap to keep his hand from trembling. "Penance, I suppose. I've been afraid of dying, I admit it, but at least now I can go out with my head held high. The burden is no longer yours, Jake. You don't need to take Vincent's life."

"He doesn't deserve your mercy."

"It's not him I'm worried about. If you used the needle on him, you would have had to carry that with you for the rest of your life. Trust me, I know what that's like. It eats away at you."

Jake put a hand over his heart, dismayed to see George withering away before his very eyes while smiling happily at the same time. If this was the end, then Jake wanted to know as much about this kind old man as he could. "George? Back when you made a bargain to heal Kelly, who did you use the needle on?"

"I was wondering when you'd ask me that."

"Who?"

"My wife. It was my Leanne who paid the price of my flesh bargain."

Jake eased back slightly in his chair, trying to disguise his shock. To further hide it, he sipped, once again, at his whisky.

George seemed to appreciate being given the space to continue, so he licked his bloody lips and spoke again. "Jing did the same for me as he did for you and sent me away with a needle. I had no enemies, and there was no one I felt truly deserved to die, but I was unwilling to lose my daughter, either. My idea was to visit an old people's home or a hospice, but…" He sipped his whisky and let out a sigh. "I never got the chance."

"What happened?" Jake wasn't sure he wanted to know.

"Leanne knew nothing about what Jing and I had done. Maybe if I had told her, she wouldn't have put her hand inside my wallet to get some change to pay the milkman."

Jake winced. "You put the needle inside your wallet?"

"I did. It should have been safe there – I thought it would be – but fate enjoys being cruel. The next morning I woke early, thinking I had several hours to complete the bargain, but Leanne woke even earlier – a habit she had from working for the Post Office. Then, of course, the milkman came at the crack of dawn."

"I'm so sorry, George."

He didn't seem to hear Jake. "For a long time, I was sure it was some kind of malicious twist of fate; like some evil, cosmic force had whispered to Leanne to go look inside my wallet, but after so many years without answers, I had to let it go for the sake of my sanity."

"What happened?" Jake asked. "After Leanne pricked her finger?"

George shuddered. It was unclear if it was his frailness causing him to have a chill or the cold memories of the past. "It happened quickly," he said. "She was making breakfast while I helped Kelly down the stairs and into her chair. Kelly said she was feeling better, but Leanne… Leanne was feeling dreadful. Her face was drained of all colour, and she was trembling like a leaf. I just thought she was coming down with the flu, so I didn't pay much attention. My mind was so preoccupied with Kelly getting better that I barely noticed my wife's suffering. Not until…"

Razor-sharp teeth gnawed at Jake's guts as he waited for George to finish.

"Not until her spine twisted like a corkscrew and her neck snapped like a twig." He put a shaking hand up against his eyes and wiped them. "Dead before she hit the ground. Kelly's screams still haunt me, like broken glass in my brain."

"George, I'm so sorry. That… That's just terrible."

"And something I couldn't risk happening to you." He shuffled in his seat, wincing in discomfort as he continued. "My Kelly got better, but she never forgot the sight of her mother's body snapping and twisting in the kitchen. I never forgot it either. The trauma left no space for a healthy father–daughter relationship, and by the time I tried to fix things, it was too late."

"I'm sorry."

George shrugged, even that seeming like a physical ordeal. "Kelly has a lovely life now, but I'm not much a part of it. I think, deep down, she knows I had something to do with her miraculous recovery. Her life was purchased with the blood of her mother."

"Why didn't you tell me this before, George? If you'd known there was a risk…"

"There's no risk, Jake. I took the needle while you were preoccupied with Lily and vowed to use it on myself. Your family will stay… they'll stay whole. It's d-done."

Jake slumped beneath a sudden weight of dread. If only what George was saying could be true.

But it's more complicated than he thinks.

"I was stabbed last night."

George frowned, his cheeks growing ever more gaunt. "What?"

"Vincent's uncle. He stabbed me. Last night. I was dying."

"Jake, I don't understand what you're—"

"I was dying, but I made it to Mr Cho's house. I made another bargain."

George coughed, spluttered, wiped his bloody mouth with the back of his arm, and then wheezed. He eased himself forward, watery grey eyes steely as they drilled into Jake. "You have a second needle?"

Jake shook his head. "I asked a favour for myself. No needle. No passing on the consequences."

"But… Jing always told me he would never make a flesh bargain for someone's direct benefit. It's against the rules. *His* rules."

"I begged him. I begged him while dying at his feet."

George sighed and then nodded knowingly. "Jing wouldn't have been able to say no. He never could bear to see a person suffer. So… what'll happen now?"

"I don't know. I've been trying not to think about it, but

after what happened to your wife... I can't risk something happening to my girls."

George leaned forward, as if trying to get up. "W-we have to go to Jing. He'll know... he will..." He flopped back in his chair, gagging. His throat bulged. His eyes opened wide.

Jake leapt out of his seat and went to him. "George? George, tell me what you need."

"C-consequences," he spluttered. "There are always... consequences."

Blood erupted from George's mouth, splattering his shirt and the arm of the chair. It caused Jake to recoil. A sudden surge of adrenaline coursed through his veins and made him dizzy. He stood back, bumping against the coffee table. "I-I'll call an ambulance. I..."

The smell of blood. So sweet.

Jake's body tingled like a firework about to go off.

George stared at him through pus-filled eyes, his nose dripping thick green mucus. It was as if some awful virus had instantly overwhelmed his system to wreak havoc.

His immune system is gone. Just like Emily's.

"What can I do?" Jake begged. "How can I help?" He couldn't help but stare at the blood on the old man's shirt. It seemed to shimmer, sending up wispy fumes. "George?"

George reached out a hand, terror on his bulging face. He gave Jake a wide-eyed stare. "W-what's... wrong... with... you?"

Jake frowned.

What's wrong with me?

Jake was about to ask what George meant, but George bucked violently in his chair and a torrent of blood spewed forth from his mouth, nose, and eyeballs. By the time it was over, his neighbour's face was a slick red mask.

George was gone.

Jake was trembling, his fingers outstretched and locked, as if he were attempting to resist having a seizure. The smell in the room was overwhelming, causing his head to spin.

I… I need to get out of here. I need to call someone.

Jake tried to pull himself away but remained fixated on the blood in the room. George was dead, no doubt about it, but his body was still warm. Hot blood still trickled out of his nose.

"I need to leave," Jake said out loud. "I need to leave right now."

But he didn't. He couldn't.

———

Jake shielded his eyes, blinded by the silently flashing lights on top of the ambulance. His headache was gone and, thankfully, so was his thirst. Of all the things to quench it, he hadn't expected it to be whisky. He felt strangely full, bloated even.

The paramedics wheeled George into the back of the ambulance. Horrifyingly, Jake realised one of the two uniformed medics had also taken Emily away yesterday. They were probably thinking the street was cursed.

Perhaps it is.

Jake had called 999 as soon as he stepped outside, informing the operator of George's death. Unfortunately, they had been unwilling to take him at his word, so had sent an ambulance. The paramedics performed CPR, then hooked George up to a ventilator, but they had clearly been going through the motions.

"Poor George," said a voice behind Jake.

He turned and realised he had back-pedalled towards Mr

Cho's house. The short, bald man was standing right beside him, with John the pug sitting without a lead by his feet.

"Jing? What are you doing out here?" Jake checked his watch, about to turn nine o'clock. "It's getting late."

"One of my neighbours died," he said. "It's the kind of thing one steps outside for." He bowed his head and said again, "Poor George."

"He had cancer," Jake said. "In his stomach."

"Yet that is not what killed him."

Jake turned to the man and narrowed his eyes. He didn't want to give anything away, so he declined to speak.

"He took the needle," Jing said. "Last night, while you were distracted. I watched him slide it into his pocket."

"What? You saw him take it and said nothing? Why?"

"George and I have been friends for a long time. If this was the ending he chose for himself, what right did I have to prevent his will? And if he was already dying, as you say, then I imagine the sacrifice gave him purpose, perhaps even peace. He left us on his own terms."

Jake ran a palm over his bristly head. His hair was growing out and needed shaving, but it was the least of his concerns right now. "This street…" He closed his eyes. "Everything started going wrong the moment we moved to this street."

"Things were going wrong for you before that, Jake. Is that not what brought you here in the first place?"

Jake sighed. Jing was right. "I thought I understood the world, but the last few days…"

"The only way to understand the world is to understand that we understand nothing."

"Ain't that the truth?" Jake let his head drop as the paramedic shut the ambulance doors and sealed George inside. It would likely be the last time either of them saw their friendly old neighbour, so it felt right to bow and remain silent.

He was a near stranger, yet he gave his life for Emily. How do I ever make peace with that?

Jake turned back to Mr Cho, keeping his voice low. "What's going to happen to me, Jing? You brought me back from the brink of death, and I feel… good. Stronger and more alert. I can smell better, hear better. What did you do to me?"

"I did what you asked. I brokered a bargain between you and… something else."

"What something else? What exactly did I agree to?"

Jing turned slightly, but didn't look at Jake directly. "I truly do not know."

The ambulance pulled away from the kerb, its lights still flashing. Despite George being dead, the driver put on the sirens. Jake noticed the predictable twitching of curtains and faces at the windows. Suddenly, the road seemed like a stage, and the terraces like long stalls on either side.

"Ghouls," he said. "Is there nothing to watch on TV?"

Jing put his hands together and averted his eyes, not watching the ambulance leave. "People fear death, Jake. Do not judge them for it."

"George told me about his wife," Jake said. "He thought the bad luck was deliberate, like fate wanted the worst to happen. He saved his daughter, but lost his wife."

The thought of the same thing happening to Jake filled him full of poisonous dismay, making him want to drop to his knees and purge himself. He still felt so bloated. A little fuzzy too.

"It was the last flesh bargain I ever facilitated," Jing told him. "Twenty years ago, and never again since. At least, not until George brought you to my door."

Jake turned to him, waiting for the man to look at him. "Is my family safe, Jing? Can you tell me if I need to worry?"

"A father must always worry, Jake. All I know is that the flesh bargain you made for Emily's future is now complete. Thanks to George, the cancer will not take her."

"What about something else? What if there are other dangers?"

Jing frowned at him. "You want me to remove all danger from life? Even I cannot do such a thing. Protect your family, Jake. Be a husband and a father. Fate will do as it pleases."

Jake could do nothing but blink. Jing's words gave him no comfort at all, and yet they were undeniably true. What else could he do, except carry on doing what he always tried to do?

I have to protect my girls.

No matter what.

"You have blood on your mouth," Jing said, pointing a withered index finger. "Did you bite yourself?"

Jake frowned, wiped at his lips, and saw a thick smear of blood along the side of his hand. "It must be George's." He licked his lips, somehow both sweet and salty. "He bled everywhere."

"Poor George," Jing replied, and then the small man turned. "Come, John, let us retire to bed. Tomorrow, we shall honour our friend and neighbour. Goodnight, Jake."

"Yeah, goodnight, Jing."

The old man trotted off with John waddling at his heels.

I want more than best wishes, thought Jake. *I want answers.*

He licked at his lips again, and didn't stop until all of George's blood was gone.

―――――

Lily put her hands to her ears, not wanting to hear any more arguing. Her mum was mad that her dad had been gone for more than an hour, and her dad was mad that she was mad.

And I'm mad that the two of you won't shut up.

"Are you a part of this family?" Maggie asked him, leaning against the kitchen counter with her arms folded. "Or are you going to spend all of your time elsewhere?"

Jake hissed. "Maggie, will you just listen? You don't understand. I popped round to thank George, but…"

"But what?"

"He's dead."

That made her mum shut up.

"He had a heart attack or something. Right in front of me, Mag. Didn't you hear the ambulance?"

Lily let her palms slap against the kitchen table and sat up straight. "What? I heard an ambulance go past, but I didn't think anything. It was for George?"

Jake nodded at her, and she then saw a disturbed look in his eyes, like a part of him was far away. "It was horrible, Lil. He… He pricked his thumb on a needle…" He tilted his head and blinked at her a few times. "Perhaps that's what caused the heart attack."

"What are you talking about?" Maggie asked irritably. "He pricked his thumb on a needle? Why would that cause a man to have a heart attack?"

Jake shrugged. "The shock of the pain or something? It happened right before he died."

Lily was glad she was sitting down, because she felt woozy. "W-was the needle the same one you had, Dad? The one that you…" How did she say it in code?

"The one I jabbed myself with too? Yeah. I thought I took it away with me last night, but George had it the whole time."

"George had it?"

"Enough!" Maggie yelled. "I don't know what secret conversation you two are trying to have, but I'm not stupid. Tell me what the hell is going on? Is this about the drugs, Lily? Did you inject yourself with a needle?"

Lily shook her head, but decided to use her mum's suspicion as the foundation for a lie. "George had this tin full of medications and stuff," she said. "Dad caught me rooting around and took it from me. He, um, pricked his finger on a syringe. There was, like, morphine and other junk inside."

Jake nodded, slipping into the lie alongside her. "I was trying to communicate to Lily that when I found George, he had just injected himself with an overdose of morphine. I tried to help him, but it was…" He shook his head, suddenly a little teary. "It was too late."

Maggie went over to the sink and leant over it, her dark hair falling in front of her face. "This street," she said. "It's one thing after another. First, you get attacked by that thug. Then he gives Lily drugs. Now this."

Lily glanced at her dad, but he looked away.

Vincent attacked him? When?

"I'm going for a long bath," Maggie announced, turning around to face them both. "Then I'm going to bed. If you have any sense, Jake, you won't bother me."

Jake winced, but he said nothing as she stormed out of the room.

Lily turned to her dad and gasped. "Vincent attacked you?"

Embarrassed, he turned and went to the fridge, grabbing a beer and twisting the cap off. "Technically, I attacked him. We got into a fight. It was nothing."

"Really? He… He never mentioned it to me."

"Probably more interested in getting you hooked on drugs."

She struck her fist on the table. "You said you wouldn't mention it!"

"I'm doing my best." He sat down and swigged his beer. "Doesn't mean I'm not still pissed off about what you did."

I knew he couldn't keep his word.

Angry, she changed the subject. "What happened to George? He pricked himself with a needle? You mean Emily's needle, don't you?"

Jake nodded, a grave look on his face. "He swiped it out of the plastic wallet when I was dealing with you at Mr Cho's. He always intended to use it on himself."

"Why?"

"I'm not really sure. He was already dying of cancer and only had a couple of months to live, so I suppose he saw it as a way to make his death mean something."

"Wow." Lily shook her head and said it again. "Wow. I can't believe we just met the guy and he did that."

"Emily is okay," Jake said, reaching out a hand to grab hers. "It's a miracle, Lil."

Lily nodded. As weirded out and as anxious as she was about everything, she couldn't deny the blossom of joy she felt growing inside her tummy. Not only was the dreadful era of cancer finally over, but Emily was going to get to live a normal life.

We can be sisters again. Eat ice cream and talk about boys. No, screw that, we can go clubbing together.

"You should get to bed," Jake told her. "Tomorrow might be a long day."

"Every day is long," she said, but when she started yawning, she decided to take his advice. "Are you gonna go to bed too?"

He grinned sheepishly and glanced towards the hallway. "Think I'd best wait until your mum's asleep, or I'll end up on the sofa."

"Try not to argue, okay? If Emily really is going to get better, then things will go back to normal soon, right? Mum just doesn't realise it yet."

"She will soon. What you and I did, Lil…"

She nodded and stood up from the table. "I'll see you in the morning."

He said the same, and she went upstairs.

Passing by Emily's room on the landing was strange. She had often imagined walking by to see an empty bed and her sister gone, but that had been in their old house. Walking past this strange room now was unsettlingly unfamiliar, but slowly she pictured Emily lying on the bed, coughing, spluttering, and calling out for her mum.

Is it really all over?

She stepped into the room, the scent of Vaseline and antiseptic thick after not even a week of Emily being there. She got so many sores. Even the smallest cut could take weeks to heal.

Is it really all over?

No more moans of pain. No more crying. No more misery.

No more pills.

If her cancer was gone, Emily's prescription would expire.

The pills she already has will just go to waste.

Lily went over to her sister's bedside cabinet and moved the alarm clock to one side. There were no pills there, nor were there any inside the drawers.

Her mood soured. *You had plenty left. I saw the pile.*

Somehow, she knew Emily had hidden the pills to spite

her. Despite everything – which included saving her frikkin' life – her big sis still thought she was better than her.

But you're not smarter than me.

Lily glanced back and forth, examining the room. There was scant furniture – a small chest of drawers and a double wardrobe – but Emily would've been too weak to get up and hide the pills in there. No, she would've hidden them somewhere she could reach from bed.

Such as the bed itself.

Lily checked underneath the pillows and found nothing except yellow patches of her sister's sweat. She then ran a hand down the side of the mattress, prodding at the divan underneath.

Bingo.

She wiggled her fingers back and forth, gathering every pill she could find. Eventually, she ended up with half a dozen painkillers and a small pile of other drugs that were of no interest to her.

"That's me sorted for the next few nights," she said, shoving the pills into her pocket.

She turned around to leave. Her mum was standing right there, watching her.

"What are you doing in here?" she asked, towel around her chest in anticipation of getting into the bath.

Lily stumbled as a swarm of bees filled her tummy. "Oh, I, um, was just thinking about Em. You think they'll let her come home tomorrow?"

Did she see me take the pills? Did she see me take the pills?

Maggie smiled. "I hope so, sweetheart. The house seems empty without her, doesn't it?"

Lily nodded, and then, to fill the silence, she said, "I'm sorry about last night, Mum. You shouldn't have been left on your own."

Maggie nodded, lips pressed tightly together. "Let's just get a good night's sleep. We can figure it all out tomorrow."

Great. Lily forced herself to smile. *That doesn't sound promising.*

But at least I have something to keep me from worrying about it tonight.

"Goodnight, Mum." Lily moved onto the landing and headed for her bedroom. The pills in her pocket were burning a hole in her jeans. She couldn't wait to take them out and swallow one.

CHAPTER FOURTEEN

JAKE WAS on his third beer when Maggie came downstairs in her pyjamas. He had hoped she might be coming to talk, but instead she stomped around the kitchen in silence.

"Hey," he said, talking to her back. "You okay?"

She went to the fridge and got milk. She often poured a glass to take up to bed.

When he didn't get an answer, Jake tried again. "Mag, I don't want to fight. I've had a rough night."

"You've had a rough night? Are you serious?"

He put his beer down and sighed. "I'm just talking about George. It was upsetting, and I wish I could talk to you about it."

She put the milk back inside the fridge and pulled out a bottle of wine. Pouring herself a glass, she came and sat opposite him at the small round table. "Fine. Tell me why you and Lily seem so heartbroken about an old man who, this time last week, you didn't even know? The two of you have been up to something. Tell me what."

"Nothing." Her mistrust wounded him, but he tried not

to show it. "George was the only person to welcome us to the street. He was kind and decent, and if you had come to have a drink with him when he invited us, you would know that."

"So that's it?" She raised an eyebrow at him. "You finally found a father figure at forty?"

"I'm thirty-eight."

"Jake, you've spent your whole life trying to keep the girls away from run-down places like this" – she shook her head and sighed – "only to end up besties with some jobless nobody."

"George was retired." He put his hands together on the table and leant forward. "Why are you being so mean about him? The man just died."

She shrugged and looked away, picked up her wine and took a swig. "I don't know. Just the mood I'm in, I suppose." She ran a hand through her damp hair and cleared her throat. "I understand it must've been traumatic for you to watch someone die. I'm just… not in a sympathy-giving mood right now."

"I can see that." He let out a sigh to match hers and flattened his hands against the table, wanting to reach out but unwilling to risk it. "Maggie, I hate this. You're my best friend."

"Really? Best friend? When was the last time we went out to dinner or a show, Jake? When was the last time we even watched a film together? You're at home all the time, Jake, yet somehow I hardly ever see you."

"You're at home too."

"I got laid off as an underpaid HR manager at a supermarket. You voluntarily closed an entire business for no reason. And you're the reason I haven't reapplied elsewhere. You wanted us both at home to take care of Emily."

He rolled his eyes. "Sorry. I didn't realise you'd rather be working."

"Don't! Don't do that, Jake. I've been here every second for our daughter. I'm a nervous wreck at the edge of a breakdown, but I've taken care of her more than anyone."

"More than anyone?" His hands clenched into fists on the table. "I would do anything for Emily. In fact, I have."

Maggie put her wine glass down and glared at him. "What does that mean? You think you're the only one who's sacrificed?"

He shook his head, not knowing how much he wanted to say. If he spilled the beans about what happened at Mr Cho's, she would laugh at him. Eventually, when she saw the proof of Emily's miraculous recovery, she would have no choice but to believe him, but right now she would think him mad. "Look, Mag, can you just trust me when I tell you Emily is going to be fine? Her cancer is gone. Really, truly, one hundred per cent gone."

"Don't be so absurd, Jake. You heard what Dr Kwami said: it's just some kind of bounceback. Not a miracle. Cancer doesn't just disappear overnight."

He smiled and reached out to take her hands. "I know you can't believe me just yet, but everything is going to be okay. Please, just trust me."

She pulled her hands away and folded her arms, eyes narrowing. "I don't trust you, Jake. Since we moved to this street, you've been angry, and secretive, and…" – she nodded at the two empty beer bottles on the worktop – "drinking too much."

"You and me both."

"Perhaps. Maybe we're both just too broken now. Maybe things have run their course."

"What? Are you talking about our marriage? Because if

you're just being dramatic…" He picked up his beer bottle. "Just make sure you don't say something you don't mean."

Maggie got up and poured the rest of her wine down the sink. "It's late. I'm going to bed. You can stay up and do whatever you want."

"I will."

Jake watched his wife storm out of the kitchen. He was stunned and angry. Didn't she see how much he had done to keep their family together? Would she prefer him to work all hours like he used to? Sacrificing sixty hours a week of his life, and for what? A swanky house and an overpriced car? Wasn't being at home with Emily more important? Wasn't family more important?

She has no idea what I've done. I fixed everything, and she doesn't even know it. Emily is going to be fine because of me.

There was a cracking sound, causing Jake to jolt backwards in his chair, its rickety wooden legs biting into the old lino. A shock ran through his palm, from thumb to pinkie.

Ouch! What the…?

He had gripped his beer bottle too hard and cracked it, just like he had the hospital vending machine. The sharp edges had cut into his palm. Clumsy.

Curiously, the pain had gone away almost as immediately as he had felt it. He examined the slender scratch; it already seemed to be scabbing over, and there was a near total absence of blood.

"Huh. Lucky break."

Jake took the broken bottle to the bin and tossed it in, then he went and wiped down the table. He considered getting another beer, but decided against it. His thirst back, and alcohol wasn't quenching it, so he went and stuck his head under the cold tap, turning on the water and gulping from the sputtering stream. Maggie would have chided him for such oafish behaviour, but he really didn't give a shit right now.

He felt himself vibrate with anger. The emotion had been building and building for a while now, long before moving to Tovey Avenue. Being stuck at home, with nothing to occupy himself except worry and lament, had not been good for his mental health. The notion of returning to work, now that Emily was better, actually filled him with an over-whelming relief, but he needed life to return to normal fast or he might not make it. He was a flailing swimmer grasping for air.

Unable to bear lying beside Maggie while he was feeling this way – and anxious she would give him the cold shoulder if he tried – Jake grabbed his jacket, closed the front door quietly behind him, and went for a walk around the block.

Perhaps Maggie was right about him constantly disap-pearing – both physically and emotionally – but what choice did he have when she was always getting at him?

I screwed up, but she needs to let it go.

His jaw locked, teeth grinding.

As he headed down the street, a slight breeze caressed his skin, like a child tickling his arms and face – a playful, tender touch. It was eleven thirty, and all was quiet. Surpris-ingly, there were still plenty of lights on inside the various houses and even the flash of a television coming from one or two. It seemed people went to bed late around here. In fact, there was someone in their front garden, right now, about six houses up.

Getting closer, Jake saw it was an old lady, wearing a duffle coat that almost swallowed her whole. She was pottering around her front garden and pouring water from a metal watering can. Jake could smell the rust on its spout.

To avoid worrying the old lady by approaching her at such a late hour, he said hello a dozen feet before reaching her. "Good evening."

She looked up, startled, but not visibly concerned. "Oh, hello there."

"I'm Jake from number twenty-six. Sorry to creep up on you at night."

"That's okay. George told me about you moving in. I'm Mary."

Jake smiled. *She doesn't know. Did she not see the ambulance?*

"Um, George mentioned you as well. Nice to meet you, Mary. Odd hours you keep."

She straightened up stiffly, the watering can appearing heavy in her hand. "I retire early these days, but I have a tendency to wake up every few hours until dawn. I do my best thinking at this hour though, so it doesn't bother me. Plus, the plants enjoy a late-night watering."

Jake moved up and peered over her garden wall at an array of bushy plants and colourful flowers. They were all well taken care of in thick ceramic pots. "You have a lovely garden, Mary."

"Thank you." She beamed, her teeth grey in the soft light coming from her open front door. "They'll all be curling up for winter soon, but they'll be back come spring. Daffodils, hyacinth, tulips. Do you do much gardening yourself, Jake?"

He laughed. "I'm good with my hands, but my thumbs are definitely not green. I'm a carpenter by trade."

"Oh, how wonderful to have someone handy on the street. I've been waiting all year for someone to fix my letter box. Let's in a right draught, it does."

Jake peered towards the letter box of the open front door, able to see it because of the light in the hallway. It was old and brass, and it hung askew from a single screw, leaving the slot exposed where there should have been wind-dampening bristles. "Seems like an easy fix," he said. "A few screws, really."

"You would think I could manage it myself," she said, "but my hands are no good with anything fiddly, and my eyesight is even worse. Part of the reason I can't sleep at night is because the bloody thing whistles like an excited girl when the wind is up."

Jake understood. Even now, with only a slight breeze, he could hear the air whistling as it slid between the hanging brass letter box and the door. "Well," he said. "I'd better fix it now then."

"Don't be silly," she said. "It's almost midnight."

"I do my best work at this hour. No noise, so it's easy to concentrate. Just let me grab some tools from my car."

"No, need. I have my husband's old toolkit inside. Come on in."

He frowned at her. "Are you sure?"

"If you planned on hurting me, I imagine you would've done it by now. Anyway, I'm seventy-six and scraping by on a state pension; you'd have to be a pretty stupid criminal to bother with me."

"I suppose you're right." He chuckled and extended a hand. "Okay, Mary, show me the way."

Maggie wouldn't believe it if I told her. Socialising with the neighbours at midnight, like it's the most normal thing in the world. Got to say I kind of like it. The night has a peacefulness about it.

If only George was still around, I could pop by for a whisky.

Am I actually starting to like the stuff?

Mary led Jake inside her house, leaving the front door wide open. It was strange for her to be so trusting when you had the likes of Vincent and co regularly hanging around the street.

George told me to stay out of their way and they would stay out of mine.

Did I bring trouble on myself? I should never have attacked Vincent. What was I thinking? And I did it twice!

Why couldn't I just keep my head down and control my temper? When did I even get a temper?

There was no point in giving himself a hard time about past events, so Jake tried to reframe things in his mind. If the only way to avoid trouble with the likes of Vincent and his uncle was to let them do whatever the hell they wanted, then he was glad to have fought back. It was right.

Mary pottered over to a cupboard underneath the stairs. "Just in here," she said, opening the door. "The big blue metal box. You might have to clear a few things out of the way to get at it."

Great. Jake smiled at her. *What did I get myself into?*

All to spite Maggie.

With only the light from the hallway, he had to squint as he peered inside the cupboard. There was something shiny inside.

"Just move that," Mary said. "It's just an old ashtray that belonged to my Eric. Family heirloom, I couldn't bear to throw it away."

He turned to her. "I take it your husband passed?"

"Five years ago now."

"I'm sorry you lost him. Must be tough."

She shrugged. "George helped me a lot in the beginning. He lost his wife so young, you know? He understood what I was going through. Salt of the earth, that man."

Jake nodded.

Should I tell her?

Not now. Not at twelve o'clock at night. I'll come by first thing in the morning to let her know. At least then she can call someone if she needs to.

As Jake's eyes adjusted to the gloom inside the cupboard, he spotted the bulky blue toolbox sitting inside, buried beneath the old ashtray and what looked like a pile of vinyl records in their sleeves. It was the ashtray that captured his attention, though. "Wow. This thing must be worth a bit of money, huh? It's beautiful."

"Real silver," Mary said proudly. "It got its use over the years too. My Eric was a pack a day smoker. What killed him in the end, most likely. God bless his soul."

Jake gave her a sympathetic smile and then turned back to the cupboard. "Okay, I'll just grab it and move it out of the way, if that's all right? Are you okay to take it from me? I don't want to damage it."

"Of course. Pass it over."

Jake reached in and grabbed the silver ashtray with both hands, expecting it to be heavy.

The pain was like nothing he'd ever felt before.

For a second, Jake thought he'd grabbed a live wire in both hands, but it was more than a simple electric shock. It was as if his soul were screaming.

He flew backwards out of the cupboard, tossing the ashtray away as if it were on fire. It clunked against Mary's head.

She staggered down the hall, lost her feet, and collapsed onto her side in the middle of the carpet. The moan that escaped her was like a cat Jake had seen get squashed beneath a truck tyre when he was nine years old. It was a horrible memory from his childhood, and he cursed his brain for bringing it to him now so lucidly.

Jake's first instinct was to help Mary, but his nerves were

in disarray, numbness and pain intermingled. His vision flashed. When he tried to walk, he staggered drunkenly. He tried to talk, but mumbled.

Everything seemed to glow, the lightbulb overhead glaring. The surrounding air pulsed. Jake felt every hair on his body rise, could feel every pore on his face open up.

Mary was half knocked out, moaning and groping at her forehead, which was split open like a cantaloupe and gushing blood.

"What the hell have I done?" he said out loud.

"H-help me…" Mary moaned, rolling onto her back and staring blindly at the ceiling. "Help."

Jake stared at the old woman, licking his lips. His body trembled.

———

V hated Tovey Avenue and its twin rows of endless houses. He hated how people nosed out of their windows whenever something was happening but never got involved or tried to help. It wouldn't surprise him if a dozen people had witnessed his uncle's actions last night, yet nobody had gone to the police. People didn't want to be bothered, nor did they particularly like having a spotlight shone on them by the authorities.

A third of the houses were customers of V – or more accurately, customers of his uncle – while another third were alcoholics. The other third were decent enough, he supposed, but they were the ones who always turned their noses up at him. They thought he was scum.

Because that's what I am. I'm a drug dealer.

My mum would be so upset.

V missed his mother every day, but the memories of her

were always painful. Every time he got a flash of her pushing him on a swing or buying him a Fredo bar at the newsagents, an image of her twisted up in a wheelchair or covered in her own shit would replace it. The MS had taken away even the happy times he had spent with her – the precious few years when he had been an ordinary kid. His mind was a junkie's forearm, covered in poisonous little track marks and festering sores that never healed.

He had just finished dealing with Brett at number nineteen, a MIG welder with a mild cannabis habit. As far as his customers went, Brett mostly had his shit together. He smoked at night to chill out and sleep, but that was it. No matter how often V offered the guy harder stuff, he never bought anything besides weed.

Business done for the night, V headed home. As he walked, last night's horror show replayed in his head. Jake had been so angry, ready to do some proper damage. V might have taken him during their first altercation, but he wasn't sure he would've stood up to the man last night.

He had a right to be angry. I gave Lily a pill.

Why did I do that? She's just a kid.

V didn't like Jake at all, but he was awash with guilt as he pictured the guy staggering off in a daze, holding his guts and not seeming to realise he'd just been stabbed.

Where did he end up? How long did he last?

Doser had texted V to say he'd seen an ambulance earlier tonight on Tovey Avenue, which must have been for Jake. Had he dropped dead in someone's front garden, undiscovered for hours? What must his family have thought when he hadn't come home last night? What must they have been thinking now that he was gone for good?

Lily must be a right mess. I should text her.

No. I can't be her friend after what happened. It would be sick.

He stopped in the middle of the road, realising it was the exact same spot where Jake and his uncle had faced off. The man's blood still stained the ground. In the orange glow of the lampposts, it showed up as a dark patch on the tarmac, with several smaller smudges leading away in a staggered line.

V was surprised by how quiet the street was tonight. It might have been buzzing with pigs earlier, but right now there was nothing going on. Where was Jake's family? At the hospital? With family?

At home?

He turned and looked towards Lily's house, wishing he could see her, talk to her. Try to make things better.

How? How do I make things better?

I should just go home.

He started walking, wanting to be away from Tovey Avenue, wanting never to come back. If not for his job, he probably never would.

And if not for Uncle Dev, I would quit.

Who am I kidding?

Vincent saved most of his money, wanting to get a car for himself, but he couldn't deny he made a good living for a seventeen-year-old. Not only that, he could imagine himself going insane working at some factory or in a shop. Being a dealer was a good gig, so long as you were smart and professional. Some people might say he was doing something bad, but the scagheads and coke sniffers were going to get high one way or another. All he was doing was meeting a need and getting paid for it. How was he any different to the billionaires overcharging people for gas or medicine?

He stepped up onto the pavement, realising he was going to have to walk past Lily's house in a few minutes. He was currently passing by Limp's place, with the overgrown garden and rotting door. The old fucker was a joke, living alone like some weirdo perv. He might never cause any trouble, but V always sensed the bastard watching him and judging.

Like he's lived a life to be proud of. I promise, when I'm his age, I won't have a rotting front door and rubbish in my front garden. Although fair play to the guy for all the weight he's lost lately. Must be one hell of a diet.

V walked a few houses further down, passing by the weird Chink's front door, with his stupid candles that were always burning and his—

He stopped in his tracks as someone came staggering out of one of the houses about twenty feet ahead.

"No," he muttered, shock gripping him around the throat. "No, it can't be."

It was Jake. V was sure of it. While it might have been past midnight, the front doorstep was lit by a hallway light, making it easy enough to see who had staggered out of the house. Wearing jeans and a long-sleeved T-shirt, Jake was alive and well. Although he seemed a little out of it, weaving back and forth along the pavement.

Jake turned in V's direction.

"Shit!" V tried to duck out of the way, but it was too late. Jake was staring right at him.

No… No, he's looking through me.

Jake's eyes were like dark marbles. He seemed unable to focus. V, standing in the middle of the pavement, appeared to provoke no reaction at all. In fact, Jake turned away and started back up the path for home, although not so quickly that V didn't notice something terrible first.

His face…
What the hell?

Jake's mouth and chin were covered in blood. It dripped from his fingertips as he staggered down the pavement.

V was rooted to the spot, too freaked out to think straight. Jake was alive, which was impossible. Impossible, but true.

He was alive.

But there's something wrong with him.

After Jake disappeared into the darkness beyond the nearest lampposts, V managed to get his feet moving. Every part of him wanted to run the other way, but he ignored his fear. He needed to look inside the house ahead of him. The house with the open front door. The house Jake had staggered out of.

Who lives there? I'm not sure.

V moved slowly, one foot in front of the other, hips lowered so he could spin around and flee if he needed to. The night was once again still, quiet as death itself. If not for the chilly breeze against his face, he might have thought himself dreaming.

Not a dream. A nightmare.

He reached the end of the garden path and turned to face the open front door. For a moment, he thought he saw a duvet lying in the middle of the hallway, but then he realised it was a thick blue padded coat. Someone was lying on the floor.

"Fuck me," V whispered to himself as he started towards the house. "Fuck me."

It took five steps to get from the garden gate to the front doorstep, and it was only after the last step that V saw all the blood. It soaked the walls, the floor, and even the ceiling. Most of all, it stained the body beneath the thick padded coat.

This can't be real. What the hell happened?

V tried to see the person's face, to work out who it was and if they were alive. Then he realised.

"Oh fuck, oh fuck, oh fuck."

V yanked the front door closed to block out the horror. Then he turned around and ran.

————

Jake dreamed of the squashed cat, its intestines popping out beneath the reversing truck tyre while it screeched in agony. In his mind's eye, the poor pet's blood was Day-Glo bright and shimmering.

He saw himself, a horrified nine-year-old boy, standing at the side of the road in tears, wishing his mum would magically materialise and take him away. He'd had this nightmare before; no one ever came to make it better.

But this time, he dreamed a little differently. He broke away from his tears and walked towards the dying cat, as if pulled by an invisible wire. The sweet, coppery scent of blood invaded his nostrils. He crouched beside the fading creature, took a deep breath in, and buried his face in its guts.

This time, he ate.

Jake sat up with a gasp. His head struck something, and he yelped before falling a short distance. Confusion took hold, and it was several seconds before he worked out exactly where he was.

What am I doing in my car?

He glanced about himself and noticed two things. Number one: he was half-asleep on the back seat on his X-Trail. Number two: he was also half-naked.

"What the hell?" Jake pulled himself from the rear footwell and onto the back seat. He was grateful that the rear windows were tinted, because his watch told him it was past eight in the morning. Anyone could have looked in and seen him sleeping.

He had zero recollection of getting there. The last thing he remembered was…

Arguing with Maggie. I stormed out of the house.

That explained it. Rather than share a bed with his wife, he had gone out to sleep in the car. He only remembered having a few beers, but perhaps he'd drank more.

Or maybe I was just so exhausted I passed out.

There was the worst taste in his mouth, like burnt pennies and olive oil. He wanted to spit on the pavement, but until he found his clothes and car keys, he was stuck inside the car. Patting around with his hands, he located not his keys, but his phone. There were two messages waiting for him.

One message was from Greg, explaining he'd left a Blu-ray player and film library in his van. He would pop round with it one morning this week.

The second message was from Maggie. It read: **Where are you? Woke up and you were gone? X**

At least her message had a kiss.

He recalled the words spoken last night, his wife suggesting their marriage may have 'run its course.' Him sleeping out in the car probably hadn't helped things. Or maybe it had. Maybe it had sent a message that he wouldn't be threatened.

"Need to get dressed," he said, looking around the back of the car. He still wore his jeans, socks, and shoes, but he couldn't see his long-sleeved T-shirt anywhere.

Then he looked over the back of the seats into the boot. For a moment, he was baffled. He was sure he'd been wearing a green shirt, not red.

It's blood. My shirt is covered in blood.

For the second time, Jake found his clothes ruined by blood.

Where did it come from this time? Was I stabbed again? I have no idea.

Somehow, Jake knew the blood wasn't his. He could smell it. Foreign.

There was a knock at the window.

"Jesus!" Jake tried to turn around, but found himself tangled up against the front seats. He had to turn his head to see who was standing outside.

Maggie pressed her face against the tinted rear window, trying to see inside. "Jake? Jake, are you in there?"

"Yeah. I, um, slept in here."

"Why?"

I have no idea.

"I figured you wouldn't want me in the bed."

There was a pause. Then she said, "That's stupid. You could have slept on the sofa if you didn't want to come to bed."

From her tone, she didn't seem angry. Maybe she regretted last night. When Jake thought about it, he regretted it too. "I'm sorry. I just wanted to clear my head after our argument."

"I don't want to talk about it right now," she said.

"Me neither. I don't want to fight."

"Are you coming out? We need to go to the hospital to see Emily."

Jake eyed his bloody shirt in the boot. He had no way to explain it. "Um, yeah, but… I need a shirt from inside the house."

"Well, come inside then."

"I will. Just give me a minute to get my shoes on and that."

She moved to the front window and peered in at him. "Can you open the car? I'll wait for you in here. Tell Lily to hurry up, will you?"

Shit! What if she sees the bloody T-shirt?

It's in the boot. She won't.

"Hold on." He reached into the boot and grabbed his shirt, wondering if he could scrunch it up and hide the blood. But there was too much. He tossed it back in the boot, trying to stuff it into a corner.

"Hurry up," said Maggie. "I'm standing out here."

He looked around for his car keys and found them in the ignition. Had he driven somewhere, or been planning to?

Why can't I remember anything?

"What's that on your face?" Maggie asked, still peering through the window. She angled her head, trying to see him better.

"What?" He rubbed at his face. Dried flakes of blood came off like dust in his hands.

"I… I must have had a nosebleed. It's dry and stuffy in here."

Maggie groaned. "For crying out loud, Jake. How much did you drink last night?"

"I… I'm not sure. I'm sorry. Maybe I'll knock it on the head for a bit."

She said nothing, still waiting to get inside the car. He had no idea how much blood was on his face, and the only thing he could think to do was to lick his palms and rub vigorously at his cheeks. By the time he was done, his hands were smeared red and his fingernails dirty.

Before Maggie complained again, he reached over the centre console and pressed the button to unlock the doors.

Maggie immediately yanked open the front passenger door. Jake, at the same time, hurried out of the rear driver's side. "I'll be quick as I can," he said as he slammed the door behind him and headed up the path. His intention was to keep his wife from getting a close look at his face.

I need to get a look at myself first.

He headed inside the house and bumped into Lily, who was putting her coat on in the hallway.

"Shit! Dad? Mum's looking for you."

"She found me."

She pointed to his face. "You have blood on you, again. Where's your shirt? What is going on with you, Dad?"

An urge prodded at him, telling him to hug his daughter and tell her everything. It was his job, as a parent, to be steadfast and strong, but these were extreme circumstances. Was it okay to have a breakdown in front of his fourteen-year-old daughter?

"I had a nosebleed," he said, trying to shrug it off. "I slept in the car and the air must have been dry."

She raised an eyebrow, clearly doubtful, but what exactly could she say? What accusation could she level at him without evidence?

"I'm going to the car," she said. "Are you coming to the hospital with us?"

"Of course I am. I just need to wash my face and put on a fresh shirt."

"Because your old one is covered in blood, I'm guessing?"

He shrugged.

"Dad, did you kill someone or something? You know what? Don't tell me. I've had enough death and weird Chinese voodoo rituals for one week."

"I think voodoo is from the Caribbean, honey. Haiti, maybe?"

She scowled at him. "Seriously? That's the part of my statement that concerns you. I'll be in the car. Hurry up and get dressed."

"Yes, ma'am." He saluted.

Jake hurried up the stairs to get dressed, but before he did, he looked in the bathroom mirror. There wasn't as much blood on his face as he'd feared, but then, any amount of blood was too much when you didn't know where it came from.

"What's happening to me?" he asked his reflection, pulling down on his cheeks and exposing his bloodshot eyeballs. "And what the hell happened last night?"

CHAPTER
FIFTEEN

EMILY WAS out of bed and standing at the window. From the third floor of the hospital, she could see the university's train platform and the surrounding suburb of Edgbaston. Birmingham wasn't usually a pretty city, but right now she saw beauty everywhere. The delicate, shimmering feathers of a magpie on a window ledge. An Audi Q7 in a delightfully audacious burnt orange. An old man sitting on a bench eating a sandwich. Life. Mundane and wonderful.

A life she suddenly felt like she might get to enjoy.

She felt not an ounce of pain. Her skinny legs once again had enough strength to lift her. Even the low-level, ever-present nausea was gone.

Dr Kwami was freaking out, of course, and half a dozen other doctors had been to see her overnight – second, third, fourth, fifth opinions being offered around excitedly. One thing was for sure: they all struggled to understand where her cancer had gone.

Could it be true? Could I actually be healthy?

After so long?

She hadn't contemplated getting to live, not for many

months now. With the notion once again a possibility, she felt overwhelmed and manic. Her senses were so alert that she somehow knew her mum was about to walk through the door before she actually did.

Her mum saw Emily standing up and gasped. "Honey? You're on your feet."

Emily beamed. "Walking and everything. Glad I didn't forget how."

Maggie came and gave her a gentle hug. "I'm so happy, honey. What have the doctors said?"

"All my results are coming back clear. Dr Kwami is contacting some medical newspaper about me, I think."

Jake and Lily entered the room and both of them grinned to see her on her feet. It was strange that they had entered several seconds behind Maggie. Had they not been walking together?

"How are you feeling, sweetheart?" Jake asked.

"Amazing," she said, doing a little twirl. Her body still had more in common with a rake than it did a teenage girl, but she was feeling stronger every second. A cartwheel might be a little beyond her, but a quick spin was invigorating enough for now. "I'm starving though."

Lily gripped the end of her bed and nodded. "Me too. I had noodles for breakfast. I'm thinking of calling Childline."

Maggie tutted. "We need to get some shopping in. There's been a lot going on."

"Can you come home?" Jake asked. "You must be bored stiff in this place."

"Eh, it's all right," Emily said. "I'm only halfway through my book and I like the quiet. Dr Kwami is coming back in ten minutes; you can ask him when I can leave."

Lily slumped down on the chair beside Emily's bed. She seemed tired and a little out of it, but she kept smiling and appeared to be in a rare good mood. "So, sis," she said, smiling at Emily. "Any hot doctors around? Kwami's a bit old for my tastes."

"There's Dr Shamov. I think he's from Romania or somewhere, but he's pretty young and hot. Has these long, dark eyelashes."

"Ooh," Lily said. "I love that. Like the sheriff in *Bates Motel*?"

Emily clicked her fingers. "Yeah, just like that guy. How long ago did we watch that show? It was so good."

"It was years ago now," said Maggie, who had watched it with them while Jake worked late as usual back then. "I can't even remember how it ended."

"I think everyone had a great big orgy," Lily said. "Then they all died of herpes."

Maggie rolled her eyes and ignored her. She looked at Jake. "Can you get us some hot drinks, please?"

"Um, sure. Coffee?"

"Yeah."

"Hot chocolate for me," Lily said.

Jake looked at Emily. "Sweetheart?"

"Nothing for me. I just had some juice."

Jake left the room a little huffily. Emily got the impression her mum wanted him gone. Clearly there was still tension between the two.

At least Lily seemed to be all right. She had her legs hooked over the side of the chair and was texting on her phone. Her blonde and pink hair was tied back in a ponytail, which probably meant it needed washing.

I'm going to get my hair back. My tits too. I can't believe it.

Before the chemo took it from her, Emily had had the same blonde hair as her mum and sister. It was only her dad who was different, with shaved brown hair and a bald patch at the back. She's seen photos of him in his younger days with long, silky hair, but she couldn't remember him ever having more than a half an inch on his head.

Dr Kwami entered. He was looking down at his notes and flinched when he almost walked right into Maggie. "Oh, Mrs Penshaw? How are you doing this morning?"

"Great," she said. "How is Emily doing? She's walking?"

"Cautiously, yes. Her muscles need to recover, so it's important she doesn't overexert herself. Please, encourage her to rest."

"I'm right here," Emily said, half looking out the window at the city below. "And I already said I'll take it easy. Stop worrying, Doc."

Dr Kwami smiled, but he was a serious man with little sense of humour. "I will do my best."

"Is her cancer retreating, Doctor??" Maggie asked, her face serious. "Is it really as good as it seems?"

"It is… miraculous," he said, moving over to stand beside Emily at the window, as if he expected her to suddenly try to attempt a dozen cheeky jumping jacks. "Every test I have run has shown a complete lack of cancer. We performed a bone marrow biopsy last night—"

Emily rubbed her lower back. "Which sucked."

"—and the results came back as perfectly healthy. Her blood tests are fine. Every scan has shown a complete lack of growths or tumours. Optimal liver function. Perfect kidney function." He shook his head, as if it were bad news he was giving instead of amazing news. "There's not a doctor at this hospital who can make sense of it. And that's what concerns me."

"Why?" Maggie asked. "Why does that concern you?"

"Because, in medicine, it is always better to have answers than unexplained miracles. It is a doctor's job to make sense of things, but in this case, I am at a complete loss."

"But ultimately," Emily said, "I'm better, right? Isn't that the thing that truly matters?"

"Forgive my negativity. It is wonderful that you seem to be cancer-free, Emily. It merely concerns me that there is no rational explanation. If I could understand it, I would be better placed to give a prognosis."

Emily waved a hand at him. "I don't need you to predict the future, Doc. The point is that I have a future. Whatever happens will happen, so let's just celebrate the win."

"That's a very healthy way of looking at things, Emily."

"When you expect to drop dead at any moment, only to find out you're actually going to be okay, then it's pretty easy to be positive."

"You're welcome," Lily muttered.

Emily looked at her. "Huh?"

"Just talking to myself," she said. She lifted her legs from over the chair and put her feet back on the floor. "So can my sis come home, Doc?"

Dr Kwami moaned. "I would really rather she stay for one more day."

"Drink up!" Jake entered the room, balancing three hot drinks in his arms. He handed one to Maggie and another to Lily. As usual, he had picked a hot chocolate for himself. "Hello, Doctor. You looked tired."

Dr Kwami seemed to blush, his complexion darkening. "Oh, well, I was working through the night. I have today off though, so I'll probably spend most of it sleeping, if my wife will allow me."

"Workaholic, huh? I used to be one of those." He looked at Maggie. "Probably will be again soon, huh?"

Maggie seemed to take the comment badly, because she

looked away and said, "Dr Kwami, can we take Emily home? Does she absolutely need to be here?"

"We can take care of her," Jake said. "Give her any medications, et cetera."

"Right now, none are needed, Mr Penshaw, although some will need tapering off, so I'll write up some guidelines on dosages. Again, I would prefer her to stay her for another day though, if possible?"

"Why?" Emily asked bluntly.

"To monitor you. You got better very suddenly, and I fear you might go the other way just as fast."

"She's fine," Jake said, beaming. He sipped his hot choco-late, even though it was hot enough to give off steam. "There's no need for her to be here."

"Let's not be hasty," Maggie said. "Let's listen to the doctor."

Jake bowed his head. "With all due respect, Dr Kwami has tried and failed to treat Emily for more than a year. The treatments didn't work. It's time to move on and finally get on with our lives."

Dr Kwami clutched his notes against his chest and wrin-kled his nose. "It's been a long, hard road, admittedly," he said. "But there is no reason to suggest that Emily's recovery is not a result of her various treatments. Without them, she would surely have died."

Rather than agree, Jake gave the doctor a smug grin. "Guess we'll never know, huh? I'm taking my daughter home, Doctor. She's doing fine, and if anything changes, you'll be the first to know."

"I still have some test results outstanding."

"Then pick up the phone. You have our numbers."

Dr Kwami sighed. "Very well. I will arrange Emily's

discharge. But please come right back to the hospital if you have the slightest worry."

Maggie glared at Jake. "Of course. We're so grateful for everything you've done, Dr Kwami."

Dr Kwami bowed and left the room.

"That was rude." Maggie said, still glaring at Jake. She moved over to Emily and started rubbing her back.

What will she do now she doesn't need to fret over me every second?

It was a relief for Emily to know she might soon be able to look after herself again, but even more of a relief that her mum could start thinking about herself a little more. Her dad too.

Lily shrugged in the chair beside Emily. "Dad's right. Emily would be dead if we left it to Dr Kwami. He wasn't able to help her."

"What?" Emily frowned at her sister. "What do you mean if we left it to him? It's not like I've been getting treatment elsewhere."

Lily pulled a face as if she'd said something she shouldn't have. "Yeah, I just, um, meant that it was fate that cured you in the end. You kept fighting until a miracle came along. It wasn't the chemo or the radiation therapy that helped you. Actually, it made you worse."

"You're being unfair. Dr Kwami has done everything he could to help me."

Maggie nodded. "I agree. We should be thanking the man, not insulting him."

"Fine." Jake shrugged, then gave Lily an odd look. "I'll apologise before we leave. In the meantime, let's get Emily ready to go home. No more hospitals for at least a year, so I don't even want to see a stubbed toe in this family."

Everyone chuckled, and even Maggie smiled. "Well, that's something we can agree on, at least. With all the bad luck we've had this last year, I think we're due a little peace."

"I'm sorry," said Emily, and when her mum went to interrupt, she spoke fast enough to stop her. "No, listen. This last year has been horrible for you all, and things aren't like they used to be. You don't laugh like you used to or even look at each other the same. All you do is take care of me. Me getting sick has been horrible for everyone, but I think it's over now, so we all need to remember that we love each other and that no one is to blame for the last eighteen months. There's no point in me being better if my family is gone."

"I'm sound," Lily said. "No grudges here."

Emily looked at her parents. "Mum? Dad?"

They looked at each other, and eventually her mum let out a sigh. "It's been a tough week. Let's just get home and see what happens. I'm sure, with some time to heal, everything will work out fine."

Jake nodded, wrapping his arm around Maggie, which she allowed him to do. "We're still the same people, honey," he said. "We're still a family, and none of us is going anywhere."

Emily smiled, but she had a bad feeling in her stomach that somehow that might not be true.

———

Eight o'clock and they were eating pizza in the kitchen again. Lily was sick to death of pizza.

Emily hadn't been discharged from the hospital until four in the afternoon, and it had become more and more obvious that Dr Kwami had been attempting to delay them, perhaps hoping it would get so late enough that they would agree to keep Emily in for another night. Jake had been having none of it, though, and actually threatened to call the police with a kidnapping complaint if they didn't let Emily go. By the time they eventually left, even Maggie had had enough of Dr Kwami.

Rather than go straight home, Jake had taken the car over to Cannon Hill Park so they could watch the ducks on the lake and have an ice cream. The afternoon had been a little chilly, but Emily didn't seem to mind. They spent two hours walking and enjoying the fresh – non-chlorinated – air.

Then they had gone home and ordered pizza.

They were all happy to have Emily home, but it was weird. She was laughing and joking, and stuffing pizza into her face like there was no such thing as the Atkins diet. It was like having dinner with a stranger. Where was the sickly, constantly exhausted stick insect they were all used to?

We're in shock. We've finally sat down with time to think, and it's too fucked up to contemplate. It'll take a few days to wrap our heads around it. Emily's okay.

Lily found she had no appetite, and had only eaten a single slice of pizza, while another lay untouched on her plate. Maggie seemed uninterested in eating as well, but she had started on her second glass of wine. Jake, however, had eaten almost an entire Meat Feast to himself.

He's being a right pig.

At least he was sticking to water for a change. Lots and lots of water. Lily didn't remember the last time he hadn't had a beer at dinnertime, but she found it a relief. In fact, she was pretty sure both her parents were drunks.

And I'm a druggie. We belong on this street, that's for sure.

They all sat for another twenty minutes, with Emily

244 OF IAIN ROB WRIGHT

doing most of the talking and only the odd comment added by anybody else. Maggie made it to her third glass of wine, Jake his fifth glass of water.

Why is he so thirsty?

Then, at around nine o'clock, the Emily show ended when she announced she was going up to bed. She had been up half of last night having tests, and a sudden wave of tiredness visibly hit her, turning her face grey and making her yawn constantly. Feeling weary herself, and not wanting to hang around with her mum and dad, Lily announced she would also retire.

Emily kissed everyone goodnight and went up to bed first. Then, when Maggie went to the toilet, Jake took Lily aside in the kitchen. "You okay?" he asked her. "It's been a crazy couple of days."

"I don't know what you're talking about. My sister randomly recovered from cancer. It happens, Dad."

He smiled at her knowingly and then gave her a hug. "It's all going to get better from here on in, I promise. I'm proud of you."

She pulled away and frowned at him, her tummy awash with strange emotions. "What?"

"I mean it, I'm proud of you. You're a pain in the arse at the best of times, but you could have given me and your mum a much harder time than you have, all things considered. I should have noticed how strong you are, but you can stop now. It's over. Just be a teenager."

The words he was saying made her happy – at least she thought so – but for some reason she felt like crying. Also added to the emotional mix was a deep, mistrustful fear. Fear of life, and the newfound knowledge that it could be manipulated by outside forces.

Her dad frowned at her. "Something on your mind?"

"I have a bad feeling, Dad. We messed with stuff we don't understand. It feels wrong. Like we cheated somehow."

"How did we cheat, honey? Emily's innocent, and she didn't deserve to die at seventeen. So, if there are rules and we broke them, who cares? The world is full of people who do whatever's best for them, no matter the consequences. Maybe what we've done is more common than you think. Maybe Bill Gates and Evers Nealy and Elon Musk are all witches, conjuring up their fortunes by making deals with the Devil. Why should they get all the luck?"

"Warlocks."

"What?"

"I dunno," she said, shrugging. "Can men be witches? Aren't they warlocks?"

He shook his head. "I have no idea."

"Wizards?"

"It doesn't matter."

"I'll ask Mr Cho the proper terminology," she said, chuckling. "I want to see if he'll do a spell to bag me a Man City player when I'm eighteen."

Her dad clasped his face in his hands. "Please, daughter, aim higher than being a footballer's wife. Especially Man City. This is an Aston Villa household."

"Don't worry. It'll only be for a couple of years. Then I'll divorce him and take all his money before starting a career in reality TV."

"God, it gets worse."

She gave him another quick hug, and as she pulled away, she studied him. "You look rough, Dad. Your eyes, they're really red."

He rubbed at them. "Allergies."

"Since when have you had allergies?"

"I'm getting old."

"Let me know when you need a walking stick. I'll help you design a cool one like…"

He nodded. "Like George's?"

She nodded, unexpectedly sad at thinking about the old man. "He was a nice guy, huh?"

"Shame what happened to him, but at least he was happy when he went. I was with him; he was okay. At peace."

"That's good. I'm glad. Anyway, I'm going to bed. Try not to argue with Mum, okay?"

"No promises." He smiled and gave her a little shove. "Go get your beauty sleep so you can bag a footballer."

Smirking, she left the kitchen and headed upstairs. When she passed by her sister's room, Emily yelled out to her. "Lily!"

Lily stopped, confused at her sister's harsh tone. She went inside the bedroom. "What is it?"

"My pills? Where are they?"

"What pills?"

Emily shook her head and tutted. Seeing her on her feet and pacing around her room again was a strange sight to see. It was almost like she had forgotten about ever being ill. "You know exactly what pills I'm talking about, Lily. They were underneath my mattress."

"Why were they underneath your mattress?"

"To keep them away from you!"

Lily took a step towards her sister, scowling. "The fuck are you talking about?"

Emily rolled her eyes and looked away, almost as if she were too disgusted to look at Lily.

Fuck you. Who do you think you are to look away from me?

"I said," Lily repeated, "what the fuck are you talking about?"

Emily turned and looked Lily in the eye. "You think I'm stupid? You have a problem. Half my painkillers have been going down your throat lately. Is that what Dad caught you with the other night?"

"No. It was just something V gave me."

"V? The local dealer? Oh great, so you're popping ecstasy as well as painkillers now."

"It wasn't ecstasy. It wore off after like thirty minutes. What's your problem?"

"My problem," Emily said, "is that you obviously have a drug problem."

Lily rolled her eyes and turned to leave. "Whatever."

"Give me the pills back, Lil, or I'll tell Mum. I mean it. Every single one. I counted them, so I'll know."

"You counted them? God, you need to chill out, Em. Actually no, in fact you should fuck right off. You're feeling better, for one day, and you suddenly think you can start this bullshit with me? I've had to put up with you dying for over a year, playing second fiddle with Mum and Dad, having to move house and look after you every time you're too weak to wipe your own ass."

Emily sneered. "You're right, I'm better now, which means I won't watch you piss your life away. Do you have any idea how lucky you are? Try going through what I have, then you'll see how fucking disgusting it is for you to play games with your health. Haven't Mum and Dad been through enough?"

For the first time in her life, Lily wanted to smack her sister in the mouth. "I should have stopped him," she muttered. "You don't deserve what we did for you."

"I don't even know what that means, Lil, but you have

two minutes to return my pills. Then you can watch me flush 'em down the toilet."

"Fine. I only needed them for my period pain, anyway. I'll just suffer instead if it makes you happier."

"You have more periods than the book I'm reading. You're not fooling anyone."

"Fuck off!" Lily stormed out of the bedroom and across the landing. She grabbed her sister's pills from the make-up box on her dresser and took them back, throwing them right at Emily's face.

"That's mature," she said, shielding herself with a bony arm.

"Choke on 'em."

Lily went back into her own bedroom and slammed the door behind her. Her mum shouted from somewhere below, but she didn't come upstairs to complain.

That bitch. That goddamn bald-headed, self-righteous bitch.

Me and Dad saved her life. We saved her life, and she dares speak to me like that?

We should have let her die.

Lily felt a little sick at herself for thinking such a horrible thing, but the anger inside her was a nasty, spiteful thing that didn't care who it hurt. What mattered was that it felt good and told her she was right. Nobody else was on her side except the angry voice inside her head, so she was happy for it to stick around.

She rooted around in her make-up box to see if, by chance, she had missed a pill. Feeling the way she did right now, she needed something to take the edge off more than ever.

But there were no pills to be found. In her offended rage, she had tossed every single one back at her sister, truly convinced she didn't even want them.

But I do. I want the pills.

She slumped forward over her table, groaning, and knocking aside hairbrushes and lipsticks. Her left hand clamped around something thin and long, and she prepared to launch it across the room, but its sleek, metallic texture caused her to stop.

Nail scissors.

The sharp stainless steel tips dug into Lily's palm as she gripped them. The pain hit pause on her anger, gave her a moment of clarity and peace. It reminded her she was alive – and that she mattered.

I matter!

The pain was good. Lily wanted more of it.

––––––––

Jake was surprised he'd stayed awake until almost eleven, seeing as he had spent last night sleeping in his car. He expected to be tired, but instead he was full of energy and felt capable of going for a late-night run. Experience told him, however, that it was best to try to keep to a normal sleep routine. With the way tempers had been flaring, he didn't want to sleep in all morning and awake grumpily.

Maggie was already in bed, so he crept quietly across the landing. Emily's door was open. He looked inside and saw her snoozing away steadily on her back. For the first night in over a year, he didn't need to worry about her. No more nightmares of finding her ice-cold beneath her duvet or finding her covered in her own vomit.

Lily's door was also slightly ajar, and her light was still on. Jake didn't want her staying up all night, so he carefully pushed her door open in order to tell her to go to sleep.

She wasn't in her bed.

Jake scanned the room, eyes passing over the vanity table, the chest of drawers…

Lily was huddled in the corner, her head pressed against the wall.

"Lily, honey, what are you doing?"

"Sleeping," she said, but her voice was barely a mumble.

Jake gripped the door frame, his fingers clawing into the wood. "Have you taken something again?"

"Go way."

"Lily, I swear to G…" He stormed into the room, approaching where she lay slumped in the corner. If this was how she was going to behave, they would have to get her into counselling, or lock her in her room until she straightened ou—

Jake paused, stumbled, and fell against Lily's bed.

His daughter was soaked in blood. Her eyes were closed, but her eyelids flickered, at least letting him know she was alive and that he hadn't been imagining her voice, but she was in a bad way.

"Lily? W-what have you done, sweetheart?"

"Let me sleep."

He pushed himself away from the bed and dropped to the carpet beside her. Without asking, he grabbed at her body, trying to figure out where the blood was coming from. She was still wearing her T-shirt from earlier, but she had kicked off her jeans and was wearing only her knickers and socks.

The blood was coming from the inside of her left thigh, a deep and grizzly gouge, its pink insides still moist. The blood had congealed into a sticky gel, stifling further blood flow, but there was at least a pint's worth all over the inside of both Lily's legs.

Jake shook her and urged her awake, but all she did was

moan sleepily, as if he were being unreasonable for both-ering her. "Lily! Lily, open your eyes and look at me."

She wouldn't.

"Why did you do this? Why? I… I don't understand it. I know I've let you down, honey, but there's no need to hurt yourself." He started to cry, wondering if these were the consequences he was due.

Please don't tell me Lily's life has been taken instead of mine. If that's the deal, I don't want it. I would rather bleed to death myself.

"You hear me?" he shouted. "I don't fucking want it!"

Dizziness and mania overwhelming him, Jake looked at his beautiful daughter and wept. Memories of her childhood swept over him, the days teaching her to swim at Cocks Moors Woods, putting his hand beneath her tiny round belly while she kicked and splashed. He thought about her fifth birthday – the last she had shared with Nanny Penshaw – when she had dropped her caterpillar cake on the floor while running to show everybody. Rather than cry, she had laughed hysterically, enjoying the moment of chaos far more than she would have the taste of the cake.

She's always been tough.

Emily is brave, but Lily is the strong one. She always wants to do everything for herself, no help from anyone.

Wants to? Or has no choice.

Moaning in misery, Jake tried to count the afternoons Lily had come home from school to an empty house, or the times she had eaten a sandwich or takeaway pizza instead of a home-cooked meal. How many times had she tried talking to him and Maggie, only to be ignored as they fussed over Emily?

I failed her. I failed Lily and now she's hurt. So badly hurt.

But her worst damage is on the inside.

Jake needed to make things right, needed to fix it all. An

overwhelming sense of power came over him, a certainty that he could do anything, and that everything would be all right. His head pounded, but there was no pain. It was like when his penis became engorged in the morning – it was a sensual throbbing, a pulsing of life.

Blood flowing.

"Jake? Jake, what the fuck are you doing?"

Jake realised he had left the present, but he came plummeting back to earth now with a brain-rattling crash. His blurred vision sharpened as his eyes came to rest on Maggie standing in the doorway. The contorted horror on her face was something he had never seen before, her mouth wide open, eyes bulging.

"Lily cut herself," he said. "We need to get her help."

"Get away from her, you freak!"

"What are you talking about? Maggie, I found her like—" He looked down and saw blood all over his hands. Had he touched her? Touched Lily?

Yes, when I tried to wake her up.

Lily moaned, her cheeks sallow. Instead of merely coating her legs, blood now stained Lily's T-shirt in a fine spatter.

Jake's mouth tasted of copper, his saliva thick – too thick. He swallowed, and then realised his face was wet.

Maggie stepped into the room, her shock replaced by aggression. "Get the fuck away from her right now."

Jake rubbed his mouth against his arm and jolted when his wrist came back smeared with fresh blood.

Lily's blood.

What did I do?

He saw the fresh puncture marks on either side of the original deep gash in Lily's thigh.

"You were feeding on her," Maggie yelled at him. "What the fuck is wrong with you?"

Jake leapt from his knees to his feet. He seemed to move too quickly, as if his body predicted his intentions before his brain even thought them.

Maggie stepped aside and pointed to the doorway. "Get out! Get out of this house right now."

Emily appeared on the landing, rubbing sleep from her eyes. "W-what's going on?" She looked inside and saw Lily, then the blood all over Jake's face. The panic was immediate. "Lil? Lil, what happened? Lily, wake up!"

Jake stood in the middle of the room, confused. Fearful.

Emily ran to Lily and started shaking her. Maggie moved to do the same, but as she passed Jake, she looked him in the eye and growled. "Leave. Leave right this second or I'll call the police."

Jake couldn't understand what was going on. He saw no other option but to do exactly what his wife demanded. He ran down the stairs, grabbed his jacket and car keys, and sprinted out of the house, covered in his daughter's blood.

CHAPTER
SIXTEEN

JAKE RAN ALONG THE PAVEMENT, once again stalking Tovey Avenue at near midnight. The lampposts seemed to burn, they were so bright, and every house along the street seemed to whisper to him, like he could sense the sleeping souls within.

I drank my daughter's blood. What the hell is wrong with me?

He didn't know what to do or where to go. Should he get in his car and leave? Would Maggie talk to him once she'd cooled off?

There's no cooling off from this.

I'm a monster.

If George had been alive, Jake might have gone there, but as it was, there was only one other place he could think to go.

Mr Cho's.

For the second time that week, Jake paid his neighbour a late-night visit. This time, Jing must have been asleep, because it took almost five minutes for the front door to open. He appeared in matching pyjama trousers and shirt.

John the pug was also wearing pyjamas, which was absurd, but the least of Jake's worries right now.

"Jake? What is it? Because of you, I have barely slept a wink this week. Are you… are you covered in blood?"

"My daughter's." Jake didn't know if he could get the words out. They were too terrible. "She cut herself, and instead of helping her, I drank her blood."

Jing gasped and teetered on the spot. "Y-you best come in."

Jake lowered his head in relief. "Thank you. Thank you so much. I have no place else to go."

Jing let him inside and closed the door. Without being asked, Jake went into the lounge and sat down in an armchair. He put his head in his hands and shuddered.

Jing sat in a chair to his right, while John hopped up onto his usual spot and went to sleep.

"Tell me what happened, Jake?"

"I… I don't even know where to start. Ever since you *helped* me, I've been feeling different. My senses are more alert, my body is stronger… Every time I move, it feels like I'm twenty years younger."

Jing appeared to give it some thought. "I suppose that makes sense. You asked to be healed, so perhaps you were healed from the effects of ageing. You assume your senses are heightened, but perhaps they've merely adjusted back to how they were before age made them deteriorate. We don't notice ourselves ageing, but if we put ten years on overnight, we certainly would. The same would be true in reverse."

"I suppose you could be right."

It was nice to make a little sense of what was going on, but…

But that's not the part I'm truly concerned about.

"I've been blacking out," Jake said. "Losing my sense of

reality. When I was drinking Lily's blood, I didn't even know I was doing it."

Jing folded his arms and crossed his slippers. He might've been cold, but it was more likely he was repulsed. "She was already bleeding?" he asked. "And you fed on her?"

"That's the word Maggie used. I 'fed' on my daughter. Is that what I was doing?"

Now that he spoke about it, he was certain it was true. He felt full – sated – satisfied. His head no longer pounded and that dreadful, persistent thirst had finally gone away.

"Have you had any other symptoms?" Jing asked, as if he were some kind of doctor sitting with a patient. "Tell me every little thing."

Jake tried to think. "I-I've had this horrible thirst that won't go away, and a banging headache that seems to get worse in the light. At night, it calms down a little. Also…" He had a flash of an image in his mind. He turned his hand in front of his face and saw that his palm was red and blistered. How had he not noticed it until now? "I think I touched something that burned me. Silver."

"Are you sure? Silver burned you?"

"I'm not certain." He closed his eyes and tried to lock down what was so close to coming to the fore in his brain. "I was helping someone. Mary. Yes, I was helping an old lady named Mary fix her letterbox. There was a silver ashtray…"

Why can't I remember? It's like there's a black hole in my mind.

Jing was staring hard at him. "How did Mary react? Seeing it burn you?"

"I… I don't remember. The last thing I recall is the ashtray burning my hand and… I think I might have tossed it away in shock. You know Mary?"

"Of course. Mary pops by to see me a few times each week to get a poultice for her arthritis. She never came by this morning though. Do you have your mobile phone on you, Jake?"

"It's in my pocket."

"I'm going to give you Mary's number. I want you to call it."

"Um, okay." He waited for the number, then entered it into his phone. After calling it, he put the phone to his ear. It rang and rang and rang. "There's no answer. It is midnight, though."

"Mary rarely sleeps at night. She would have answered if she could."

"If she could?"

Jing looked over at the slumbering John, letting out a long, weary sigh. "It is as I feared. You have paid a grave price for what you asked."

"What do you mean, Jing?"

"I fear the reason you are struggling to remember things, Jake, is because it is better that you forget them. I fear for Mary."

"Don't be silly. I'm sure she's fine. I wouldn't hurt an old lady."

Jing looked him in the eye, almost like he was trying to peer inside him. "I believe *you* wouldn't hurt anyone, Jake, but I'm not sure you're fully in control of your own actions. I think you let something in."

"Let something in? You mean I'm possessed?" He smirked, although he wasn't finding it at all funny. In fact, he hated the fact he couldn't immediately dismiss the suggestion as ridiculous. The bizarre had become normal on Tovey Avenue.

"Not possessed exactly," Jing said.

"Then what? Tell me what's wrong with me."

"Wait here a moment." Jing got up and left the room. When he returned, he was holding a thick, ancient-looking book with lots of loose pages sticking out of it. He set it down at the coffee table and bid Jake to join him on the cushions.

Jake plonked himself down and peered at the book – upside down to him. It was full of Chinese writing and faded pencil drawings.

"The legacy of my family," Jing explained. "My great-great-grandfather began this book and passed it down. As the last Cho Zhou male, it now belongs to me, but after I'm gone, it will likely be forgotten."

Jing spun the heavy book around on the table with noticeable effort. He then leafed through the various pages until he got about halfway. "I told you and your daughter that I do not know the entities beyond this realm, but that was only partly true. A few are known to me. This being is one of them."

Jake frowned, looking down at the indecipherable text. All he could make sense of was the drawing. It showed a creature much like a bat, but with double wings like a drag-onfly. Its belly was blistered and bulging with what looked like egg sacs. Its eyes were red, and in its mouth was the bloody corpse of a human being. The creature appeared to be huge. "What is this? The Cho Zhou guide to demons?"

"In a way, yes. My ancestors were what you might call Shaman, men and women tasked with protecting the villages in which they lived. There was once a time in human history when we were not alone, nor were we top of the food chain. Monsters preyed upon us in the night and took us in our sleep. My bloodline fought back against those monsters."

"Things just get weirder and weirder with you, Jing. Last week, I was worried about settling into a new house. Now I'm talking about bat monsters preying on human beings."

Jing smiled, although it was pitying. "The monsters are mostly gone in these days of technology and mechanical warfare, but I believe you and I brought one back. This creature. Its name is Xindrac."

"Xindrac? Cooler than Henry, I suppose."

"Xindrac first appeared in China during the contentious Three Kingdoms era. After a particularly gruesome battle, in what is now the Szechuan region, a cloud of horseshoe bats from a nearby cave emerged to feast upon twelve thousand dying warriors, attracted by their screams and the stink of their blood. The bats drank their victim's lifeblood as it left their body, still hot and steaming. One particular dying man, a vicious warlord named Bo Lin, refused to obey fate, and his soul seeped into of one of the bats feasting upon him." Jing tapped the page of his book. "And so, on that day, in the middle of a blood-soaked battlefield, a new creature was born. Xindrac – the winged devourer."

"And you're saying this thing is inside me now?" Jake uttered, wide-eyed.

Jing nodded. "I believe that, in order to save your life, you had to take in a spirit, one strong enough to keep your body alive. You see, whenever we contact the entities beyond the earthly veil, it is much like an auction. We make a request and multiple beings consider fulfilling it. It appears Xindrac took your contract when it was offered. He is back now, inhabiting you as he once did that lowly bat on the killing fields."

Jake couldn't help but chuckle, despite the shiver up his spine and the gooseflesh on his arms. Something in his guts was twisting and squirming, like a tapeworm learning it had been discovered. "What makes you think this monster set up shop inside me?"

"Because Xindrac feeds on the blood of the living." Jing pointed to the Chinese text, ignoring that Jake couldn't read it. "After the Three Kingdoms war finally ended, the new emperor had his forces drive Xindrac out of China, all the way into Eastern Europe, where he eventually settled in Romania. There, for over a thousand years, he was a scourge on the land, devouring peasants and nobility alike. Xindrac enslaved land owners and took their homesteads, killed farmers and controlled the local food supply, and, of course, bought favour with those in high power, which allowed him to act with impunity and even grant himself an earldom. Xindrac went by many names during those dark times, the most common being Drac, Vlad, and Lord Vampyre."

"You're kidding me. Jing, are you giving me the Chinese version of Dracula?"

"I am only telling you what my ancestors recorded. Have I seen these things for myself – of course not – but I do trust the word of my bloodline."

Jake rolled his eyes. "So what happened to Xindrac according to your ancestors?"

"In 1476, a furious mob stormed his castle in Transylvania. They cornered the beast in his wine cellar and beheaded him, finally sending him to the great beyond, where we would later contact him in 2023."

"That still doesn't cut it for me." Jake chewed at his lip for a second. "You're saying there's a bloodthirsty monster inside me, but it doesn't feel that way. I'm still me. I'm not a killer."

"Was it you who fed on your daughter's blood?"

Jake couldn't answer.

Jing tapped the pages of his book again. "Xindrac fed on

the blood of the living. He was emboldened by the night and weakened by the light. Silver, allegedly, burned him like a fiery blade, and while as strong as ten men, he was constantly unfulfilled, needing to feed regularly lest he become infirm."

"What else? No reflection? Repulsed by garlic?"

"Repulsed by smells."

"What?"

"It is written that Xindrac's senses were so heightened that powerful smells and high-pitched sounds would aggravate him greatly. There is no mention of mirrors, but it says that if cut, his blood would boil upon contact with wood, leather, or human flesh."

"I have acid blood." Jake closed his eyes, wondering where it all ended. "Well, we can test that out, right?"

Jing stared at him. "Yes, I suppose we can."

Jake waited while Jing went inside his little drawer. The sight of another needle made him groan, but he was eager to prick himself and prove that all this was complete nonsense.

"You should do this yourself," said Jing, offering him the needle.

Jake wasted no time. He took the needle and jabbed it firmly into the pad of this thumb, immediately drawing blood. Rather than grab a sheet of paper, he inconsiderately squeezed his injury over the old parchment inside Jing's book. Jing cringed, but he didn't object to the despoiling.

A drop of blood fell, struck the edge of the page, and spread throughout the old fibres.

Nothing happened.

"Well, that's disappointing." Jake grunted. "I thought I was the new Dracula."

Jing stared at him, fear in his eyes. "Jake?"

"What? What is it?"

"Your face…"

Jake touched himself but felt nothing wrong. Not seeing a mirror in the room, he pulled out his phone and opened up the selfie camera. What he saw pierced his chest like an icy spear. "What is this? A joke?"

"No joke, Jake."

Jake's face had distorted, his brow thick like a caveman's, his lower jaw grossly oversized. He felt sharpened fangs against his tongue, which itself was now different.

My tongue is forked.

Like a freaking snake's.

The shock threatened to overwhelm Jake. He clutched the coffee table to keep from falling forward. Curved fingernails the length of hairpins gouged thin lines into the wood.

"Stay calm, Jake." Jing put a hand up. "Stay calm."

"Stay calm?" He now spoke with a lisp. "Stay fucking calm?"

"The pain of pricking your thumb must have brought out the beast, but it is not in control. You are, Jake. Stay calm, and don't let Xindrac take over."

Jake slammed his phone face down on the table, unable to look at himself any longer. "What do I do? How do I fix this?"

"You can't fix it! It was the bargain you made. There's a cruel, insatiable beast inside you, and it will devour everyone around you unless you control it. I… I'm sorry. Jake…"

There was a hissing sound. At first, Jake thought it was him, but then he realised it was coming from the book on the table. The corner of the page was bubbling. The drop of his blood had turned jet-black and was stewing like oil spat from a hot pan.

"Xindrac is inside you," Jing said. "Y-you're…"

"A vampire." Jake leapt to his feet, flipping the coffee table over and sending it across the room. John, the pug, immediately started barking and hopped down off the sofa. "You need to fix this, Jing. Fix it, or I'll rip your goddamn throat out."

Jing clambered to his feet and backed off, suddenly seeming very frail. "I think you should leave, Jake. P-please."

"Leave? You did this to me, Jing? You need to help me."

"It is beyond my power. Forgive me."

John jumped up against Jake's leg, still barking, but the stocky little dog was too small to bother him, or even unbalance him, so he kneed the pooch out of the way.

Jake stepped towards Jing.

I'm going to tear him apart.

How could he do this to me? I want to see him bleed.

He set his feet apart, preparing to leap. Preparing to explode with ferocious strength and speed, all of it aimed at the small man cowering before him.

An awful stench washed over Jake.

He stumbled, groaned, and held his nostrils closed with thumb and forefinger. The vile smell wouldn't go away. He searched for its source, able to trace it through the air by sensing the individual molecules drifting towards him.

John! That disgusting dog has let one go again.

Jake was furious, the smell so bad it was almost debilitating. He let out an inhuman roar, his fangs bared, forked-tongue hissing.

"Leave now," Jing demanded, cowering in the corner. "You are not welcome here any more."

———

"Uncle, this is a bad idea. I saw the guy leave; he was covered in blood, and the old lady…" V tried to swallow, his mouth dry. "She had no fucking face, man. He tore her to shreds like a goddamn animal."

His uncle stopped the Range Rover at the edge of the road and turned off the engine. Then he glared at V in the back seat. "I stabbed this guy twice, and he's still walking around. That's a problem, nephew. At the very least, I'm going to go have a talk with him and see what's up. Seems all he's done since moving in is cause trouble. But it stops tonight. Nothing like a midnight visit to shit a guy up."

Bekim, filling out the front passenger seat, smashed his fist against his meaty palm. "Even if I have to cut man into little pieces and bury him."

"He's got family, right?" said Doser, sitting beside Vincent in the back seat. "We could always threaten to hurt them if he doesn't keep quiet."

"Leave the thinking to me, sweetheart," Dev warned him. "We don't want to start a fire because you overused that single brain cell of yours."

Doser chuckled as if it were a good-natured joke, but in reality, Dev had no time for V's mates. They were just low-level pushers destined for a long stretch.

V watched Doser pull his jacket zip up to his neck, hiding half his face.

It's a nervous gesture. He does it all the time. All the designer gear is just a place for him to hide. How much front does he put up? How scared does my uncle really make him?

How scared does he make me?

Dev got out of the car and ordered everyone else to do the same. V did so reluctantly, not wanting to be on Tovey Avenue again, or anywhere near the bloodshed he knew lurked behind the front door of one of the houses.

Mary. I'm sure the old girl was called Mary. She was harmless. Why did Jake kill her?

"Which is the guy's house?" Dev asked V.

"Um, I'm not sure."

Doser pointed down the street. "That one. Twenty-six, I think."

V really didn't want his uncle visiting Lily's house. It wasn't out of the question that he would set Bekim loose, breaking fingers or sticking his dick in…

I won't let that happen. I can't.

But what the fuck can I do?

Everyone started walking, but V flinched and hopped back towards the car. "Fuck me! Unc, that's him. Right over there."

Jake was storming out of a house further up the street. It looked like the old Chinese guy's place. At least he wasn't covered in blood this time, but there was something different about him. He strode more like a lion than a man, crouched down like he was about to pounce. He moved like a predator.

"Unc, I really think we should just leave it."

V yelped as Bekim shoved him back against the car with a powerful fist. His head smashed against the Range Rover's rear window, but he didn't dare complain.

Doser immediately grabbed V and pulled him out of the way, making it look like he was trying to get him moving and doing what he was told, but really he was shielding him from Bekim, who looked ready to launch a follow-up attack.

"Just let your fam do what he wants, V," Doser whispered in his ear. "No point standing in the way and getting a slap, is there?"

V was worried about Lily, and about Jake, but also about his uncle's anger, so he got moving and quickly caught up.

Bekim and Dev were already on the pavement, storming towards Jake as he came the other way.

"Hold up there, sunshine. We meet again." Dev spoke in a friendly manner, which was a little sick considering he had recently stabbed the guy coming towards them.

Jake froze and seemed confused. He'd obviously been in a world of his own, because he gazed vacantly at Dev for a moment as if they'd never met. Slowly, however, things seemed to dawn on him. "You…"

"Yeah, me. We had a little chat the other night, remember?"

"You stabbed me."

Dev looked around, clearly disliking the accusation. "Don't know anything about that, mate, sorry. You're looking pretty good, though, for someone who reckons they got a shanking."

"I heal fast." Jake's expression was non-existent. V couldn't tell if he was afraid, angry, or totally uninterested.

Dev took another step closer.

Bekim did the same, flexing his thick arms and puffing out his chest. "That is some very fast healing, mister. I think maybe you were not stabbed at all."

Jake's expression finally arrived, settling on a crooked grin. "Oh, I was stabbed all right. Twice." He tapped his stomach underneath his grey woollen jacket. The same one he'd been wearing the other night. "Right here."

"Well," Dev tutted, "you must've done something to deserve it, sunshine."

Jake turned to face V, causing V to step back cautiously. "What do you think, Vinnie? Did I deserve it? Did I do anything wrong when I moved here to look after my family? Or was I just minding my own business, trying to get through the day?"

"I…" V was about to agree that Jake had done nothing to start this war, but then he saw his uncle's glare and reconsidered. "You were disrespectful to me, bruv, which means you had to get taught a lesson, innit?"

Dev smiled at Jake. "You see? This is a dangerous place, and if you go around making noise, someone's going to come along and shut you up. Do you understand what I'm telling you?"

Jake started laughing.

V groaned inwardly. *Don't fucking laugh. Just promise to keep your head down and beg for mercy. Wasn't getting stabbed twice enough for you?*

"Did I say something funny?" Dev was growing visibly angry, his fists clenched, his eyes narrowing. "Because I ain't a fucking comedian, mate. Don't mistake me for one."

Jake took a step forward, grinning so widely that his teeth caught the light of a nearby lamppost. "I don't think you're a comedian. I think you're a fucking clown, mate. A pathetic little clown who can't do anything useful, so he deals drugs to convince people he's not a sad, lonely clown." His grin stretched even wider. "But beneath that silly goatee and the slicked-back hair, I can still see your face paint, buddy. I still see the miserable, sad little clown." Unbelievably, Jake balled his fists and made a theatrical crying gesture in front of his eyes with them.

"Do you have any idea who the fuck you're talking to?" Dev demanded, red in the face.

Jake took another step forward and grinned manically, right in his face. "Yeah, of course I know who I'm talking to. You're Bobo the fucking clown."

Bekim didn't need to be asked. He swung a knuckle-duster at the side of Jake's head.

Jake stepped lazily out of the way, as if he'd known the

punch was coming. The big Romanian overbalanced and went stumbling down the pavement.

"Missed me." Jake shook his head at Dev, tutting like a disappointed parent. "That's what happens when you hire children and monkeys to do your dirty work."

Dev's fists were clenching and unclenching at his sides. He was breathing heavily, that familiar rage overtaking him. "I'll work you myself, mate, if you're not careful."

Doser looked at V. He clearly couldn't believe what he was seeing, and neither could V. Strangely, a part of him was enjoying it. He liked seeing Uncle Dev made a fool of.

But he's not going to take this. It's about to turn very ugly.

"You want to be a tough guy?" Jake fronted up against Dev, their noses almost touching. "Try doing an honest day's work. Try paying the bills and taking care of a family. You think being a criminal makes you a hard man? Buddy, it's the easiest fucking thing in the world. You deal drugs and throw your weight around because you're weak. Weak and afraid."

Bekim flew in with a second punch, but Jake once again stepped out of the way without even flinching. This time Bekim bellowed in anger, and as soon as he regained his balance, he threw a tackle at Jake's legs. Instead of dodging, Jake brought his knee up and caught the Romanian on the side of his lowered head. It didn't knock Bekim out, but it sent him sprawling into the middle of the road, where he landed hard on his hands and knees.

For the first time in V's life, he saw his uncertainty in his uncle's eyes.

"You're making some pretty big mistakes here," he warned Jake.

But it didn't cow Jake in the slightest. Something about him had changed. He glared at Dev now, no longer smiling.

"You listen to me, Bobo. It's over, okay? If I see you, or any of your teenage drug dealers, on Tovey Avenue again, I'm going to come visit you where you live and slice your fucking neck while you sleep."

"Don't threaten me. Do not make that mistake."

"I'm threatening you. What are you going to do about it?"

"You don't want to find out."

Jake's smile returned. "If I were you, Bobo, I would put some fresh face paint on and go back to juggling at the circus, because your days of dealing junk on this street are over. You had your shot, and I'm still here. Next time, it'll be you who walks away bleeding."

Bekim got to his feet and stormed towards Jake, but he stopped in his tracks when Dev put a hand up. "Don't bother," he barked. "We're not doing this now."

Bekim was nothing if not obedient, so he stepped back into the road. V couldn't be sure, but he thought he saw a look of relief on the big man's face. Bekim was glad the fight was over.

Because he was getting his arse handed to him.

Jake grinned at Dev for a moment more, then pushed past him and carried on down the street, whistling a merry tune that sounded a lot like ghostbusters.

Dev was clearly furious, so nobody said anything as he stood there – not even Bekim. Doser and V shared another look of disbelief, but they knew this wasn't the end of it. There was no way Dev would just stop dealing on Tovey Avenue because someone told him to. He would need to deal with this.

And he wasted no time.

Dev got on his phone and made a call.

All V could think about was Lily.

———

Jake had thought about trying to go home, but what Jing had told him scared him. Left him afraid of himself. What if he tried to hurt his family?

While the story of Xindrac was farfetched and fanciful, he couldn't deny there was something inside him, something powerful he couldn't control.

But I'm still me.

I think.

Awakening from his thoughts, Jake found himself sprinting through alleyways and hopping over fences, a rabid beast tracking the grumbling Range Rover with his ears alone. He stayed close to the main roads, attuning himself to the particular, unique sound of the car's engine. He could hear it at a distance, and followed it towards its destination.

Jake intended to take care of his enemies once and for all tonight.

He was thirsty again.

His body surged with power.

The Range Rover came to a stop in an old part of town, a place where converted factories were now discount furniture shops and Polish supermarkets. His prey stopped right outside what appeared to be a snooker hall.

Jake watched Vincent and his friend run inside the building, followed by the kid's uncle. The big, clumsy, stinking guy stayed in the car, though, and quickly drove off.

I'll have to deal with him later.

Jake crept up to the steps at the front of the building and winced when a floodlight came on and shone in his face. He hissed, once again detecting a forked tongue in his mouth.

The vampire inside him had come out, unable to hide in bright lights. Good, he would put it to good use.

Am I doing this? Is this me?

Rather than think too hard, Jake went inside the building, moving quickly while somehow still able to creep. A flight of carpeted stairs led immediately upwards. Jake sensed a dozen heartbeats above.

Each one seemed to call out to him. Each one sang its own unique tune.

He saw human-shaped outlines, pulsing in and out of his vision like blips on a sonar screen.

Jake paused at the bottom of the stairs, a little dizzy, a little disorientated. A voice whispered in the back of his head, but he couldn't work out if it was urging him forward or calling him back.

Several minutes passed like seconds, and Jake barely moved a millimetre until he was alerted by half the heartbeats upstairs suddenly retreating. There must have been another exit somewhere, because they exited the building on its far side.

Still plenty left.

Jake stalked up the stairs and pushed open the door at the top. His inner vampire had gone back into hiding, but it was still there, right at the surface. He scanned the room, seeing everything all at once, smelling and hearing and feeling the very air itself.

None of these people were the prey he was looking for.

There were two pairs of men drinking beers and playing snooker, but no sign of Vincent or Dev. The strangers glared at Jake, but then went back to their game. The stench of weed hung in the air, disgusting and acrid.

"Where's the boss?" Jake asked, almost in a bellow.

All four men straightened up and glared in his direction

again. One man, a large black guy with dark ink up both arms, ambled towards him. "The fuck you on about, mate? This is a private club, and it's after hours."

"Where. Is. The. Boss? You know, has a fabulous goatee and drives a three-litre penis extension that is likely to break down on him before the year is through." Jake shook his head and tutted. "I mean, seriously, Range Rovers are rotten for reliability."

"Dunno who you're on about, mate, but I suggest you stop talking and get the fuck out of here." He cracked his neck to the side. "Before you get hurt."

Jake tilted his head and studied the well-muscled man. His flesh was beautiful, so smooth and clean. It seemed to breathe. Unlike the other three men, this one hadn't smoked or drunk anything tonight. He was pure, like bottled mineral water. "Either you tell me where Billy Goatee is right now or I'm going to hurt you."

All four men broke out in hysterical laughter. Jake laughed too, finding the sound of him making such a threat mildly comical. Laughing most of all, however, was the large, angry man to whom he had made the threat.

"You're hilarious, mate, and you're lucky I'm still on licence or you'd already have gone out the fucking window. Leave now, while you can still walk."

"Last chance," said Jake, meeting the man's glare with a smile. "Tell me where I can find Bobo and I'll leave you intact."

The guy looked back at his friends and murmured. "This guy? Can't say I didn't give him fair warning, right?"

Jake looked down at his own shoulder as a large hand was clasped around it. Meanwhile, another hand swung towards his navel. It struck him at high speed, four large knuckles crashing against his abdominal muscles like a freight train. Mike Tyson himself could not have hit any harder.

"Ouch!" said Jake, frowning. "That the best you got?"

Despite his foe's obvious strength, the blow hadn't even caused Jake to take a step back, or even flinch. It clearly unnerved his attacker, but not enough to send the man running.

"What's your name?" Jake asked politely. "Would be nice to know who I'm about to kill."

The man grabbed a pool cue from one of his mates and swung it like a baseball bat. It crashed against Jake's ribs and snapped in two. The blow sent him stumbling to the side a couple of steps, but he soon straightened up and breathed through the brief flare-up of pain. Clearly, he could still be hurt, but it wasn't that much of a big deal.

Now the four men were visibly unnerved. They glanced at each other, as if seeing who would dare attack next, but none of them did. Even their big, scary leader had backed off.

Jake stepped forward, grabbing the big guy by his dark, tattooed wrist and snapping it like a twig. He fell to his knees immediately, squealing like a blood-filled pig. "Please!" he said. "It hurts."

"Goatee? Where is he?"

One of the other men spoke. "Dev went out back with the others. You just missed him. H-he was all tooled up and ready to go off somewhere."

Jake scowled. "He's looking for me. Tell him I'm here."

The big man with the broken wrist cowered on the floor. Jake found his fear intoxicating. He wanted more of it. He reached down and dragged the guy to his feet, pushing him back against one of the snooker tables. "Any last words before I eat you?"

The man quivered and tried to get some words out, but all he could manage was, "Y-your face!"

Jake felt canines the size of shark's teeth inside his mouth, jutting out past his lower lips. He licked his lips, ready to indulge his rapidly growing thirst. "You're about to meet my dark passenger and I… No, no wait, I can do better than that." He cleared his throat. "You're about to meet my wetter half. No… that's still awful. Oh, sod it, I'm too hungry to think."

Jake opened his mouth and inhaled the man's screams.

A pitiful voice cried out to him. "Mr Penshaw!"

Jake closed his mouth and growled. He smelled urine, and realised it was coming from the trembling man he was holding, so he tossed him aside with a disgusted sneer. He then turned to face the one who had called out to him.

"Who's interrupting my dinner?"

Vincent was trembling, as were the three men standing beside him with pool cues, shoulder to shoulder like a line of spearmen. "It's me."

"Vincent? Oh, you're just what I'm in the mood for." He stalked towards the lad, and to his credit, he stood his ground.

"What happened to you, Mr Penshaw? Y-your face? It's all messed up."

"Careful," he said around his oversized fangs. "You'll hurt my feelings."

The three men took their opportunity to run, sprinting for the exit and leaving Vincent – a teenage boy – behind to fend for himself. The piss-soaked big guy went after them, clutching his broken wrist and sobbing.

"Looks like you're more of a man than they are," Jake said. "I bet you taste better too. I've been waiting for this."

Vincent shook his head, a lump bulging in his throat as

he swallowed. "I ain't a man. I thought I was, but it was all bullshit. Truth is, I'm about ready to piss my pants."

Jake wrinkled his nose. "Don't. I dislike the smell."

"Yeah, it was, um, a figure of speech. I'm not a man, but you are, Jake."

Jake flicked his forked tongue. "Are you sure about that?"

"Yeah. Lily told me about all the sacrifices you made to look after Emily when she got sick, about how hard you worked to build a business, and how you wanted more for your family than what you had growing up. You came up on the streets too, yeah?"

"But I left them. I didn't take the easy path like you. I never made victims of other people."

Vincent looked towards the door where the four men had fled. He would have to get past Jake to escape. "Think I'll disagree there, bruv. You were just about to eat Gary Dobson."

Jake leapt into the air, covering ten feet like it was nothing. He landed right up against Vincent, his teeth bared and a high-pitched screech emanating from his throat. "Your days of hurting innocent people are over."

"Lily's in danger."

Jake recoiled. "What?"

"Uncle Dev is on his way down your ends right now to fuck you up, but you're standing here, innit?"

"So tell him to come get me. I'll be waiting."

Vincent was trembling like a leaf, but his voice was even and firm. "It ain't like that now, bruv. He's gonna make an example of you. My uncle's a sick fuck and you humiliated him in front of the mandem."

"Why are you warning me? Your uncle won't like that."

"So what? I fucking hate him. When my mum died, I

thought he was a good guy, taking me in when he didn't have to, but all he's ever done is use me. He was gonna let me take the fall for stabbing you. My own flesh and bl—"

"I don't care about your problems!" Jake hissed, his tongue flickering.

"Yeah, okay, you got bigger problems than me, I get it. Look, I'm sorry for the beef I caused – seriously, I wish I could take it all back – but listen to what I'm telling you, fam. My uncle is on his way to your gaff right now to do some proper bad shit. You need to leave."

Jake stared at him, his mind vibrating and full of smoke. Vincent's blood called out to him, pulsing through his neck, behind his eyes, and down both arms and each of his legs.

I'm not in control. This isn't me.

"Believe me or don't, bruv, but I care about Lily."

"You gave her drugs." His forked tongue escaped his mouth again, flicking against Vincent's cheek and making him squirm. "You took advantage of her."

"I fucked up, bruv, but I'm trying to fix it. Get in your goddamn car and floor it. You and me can wait."

"I didn't drive here, I ran."

Vincent frowned. "That's impossible."

"Look at my face and tell me what's impossible."

"Please, just go. Your family needs you."

The entry door opened at the front of the snooker hall. Someone walked in and gasped. "V, that you, bruv?"

Jake turned to see a black youth swaying back and forth, either drunk or incredibly high. He obviously didn't see Jake's face because he carried on talking to V.

"Your uncle's called for the troops, fam, innit? Shit's going down on Tovey Avenue and we all gotta go."

Vincent reached out and grabbed Jake's arm, looking him in the eye and showing no fear at what he was. "If you're still Lily's dad in there, then get the fuck out of here now. Go!"

Something shifted inside Jake. The thirst and hatred ebbed away, the smoke inside his mind clearing. He nodded at Vincent, not quite able to say thanks, but appreciating that the lad was actually trying to help him.

"Stick yourself in the microwave. I'll eat you later."

"Bruv, that was lame."

Jake had no time to argue. He sprinted away, almost knocking the intoxicated kid over as he rushed past him to the stairs, faster than any human being ought to move.

I may be a monster, but no one is hurting my family.

CHAPTER
SEVENTEEN

LILY WAS STILL WOOZY, but the three pints of water followed by a ham sandwich and crisps had brought her back to life. Emily kept demanding they call the hospital, but Maggie wouldn't have it. Instead, she had cleaned Lily's wounded thigh and wrapped it in bandages herself.

Lily's sliced flesh throbbed, hot and painful. Her shame ached even worse.

"If we take her to see a doctor with self-harm," Maggie argued with Emily again, "she'll never be able to move past it. It'll be on her file forever. What if they keep her in for observation, or… or take her away into care?"

"What if she keels over and dies from blood loss?" Emily hit back, hands on her hips.

It was weird for Lily to see her sister up and about, yelling and making demands. She still resembled a skeleton, but already she seemed to have put on weight. In fact, she had hardly stopped eating.

"I'm fine," Lily said. "If I was going to pass out from blood loss, I would've done it already. I just want to go to bed; it's past one in the morning. And where the hell is Dad?"

Maggie handed her another pint of water. "You're not going to sleep until I'm convinced you're okay." Her voice was a mixture of angry and sad, but her expression was more desperation and confusion. She put a hand against her head and moaned. "Perhaps your sister's right. Should I be taking you to the hospital?"

"I'm fine. Where's Dad?"

Emily and Maggie looked at each other.

"Don't worry about it right now," Maggie said. "Oh Lily, why did you do something so stupid? Why would you do this to yourself?"

"Because she's a messed-up druggie," said Emily, and then gasped as if she were shocked at herself.

"You bitch!"

Maggie shook her head. "What is she talking about, Lily?"

"She's just taking a dig at me for getting high the other night. I already apologised."

Emily smirked. "Just the once, was it?"

"What are you doing?" Lily tried to look her sister in the eye, but her head was too heavy and it lowered towards the table. She was so weak, like she could fall unconscious at any moment. "Why are you being spiteful?"

"Because I'm worried about you. Now that I'm finally getting better, it's time to take care of you."

Lily rolled her eyes. "Way to be condescending, sis. Look, you don't need to worry about me. In fact, you should be thanking me."

"Thanking you for what?"

Lily grunted. "If only you knew."

"Knew what?" Emily folded her arms, growing impatient.

"Stop it!" their mum yelled, which seemed unnecessary seeing as they were barely even bickering. "Stop getting at each other, okay? I'm dealing with this by myself – again! – so I need you to be kind. Please, just be kind."

"Where's Dad?" Lily asked again, realising that her mum was obviously dealing with something. Where could he possibly be at two in the morning?

Lily had a sense her dad had been there, had been the one to find her in her room, but now he was gone and no one would say why.

"Did you chuck Dad out of the house? I swear, you two arguing is getting out of hand. He's not perfect, but he doesn't deserve to be—"

"Just leave it," Emily said. "Seriously."

"Leave what? What did Dad do?"

There was a knock on the door.

Maggie and Emily flinched.

Lily leapt up. "Is that him? It must be."

"Hold on," Maggie called, going after her. "We don't know it's your dad."

"Who else could it be in the middle of the night?"

Lily went into the hall and unlocked the front door. She opened it, expecting to see her dad. Instead, it was a stranger who punched her in the face.

———

Jake spotted the black Range Rover as soon as he turned the corner into Tovey Avenue. It was boxed in by a pair of silver BMWs. Vincent's uncle had obviously brought backup. All three cars were parked right outside Jake's house.

If he hurts my girls…
What if I'm too late?

Jake's stamina was faltering after sprinting all the way from the snooker hall. He was strong – almost indestructible – but he wasn't invincible, and he had to slow down a little to suck in air and replenish his stamina. As desperate as he was to get inside his house and protect his family, he was hesitant.

My family isn't safe while I'm like this.

I can feel myself being pushed aside and something else moving in.

Despite his fears, Jake had no choice but to go home. This was all his fault. He had moved his family away from a safe area and brought trouble down upon them. If he didn't fix this, then there was no telling what Vincent's uncle might do.

Once again, he sensed the beating hearts inside the houses of Tovey Avenue. He smelled people's rubbish bins and heard their muffled snores.

Two heartbeats beat louder than the others.

Jake stalked down the centre of the road, crouching low and blending into the night. He sensed two men standing outside his house. A thick fog surrounded them, the acrid scent of weed. A pair of deadbeats.

Anger brought Jake out of his crouch, and he approached the two men casually, not caring if they saw him. One was only a teen, but the other was a fully grown man holding a hammer. He didn't look like he was preparing to do some DIY, and when he saw Jake, he puffed up and moved into the middle of the road to meet him.

"Can I help you, mate? Bit late to be taking a stroll, ain't it?"

"This is my house. You need to leave."

The man was obviously surprised, because he frowned and went, "Huh! Thought you was already inside. Lot of people here to see you, mate."

"I'm a popular guy."

The younger man stepped out into the road. He had short dreadlocks and seemed half-asleep. "Shit, boy, you need to go deal with your shit. Bossman wants your head on a block."

The man with the hammer stepped up to Jake and scowled. "Inside, mate. Now."

Jake didn't move. He nodded at the hammer in the man's hand. "You planning on putting some shelves up?"

"I'll nail you to the fucking wall if you don't move it. The bossman wants a word with you. Inside. Now. You fucking muppet."

"I'll get to your boss. First, you're both going to piss off out of my street. Tovey Avenue belongs to me now."

The doped-up teen sucked at his teeth and then chuckled. "Man is making a play. He's a tough guy."

"You have no idea," Jake said.

The goon with the hammer waved it in front of Jake's face. "I ain't playing games here, mate. Get in the house or I'll cave your fucking skull in."

"You really don't want to see the inside of my head, buddy. It's frightening."

The goon shook his head, irritated – and then he swung his hammer low, aiming for Jake's thigh.

Jake shoved the man in the chest, interrupting his swing and throwing him ten feet backwards. He landed on his back in the road, his lungs exploding. He rolled back and forth, trying to suck in air.

The young lad stepped in front of Jake and put a hand

out. "Whoa, bruv, chill. You just fucking launched Craig Masters. Do you know who his family is?"

"The only family I care about," Jake said, "is my own."

He grabbed the stoner kid and bit into his neck, his fangs extending and his mouth sucking hungrily. His entire body surged like an overcharged battery. Thoughts and feelings flooded through him that were not his own, and suddenly he knew everything about the kid he was feeding on.

Kaydon. He's name's Kaydon.

He deals drugs to take care of his younger sister and mother. He's been smoking cannabis since he was twelve and can't sleep without it. Besides weed and his family, Formula One is the only thing he cares about. Lewis Hamilton is his idol. And he's… afraid. So afraid.

Afraid of dying.

Suddenly nauseated, Jake shoved Kaydon away from him. The lad collapsed in the road, clutching at his bleeding neck.

Jake looked up at the moon and sprayed a mouthful of sour blood into the air. Then he turned to his half-finished meal in disgust. "You taste like old coffee grounds and cigarette ash."

"I'm sorry, man." The kid cowered against the kerb. "Don't hurt me. My lil sister…"

Jake nodded. "She needs you. Maybe try to stay out of prison or the morgue?"

The older man was recovering, clutching his ribs and sucking in great gasps of air. Somehow, he had kept hold of his hammer, but the weapon didn't concern Jake in the least. He leapt over to the man and crouched beside him, his forked tongue flickering. "I did warn you."

"Y-you're a fucking dead man," he warned Jake.

"I'm not sure of the exact details," Jake said, "but you might be right. Let's see if you taste better than your friend."

The man frowned in confusion, and then screamed as Jake tore into his throat and opened up his jugular. The veins were stringy, like calamari, but the blood inside was like champagne. A straggler in a desert, dying of thirst, Jake gulped the man dry, his throat bulging and convulsing greedily. All of his tiredness went away, and he felt powerful once again.

He felt…

Strange.

A dizziness washed over Jake, not unpleasant, but rapidly increasing. He felt sleepy, confused, and…

High. I'm fucking high.

Jake threw the man down on his back, where he lay still. Dead. Drained of too much blood. His unkind face was frozen in pale shock, his mouth wide open. A monster's prey.

Horrified by what he'd done, while also ecstatic at the power coursing through his veins, Jake staggered backwards in the road. His legs crossed over themselves, as if he could no longer tell which way was which. His vision spun. Stomach acids mingled with swallowed blood and leapt into his throat – a thick, burning potion. Eyelids falling, he looked towards his house, knowing there were more monsters inside – ones that might even be worse than he was.

I… I need to get inside. I need to help my family.

The young lad was still lying on the floor, but he was propped up now on his elbow and staring. He seemed more with it than before Jake had bitten him, like the blood loss had sobered him up.

"You…" Jake said. "I drank your blood, but it was tainted. Foul. Spoiled."

The lad continued staring, as if dumbfounded and unable to speak.

"H-how much weed have you smoked, boy?"

Finally, the lad seemed confident enough to talk. Still clutching his neck, he shrugged. "Enough to kill a Shetland pony, bruv. Man has bare tolerance, innit?"

"Junk food," Jake said, and he fell down to one knee. His head was spinning, his thoughts were like spinning waltzers in his brain, making him feel sick. Sleep screamed at him, determined to take him down into the muddy well of oblivion. Powerless to fight, too tired to stay awake, he gave in.

As he faded, he thought he saw someone running across the road towards him, but before he could figure out who it was…

All was black. All was darkness.

A place for monsters.

―――

Lily's eyebrow throbbed. The flesh there, right over the bony ridge above her socket, had thickened and become puffy, like her face was made of Play-Doh. The nasty punch hadn't knocked her out though, which she was strangely proud of. It made her feel slightly less vulnerable as she sat there in nothing but knickers and a T-shirt.

Every other emotion she felt was overwhelmingly horrid. Panic, confusion, anger, and terrible, terrible fear.

Who are these people?

What are they going to do to us?

Lily, Emily, and Maggie were sitting in the lounge, side by side on the main sofa. Standing in the room with knives, hammers, and even a baseball bat were five violent men. Violent men who had punched Lily and kicked Emily on the ground until she had almost fallen unconscious. Sadistically, they hadn't touched their mum, only made her watch. Her face was covered in snot and tears now as she sat between her bruised daughters.

"What do you want?" Emily asked huskily, her jutting ribs battered by multiple blows. The sound of her sister screaming inwardly, unable to breathe, had been the worst thing Lily had ever seen. She and her mum had both screamed for help, sure that someone would come – or that a neighbour would call the police – but it had been twenty minutes now and nobody had come. Their lounge lay in tatters, the TV smashed in and the coffee table upended. These five evil men didn't care about causing a ruckus.

The window in the lounge showed only a black feature-less night. No heroes planning a rescue. Not even her dad.

It's the middle of the night. Nobody is going to get involved, even if they hear something.

The clear leader of the group was a weird-looking guy with thick gold bracelets rattling on both wrists, and slicked-back hair like an old-fashioned gangster. His goatee was jet-black, almost like it was spray-painted on. He glared at Maggie like she was an idiot. "I want your fucking husband, sweetheart, and for every minute he don't turn up, I'm gonna take it out on your pretty little daughters."

"I texted him a dozen times," she spat. "I don't know where he is."

"Well, he was wandering around the fucking street earlier tonight, love, and he made some very serious threats against me and my business interests."

"He won't do anything," Emily muttered. "Just leave and he won't do anything, we promise."

"We don't even know who you are," Maggie said desperately. "We just want to be left alone. My daughter hasn't been well. Leave and we won't tell a soul."

"Your daughter's been ill?"

She nodded.

"So fucking what?" he asked. "I don't let people threaten me and get away with it. Your husband needs to be taught a lesson, and this time he ain't gonna walk it off."

Lily frowned. "What do you mean?"

The guy looked at her and actually seemed respectful for a minute, as though he was impressed by what he was about to tell her. "I shanked your old man twice in the guts. Next day, he's walking around like nothing happened."

That was why he was covered in blood, Lily realised, remembering her dad walking down the street in a bloodstained shirt.

"You're V's uncle," she said, putting two and two together.

That was enough to get a reaction from him. He raised a thick black eyebrow. "You know V? Small world."

"He's my friend. He wouldn't want you to be doing this."

One of the other guys in the room laughed. There was an 'otherness' about him, like he wasn't from this country, and when he spoke he confirmed it with an Eastern European accent. "Ah, I think she might be V's girlfriend, boss. Should I break her in for him and teach her what to do?"

"Maybe later, Bek. Gotta give Jake a little more time to get here, but you can cause a little pain if you want to."

Lily gasped as the big man strode towards her and grabbed a fistful of her hair. He yanked her to her feet and swung her by her roots, her scalp burning. Maggie and

Emily screamed and begged, but the men in the room only laughed.

"Why don't you talk about how much V would not like *this*," the big man said, thrashing her back and forth like a bone in the jaws of a pit bull. "You tell him what Uncle Bekim did to your pretty blonde hair."

He tossed her back onto the sofa, where she fell across her mum's lap, sobbing. A thick tassel of her hair drifted down to the carpet, released from the brute's large hand. Lily prodded at her scalp and felt a bald spot the size of a fifty-pence piece.

She should've been more afraid, but instead she felt less scared, the emotion replaced by an inhospitable rage fighting to release itself. "Pig," she said, and snorted like an animal. "Pathetic pig."

The big man – Bekim – smirked at her. "I think you're confused, little lady. Pigs are the ones who wear uniforms and play with each other's dicks. We are wolves, and we eat little lambs like you."

"You have no fucking idea who you're dealing with," Lily said. "The things I'm capable of."

"Quiet!" said the one in charge, V's uncle. *Uncle Dev.* "Save your anger for your old man, blondie. He's the cause of all this. It's his fault you're never gonna forget this night as long as you live."

She sneered. "I bet most women forget a night with you by the time morning comes around."

Dev actually flinched at her comment, and it was wonderful. Lily knew pain was probably coming her way, but that little moment of seeing his pride hurt was worth it.

Surprisingly, he didn't strike her. He laughed instead, seeming genuinely amused. "Oh, I can see why my nephew likes you, sweetheart. A lot of front, just like him. Maybe I should put you to work. You'd probably do a better job than some of the muppets I have to put up with."

Lily noticed that some of the younger men in the room blushed. She wasn't sure, because they were wearing hoods and balaclavas, but she thought a few of them were friends of V. Teenagers, like her.

Doser, Fat Ryan, and… Mikey?

She wondered if V knew about what was happening, and decided he must do. These were his friends and family. He'd been ghosting her a while. Now she knew why.

I was wrong about him.

"Why don't you just go after my dad?" Emily said, still rubbing at her ribs. "Mum kicked him out for being a freak, so leave us out of it. You can have him."

Lily looked past her mum and glared at her sister. "Em, what the fuck?"

"What? If Dad has made enemies, then it's his problem. Us and Mum shouldn't have to suffer."

"Are you for real? I swear, ever since you got better…" She shook her head. "We should never have helped you."

"What are you talking about? Why do you keep saying things like that?"

"Because," Lily spat, "Dad saved your ass, and now you're throwing him under the bus."

Emily pulled a face. Maggie was silent between the two of them, staring at the carpet like her mind had drifted away. This week had finally broken her. "What the hell are you saying, Lil? How did Dad save my ass?"

"Magic. He went to Mr Cho down the street and did this weird ritual. Next thing you know, you're miraculously out of bed and acting like a bitch."

"You're insane."

"Yeah, it feels like it sometimes, but I'm telling it to you like it is. You were dead, rushed to hospital in an ambulance, but the very next day you're cancer-free and feeling fine. Ever wonder why Dad didn't make it in to see you at the hospital for so long? It's because he was with me at Mr Cho's making a deal for your life."

"What kind of deal?" Emily asked, smirking like a smug snake.

Lily shrugged. "It don't matter. He accepted the consequences. He wanted you to live, just like he always has. Dad has done whatever it takes to be there for you. I can't believe you don't appreciate how much h—"

"He was drinking your blood, Lily!"

Their mum retched, like she'd been holding in her lunch and couldn't any more.

Emily lowered her voice and repeated herself. "After you cut yourself, Dad found you and started drinking your blood. Mum caught him doing it and threw him out. If this bullshit about magic rituals is true, then it must have turned Dad into a goddamn vampire, because he's a freak."

Lily sneered. "He's not a vampire. He's… He's…"

V's uncle had his arms crossed and had been listening to them argue like he was spectating a tennis match, head bobbing back and forth. Now that a gap arose in the conversation, he took a long breath and blew it out of his mouth. "You people are fucking mental. Are you seriously talking about magic rituals and curing cancer?" He looked at Emily. "I admit, you look like shit, sweetheart, but your sister is messing with your head."

Emily nodded. "I know she is. I might have a sick body, but she has a sick mind."

"Seriously." Lily rolled her eyes. "Believe me or don't, it doesn't change anything. You should be dead."

"Just like your old man," Dev said. "I stuck him twice

and he's fine. In fact, he grew some balls overnight and decided he wanted to be a player. That's what this is all about."

"I thought it was V who attacked him?" Lily said.

"My nephew had a run-in with him first, but I finished it." He shook his head and grunted. "I fucking know that I finished it. Makes no goddamn sense. He was bleeding all over the road."

"Wait." Lily frowned, trying to think. "You really stabbed my dad?"

He looked her in the eyes and nodded. There was no shame or regret. No remorse whatsoever. In fact, his eyes were empty.

"Then…" Lily tried to think. "Maybe he went to Mr Cho again. Maybe after you stabbed him he made another deal. A deal to save his life."

Bekim was silently gawping at his boss, as if waiting for him to react in some way. Of course, what Lily was saying to them must have sounded utterly absurd, but for some reason V's uncle seemed to give it some thought.

Emily was looking at Lily and shaking her head. "You've lost the plot."

Lily's anger was gone. She only felt tired. It was the middle of the night, and she was short on blood. "Just think about it, Em. How else can you explain your cancer going away? You've been fighting it for over a year, and it's been kicking your arse. Do you really think it's normal that you suddenly feel fine? And what about Dad? I saw him covered in blood" – she looked at Dev – "as though he'd been stabbed. But he was fine. How? It's all because of Mr Cho."

"I've heard things about him," Dev said before Emily could speak. "There's been rumours about the old Chink for years, stories about him helping people out with their pains.

For a while, I wondered if he was dealing weed and I needed to pay him a visit, but the old guy keeps to himself."

Bekim closed his mouth and nodded. "I once hear this Mr Cho help old lady get rid of cataracts. Miracle, they say."

One of the young guys in a balaclava grunted. "My nan goes to see him once a month for some special tea that helps her sleep. Swears he's proper legit, she does, and when I got meningitis as a kid, he gave my mum something to stop my fever. It's proper legit old Chinese medicine."

Emily closed her eyes and leant forward. "What is happening here? Has everybody lost it?"

Dev shook his head, like he agreed with her and thought himself mad. "Let's go get the Chink out of bed, aye? Let's see how magic he really is."

Bekim nodded and headed for the door. "House with red door, yes? I go get."

"Be gentle," Lily warned him. "He's old."

"Old and magic," Emily said sarcastically. "Don't forget the magic part."

Lily glared at her. "Bitch."

CHAPTER
EIGHTEEN

JAKE OPENED his eyes and saw a dirty ceiling that might once have been white but was now stained the dirty yellow of a smoker's fingers. He turned his head and found himself lying on a worn carpet littered with cigarette buts and beer cans. The room stunk of piss and shit. Piss, shit, and noxious chemicals.

"Where the hell am I?"

"Relax, fam. You're safe."

Jake sat up, dizzy and weak, like he was awaking from a hundred-year sleep. His vision was blurry and it took a moment to focus. "Vincent? I'm going to make you—"

"I helped you!" The lad was standing to Jake's left and clutching at himself nervously. Behind him, several people slept, sprawled out on mangy sofas and sleeping bags. "You drank Kaydon, bruv. I think it gave you a big hit of whatever was in his bloodstream."

"Shit still stings," said another voice. The lad with the dreads, the one who Jake had bitten, appeared on Jake's right. He looked ill, his face ashen, eyes bloodshot. "V says you're not yourself though, fam, so I'll call a truce, yeah?"

Jake realised he was unhurt, and he had a vague memory of passing out. "I… I got high from bad blood?"

The lad sucked his teeth. "Ain't nothing wrong with my blood, wasteman. You never had to go drinking it, anyway."

"Like Kay said," Vincent spoke in a diplomatic tone, "it's water under the bridge, innit? We need to get you sobered up and back on your feet. Uncle Dev's still at your gaff."

Jake tried to spring up onto his feet, but he almost fell back down. The two lads had to grab him and steady him. "Where am I? Why are you helping me?"

"I ain't helping you," Vincent said. "I'm helping Lily."

"As for where you is, bruv." Kaydon shrugged. "Number nine, Tovey Avenue, innit?"

"This is Tovey Avenue?" Jake looked around, his nose wrinkling at the smells. "It's disgusting."

"It's a dosshouse," Vincent said. "Been abandoned for a year now, but no one wants the cost of fixing it up."

"People sleep here?"

"If you can call 'em people."

Jake scowled and some of his dizziness washed away. "You made them like this. They're all probably messed up on the drugs you sold them."

Vincent turned away and actually seemed ashamed. "We ain't got time for that discussion right now, fam. You need to get back in the game. You took out one of my uncle's soldiers, but there're more inside your house. It's time you went home."

Jake nodded, testing out his limbs and feeling his strength slowly coming back. "I… I'm okay. Get me out of this place and I'll take care of it."

"Safe, bruv. Let's get you out the front door so you can do some damage."

Jake started to follow the two lads, but then he stumbled

weakly. To keep from falling down, he had to grab the arm of a battered leather sofa. A young girl, not much older than Emily, lay asleep on it, her face covered by filthy brown hair. He felt her heart beating – it drummed inside his head like the flapping wings of a delicate butterfly.

Vincent stopped and turned back. "Jake? Come on, you need to go, man."

"I… I can't. Too weak. Need a pick-me-up."

He felt something change, his jaw swelling, his senses heightening. The vampire was out. Xindrac was hungry. He heard the beast hissing inside his skull. Laughing. Mocking.

Vincent and Kaydon moved back against the wall, but Vincent put a hand up to Jake. He was trembling, but he lifted his head confidently. "Jake, whatever it is you're about to do, take a breath first, yeah? No one here is your enemy."

"I need to feed." He eyed the sleeping girl. His mouth began to water. Saliva dripped from the end of his needle-like fangs. Who would miss her?

"I get that," Vincent said, "but all of these people in here are junkies. You think Kaydon tasted bad? You don't even want a sip of Cheryl Renner's blood."

Jake looked down at the sleeping girl. "Cheryl?"

"Yeah. She's nineteen, bruv. Think her stepdad did some nasty shit to her and messed her up nice and early. Started out on the booze, but then she moved onto the hard stuff. She was already deep by the time I started supplying her, so it ain't on me. Maybe you can help her, Jake. Once this is all over, you could try, right? You want to make Tovey Avenue a better place for your girls, then do it, bruv. Starting with my uncle."

Jake licked at his teeth and felt them vibrate. The girl's heartbeat still fluttered inside his head, and it was getting louder. He clenched his fists, eager to tear flesh and break bone. To keep from losing control, he put his hands inside his pockets.

Burning. Fire. Pain.

Jake hissed, his forked tongue flickering. Electricity sparked inside his chest and shot up and down his arms. The agony froze him in place, made it impossible to think straight.

It lasted only a split second, but it left him panting.

Kaydon pressed himself back against the wall even further. "You good, bruv?"

Jake's mind slowly cleared. The thirst and the fury bled away as the vampire went back inside its shell.

Something inside his pocket had burned his hand and sent Xindrac away.

Gritting his teeth, Jake reached inside his pocket again and pulled out the object. It felt like grabbing hold of fire, somehow ice-cold as well as infernally hot. A terrible stench filled the room, his hand giving off tendrils of black smoke. He was cooking.

Vincent and Kaydon groaned as he pulled the Cho Zhou symbol out of his pocket and held it aloft. He readjusted his grip and took it in his other hand, avoiding the silver tips. The pain stopped. But the damage was done.

Jake examined his palm and saw a deep, sticky burn. While he might have been nigh-on invincible, he could clearly still be hurt. Hurt by silver.

"You okay, bruv?" Kaydon asked again. "You should really get some cold milk on that. It'll soothe it and keep it clean from infection."

Jake huffed. "I don't think I need to worry about infections, kid, but thanks for your concern."

"Can't take no chances with burns, bruv."

Vincent stepped away from the wall. "What is that, Jake?"

"Something Mr Cho gave me. A protective symbol."

"Is that silver around the edges?"

Jake nodded.

"And it burned you?"

Jake nodded again. "But it burned the monster worse. Sent it away and brought me back."

"Good to know. You ready? Ready to go take care of your family? And my uncle?"

"Yeah, fam." Jake nodded and put the symbol back in his pocket. "It's time to go be a man."

———

Lily's jaw ached terribly, swollen and hot. It was her first time getting walloped by an East European gangster, and she sincerely hoped it would be the last. Everyone was standing or sitting in silence, waiting for Bekim to return with Mr Cho. Uncle Dev – or just Dev, she supposed – was the most anxious of all, fidgeting and scratching at his arm with a nasty-looking blade he had produced. His remaining thugs looked bored, either thirsting for violence or yearning for home and their beds.

Lily looked at the black square outside the window, wishing for blue and white flashing lights or even a hint of approaching daylight. But help wasn't coming. There probably no one even awake to know about the misery going on inside 26 Tovey Avenue.

What time is it? Must be like three in the morning.

I really should have cut myself deeper and avoided all this bullshit.

Bekim had been gone a while. Lily hoped it wasn't

because poor Mr Cho had put up a fight. She had dragged him into this by mentioning his name, but he was the only one who could back up her version of events.

"Who is this Mr Cho?" Emily asked quietly, better able to breathe now that the pain in her ribs had subsided a little. "You talk about him like he's some kind of a witch."

"Warlock," Lily corrected her, "or maybe a wizard."

"Who is he?"

"Just an old man who lives up the street. He knows things. Things other people don't."

Emily clearly wasn't buying it. Her tone was mocking. "And you think he cured my cancer?"

"He *did* cure your cancer. Dad made a deal."

"Uh-huh."

The front door opened, and a cold gust entered the house. The ceiling light flickered, no doubt from the house's old wiring.

Mr Cho waddled into the room with John the pug. Both man and dog wore matching light blue pyjamas, which was as cute as it was absurd. Bekim walked behind Mr Cho, prodding him in the back. "I am here," the old man said. "No need to put your hands on me any further."

Bekim smirked. "Here's the Chinese you ordered, boss."

Mr Cho stood in the centre of the living room and looked around at the mess. It clearly saddened him, and he bowed his head.

"Jing?" Lily gave the man an apologetic smile. "I'm so sorry."

"As am I, child. It appears my meddling has done great harm. Where is your father?"

"We don't know. He… He…" She looked down at her bandaged thigh.

Mr Cho bowed his perfectly bald head. "Jake visited me

earlier. He told me what happened. I'm afraid something very dangerous has taken nest inside him. His actions are not his own."

Lily smiled weakly. *Good to know that Dad wasn't drinking me like a mojito because he liked the taste of me.*

Maggie snapped out of her daze and glared at Mr Cho. "Is this all because of you? What have you got my family involved in?"

"You must be Maggie. It is good to meet you, but I fear your accusations might be correct. Your husband came to me asking for help. I should have closed my door, but I allowed myself to be persuaded. I thought I was saving a life, but it appears all I have done is aid death and misery."

"George." Lily licked her lips. "Do you know about what happened?"

Mr Cho bowed his head. "An old friend already dearly missed."

He looked at Emily. "I am glad to see your health improving. At least something came of this."

Emily frowned at the old man and gave no reply.

"Enough chit-chat," Dev barked. "I didn't bring you here for tea, old man. I brought you here because blondie says you can do magic."

"Magic is make-believe, sir. I suggest you hire an enter-tainer if you wish to see card tricks."

Dev moved up to Mr Cho and put the knife against his weathered cheek. "Don't mug me off, old man. I'm in a really bad fucking mood."

Mr Cho didn't seem afraid at all, merely tired. "What is it you want from me?" he asked, blinking slowly and sighing.

"The truth. Did you cure this skinny bitch's cancer? Furthermore, did you heal her old man after I stuck him with this very knife pressed against your cheek?"

"I helped Jake, yes, but it was not I who did the things you mentioned. I merely helped broker a deal with one who could."

"A deal?" Dev looked at his thugs and laughed. "So you're just a middleman, huh? Well, who's the one in charge? Who do I need to talk to?"

Mr Cho laced his hands together and looked at the floor. "Nobody is in charge. If you think there is order and hierarchy to the universe, then I am sorry to disappoint you. Even the most powerful of entities are greedy and self-serving."

Dev grabbed Mr Cho by the back of his pyjamas and almost lifted him up. Immediately, John the pug leapt at the brute's ankles, snapping and biting. "Bloody mutt. Bekim, stamp on this thing, will you?"

Bekim moved forward.

Lily cried out for mercy. "No, he's just an animal."

"He's about to be a dead animal." Dev shook John loose and reared back to kick him.

"Please," Mr Cho begged. "I will answer all your questions. There is no need for cruelty."

Dev let go of the old man and growled. "Then call your bloody dog off before I cut its throat."

"John! Now is not the time for violence."

The pug backed off, but he didn't take his eyes off Dev.

Dev turned his attention back to Mr Cho. "Did you save Jake's life after I stabbed him?"

"Yes."

Lily looked at Emily and her mum, observing as they both tried to process what they were hearing. Did they believe it?

"And you helped cure her cancer?" Dev nodded his head sideways at Emily.

"I… aided her father in doing so, yes."

"How? You say you brokered a deal? The fuck does that mean?"

Mr Cho clearly didn't want to answer, but when he hesitated, Dev moved towards John. The threat was clear and it got the old man talking. "I put Jake in touch with entities beyond our perception – ancient beings with powers beyond our own."

Dev put a hand against his face and smoothed down his goatee. "You mean the Devil?"

"Not the Devil," Lily muttered. "I thought that too."

"I doubt very much the Devil is a being who exists," Mr Cho said. "Nonetheless, names don't matter, only the terms of the bargain."

Dev turned then to look at Lily. "All this time, Mr Magoo has been living on Tovey Avenue; quiet as a mouse, until your family got here. Do you see all the trouble you've caused?"

"It's not their fault," Mr Cho said, rising up and speaking firmly. "I chose to meddle. The blame lies with me."

Dev looked around, his brow furrowing as he seemed to think things through. His attention eventually settled on Bekim, and then on the younger lads behind him. "What d'you lot think about this? A load of fucking nonsense, right?"

Bekim shrugged. "He is Chinaman. They eat cats and sell babies. Who knows what else they do?"

"Bit racist," said Lily, giving Mr Cho an apologetic smile.

"I prefer dog," said Mr Cho, and then he began chuckling to himself. He looked down at John and apologised. "I am just joking, John. Don't look at me like that."

"Boss?" said one of the younger guys. "Way I see it, you got nothing to lose, innit? Ask for something, and if the old guy really is magic, then you'll get it. If not, well… we can do what we came here to do."

Dev looked at the eyes inside the balaclava and slowly nodded. "You putting that brain cell to work, Dose? Nah, you're right. What do I have to lose?" He turned back to Mr Cho. "All right, old man, you got a choice. Either I gut everyone in this room while the mum watches, or you do your magic and give me whatever I ask for. Deal?"

Maggie and Emily moaned.

"It doesn't work like that." Mr Cho brought his hands up to his chest and held them together, almost like he was praying. "If you ask a favour for yourself, bad things will happen. Jake is proof of that. I'm sorry, but my answer is no. Whatever you do in this room will not be as bad as what might happen if I help you."

"Please," Maggie said, hugging Lily and Emily closer to her. "Just go. You don't have to hurt anyone."

Mr Cho nodded. "You can put a stop to this right now. Be a decent man and go."

Dev grunted and stepped back. "It's so disappointing when people drag things out, you know? Well, it's disappointing for me; Bekim here loves it when people fuck around."

Bekim strolled towards Mr Cho, smashing a fist against his palm. "Time to make chop suey."

"Seriously," Lily said. "Stop with the racism. Or at least do it better."

Mr Cho did not cower. He put his hands down in front of his waist and bowed his head. He muttered something in another language; not a prayer exactly, more like he was speaking to someone inside his own head. He looked up, just as Bekim reached him. "I forgive you," he said. "I'm sorry you have to do this."

Bekim frowned, appearing genuinely confused. "I'm not."

Mr Cho bent forward and moaned as a fist hit him in the stomach. The old man was so frail that he didn't seem to have much air inside him, and he deflated like a half-filled ballon. As he doubled over, Bekim used his fist like a hammer and hit the old man on the back of the neck. Mr Cho dropped face first onto the floor without a sound. His hands grasped at the carpet and his left leg bent slightly, but he was too beaten to recover.

Bekim stood over him, grinning.

John the pug leapt at Bekim's legs, biting him on the knee and holding on like a pit bull.

Bekim growled, matching the noises coming from the dog, then unloaded a horrible punch into the top of John's skull. The dog yelped and tumbled backwards, shaking his head and grunting.

"Leave them alone," Lily cried, leaping up off the sofa, but one of the lads in balaclavas grabbed her right away and stopped her from interfering. "Been waiting to get my hands on you," he said as he wrapped his arms around her waist.

"Stop this," Emily cried.

Maggie started yelling hysterically. "Jake? Help! Jake, we need you."

Dev stood in front of Maggie, his crotch almost in her face. "Hubby ain't here, love. You want a real man to look after you? It can be arranged."

"You're disgusting," she said, fighting back her tears. "I would rather fuck a broom."

"Nice! I see where your daughter gets her smart mouth from. How about I fill it?"

Lily bucked and tried to get away from the groping arms

around her. She glared at Dev the whole time. "You couldn't even fill one of my cavities," she said.

"Seriously?" Dev glared, his thick black eyebrows pointed downwards in a V. "I've already given you one pass, blondie. Time you learned how to behave."

Lily yelped as he backhanded her across the face. She tasted blood and almost spat it in his face, but this time the pain rattled her too much to fight back. She swallowed the blood in her mouth and fell back onto the sofa, finally let go by the sonofabitch she was now sure was Fat Ryan. When another hand grabbed her, she jolted, but it was just Emily. Lily's sister hugged her as she fought back sobs.

Bekim kicked Mr Cho in the side, causing the old man to heave. John the pug grumbled but was still dazed from being punched.

Dev checked his watch. "Fuck, this shit is getting old. We'll deal with hubby later. Let's just leave him something nice to come home to. Put yourselves to work, boys. I want this room painted red."

The young lads in the balaclavas glanced hesitantly at each other, but then they raised their weapons and moved towards the sofa. They were either remorseless thugs, or too weak to disobey Dev's orders. Once again, Fat Ryan came towards Lily with groping hands.

The living room window exploded. Not like a rock had been thrown through it, more like a wrecking ball had struck the house.

But instead of a wrecking ball, it was Jake who crashed through the window. He seemed to arrive in slow motion, a thousand tiny shards surrounding him like a swarm of twinkling wasps as he leapt into the room from outside.

Everyone staggered backwards, shielding their faces.

Jake landed in the middle of the living room, right next to Mr Cho. Like some kind of superhero.

Except his face was all wrong. Distorted. Horrific.

Lily covered her mouth in horror.

Is it Dad? Or something else?

Bekim was the first to react. He balled his fists up and launched himself at Jake.

Jake ducked a flurry of punches, almost like he was dancing to a choreographed routine. Try as he might, Bekim just couldn't land a blow. After only ten seconds, the big man grew tired and his punches slowed. He was huffing and puffing.

Jake wore a wolf-like grin, his teeth too large and his jaw too wide. When he spoke, he did so with an unfamiliar lisp. "Your hands can't hit what your eyes can't see. Float like a butterfly, sting like a bee." He then did a foot shuffle like a professional boxer and threw a punch that would have put Tyson Fury down for a month.

Lily shook her head, wondering what she was seeing.

Bekim flew backwards, his legs pumping strangely out of time before giving out completely. He crashed into Dev before flopping onto his back with a resounding thump. Both his arms were stuck out bizarrely in front of him, like he was trying to grab an invisible steering wheel.

Lily heard Emily and her mum gasp. Then she realised why.

Bekim was dead – he had to be dead – because where his face used to be was now a misshapen crater. Blood flowed from his nose. It found a crevice and flowed down his crushed left cheek, leaving the rest of his face strangely bloodless. His arms stopped reaching for that invisible steering wheel and flopped lifelessly at his sides.

Dev backed off towards his other thugs. "The fuck!"

"*Sangele tau ma va hrani.*" Jake spoke in a voice that wasn't his, a hissing, angry tone like white-hot metal being doused in water. His smile was also foreign, the feral gaze of a predator. All the same, Lily felt a wave of relief crash over her as he stalked towards Dev.

"What the fuck is wrong with you?" Dev demanded, his voice fraught with nervousness. "You're a goddamn beast."

"There is much to be learned from beasts." Jake said, tilting his head and smiling. "Allow me to show you."

Dev lifted his knife. Jake pounced.

Lily screamed.

———

Once again, Jake felt strong. The tainted blood he'd drunk still affected him, and weakened his grip on reality, but there was no doubt in his mind about who his enemies were.

Vincent's uncle. I'm going to tear his throat out and inhale his blood.

Then I'm going to slaughter his nephew and his entire remaining bloodline.

His prey stood directly in front of him, the stupid black goatee insufficient at covering the obvious fear on its face.

Jake lunged at Dev.

Dev grabbed a younger man in a balaclava and dragged him in the way, trying to delay his inevitable demise. No matter. No rush. Slaughter was not something to be rushed. They had all night.

Empowered by the screaming and shouting filling the room, Jake grabbed the young man in front of him and glared at the eyes peeking out of the balaclava. He wielded a baseball bat and tried to bring it to bear, but Jake grabbed his wrist and twisted it three hundred and sixty degrees, almost tearing his entire arm away at the shoulder.

Wailing so loud that he could probably have cracked crystal if there were any in the house, the young lad whimpered and grabbed at the zipper of his tracksuit, pulling it up to his Adam's apple. "Please," he begged. "Please…"

"Don't mind if I do," said Jake, and he sank his sharp fangs into the young man's neck.

As he drank, he discovered his victim was only fifteen, a child. But. despite his revulsion, Jake couldn't pull away. The beast inside him – not Xindrac, but the rage that had slowly been filling him over the last eighteen months – would not tolerate mercy. Mercy was weak. Mercy was an acceptance of being treated poorly, and that was something he was no longer willing to do.

The boy's memories – Dean 'Doser' Oswald – flooded through Jake's mind, and he realised it was his victim's life passing before his eyes and draining out of him alongside his life's blood.

Doser was born with heroin in his system, and went on to have a childhood plagued with ADHD, dyslexia, and burgeoning bipolar disorder. The kid never had a chance at a normal life, never had a glimpse of a future where he might become a doctor or an accountant. He was damaged, highly vulnerable, and without a single decent adult to help or guide him. A victim bred to make victims. Hurt people hurt people.

And now he was dead.

Jake let go of Doser and let his limp, drained corpse collapse to the floor.

Jake's soul ached with what he had just done, but his body surged with life – a life stolen and absorbed. Energy pumped through every muscle, filling him with strength, power, and clarity.

His family sobbed on the sofa, Maggie pulling Lily and Emily close and covering their faces. They were terrified.

Terrified of me, Jake realised, but the part of him that would care about such things was currently closed off.

He turned to Dev and grinned, his fangs dripping blood. "I'm gonna let you watch while I take your thugs apart. Then I'm gonna make you beg."

Dev sneered defiantly, but it was only an act – and an amateur one. The man was afraid like he'd never been afraid before, and when he lifted his knife, his hand shook. "Come on then, you fucking mug. Let's do this."

Despite his fighting words, Dev melted back behind his remaining backup, leaving a bunch of young lads to face Jake.

Jake tore through them with ease, breaking their arms to keep them from struggling before tearing open their jugulars to feed. The first was a boy named Ryan – who liked to eat junk food to comfort himself and watched far too much hardcore pornography. He called out for his mother as Jake drank him. The second was a lad named Mikey, who hopped up and down comically as he bled out. The third and final was an older man in his thirties called Kevin McCallister who had been relentlessly bullied at school for sharing the same name as the kid in *Home Alone*. Over time, he had become the bully and done many terrible things. Jake enjoyed drinking him the most. Evil had a tang to it.

When the carpet was littered with twitching bodies and blood, Jake turned to face Dev once again. "You're all out of bodies. What you gonna do now?"

Dev didn't answer. He hopped over Mikey's body and lunged at Jake with a knife.

Jake met him head-on and grabbed his wrist. He intended to snap Dev's arm, but he was surprised when something sharp struck him in the ribs. A second knife.

Dev leant in close, his mouth pressed against Jake's ear. "Let's see you walk this one off, Fido."

Jake was overwhelmed by a spreading pain, his lungs seizing in his chest. It took great effort to force the words out of his mouth. "I'm. A. Vampire."

His fangs erupted even further from his mouth. He reared back, staring Dev in the face so he could see the man's look of horror before he was devoured.

But Dev only smiled. "You and me both, mate." He twisted the knife, causing Jake further agony. Then, to his absolute shock, Dev buried his face in the side of Jake's neck and clamped down with his teeth.

Lily screamed obscenities from nearby, and Jake was vaguely aware of her approaching. "Get away from my fucking Dad!"

Dad. I'm Dad. Not a monster.

Jake locked his jaw and tried to push aside the pain in his ribs and in his neck. Dev was chewing and gnashing, drawing blood and sucking it down. Was he a vampire too?

No, just a sick and violent man.

Jake got control of his arms and shoved against Dev, but he was momentarily weak. It was barely enough to break Dev's hold and send him back a step.

There was blood all over his face.

My blood.

The black-red stains on Dev's chin bubbled and hissed, burning like acid. He began to panic, clutching at his face and wiping. "What the fuck? It's burning me."

"Drinking is bad for you," said Jake as he prepared to lunge at the man.

Lily got there first. She crashed into Dev and beat both fists against his chest, pummelling him over and over again. "You fucking piece of shit," she screamed. "You bastard."

Dev's movement was already hastened by his panic, so he reacted quickly. Growling, he threw out both arms and spun Lily around. Before Jake could do anything, the man had his daughter in a chokehold and a blade pressed against her eye. "Stay back, you freak! Stay away."

Maggie screamed for help. Emily joined in.

Jake reached down and noticed the knife still sticking out of his ribs. With great effort, he yanked it out and pointed it at Dev. "You hurt one hair on her head and I'll take you apart piece by piece."

"You take another step and I'll open her up like a fish." Dev turned to the sofa. "Same thing will happen if you two don't shut the fuck up!"

Emily stopped screaming, then hugged her mum to try and calm her too.

Jake felt his strength returning, buoyed by the amount of human blood he had devoured. Feeding had made him stronger, but he also felt it take something away from him. It sent Jake the father and husband into the background and brought forth the beast. He almost didn't care about Lily's plight, so eager to kill this man that he was willing to disregard all risk.

He reached into his jacket pocket and clutched the Cho Zhou symbol. Xindrac hissed. The flash of white-hot pain brought Jake back.

"Don't hurt her," he said, loosening his stance and stepping away from Dev. "Please, don't hurt my daughter."

Dev twisted the knife under Lily's eye, making her moan. "Then you better do exactly what I fucking well say, sunshine."

CHAPTER
NINETEEN

JAKE CONTINUED to grip the silver points on the symbol in his pocket periodically, to ensure that he remained present. The blood in the room was making him dizzy, like he was breathing in petrol fumes. Every few seconds, he had to fight the urge to bury his face in the entrails of his victims.

Kids. I slaughtered a bunch of kids.

I'm out of control.

No. No, I'm here. I'm me.

The way Maggie and Emily were looking at him told Jake he wasn't the man they knew, even now that he had calmed down enough to send the monster away. His fangs were gone, his face had returned to normal, but he was still a beast soaked in blood.

Lily was the only one who looked at him the same way she always had, although she was fraught with terror as Dev dragged her backwards into the kitchen. He still had the knife pressed beneath her eye.

One of the bodies lying on the carpet moved and let out a moan. It was Mr Cho. The old man turned onto his side and looked around in a daze. John the pug was also in the room, appearing from the debris of the coffee table. He licked his master's face and wagged his curly tail.

"Jing?" Jake crouched beside him, ignoring John's snarls. "Jing, are you okay?"

The old man rose up onto his knees and looked around. Each body his eyes fell upon caused him to flinch. "What have I done?"

"You haven't done anything," Jake said. "These people broke into my home and threatened my family." He straightened up and turned towards Dev in the kitchen. "And they haven't all been dealt with yet."

Jing reached out and grabbed his hand. "Jake, you have to stop this carnage now. Do not let the beast inside you get what it wants."

"Who said anything about the beast getting what it wants?"

Jake looked at Maggie and tried to smile, but he couldn't manage it. The fear on her face made it impossible. Emily couldn't even meet his gaze. Did they think he would hurt them?

I would never…

Jake marched towards the kitchen, stopping in the doorway. Dev still had a hold of Lily, and he was trying to leave through the back door. But the handle wouldn't turn.

Jake reached into his pocket and brought out his keys. He dangled them in the air. "It's locked. You're not going anywhere. Unless you let my daughter go."

Dev glared at him over Lily's shoulder, his burned chin pink and raw. "You think I'm stupid? I let her go and you'll tear me apart."

"Maybe you'll get lucky and I'll be the one who comes off worse."

"Three times I've stabbed you now. You ain't fucking human."

Jake fought to stay calm. It was a difficult thing to do while his daughter was in danger, but he couldn't risk the beast coming out and putting her in harm's way. "So what do you want to do, Dev? How do we put an end to this situation?"

Dev bared his teeth; they were stained dark with Jake's blood. "There is no end to this. Your living room carpet is littered with my lads. Am I just supposed to forget that?"

"I don't care what you do. I just want you out of my house and away from my family. For good. Promise me that and I'll let you walk away."

Dev closed his eyes for a second and let out a breath. Jake might have been able to use it as an opportunity to attack, but he kept himself back and let his enemy continue speaking. "What the fuck happened to you? You cheated death and turned into a monster."

"It takes one to know one."

"Seriously. What did the Chink do to you?"

"He saved my life and the life of my daughter. It came with a price tag. Something is inside me now, but I can control it. I can learn to keep it away."

Dev nodded thoughtfully, and seemed to fully believe what he was hearing. "You're unkillable. Strong. Fucking vicious. You're everything a man in my business needs to be. I want what you have."

"No, you don't. You've seen what I can do."

"Exactly. Everyone, back into the living room. I want to make a deal. Come on, don't make me cut blondie's pretty face."

Jake considered his options, but when Lily looked at him

pleadingly, he decided to keep things moving along semi-peacefully for the time being. "Fine."

They moved cautiously back into the lounge, where Mr Cho was now sitting on the sofa beside Emily and Maggie. All three of them gazed, in shock, at the massacre covering the carpet. Four dead bodies.

"Step away," Dev ordered Jake, and then he positioned himself behind Lily in the corner of the room. He looked at Mr Cho, nodded. "I want to make a deal. The exact same deal Jake made. Put a beast inside me so I can tear through my competition and run this fucking town. Do that for me, and I promise I'll personally see to it that Tovey Avenue isn't even bothered by so much as a Jehovah's Witness. No retribution. Clean slate."

"I cannot do what you ask," Mr Cho said. "The thing inside Jake is there by choice. He made a bargain with Xindrac directly, and the creature now resides inside him."

"Fine, give me something else then, so long as it makes me invincible."

"It's not something I can guarantee. When you ask a favour for yourself, the results are unpredictable. That is why it is safer to ask favours on behalf of another, like when Jake first came to me and asked me to take away Emily's cancer in exchange for passing it on to someone else."

"What?" Emily spluttered and sat forward. "What do you mean?"

Jake looked at her, glad when she was able to maintain eye contact with him. "Mr Cho placed your cancer onto the head of the pin and George purposely pricked himself with it. If we didn't pass it on to someone else, your cancer would've come back and you—"

"Would have died like I was supposed to?" Emily stared

at the carpet, her gaze growing vacant as she tried to digest what she was hearing.

"Wait a minute," Dev said, readjusting his grip around Lily's waist. Her bare feet stood in a puddle of blood, causing her to look down and moan. "So, you can take someone's condition away and give it to someone else? That's how it works?"

Mr Cho nodded. "A selfless act has power. The bargain made must be fair and balanced. An eye for an eye. A life for a life."

"So you put Jake's inner beast on a pin and you stab me with it. Will that pass it on?"

"I do not know. The ritual is not something to experiment with. All I can tell you is what was passed down to me. Never have I dealt with such destruction as what is happening here this night." He looked out the window, at the dark night that seemed to be lifting. "May my ancestors forgive me for what I have done."

"I'm sorry, Mr Cho," Jake said. "If this is what it takes to end this, then let's just get it over with."

"Don't do it, Dad," Lily said. "If you pass on your strength, you won't be able to protect us. Dev won't keep his word."

"I will," Dev protested. "Believe it or not, I have honour. No one in this room will be harmed so long as I get Jake's power. You have my word."

Jake shook his head at the man, wondering if he was just dumb or completely evil. "It's not power. It's a curse. Don't you see that?"

"One man's trash is another man's treasure. You leave the worrying to me, sunshine."

"We would need someone to ask for the bargain," Mr Cho said, rubbing the side of his face as if trying to keep himself awake. "It cannot be you, Jake, because asking to be rid of Xindrac is a self-serving request."

Jake nodded. "Fine."

"I'll do it," Lily put a hand up, as if she were in school. "Also, what the hell is Xindrac? Is it like herpes?"

"It's the name of the monster inside me," Jake said. "It's a little bit like herpes. If herpes caused you to eat people."

"Usually, it's the eating people that gets you herpes," Lily quipped, and she managed to summon half a smile. She was being brave, Jake could tell. He loved her for it.

Maggie moaned. "Seriously, Lily. We need to have a talk about your sense of humour."

"Later, Mum. I'm a hostage right now."

"And you're staying one," Dev growled. "I can't let you go until it's done."

Emily suddenly stood up, her twig-like legs wobbling beneath her. "I'll do it. This all started because of me, so I'll do whatever needs to be done." She looked at Mr Cho. "I just need to ask a favour? Ask for my Dad to be cured?"

Mr Cho nodded. "Essentially."

"And the monster will go out of Dad and into the end of a pin, and then into whoever I stab with it?"

"I… believe so. It is not certain."

Jake took a step towards Dev and looked him in the eye. "Your word. I need to you give it to me again. You don't harm anyone in this room. You get what you want and you leave."

Dev pressed the knife against Lily's cheek, a nervous response to Jake stepping towards him. He was on edge, probably exhausted, and prone to doing something stupid. "You have my word, Jake. Give me your inner monster and you will be forgiven. Call it payment for the muscle you robbed me of tonight. Some of those lads made me good money."

Jake turned to Mr Cho. "Should we do this? Do we have a choice?"

"I don't know, Jake. Whatever we do, a great evil has been unleashed upon the earth, and that is something we must live with. I will do whatever you decide."

Jake turned to look back at Dev, trying to read the man's face. He could sense his heart beating in his chest, drumming rapidly. It whispered to Jake, told him secrets. Right now, all Dev was focused on was power, and the ability to rip through his enemy without consequence. There was a real chance that he would forget his grudge with Jake if he got what he wanted.

And it might be my only chance to get rid of Xindrac. If I don't do this, the monster could be with me forever, and my family will never be safe.

"Okay, Dev. You have a deal. You take the beast from me and leave. No more bloodshed."

Dev grinned. "Glad we could do business. Let's fucking get on with it."

Emily stepped forward, trying to avoid the bodies of the dead. Mr Cho gave her a gentle smile, but it was full of fear.

––––––––––

Lily's cheek had grown numb from the constant pressure of Dev's blade. As time passed, her heart stopped beating quite so fast, and she became hopeful she might just get out of this without losing an eye. Her main worry was what the hell was wrong with her dad, and what the hell would happen if a maniac like Dev got super monster powers?

Lily just wanted her family to be okay. If there was something evil inside her dad, then she wanted it out. Maybe Dev really would keep his word and leave them all alone, and if so, the only problem left would be explaining four dead bodies in the living room.

Emily and Mr Cho went into the kitchen, which wasn't covered in blood and debris like the living room was. They sat down at the circular table opposite one another. Dev took Lily to join them and stood at the back of the room. Jake reached out to Maggie on the living room sofa. She clearly didn't want to take his hand, but when he insisted, she stood up and went with him into the kitchen. It was cramped, but they all managed to squeeze in somehow.

Several times, Lily thought about trying to stamp on Dev's foot and make a run for it, but for the time being things were progressing calmly, so she followed her dad's lead, which seemed to be to play along for now. If it meant his 'Jaws' face stayed inside, she was all for it. When he changed, he stopped being her dad. She felt afraid.

Would he hurt me?

He already drank my blood.

Lily ran a hand over the bandage on her thigh, suddenly angry at herself for having done something so stupid. So much pain in the world; why had she tried to add to it?

"I need silence in the room," Mr Cho said, his hands flat on the table. "And a needle of some kind, something that can draw blood with two separate ends."

Lily watched as her mum moved away from her dad and went over to one of the kitchen drawers. She pulled it open and reached inside. What she pulled out was long and thin, a metal kebab skewer that her dad sometimes used on their old barbecue. "Will this do?" she asked emotionlessly.

Mr Cho nodded. "It is a little unwieldy, but will meet our needs. Thank you, Maggie. Okay, everyone. Silence, please."

Jake frowned. "Don't you need your candles and powders and stuff?"

"No, that is all just for ambience. I find it helps focus people if you add tiny details, but we're past that."

"What? So the whole ritual was for show?"

"Yes, Jake. All I actually need to do is focus and communicate. It is a skill passed down to me by my grandmother. It allows me to navigate the tapestry of existence, to see the threads of life and speak to the beings living in the gaps between."

Dev nodded appreciatively. "All my nanna left me was a shitty piggy bank collection. Barely got a hundred quid for it."

Mr Cho ignored him and started to speak the words he had spoken several days ago when all this had started, when he had helped Emily. He spoke to ancient beings, old and wise and merciful.

But they're not merciful, Lily thought. The thing inside her dad had showed no mercy when it had been ripping Dev's lads to shreds.

I think some of them were friends of V.

Where is he right now? How come he isn't here with his uncle?

Listening to Mr Cho's words, Dev pinched the bridge of his nose and exhaled as if he were suffering from a headache. "Can we hurry this the fuck up? The bloody sun will be up soon."

Mr Cho continued to ignore everyone else in the room and spoke the words he needed to speak. "We seek to benefit the man, Jake Penshaw, who stands in this room. He is afflicted by an unwanted presence inside him. Please, give him your mercy and restore him. I offer the blood of she who asks this favour."

Emily frowned as Mr Cho offered the end of the kebab

skewer to her, but it quickly dawned on her what he was asking. She pushed her palm against the metal spike, wincing, and then grunting. "It's pretty blunt."

"It must be done."

"Shit!" She pushed harder and then squealed as her flesh suddenly gave way and the skewer punctured her palm. She yanked her hand away, swearing some more as blood trickled down her wrist.

Lily watched her dad fidget uncomfortably at the back of the room.

Dev still had an arm around her waist, and a knife against her cheek, but his grip was looser now. In fact, he was trembling as if the exertion was too much.

He's getting distracted. Should I do something?

"To complete the bargain," Mr Cho said. "We will shed the blood of another." He offered the skewer back to Emily, this time for her to take from him. She did so and examined it, particularly the end with her blood now dripping from it. All that was left was for her to stab the other end into Dev.

Then Dad will be back to normal and Dev will be a vampire.

Who will slaughter us all.

He was still trembling behind Lily. She saw sweat beading on his forearm pressing against her stomach.

Emily looked at Mr Cho. "What do I do now?"

Mr Cho was frowning, as if lost in thought. He flinched at the sound of her voice and took a breath. "You must pierce the flesh of the one you wish to curse with Jake's affliction."

"I just stab them? And then that's it?"

"Nothing is certain, but yes."

Dev shuffled forward, still holding on to Lily. She was feeling sick from his aftershave, and hated the growing heat of his sweaty body against hers. At least he didn't have a hard-on pressed against her back, which would have made her puke. "Stab me," he said, holding out his palm. "Come on, do it!"

Emily held the skewer in her right hand, her left placed flat against the table. She looked at Dev and seem hesitant to act.

"Come on," he said again. "Do it."

Emily nodded. "Okay."

To everyone's audible shock, Emily turned the skewer downwards and drove it into the back of her flattened left hand. She yelled out in agony, cursing and spluttering and letting out a long stream of obscenities. "Motherfucking racoon fucker bitch."

Lily's eyes were glued to the metal spike sicking out of her sister's hand, standing straight up on its own. There was only a tiny amount of blood, welling around the edges of the puncture wound, but the metal had gone in deep. "Sis…? What did you do?"

"You bitch!" Dev tensed up behind Lily, his anger physical. "You were supposed to stab me."

"I know that, you idiot." Emily turned her head and sneered at him. "You think I'm about to give you demon powers after you broke into my home and terrorised my family? You're a monster. I'm not about to make you stronger."

"Bitch!"

This is about to get ugly, Lily realised. Now was the time to act. Emily had put her in harm's way, but it was also an opportunity to end this.

Dev removed the knife from Lily's face and lunged at Emily.

Lily was ready. She shoved Dev as hard as she could, knocking him sidewards into the fridge. Jake made a grab for him then, but he unexpectedly missed. Dev was surprisingly fast and agile, ducking and spinning out of the way like a martial artist on speed. He ended up behind Mr Cho, his knife held out to keep everyone else at bay.

"It's over," Jake growled, his face contorting and beginning to change.

Lily frowned. "Dad, you're still… ugly."

He put his hands to his face, feeling at the two twisted fangs poking out between his lips.

"I don't feel any different," Emily said. She yanked the skewer out of her hand and shuddered in pain. "Did it work? Is there a monster inside me now?"

"No." Mr Cho shook his head, and squinted as if trying to hear something over everybody talking. "The bargain was refused."

Dev grabbed him by the scruff of the neck from behind. "The fuck does that mean?"

Mr Cho turned to Jake. "The entities beyond are angry that Jake made a deal for himself, and they want nothing to do with Xindrac. They consider him an unclean thing."

Jake licked at his fangs. "So I'm stuck like this?"

Dev bellowed and lowered his knife around Mr Cho's throat. "You fucking idiots. Who do you think you're messing with? What do you… do you…" He looked dizzy, like he was about to fall over.

"It's over," Jake said. "Drop the knife."

But he didn't drop the knife. Instead, Dev shocked them all by grabbing Mr Cho from behind and biting into his neck. Blood spurted across the kitchen table, staining the wood.

John the pug let out an awful, human-like scream.

Jake tackled Dev from the side, forcing him away from Mr Cho and back against the fridge. The metal door dented under their combined weight. "The hell are you doing?"

Dev punched Jake in the throat and sent him staggering back towards the sink.

Everyone in the room gasped. Maggie called out to Jake, pleading for him to stop all of this madness, as if he could simply snap his fingers.

"I don't understand," said Emily, over and over again. She was staring at the hole in the back of her hand.

Mr Cho clutched at his neck, but it was torn wide open and his blood was going everywhere. It spurted all over Maggie standing next to him, but she seemed not to notice, staring at both Dev and Jake in horror. She continued begging for it all to stop.

Two vampires in the room.

Dev had changed. His face was distorted like Jake's, his brow too large and his jaw too wide. A pair of razor-like fangs jutted out of his mouth and his fingers were like claws.

"H-How?" Mr Cho gurgled and spluttered. Then he slumped face down on the table, his blood pooling all around him.

Dev felt at his face in confusion, running an elongated finger along his new fangs. Slowly, a grin surfaced on his face. "This is interesting."

Jake lunged at him.

Dev caught Jake in mid-air, turned, and then slammed him down right in the centre of the kitchen table. The legs snapped and the whole thing came apart in a pile of wood and splinters. Everyone retreated to the edges of the room, crying out in shock. John the pug cowered against Lily's leg.

Dev landed on top of Jake and immediately started pummelling him in the face. After several horrible, thudding blows, he threw his head back and hissed, a forked tongue escaping his mouth.

"Y-You gave your word," Jake moaned on his back, his

face bleeding. "You promised."

Dev looked down at him and grinned. "I lied."

He bit into Jake's neck and began to drink.

Lily screamed, frozen in horror.

The only one in the room who moved was Emily. She knelt down, picked up a piece of broken table leg, and drove it with both hands into Dev's back. It was blunt and thick, but she managed to bury it several inches into his flesh. He reared back and roared, blood spraying from his mouth and arcing in the air. Beneath him, Jake gurgled and choked as dark liquid spilled from his neck.

Lily tried to help her sister, but she couldn't move. The events of the last few days had finally caught up with her, and PTSD ignited inside her skull and turned her into a blubbering, inert mess.

Snarling and in pain, Dev thrashed and flailed. He lashed out with an arm, his hand like an eagle's talon, curled inwards and grasping.

Emily staggered backwards, blinking slowly, over and over again. She seemed confused. Shocked. The air in the room seemed to go still. All noise paused as a thin red line opened across the front of her neck, slowly lengthening from jowl to jowl.

Then the line widened into a wet, sucking mouth.

Maggie screamed out her daughter's name.

Lily could only speak in a horrified whimper. "E-Em?"

Emily's throat had been slashed wide open by Dev's swiping fingernails, like razor tips on the end of each finger. She fell back against the fridge and slowly slumped to the floor, trying to keep the blood inside her neck with both hands – but failing miserably. It seeped between her fingers and spilled out of her mouth. Her eyes turned to Lily, wide and confused. Frightened.

Lily broke out of her daze and went to her. Her mum was already there, kneeling beside Emily.

Her dad was still incapacitated, unaware of what was happening. He didn't know that they needed him. That his eldest daughter was dying.

Dev hissed, the length of wood still jutting out of his back. He reached behind himself to get at it, but couldn't reach with either hand. In an increasing fury, his focus turned to Emily. What he had done to her might have been an accident, because as he looked at her now, he seemed surprised. Maybe even sorry.

Dev turned and stumbled out of the kitchen and into the hall, the broken shaft of wood still buried in his back.

Emily lay choking on her own blood.

So did her dad.

"What do we do, Mum?" Lily asked. "What do we do?"

But all her mum did was look at her. She gave no answers.

———

For the first time in his life, Vincent considered calling the police, hoping for them to arrive and arrest his uncle. But part of him knew his uncle would get out on bail and kill anyone he considered a witness. That wouldn't save Lily or her dad.

What the fuck happened to him? He's turned into fucking Morbius.

Despite being some kind of monster, it was Jake who Vincent decided to pin his hopes on. Whatever had happened to the guy had made him deadly and unafraid. If anyone could take care of Uncle Dev, it was him.

Maybe Uncle Dev was already dead, torn apart like the thug he'd left to guard the house with Kaydon.

If I hadn't arrived when I did, Kay would be dead too.

The two of them now stood in the middle of Tovey Avenue, wondering what to do. Lily's house was fifty metres ahead, and from outside and at a distance, you wouldn't know anything was wrong. The lights were off, the front door closed.

Dawn was on its way, the night sky stained bloody at its bottom, the highest of the sun's rays making it over the curve of the earth. It was beautiful in a way, spoiled slightly by the artificial glare of Tovey Avenue's buzzing lampposts.

"We're dead man if the bossman finds out we helped the man he came here to shank," Kaydon said.

"I know," Vincent said. "So why are you with me?"

"You're my best mate. Where else would I be, fam."

Vincent gave Kaydon a smile, one without any front or hard man act. In that moment, all he wanted to do was hug his friend.

Screams came from Lily's house.

"Shit!" Vincent started forward. "We need to do something."

I have to stand up to my uncle before it's too late.

The truth was V was bricking it. This whole night had been like something out of a horror movie, and while Jake hadn't killed V earlier when he had had the chance, there was a good chance he still wanted to tear him apart.

I called a truce with him. He knows I tried to help him.

"It sounds like a massacre in there, fam." Kaydon was shaking his head, and he reached into his pocket and pulled out a small baggie full of pills. He poked a finger inside to fish one out.

"Yo," V said. "What are you doing? I need you on this."

"Bruv, I can't deal with any more of this night of the living dead shit. Man needs a chill pill."

"What even is that?"

Kaydon shrugged. "Just a little Special K, left over from last month's supply. Weak as shit, but they take the edge off. You want one?"

"I don't do that shit, man, and you know it. We know the damage it does."

"True dat, V. I'll quit tomorrow, innit?"

V sighed. Kaydon was a loyal friend, and pretty level-headed, but he was no good in a crisis. The merest hint of stress and he'd light up a spliff or pop a pill.

A front door slammed, and when V turned to look, he was shocked to see his uncle staggering out of Lily's house. He was covered in dark stains that must've been blood, and his face was a mess like he'd had a beating, all swollen and broken.

"No…" V shook his head. "Uncle Dev, he's…"

"Fuck me." Kaydon moved up beside V. "Bossman's got the werewolf thing too."

"It's not werewolves, Kay. This is some other shit. Fuck, if Unc has what Jake has, then there'll be no stopping him. He was already psychotic enough."

Kaydon popped another pill, straightening his neck to swallow it. "Man will go on a killing spree, fo' sho."

V watched his uncle move into the centre of the road, backed by twilight. Something was sticking out of his back, a short length of wood. Someone must have stabbed him with it.

Pity they didn't finish the job. He's going to unleash hell.

V had never seen his uncle kill anyone, but he had seen plenty of people cross him and disappear. There was no ambiguity about what he was capable of doing when angry.

Dev thrashed and spun around in the road until the length of wood finally came loose. The relief was obvious, and he immediately calmed down – but then he threw his head back and roared like a beast.

"We have to stop him," V muttered. "We have to stop him before he hurts anyone else."

"Fuck that," Kaydon said. "I already got sucked on once tonight, and your uncle scares the shit out of me." He pulled out a third pill and swallowed it before V could stop him. "He'll drink you dry, fam. Let's just get the fuck out of here."

So far, Dev hadn't noticed them standing there further up the road, but if they didn't get out of there quickly, it was only a matter of time before he spotted them. Either that, or he would go back inside Lily's house and finish what he'd started. The screams inside were dying off, but V kept hoping that Lily was okay. He didn't even want to think about where Doser, Mikey, and Ryan were.

I can't believe they turned up for this. When did torturing innocent families become okay?

Who am I kidding? We all knew what life we were signing up for.

But I'm signing out. I don't want this any more.

Kaydon was rubbing at his neck where Jake had bitten him. He still held the baggie full of pills in his other hand, and V couldn't help but stare at it. When Kaydon saw him looking, he offered it to him. "Thought you said you didn't want any?"

"I changed my mind. Hand it over."

"How many?"

"The whole bag."

"Shit, bruv. Go easy."

V chuckled. "Not me. I always go hard."

He downed a handful of pills in one go.

CHAPTER
TWENTY

JAKE'S VISION WAS SPINNING. He felt empty, like his skin was dried-out sandpaper wrapped around brittle cardboard tubing.

So thirsty.

He was lying in the kitchen amidst a pile of broken wood. The linoleum all around him was wet, and when he turned his head to the side, he saw Mr Cho lying on his back, the side of his neck torn wide open. John nuzzled against his side, whining.

He's dead. Did I do that?

Jake tried to feel the ground beneath him, his fingertips spreading out amongst the wooden debris. He sensed a presence in the room, heard a woman's sobbing.

Maggie? That's Maggie.

Jake rolled towards Mr Cho, then reversed and used the momentum to roll the other way and end up on his side.

What he saw chilled his bones.

"No. No." He reached out to Emily, locking eyes with her. She was still alive, sitting up against the fridge, but her throat was slashed across the front. Not like Mr Cho's though – she hadn't been bitten and drained. Something else had happened.

I did nothing to save her. I couldn't protect my family.

Maggie was slumped beside Emily. Her phone was in her hand, with a tinny, quiet voice coming out of the speaker. She'd obviously called for help but didn't have the strength to keep on talking to whoever was on the line. Hopefully an ambulance was already on its way.

Jake crawled his way towards them, tears streaming down his cheeks. "Emily? Honey, it's going to be okay."

She couldn't speak, but her eyes flickered with emotion.

"Help her," Maggie said, her voice thick with despair.

"How?" Jake shook his head, his lip quivering. "What should I do?"

"Let her drink your blood," Lily said.

Jake turned his head and saw his other daughter standing in the kitchen doorway, slumped against the frame. She had blood all over her legs, staining her bandage red. Her hair, too, was streaked with gore.

He shook his head in horror. "What do you mean?"

"Dad, if she drinks your blood, she'll become a vampire like you. It'll save her life."

Maggie moaned. "Lily. Please, just go get help."

"It's on its way," she said, "but it'll be too late. Look at her!"

Emily grunted, more blood seeping through her fingers. She gave her sister a look that suggested she understood it was true. She almost seemed to accept it.

"Lily, what are you talking about?" Jake asked. "I'm not a bloody vampire. It's nothing like that."

She sighed and rolled her eyes. "The ritual didn't work, did it? Emily stabbed herself with the skewer, and Mr Cho said no one took the bargain anyway, but Dev turned into a vampire all the same. Why? Because he bit you in the living room when you were fighting. The sicko drank your blood. Now he's a vampire. Ironic, he got exactly what he wanted just by being a twisted sonofabitch."

"He's not a vampire, he's—"

"Call it what you want, but he's the same as you, Dad. We all saw it."

Maggie stared at Jake. "She's right. Honey, she needs you to save her."

"That's all I've ever tried to do," he said, unable to keep from sobbing.

"When you were dying, becoming a monster saved you," Lily said, stepping into the room and standing over him. Both her hands shook by her sides. "It can save Emily too. Drinking your blood makes people into vampires. Dev proved it."

Maggie took his hand, and the touch of his wife was a wonderful thing, something he feared might have been lost forever. "It's okay," she said. "We need to do this."

Jake shook his head, finding the suggested plan absurd – but then everything had been absurd since moving to Tovey Avenue. "Okay, if there's a chance."

They looked at him, and for a moment, he didn't know what to do. Emily needed to drink his blood. He needed to bleed. How did he do this?

He bit into his wrist, urging his fangs to come out. They did so, but only partially. He was weak, the monster inside him buried deep, too much of his blood drained.

Emily gargled. Her face was the colour of chalk.

Jake's wrist bled slowly, but within a few seconds there was enough for her to drink. He offered the ragged wound to his daughter, moving it towards her mouth.

She turned her head away.

"Emily, honey," Maggie said, now fully on bored with the surrealness of the situation. "You need to drink. Just a little."

Jake tried to make her suck on his bleeding wrist again, but she turned her head back and forth, dodging him. "N-no…" The word came out in a croak. "No more…"

Maggie started shaking her head. "What? Honey, you need to do this."

"Time…" She choked on her own blood. "Time to… accept."

"I don't understand," Jake said. "If you don't do this, you'll die."

Emily nodded and smiled. Her eyes seemed to dry up, the reflection in them dying. He could sense her heart beating in her chest, getting slower and slower. She was fading.

Her soul. It's leaving. I can almost see it happening – like electricity in the air.

She spluttered and coughed. Blood struck Jake's face, causing his entire body to surge. The hungry emptiness inside him cried out for relief.

"She doesn't want to be a burden any more," Lily said, crouching down beside her sister and clutching her hand. Something passed between the two of them, an understanding. "After eighteen months of cancer, she doesn't want to carry on living with something terrible inside her. She doesn't want our lives to still be on hold worrying about her."

Emily nodded weakly. "L-love you… all."

"No," Maggie said. "No."

Emily's eyes didn't close, but they stopped seeing. The subtlest of changes. She was gone.

Jake swallowed.

My daughter's dead.

"No." He wouldn't accept it. He placed his bloody wrist against Emily's mouth and mushed it against her lips, wiping back and forth. It made her head flop from side to side, but her tongue was buried in the back of her throat and her lips were flat and lifeless. "Come on, honey. Drink. Wake up and drink."

"Dad, she's gone." Lily was crying and holding herself, but she seemed strong as she crouched beside him. "Stop."

Maggie grabbed his shoulder and eased him back. "Jake…?"

"No. No, I won't have it." He rubbed his wrist against her mouth again. "We can save her. She can fight it."

"She's done fighting," Lily said.

Maggie flopped her head against Emily's chest and wept. It was a terrible sound, high-pitched and keening. It rattled Jake's nerves.

Xindrac came to the surface like pus from a boil.

Emily's blood whispered to Jake. It coated her chest, neck, and chin. Even now, it seeped out of her pale, torn-open throat.

So easy to lean forward and take a drink. So easy to fill this empty hole inside me.

My daughter is dead. She's not a piece of meat.

He reached into his pocket and squeezed the Cho Zhou symbol. The pain was instant and immense, but he welcomed it now, knowing it hurt the beast more than it hurt him. This was his safety valve, the shut-off switch for when he was losing control.

The thirst went away, the emptiness a little less hollow. Reaching out to his dead daughter, he ran a hand against her cheek. "You fought with all you had, baby, and I fought too, but I guess sometimes it just doesn't matter. For whatever reason, the universe wanted you back." He closed her eyes and took a long, steadying breath. "I love you, Emily. I hope you felt that."

Maggie reached out to him and touched his hand. "She did."

Loud voices came from outside. For a moment it didn't register, but eventually Lily stood up and looked towards the window in the living room. "Dad. It's not over yet. Dev is still out there. What if he comes back?"

Jake looked at Maggie. He saw the love in her eyes, but also the sadness. There was no coming back from this. Too much had changed. Too much of it hurt. "I love you too, Maggie," he said. "My best friend forever."

She nodded, tears dripping off the tip of her nose. "I love you too, Jake. I always will."

Jake stood up and turned around to join his remaining daughter. Lily was dressed only in a T-shirt, and covered in blood, but it only made her look capable – like a battle-hardened warrior. "Stay here," he told her. "I'll be back soon."

As soon as I kill a drug-dealing dirtbag who I turned into a vampire.

Jake stepped over the bodies in the living room and went out into the hall. He already knew Dev was still out there because he spotted him through the broken front window. What surprised Jake was that he wasn't alone.

More backup probably. No end to mindless thugs in this world. I'm about to make sure there's a few less.

Jake went out the front door and down the garden path. He encountered Dev in the middle of the road, where he was now fully upright and free of the wooden stake in his back. It lay at his feet. Vincent and Kaydon were there too, and it became immediately clear that they weren't there to help Dev.

"You should have left me on the street, Unc," Vincent

said with a sneer. "I'd rather live off dead rats than be related to you. Mum wanted nothing to do with you. I used to think Dad was a piece of shit, but he was the good brother. You're worse."

Dev glared at his nephew and stalked towards him. He was clearly on the edge of lashing out, but Vincent didn't seem to care. In fact, the kid seemed to want his uncle to react violently. His friend Kaydon stood beside him, but he seemed half-asleep. Vincent, too, seemed a little sluggish as he moved back and forth in the road.

They look like they're on drugs.

"Fuckin' loser, Unc, that's what you are." Vincent snickered. "And look at you now, all ugly and shit."

Lily appeared behind Jake, making him jump. She was holding a length of wood she must have got from the broken kitchen table. It looked identical to the table leg Emily had buried in Dev's back. "We need to finish this, Dad," she said.

Jake sighed. "You never keep quiet and stay out of trouble, do you?"

"Not my style. Come on, V needs us."

"Seriously? His name is Vincent. It's not a letter."

Lily stepped forward, giving Jake no choice but to do the same. "Whatever, Dad. The lad owes me some answers, and he's not dying before I get them."

Jake couldn't help but laugh, glad that it wasn't him who was on the wrong side of his daughter.

———

With her dad beside her, Lily felt safe; felt sure that nothing could hurt her. The last week had changed everything. She and her dad had shared something and bonded. George, Mr

Cho, and everything that had happened since moving to Tovey Avenue…

I'm going to need lifelong therapy, but I see the world is bigger than just my own bullshit now.

Emily's gone.

It was always going to be this way. Deep down, I always knew I was going to lose my sister.

But I won't lose anyone else.

Like a lunatic, Lily raced into danger, not caring about the risk, just wanting to do damage to anyone threatening her family. A black Range Rover and two other cars blocked the road, but she quickly dodged around them and saw V. She wanted to get to him, needed to reach him.

She was too late.

As she raced into the road, V continued to insult and jeer his uncle. The man had clearly been prone to violence before becoming a vampire, but now he was downright savage. With no concern about attacking his own flesh and blood, Dev grabbed V and tore into his neck like a lion. Kaydon, V's mate, yelled out for help, but his volume was barely above normal speech. His words were slurred too, and when he moved to help V, he wobbled all over the place.

I can't let V die. Not until I know the truth.

Was he involved in this? Did he know his uncle was going to hurt my family?

Lily raced off the pavement and into the road. The table leg had grown heavy in her hands, but she managed to loft it above her head and bring it down like a hammer at a fairground.

Gotta hit that bell.

The wood cracked over the back of Dev's head. She didn't know if it was pain, or merely surprise, that caused him to turn around, but he let go of V, and V collapsed to the ground.

"Bitch!" Dev backhanded Lily for the second time that night and it sent her spinning. She landed on her backside in the centre of the road.

Kaydon went in, swinging a punch at Dev but missing by a mile. Dev grabbed his arm as it sailed past and twisted it around. The sound of it snapping reverberated down the street.

Kaydon screamed, but not as much as you might expect. He flopped to the ground and scurried away, moaning and muttering about it being the *worst day ever*. Then he seemed to lose consciousness.

With both lads on the ground, Dev turned his attention back to Lily. She clambered to her feet, dizzy from the smack to her face. It continued to impress her, her tolerance for staying conscious when punched, and she wondered if she had a future career as a boxer. That depended on her not dying tonight, though.

Dev stepped towards her, his fangs extended almost down to the tip of his chin. He was different to Dad, his brow not quite as pronounced, but his hands were twisted into claws far larger and his overall demeanour more animal-like. There was a lack of intelligence in his eyes, which had not been there before. He was more beast than man.

"I'm going to drain you dry and fuck your corpse," he growled, his forked tongue flicking in and out of his mouth.

"Wow, you really know how to turn a girl on."

He leapt into the air like a great ape, his shadow falling over Lily.

Jake shoved her out of the way and smashed Dev in the face with both hands as he landed. The blow would've killed an ordinary man, but Dev stayed on his feet, dazed but not beaten.

Jake stepped in front of Lily, his claw-like hands out on either side of him like daggered gloves. "I'm shutting down your business," he said with a snake-like hiss. "Tovey Avenue is now drug free."

Dev snarled. "People are just meat. They inject themselves with whatever will quicken their miserable demise. Feeding on them is a better ending than they deserve, and once I've dealt with you, I'm going to drink this entire street dry."

"You won't even make it till sunrise," Jake told him. "You're going to die here, right now, and no one will do a thing to save you."

Lily's adrenaline was draining out of her system, and she realised this was a fight that should not involve her. Stepping back onto the pavement, she looked up and down Tovey Avenue. Lights had begun to flick on up and down the street. People were waking up, finally disturbed by the chaos and murder outside.

Dev leapt at Jake, but he swatted him away like a fly, clearly stronger, and possibly bigger, as if he'd gained a foot in height. "You might be a vampire," he said, "but you're a pale imitation. I have an ancient warlord inside me, but all you have is a tiny echo. You're my bitch."

Dev snarled, blood leaking from his mouth. "You might have an ancient warlord inside you, but I am a warlord. These are my streets. You hear me? My streets!"

Jake launched himself forward, but Dev dodged to the side.

Lily assumed he was running scared, but he wasn't. He might not be as strong as her dad, but he was cunning and wicked. Instead of fighting, he grabbed Lily around the throat and lifted her off her feet. Turning around with her, as if she were no heavier than a teddy bear, he warned Jake back. "I'll snap her neck. Easiest thing in the world."

Lily choked, unable to breathe. Her legs kicked uselessly in the air.

"Leave her alone!" someone yelled.

Both Jake and Dev looked towards the far end of Tovey Avenue. Someone was standing out in their front garden and waving a fist.

"Fuck off, you scumbag," someone else shouted from nearer by.

Dev let go of Lily and turned in a circle. He seemed confused, then angry. "Do you know who the fuck you're talking to? I run this town. Heathskil is mine, and if you have a problem with it, just step on up and—"

Something flew through the air, glinting in the orange glow of the street lamps and the rising gaze of the sun. It struck Dev right between the eyes, sending him back a step. It landed in the road – an unopened can of Aldi baked beans.

Then somebody a few doors down threw something else.

A moment later, rubbish, tins of food, and even a brick came sailing through the air. Nearly all of it missed Dev, but it was enough to distract and enrage him. He bellowed at the residents of Tovey Avenue, threatening to murder them all.

But the residents walked down their garden paths and stood in the street, jeering and heckling.

"This used to be a nice place."

"You're not welcome."

"I'm calling the police. I don't care how much you threaten me."

"Clear off out of Tovey Avenue."

"Piss off out of it!"

"Get lost."

"Sling yer hook."

Lily had seen very few things in her short life worth remembering, but she knew, right now, that she was witnessing something that would stay with her forever. People coming together and facing down evil. Like a medieval village assembling to take down a dragon, it was almost fantasy. But it was happening.

Jake stepped in front of Dev, ignoring the debris sailing through the air and almost hitting him. "Looks like you're not welcome any more. Time for you to leave."

Dev was so enraged that he didn't even bother to acknowledge Jake. Instead, he wobbled back and forth, throwing up his arms and wailing threats back at the various residents. But even as his threats became more vicious, more lights switched on in various houses and more people walked out onto their front lawns.

Sirens sounded a mile away.

Lily rubbed at her neck and groaned.

Help was finally coming. Way, way too late.

Jake put a hand out and pointed a finger. "Go."

Dev turned his head and stared at Jake and Lily. Lily shivered under his gaze, but she quickly realised he wasn't really seeing her. He opened his mouth to speak, glancing back and forth like he didn't know where he was. "What is it? Who do you… what is you? What like?"

Lily frowned. "You're not making sense."

Dev tried to focus on her, but his eyes were like hockey pucks. The vampire inside him had retreated, and he was once again just a funny-looking dude with a bad goatee.

Dev collapsed onto one knee.

Lily looked at her dad, and he looked back at *her*. Neither of them understood what was happening. Instead of strong and dangerous, Dev now seemed pitiful and weak. The residents of Tovey Avenue were still leaving their properties and stepping into the road to yell at him.

Jake moved in front of Lily and seemed ten feet tall.

Vincent was stumbling about, while his friend Kaydon was slumped on the ground in a heap, his broken arm lying across his waist.

The threat was gone. Dev was no longer fearsome.

But he was still a vampire.

Dev shook himself, and the beast woke up. His fangs lengthened, his hands turned into claws. For some reason, his attention fell upon Lily. "You! Blondie! I should... I should never have listened to... to you!"

"The fuck did I do?" She took a step back, shielded by her dad.

Rather than answer her question, Dev staggered forward. His eyes were rolling all over the place, like he was fighting to stay conscious. He could barely place one foot in front of the other. "What... what is wrong with me?"

V appeared in the road behind his uncle. He, too, looked ready to pass out, and blood stained the side of his shirt, leaking from his neck. "You got high off your own supply, bruv. I gave you one hell of a roofie."

Lily frowned, not understanding, but she noticed her dad was smiling as if he did.

V knelt down in the middle of the road to pick something up. It was the length of wood that Emily had buried in Dev's back. Seeing that this was it, Lily moved a few feet to her left and grabbed the other table leg that she had brought out. Her dad didn't need a weapon; he had fingernails the size of razor blades.

V struck first. He swung the length of wood clumsily at his uncle, walloping him in the lower back. Before Dev could react, Lily leapt forward and smacked him around the side of the head. In his weakened state, the blows rocked him and sent him tumbling to the ground. Although hurt, he wasn't beaten, and he quickly turned to face the next attack.

"I took a shitload of downers before you fed on me," V said, his words slurring as he raised the piece of wood to strike his uncle again. "You fell right for my plan, you muppet."

Dev snarled, his face flickering as the vampire fought to stay present. "I should've smothered you when you were born. Your bitch of a mother had no right bringing you into this world. I told her. I told her I never wanted a kid."

V staggered, the piece of wood in his hands lowering. "Wh-what?"

Dev didn't answer. He just attacked, grabbing Vincent around the throat and squeezing. He glared into his nephew – his son's – eyes and expressed utter hatred and disgust. "Worst mistake I ever made," he snarled.

Lily stepped forward, ready to swing at Dev again. She needed to save V.

"Leave the kid alone."

Jake stepped in front of her. He held something in his hand, some kind of a metal object that seemed to burn him and give off smoke. Lily thought she recognised it from somewhere.

Dev turned his head, still throttling V with one hand.

Lily watched her dad drive the metal object into Dev's face, stabbing him right in the eye with its pointed end. The wound gave off a flash, followed by a puff of foul green air.

Dev recoiled, letting go of V and clutching at his face. Wispy black fumes escaped his eye socket and passed between his fingers. The bellow he let out echoed up and down Tovey Avenue and sent people hurrying back inside their homes.

The distant sirens were getting closer.

In agony and panicking, Dev staggered away from Jake and the others, seeming to want no further part of the fight. Lily watched him go, wondering if he would recover and come back, but he kept on going, all the way to the end of the street.

The sun came up, almost like it had suddenly decided to leap up over the rooftops. Its rays hit Jake's face and made him recoil. His brow flattened and his teeth retracted. For one, terrifying second, Lily expected him to burn up and turn to ash. Instead, he just turned back into her dad. The vampire went to sleep.

He walked in the direction Dev had gone. "I need to finish this."

"Dad? Don't. No more, please." She turned around and saw V lying on the ground, barely conscious. His eyes were rolling back in his head and his mouth was foamy. "Shit! He needs help."

For a moment, it looked like her dad was going to go after Dev, but then he came and crouched beside Lily and V. "Get him on his side. He's choking."

Lily grabbed V's arm and pulled, working with her dad to roll him over. As soon as he made it onto his side, he vomited. Her dad rubbed his back and more came out.

The sirens were right around the corner.

"Help's coming," Jake said. "It's time for me to go."

"What? What do you mean? You have to stay and sort this out."

He looked at her, so sadly that it made her want to cry in response. "I can't stick around, honey. You're not safe. Tell the police that Dev did all this, okay? Let them go looking for him. You and your mum were nothing but innocent hostages."

Lily looked down at V. "What about him?"

"You tell them the truth, that he tried to save us. He's a good kid."

Lily nodded and smiled, but her eyes streamed with tears. "You can't leave, Dad. I need you."

"You've needed me for a while, but I haven't been here. I'm so sorry. You're strong enough without me. In fact, you're stronger than anyone I know."

He stood up. She reached out to grab him, but he stepped around her and moved onto the pavement in front of their house. Her mum was standing in the doorway, looking out at her dad and shivering in the morning chill. It seemed like she might step onto the path to meet him, but instead they just stared at one another for what seemed like minutes and then broke apart.

Jake walked away – away from the approaching sirens.

A van came speeding up the road and skidded to a halt alongside Jake's X-Trail. The driver had almost run straight over Kaydon, who was unconscious in the road.

Jake looked at his watch. "Seven a.m. A new day."

Lily stroked Vincent's back and watched her dad stand and wait for the van's driver to get out. It was Greg. He stepped out onto the road with a cardboard box and immediately surveyed the confusing scene in front of him. "J-Jake?"

Jake smiled, clearly glad to see him. "Greg? What are you doing here?"

"Sorry, it's early, I know, but I figured the girls would be up for school. I wanted to drop your Blu-ray player around to you like I promised. What the hell happened here, mate?"

"Something I could never explain." He moved and put a hand on Greg's shoulder. "I'm sorry we stopped making you part of the family, but I need to ask your forgiveness. Look after my girls for me, okay?"

Greg frowned. He tried to speak, but Jake turned and hurried away, disappearing as morning arrived.

Lily called after him, but he wouldn't stop – so she just cried and waited for the sirens to arrive.

CHAPTER 21

12 months later…

Lily hopped off the middle of the seesaw and turned around, threading herself between Vincent's legs as he continued to dangle them. She put her lips against his and enjoyed their hundredth kiss of the day. "I need to get going in a minute," she said, breaking away. "Mum is taking me to the cinema."

"You think she'll ever accept me?"

She gave him a playful nudge. "She doesn't have a problem with you. Things have just been tough on her since Dad left. She barely even spoke for the first few weeks. I think you bring back bad memories, but she's getting over it."

Vincent nodded, his eyes locked on hers. "It's been tough on you too, Lil. It was rough. The whole thing."

"You mean your uncle trying to murder my entire family and then turning into a vampire?"

"My dad," he corrected her. "Fucker was my dad all along."

"No, he wasn't. You're nothing like him."

John the pug woofed at something behind them. Lily gave his lead a gentle tug to bring him back over to the seesaw.

Vincent let out a sigh and seemed to get lost in thought. The memories weighed heavy on them both, and some nights, when they lay together at his flat, they tossed and turned all night, kept awake by chomping nightmares.

Dev hadn't turned up since fleeing Tovey Avenue, but wherever he was, he was half-blind and wanted by the police. Lily and her mum had explained the massacre away by claiming to know very little. Lily was beaten, Emily dead, and their dad missing. While the story was clearly incomplete, Lily and her mum were the victims, and the police couldn't target them for prosecution. Eventually, the events had been chalked up to Heathskil drug pushers targeting an innocent family who knew too much about their activities. The locals of Tovey Avenue had been happy to condemn Dev and his thugs, which had very nearly dragged Vincent down too, but his actions in trying to help Lily and her family had been enough to save him.

The massacre had made the national news.

Then it had all died down.

You could even say life had gone back to normal, but for Lily, and the other survivors of that night, there was no normal. Theirs was a life of vampires and butchery, something that couldn't be forgotten.

"Will I see you afterwards?" Vincent asked her.

She shrugged. "I don't like being away from Mum too much. Maybe I'll stay tomorrow night."

Because I'm sixteen and I can do that now. I swear, I feel thirty.

To think most people would still think me a kid, after the fucking nightmare I survived.

Vincent nodded, disappointed but not upset. "No problem. Just text me to say goodnight. What you seeing, by the way?"

"Dunno. Probably whatever romcom is playing. Definitely not a horror. I'll call you afterwards if I'm not too tired."

She turned to walk away and get going, but she froze in absolute shock when she found herself face to face with someone she never expected to ever see again. "D-Dad?"

He smiled, no hint of a vampire, but then it was the middle of a sunny day. "You're growing up so fast. I've missed you, honey. So much!"

For a second, she thought about whacking him in the face, but then she reminded herself that he hadn't asked for any of what had happened. He had just been trying to save Emily. So she hugged him and squeezed him, harder than she'd ever hugged anything. "I've missed you too. I didn't know if you were still alive."

He eased her back and seemed apologetic. "I had some work to do on myself. I couldn't come see you if there was any danger of me hurting you."

"You would never hurt me, Dad."

"I…" He turned and noticed Vincent, still sitting on the seesaw. "You?"

He hopped off the seesaw and put his hands up. "Hey, Mr Penshaw, I… I'm different now. I…"

Jake stepped towards him, and Lily's heart sank, but then he offered out his hand to shake. "I appreciate what you did for me that night." Then he shrugged. "Although, I could say that everything that happened was your fault to start with."

"I-I'm so sorry. I…"

Jake grunted. "Just keep your nose clean, because if you

hurt my daughter, I'll visit you in the night and drink your blood."

Vincent nodded, taking the threat very seriously.

"You're working at a garage now, right?" Jake asked.

"Um, yeah. How'd you know?"

"I've been keeping an eye on things from a distance." He let out a sigh and seemed to loosen up a bit. "You should be proud of yourself, V."

"It's just Vincent now."

"Even better. Hey, so, do you mind?"

Vincent frowned, then understood. "Oh, yeah, of course. I'll leave you both to it. Call me later, Lil, yeah?"

She nodded. "I will."

Vincent took John's lead and led the pug away to go home to their flat. Jake and Lily both waited until he was gone and then Lily blurted out, "We're having sex."

Jake shied away like she'd slapped him. "Yeah, I figured, honey. I'd rather not talk about it though."

"You're not mad?"

"Do I wish you were a bit older? Yes! But I'm hardly in a position to play the dad card. I trust you, honey. You'll be smart about it. And I'm sure you waited until you turned sixteen, right?"

She pulled a face a looked away. "Yeah, so… I expected to see you at Emily's funeral. When you didn't turn up, I figured that would be it."

"I was there, watching. It was beautiful, the whole thing. Believe me, I wanted to come out and hug you and your mum, but I couldn't. I needed to get control over the monster sharing my body first."

"And have you?"

He shook his head and sighed. "Only enough to come see you like this. I figured a few things out though. Xindrac can't come out in the sunlight, even though I'm still stronger than I was before. Churches are off limits, and in fact I can't even mention the word G… G…" He chuckled. "You see? Garlic makes me want to puke and silver burns like hell. In fact" – he reached into his coat pocket and pulled out the Cho Zhou symbol – "this is the only thing that keeps the monster from coming out when I'm really angry. Xindrac's with me every night, always hungry and forever full of rage, but he knows I can hurt him if I need to."

It sounded good, like he was in control, but then she had a question she didn't truly want to ask. "Do you have to feed?"

He let out a sigh and couldn't look her in the eye for a moment. "Every few days. I try not to kill, but sometimes I can't stop myself in time. The only thing I can do is target the people who society is better off without."

"You mean you feed off bad guys? Like some kind of dark superhero."

"There's nothing heroic about me, Lily, but I promise you will always be safe. I've cleared out every criminal in a three-mile radius of Tovey Avenue."

"Did you find Dev?"

"No, I've been looking for him, but there's no sign. That's part of the reason I'm here. The other night I sensed something, another vampire, but it wasn't Dev. It was some junkie with track marks all up his arm."

She frowned. "I don't understand."

"I think Dev is recruiting himself a new gang – one that's a lot harder to kill."

"Shit! Are we in danger?"

"I don't know, but I get the feeling we haven't seen the last of Dev. He'll be coming for Vincent at the very least."

"We need to warn him."

"You can tell him later. For now, Dev seems to be lying low, and if I find out where he's hiding, well…" He let out a deep breath, which suggested he wasn't a walking corpse like the vampires on TV. In fact, when they had hugged, he'd been warm. Her dad was still alive. Just cursed. "Look," he told her. "Nothing bad will happen while I'm around, I promise. I can't be in your life, but I'll always be near. One day, if I ever find a way to get rid of Xindrac, I'll be back for good."

She huffed. "If Mum will have you."

That seemed to hurt him, and she regretted saying it.

"How is she? Your mum?"

"In pain. She cries a lot still, but she won't ever talk about you. A few weeks ago, she started a job cooking meals at a pub, but I don't think she really enjoys it. Gets her out the house a few evenings a week though, which is good. Greg visits us for dinner once a week to check up on her. She misses you, Dad, but…"

"But sometimes that's not enough."

"We can hope though, right? Maybe, with enough time, things might change. Tovey Avenue has, after all. Now that Dev's thugs are gone, people have started coming out more and spending time with each other. It's a nice community; we all look after one another."

Jake smiled. "That's nice to hear. At least some good came of things. You're not…"

"What?"

"Still cutting yourself."

"No. No, I stopped all that. I have a lot of shit to deal with, but I'm working through it. Why are you back, Dad? Why now? If Dev isn't a threat yet, then there must be something else."

"Nothing gets past you, does it?" He shook his head at

her with a smirk. "I needed to let you know that I'm still here, and that I think about you every day. But I also wanted to give you this."

Lily frowned as he turned around and grabbed something from the grass behind him. It was a black holdall. He dumped it down at her feet and unzipped it. It was stuffed full of money.

"Fuck me, Dad!"

"Language," he chided her, but he laughed at the same time.

"Where the hell did you get all that?"

"Turns out, when you prey on criminals, they have a lot of loose cash lying around. I took out a people-smuggling gang in Hall Green last week and this was just sitting there. Figure your mum could put it to good use. You know…" He chuckled to himself. "She always had this sweet little dream of setting up a cake-making business with you and Emily. Who knows, perhaps it could happen."

Lily's instinct was to mock the idea, but she actually liked the image it conjured in her mind. The only thing that ruined it was the faceless silhouette where Emily should've been standing. "I miss Emily," she said, fighting back tears.

"Me too. She was a fighter, huh?"

"Yeah, she really was. I wish I'd got to spend more time with her. More happier times."

They were both silent.

Jake picked up the duffel bag and handed it to her. "Try not to waste all of it."

"And what do I tell Mum?"

"The truth. Never lie to each other. Use this money to make yourselves as happy as you can. If I find more, you'll get that too. In the meantime, I'm going to keep trying to find my way back to you. I'm sure I can find a way to fix this, honey."

"I hope so. I really hope so."

He wrapped his arms around her and squeezed. "Hold onto that hope, sweetheart. It's the thing that makes us human."

"But it's not the only thing. I love you, Dad."

"I love you too, Lily. I'll see you soon."

She smiled and breathed him in. "I hope so."

EPILOGUE

DEV PEERED through one good eye at the group of unclean men and women lurking in front of him in the dark. Each was a vile, irredeemable degenerate. Druggies, rapists, and petty criminals alike. They were the kind of lowlife that even lowlife wanted nothing to do with.

And now they belong to me.

My glorious army, growing day by day.

Thirty-six soldiers. That's what he had so far. The black blood in his veins was like magic, turning ordinary lowlifes into powerful and obedient warriors. They lived to feed and butcher and torment, and soon Dev would set them free.

I'm coming for you, Jake. You too, Vincent. I'll tear open the necks of every soul on Tovey Avenue. And then I'll slaughter the entire city. If people thought I was bad before, they have no fucking idea now.

Dev stepped out into the silvery moonlight coming through the cracked ceiling-height windows inside the condemned hospital's lecture hall. His senses heightened, he threw back his head and flicked his forked tongue in the air. Immediately, his small army of vampires did the same, filling the air with the sound of vipers. Soon they would feed. Soon they would become living nightmares to all who met them. And he would be their king.

Once we begin, there'll be no hope of stopping us. No hope left at all.

Breed. Feed. And kill.

He said it out loud. "Breed. Feed. And kill."

His army chanted the words back to him, over and over again. "Breed. Feed. And kill."

Dev grinned, his fangs dripping with fresh blood.

WANT FREE BOOKS?

Don't miss out on your FREE Iain Rob Wright horror pack.
Five terrifying books sent straight to your inbox.

No strings attached & signing up is a doddle.

<u>Just click here</u>

PLEA FROM THE AUTHOR

Hey, Reader. So you got to the end of my book. I hope that means you enjoyed it. Whether or not you did, I would just like to thank you for giving me your valuable time to try and entertain you. I am truly blessed to have such a fulfilling job, but I only have that job because of people like you; people kind enough to give my books a chance and spend their hard-earned money buying them. For that I am eternally grateful.

If you would like to find out more about my other books then please visit my website for full details. You can find it at:

www.iainrobwright.com.

Also feel free to contact me on Facebook, Twitter, or email (all details on the website), as I would love to hear from you.

If you enjoyed this book and would like to help, then you could think about leaving a review on Amazon, Goodreads, or anywhere else that readers visit. The most important part of how well a book sells is how many positive reviews it has, so if you leave me one then you are directly helping me to continue on this journey as a full time writer. Thanks in advance to anyone who does. It means a lot.

ALSO BY IAIN ROB WRIGHT

Iain Rob Wright is one of the UK's most successful horror and suspense writers, with novels including the critically acclaimed, THE FINAL WINTER; the disturbing bestseller, ASBO; and the wicked screamfest, THE HOUSEMATES.

His work is currently being adapted for graphic novels, audio books, and foreign audiences. He is an active member of the Horror Writer Association and a massive animal lover.

www.iainrobwright.com
FEAR ON EVERY PAGE

For more information
www.iainrobwright.com
iain.robert.wright@hotmail.co.uk

Printed in Great Britain
by Amazon

38736684R00212